SACRAMENTO PUBLIC LIBRARY
828 "I" Street
Sacramento, CA 95814
04/19

D0020772

P

When

"Bold, unconventional Bea... thrilling, thought-provoking read!"

—Kate Quinn, ...of ...*k*

"A gorgeously atmospheric hom... brates with emotion on every pa... d a Kennedy-esque romance make this novel a rich read, but the addition of a formidable heroine truly makes it unputdownable. This is not just historical fiction, but also an unrequited love story for a country and a way of life, as well as a journey of self-discovery for a woman torn between love and the two countries she calls home."

—Karen White, *New York Times* bestselling author of *Dreams of Falling*

"Cleeton once again delivers a masterful tale of political intrigue tinged with personal heartbreak. Her ferocity and fearlessness can be found on every page, and Beatriz's story—one of vengeance, betrayal, and bravery—astonishes and thrills."

—Fiona Davis, national bestselling author of *The Masterpiece*

"Atmospheric and evocative, *When We Left Cuba* captivates with its compelling portrayals of the glamorous Cuban-exile community and powerful forbidden love set against the dangerous intrigue of the Cold War. Unforgettable and unputdownable!"

—Laura Kamoie, *New York Times* bestselling coauthor of *My Dear Hamilton*

"Powerful, emotional, and oh so real. One woman's fight to reclaim her own country, against all odds and no matter what the cost is intertwined with the real history of our lifetime and creates an unforgettable story."

—Rhys Bowen, *New York Times* and #1 Kindle bestselling author of *The Tuscan Child* and the Royal Spyness Mysteries

"Oozing with atmosphere and intrigue, *When We Left Cuba* is an evocative, powerful, and beautifully written historical novel, which had me completely captivated from the first page to the last. Take a bow, Chanel Cleeton!"

—Hazel Gaynor, *New York Times* bestselling author of
The Lighthouse Keeper's Daughter

"With a sure hand for historical detail, an impeccable eye for setting, and a heroine who grasps hold of your heart and never lets go, Chanel Cleeton has created another dazzlingly atmospheric and absorbing story of Cuba and its exiles. A beautiful and profoundly affecting novel from a writer whose work belongs on the shelves of every lover of historical fiction."

—Jennifer Robson, *USA Today* bestselling author of *The Gown*

"Rich in historic detail, *When We Left Cuba* has it all—the excitement of a page-turning thriller, the sizzle of a steamy romance, and the elegant prose of a master storyteller."

—Renée Rosen, author of *Park Avenue Summer*

"Cleeton draws you into the glamour, intrigue, and uncertainty of the Cuban-exile community just after Castro's coup through a heroine who could give Mata Hari a run for her money. . . . You'll be rooting for Beatriz to change the course of history—and find her own hard-won happily ever after."

—Lauren Willig, *New York Times* bestselling author of
The English Wife

"A compelling unputdownable story of love—for a man, for a country, for a past ripped away, and a future's tenuous promise. *When We Left Cuba* swept me away."

—Shelley Noble, *New York Times* bestselling author of
Lighthouse Beach

"By turns a captivating historical novel, a sweeping love story, and a daring tale of espionage—I absolutely adored this gem of a novel."

—Jillian Cantor, author of *The Lost Letter* and *In Another Time*

"Scintillating. . . . An intriguing dive into the turbulent Cuban-American history of the 1960s, and the unorthodox choices made by a strong historical woman."

—Marie Benedict, author of *The Only Woman in the Room*

"With a richly imagined setting and a heroine worth rooting for from the start, *When We Left Cuba* is thrilling and romantic, and timely to boot."

—Michelle Gable, *New York Times* bestselling author of *The Summer I Met Jack*

"Electric and fierce. Beatriz Perez's romance with a handsome, important senator will sweep you away, but it's her profound loyalty to Cuba and her formidable determination to be her own woman despite life-and-death odds that will really hold you in thrall."

—Kerri Maher, author of *The Kennedy Debutante*

"Beatriz Perez's brand of vintage-Havana glamour dazzles with equal parts intrigue, rebellion, and romance to make for an unforgettable story."   —Elise Hooper, author of *The Other Alcott*

"A breathtaking book, and it captures what I love best about historical fiction."   —Camille Di Maio, author of *The Way of Beauty*

"In a tale as tempestuous as Cuba itself, *When We Left Cuba* is the revolutionary story of one woman's bold courage and her many sacrifices for her beloved country. An absolutely spectacular read!"

—Stephanie Marie Thornton, author of *American Princess*

"A slow burn in all the right ways, Beatriz's story is a cohesion of romance, revenge, and loyalty that kept me turning the pages until I learned her ultimate fate. Immersive and stirring!"

—Jenni L. Walsh, author of *Becoming Bonnie*

"An absolute gem of a book."

—Sara Ackerman, author of *Island of Sweet Pies and Soldiers*

"A gorgeously rendered story. . . . Part spy novel, part romance, and part political thriller, readers will no doubt find this book as hard to put down as I did."

—Alyssa Palombo, author of *The Spellbook of Katrina Van Tassel*

"Grabs you from the first page. . . . A passionate, patriotic heroine pulled into espionage, a tension-filled era in Cuban-American relations, and a romance that could ruin the political ambitions of a man groomed for power—this book has it all."

—Janie Chang, author of *Dragon Springs Road*

"A WOW book! Cleeton gives us a heroine to love—conveying in well-crafted prose, the journey of a remarkable woman as she grows in self-assurance and power. *When We Left Cuba* simply crackles with political and personal tensions!"

—Sophie Perinot, author of *Médicis Daughter*

"An immersive and gorgeously crafted tale of forbidden love, family, loyalty, and intrigue."   —Victoria Schade, author of *Life on the Leash*

PRAISE FOR
Next Year in Havana

"A beautiful novel that's full of forbidden passions, family secrets, and a lot of courage and sacrifice."   —Reese Witherspoon

"A sweeping love story and tale of courage, and familial and patriotic legacy that spans generations."   —*Entertainment Weekly*

"This Cuban-set historical novel is just what you need to get that extra-summery feeling."   —Bustle

"The Ultimate Beach Read."   —*Real Simple*

"*Next Year in Havana* reminds us that while love is complicated and occasionally heartbreaking, it's always worth the risk."   —NPR

"A flat-out stunner of a book, at once a dual-timeline mystery, a passionate romance, and paean to the tragedy and beauty of war-torn Cuba. Simply wonderful!"

—Kate Quinn, *New York Times* bestselling author of
The Alice Network

"Cleeton has penned an atmospheric, politically insightful, and highly hopeful homage to a lost world. Devour *Next Year in Havana* and you, too, will smell the perfumed groves, taste the *ropa vieja*, and feel the sun on your face."

—Stephanie Dray, *New York Times* bestselling coauthor of
My Dear Hamilton

"Don't miss this smart, moving, and romantic story."

—HelloGiggles

"A vivid, transporting novel. *Next Year in Havana* is about journeys—into exile, into history, and into questions of home and identity. It's an engrossing read."

—David Ebershoff, author of *The Danish Girl* and *The 19th Wife*

BERKLEY TITLES BY CHANEL CLEETON

Fly With Me
Into the Blue
On Broken Wings

Next Year in Havana
When We Left Cuba

WHEN WE LEFT *Cuba*

CHANEL CLEETON

BERKLEY
NEW YORK

BERKLEY
An imprint of Penguin Random House LLC
1745 Broadway, New York, NY 10019

Copyright © 2019 by Chanel Cleeton
Penguin Random House supports copyright. Copyright fuels creativity, encourages
diverse voices, promotes free speech, and creates a vibrant culture. Thank you for
buying an authorized edition of this book and for complying with copyright laws by not
reproducing, scanning, or distributing any part of it in any form without permission.
You are supporting writers and allowing Penguin Random House to continue to
publish books for every reader.

BERKLEY and the BERKLEY & B colophon are registered trademarks of
Penguin Random House LLC.

Library of Congress Cataloging-in-Publication Data

Names: Cleeton, Chanel, author.
Title: When we left Cuba / by Chanel Cleeton.
Description: First edition. | New York : Berkley, 2019.
Identifiers: LCCN 2018009614| ISBN 9780451490865 (softcover) |
ISBN 9780451490872 (ebook)
Subjects: LCSH: Cuban American women—Fiction. | GSAFD: Love stories.
Classification: LCC PS3603.L455445 W48 2019 | DDC 813/.6—dc23
LC record available at https://lccn.loc.gov/2018009614

First Edition: April 2019

Printed in the United States of America
1   3   5   7   9   10   8   6   4   2

Cover art: *Cuba* by Pavel Samsonov / Shutterstock;
Two women by Karen Radkai / Conde Nast via GettyImages
Title page art: *Floral Border* © by IndiPixi / Shutterstock Images
Book design by Kristin del Rosario

This is a work of fiction. Names, characters, places, and incidents either are the product
of the author's imagination or are used fictitiously, and any resemblance to actual persons,
living or dead, business establishments, events, or locales is entirely coincidental.

For the dreams that slip through our fingers.
May we hold them in our arms one day.

prologue

NOVEMBER 26, 2016

PALM BEACH

It arrives just after midnight, in the waning hours of night, those magical haunting hours, bundled in an elegant basket adorned with an exuberant red bow, delivered by an officious man in a somber suit who leaves as quickly as he comes, ferried away from the stately Palm Beach address in a silver Rolls owned by one of the island's most notorious residents.

The woman takes the basket, her evening winding down until she unwraps the contents in the sanctuary of the sitting room decked out in vibrant colors, recognition dawning as familiar French words greet her.

A tear trickles down her cheek.

The foil is crisp against her palm, the glass a cooling balm on her skin as though it's been chilled and waiting for her all these years. She lifts the bottle from the basket, carrying the champagne to the bar in the living room, her jewel-clad fingers trembling over the seal, fumbling with the top.

The defiant pop of the cork breaks the silence of the night. Despite the late hour, it is too important an occasion to be denied, and soon her peace will be disturbed by other noises: the ringing phone, the chatter of friends and family, a celebration of sorts after an interminable war. But for now, there is this—

The champagne explodes on her tongue. It is the taste of victory and defeat, of love and loss, of nights of revelry and decadence in Havana and days in exile in Palm Beach. She lifts the glass in the air in a silent toast, the sight of her hand—no longer a young woman's, but something more seasoned—still catching her off guard, the wrinkles no number of trips to the plastic surgeon can erase, a subtle taunt that time is the cruelest thief of them all.

When did she get so old?

There is no note in the basket, but then again, there's no need. Who else would send her such a gift: extravagant, poignant, perfectly her?

No one but him.

chapter one

The thing about collecting marriage proposals is they're much like cultivating eccentricities. One is an absolute must for being admired in polite—or slightly less-than-polite—society. Two ensure you're a sought-after guest at parties, three add a soupçon of mystery, four are a scandal, and five, *well*, five make you a legend.

I peer down at the man making a spectacle of himself on bended knee in front of me—*what is his name?*—his body tipping precariously from an overabundance of champagne and folly. He's a second cousin to the venerable Preston clan, related by marriage to a former vice president, cousin to a sitting U.S. senator. His tuxedo is elegant, his fortune likely modest if not optimistic for the largesse of a bequest from a deceased aunt, his chin weak from one too many Prestons marrying Prestons.

Andrew. Maybe Albert. Adam?

We've met a handful of times at parties such as this one in Palm

Beach, fetes I once would have ruled over in Havana, to which I now must bow and scrape in order to gain admittance. I likely could do worse than a second cousin to American royalty; after all, beggars can't be choosers, and exiles even less so. The prudent thing would be to accept his proposal—my auspicious fifth—and to follow my sister Elisa into the sacrament of holy matrimony.

But where's the fun in that?

Whispers brush my gown, my name—*Beatriz Perez*—on their lips, the weight of curious gazes on my back, words creeping toward me, clawing their way up my skirts, snatching the faux jewels from my neck and casting them to the ground.

Look at her.

Haughty. The whole family is. Someone should tell them this isn't Cuba.

Those hips. That dress.

Didn't they lose everything? Fidel Castro nationalized all those sugar fields her father used to own.

Has she no shame?

My smile brightens, flashier than the fake jewels at my neck and just as sincere. I scan the crowd, sweeping past Alexander on his knees looking like a man who hasn't quite acquired his sea legs, past the Palm Beach guard shooting daggers my way, resting on my sisters Isabel and Elisa standing in the corner, champagne flutes in hand. The sight of them, the reminder to bow to nothing and no one, emboldens me.

I turn back to Alistair.

"Thank you, but I must decline."

I keep my tone light, as though the whole thing is a jest, and a drunken one at that, which I *hope* it is. People don't go falling in love and proposing in one fell swoop, do they? Surely, that's . . . inconvenient.

Poor Arthur looks stunned by my answer.

Perhaps this wasn't a joke after all.

Slowly, he recovers, the same easy smile on his face that lingered moments before he fell to his knees returning with a vengeance, restoring his countenance to what is likely its natural state: perpetually pleased with himself and the world he inhabits. He grasps my outstretched hand, his palm clammy against mine, and pulls himself up with an unsteady sway. A grunt escapes his lips.

His eyes narrow once we're level—nearly level, at least, given the extra inches my sister Isabel's borrowed heels provide.

The glint in Alec's eyes reminds me of a child whose favorite toy has been taken away and who will make you pay for it later by throwing a spectacularly effective tantrum.

"Let me guess, you left someone back in Cuba?"

There's enough of a bite in his tone to nip at my skin.

My diamond smile reappears, honed at my mother's knee and so very useful in situations like these, the edges sharp and brittle, warning the recipient of the perils of coming too close.

I bite, too.

"Something like that," I lie.

Now that one of their own is back on his feet, no longer prostrate in front of the interloper they've been forced to tolerate this social season, the crowd turns their attention from us with a sniff, a sigh, and a flurry of bespoke gowns. We possess just enough money and influence—sugar is nearly as lucrative in America as it is in Cuba—that they can't afford to cut us directly, but not nearly enough to prevent them from devouring us like a sleek pack of wolves scenting red meat. Fidel Castro has made beggars of all of us, and for that alone, I'd thrust a knife through his heart.

And suddenly, the walls are too close together, the lights in the ballroom too bright, my bodice too tight.

It's been nearly a year since we left Cuba for what was supposed to be a few months away until the world realized what Fidel Castro

had done to our island, and America has welcomed us into her lov-
ing embrace—almost.

I am surrounded by people who don't want me here even if their
contempt hides behind a polite smile and feigned sympathy. They
look down their patrician noses at me because my family hasn't been
in America since the country's founding, or sailed on a boat from
England, or some nonsense like that. My features are a hint too
dark, my accent too foreign, my religion too Catholic, my last name
too Cuban.

In a flash, an elderly woman who shares Anderson's coloring
and features approaches us, sparing me a cutting look designed to
knock me down a peg or two. In a flurry of Givenchy, he's swept
away, and I'm alone once more.

If I had my way, we wouldn't attend these parties, save this one,
wouldn't attempt to ingratiate ourselves to Palm Beach society. It
isn't about what I want, though. It's about my mother, and my sisters, and my father's need to extend his business empire through
these social connections so no one ever has the power to destroy us
again.

And of course, as always, it's about Alejandro.

I head for one of the balconies off the ballroom, the hem of my
gown gathered in hand, careful to keep from tearing the delicate
fabric.

I slip through the open doors, stepping onto the stone terrace,
the breeze blowing the skirt of my dress. There's a slight chill in the
air, the sky clear, the stars shining down, the moon full. The ocean
is a dull, distant roar. It's the sound of my childhood, my adulthood,
calling to me like a siren song. I close my eyes, a sting there, and
pretend I'm standing on another balcony, in another country, in
another time. What would happen if I headed for the water now, if
I left the party behind, removing the pinching shoes and curling my
toes in the sand, the ocean pooling around my ankles?

A tear trickles down my cheek. I never imagined it was possible to miss a place this much.

I rub my damp skin with the back of my hand, my gaze shifting to the balcony's edge, to the palms swaying in the distance.

A man leans against the balustrade, one side of him shrouded in darkness, the rest illuminated by a shaft of moonlight.

He's tall. Blond hair—nearly reddish, really. His arms brace against the railing, his shoulders straining his tailored tuxedo.

I step back, and he moves—

I freeze.

Oh.

Oh.

The thing about people telling you you're beautiful your whole life is that the more you hear it, the more meaningless it becomes. What does "beautiful" even mean anyway? That your features are arranged in a shape someone, somewhere, arbitrarily decided is pleasing? "Beautiful" never quite matches up to the other things you could be: smart, interesting, brave. And yet—

He's beautiful. Shockingly so.

He appears as though he's been painted in broad strokes, his visage immortalized by exuberant sweeps and swirls of the artist's brush, a god come down to meddle in the affairs of mere mortals.

Irritatingly beautiful.

He looks like the sort of man who has never had to wonder if he'll have a roof over his head, or fear his father dying in a cage with eight other men, or flee the only life he has ever known. No, he looks like the sort of man who is told he is perfection from the moment he wakes in the morning to the moment his head hits the pillow at night.

He's noticed me, too.

Golden Boy leans against the railing, his broad arms crossed in front of his chest. His gaze begins at the top of my head where Isabel and I fussed with my coiffure for an hour, cursing the absence of a maid to help us. From my dark hair, he traverses the length of my face, down to the décolletage exposed by the gown's low bodice, the gaudy fake jewels that suddenly make me feel unmistakably cheap—as though he can see I am an impostor—to my waist, hips.

I take another step back.

"Am I to call you cousin?"

His words stop my movement, holding me in place as surely as a hand coming to rest on my waist, as though he is the sort of man accustomed to bending others to his will with little to no effort at all.

I loathe such men.

His voice sounds like what I have learned passes for money in this country: smooth, crisp, devoid of even a hint of foreignness—the wrong kind, at least. A tone of voice secure in the knowledge that every word will be savored.

I arch my brow. "Excuse me?"

He pushes off from the railing, his long legs closing the distance between us. He stops once he's close enough that I have to tip my head up to meet his gaze.

His eyes are blue, the color of the deep parts of the water off the Malecón.

Without breaking eye contact, he reaches between us, his thumb ghosting across my bare ring finger. His touch is a shock, waking me from the slumber of a party I tired of hours ago. He quirks his mouth in a smile, little lines crinkling around his eyes. How nice to see even gods have flaws.

"Andrew is my cousin," he offers by way of explanation, his tone faintly amused.

I find that most rich people who are still in fact rich manage to pull this off as though a dollop more amusement would be atrociously gauche.

Andrew. The fifth marriage proposal has a name. And the man

WHEN WE LEFT CUBA · 9

before me likely has a prestigious one. Is he a Preston or merely related to one like Andrew?

"We were all waiting with breathless anticipation to see what you would say," he comments.

There's that faint amusement again, a weapon of sorts when honed appropriately. He possesses the same edge to him that everyone here seems to have, except I get the sense he is laughing with me, not at me, which is a welcome change.

I grace him with a smile, the edges sanded down a bit. "Your cousin has an impeccable sense of timing and an obvious appreciation for drawing a crowd."

"Not to mention excellent taste," Golden Boy counters smoothly—*too smoothly*—returning my smile with another one of his own, this one even more dazzling than the first.

He was handsome before, but this is simply ridiculous.

"True," I agree.

I have little use for false modesty these days; if you're not going to fight for yourself, who will?

He leans into me a bit more, as though we share a secret. "No wonder you've whipped everyone into a frenzy."

"Who? Me?"

He chuckles, the sound low, seductive, like the first sip of rum curling in your belly.

"You know the effect you have. I saw you in the ballroom."

How did I miss him? He doesn't exactly blend in with the crowd.

"And what did you see?" I ask, emboldened by the fact that his gaze has yet to drift away.

"You."

My heartbeat quickens.

"Just you." His voice is barely loud enough to be heard over the sound of the ocean and the wind.

"I didn't see you." My own voice sounds husky, like it belongs to someone else, someone who is *rattled* by this.

My gaze has yet to drift from him, either.

His eyes widen slightly, a dimple denting his cheek, another imperfection to hoard even if it adds more character than flaw.

"You sure know how to make a guy feel special."

I curl my fingers into a ball to keep from giving in to temptation, to resist reaching out and laying my palm against his cheek.

"I suspect plenty of people make you feel special."

There's that smile again. "That they do," he acknowledges.

I shift until we stand shoulder to shoulder, gazing out at the moonlit sky.

He shoots me a sidelong look. "I imagine it's true, then?"

"What's true?"

"They say you ruled like a queen in Havana."

"There are no queens in Havana. Only a tyrant who aims to be king."

"I take it you aren't a fan of the revolutionaries?"

"It depends on the revolutionaries to whom you refer. Some had their uses. Fidel and his ilk are little more than vultures feasting on the carrion that has become Cuba." I walk forward, sidestepping him so the full skirt of my dress swishes against his elegant tuxedo pants. I feel him behind me, his breath on my nape, but I don't look back. "President Batista needed to be eliminated. In that, they succeeded. Now if only we could rid ourselves of the victors."

I turn, facing him.

His gaze has sharpened from an indolent gleam to something far more interesting. "And replace them with who, exactly?"

"A leader who cares about Cubans, about their future. Who is willing to remove the island from the Americans' yoke." I care little for the fact that he is an American; I am not one of them and have no desire to pretend to be. "A leader who will reduce sugar's influence," I add, my words a break from my family's position. Despite the fortune it has brought us, it's impossible to deny the destructive influence the industry has had on our island no matter how much our father attempts to do so. "One who will bring us true democracy and freedom."

He's silent, his gaze appraising once again, and I'm not sure if it's a result of the wind, or his breath against my neck, but goose bumps rise over my skin.

"You're a dangerous woman, Beatriz Perez."

My lips curve. I tilt my head to the side, studying him, trying desperately to fight the faint prick of pleasure at the phrase "dangerous woman" and the fact that he knows my name.

"Dangerous for who?" I tease.

He doesn't answer, but then again, he doesn't have to.

Another smile. Another dent in his cheeks. "I'll bet you left a trail of broken hearts behind you."

I shrug, registering how his gaze is drawn to my bare shoulder.

"A proposal or four, perhaps."

"Rum scions and sugar barons or wild-haired, bearded freedom fighters?"

"Let's just say my tastes are varied. I kissed Che Guevara once."

I can't tell who is more surprised by the announcement. I don't know why I said it, why I'm sharing a secret not even my family knows with a total stranger. To shock him, maybe; these Americans are so easy to scandalize. To warn him I am not some simpering debutante; I have done and seen things he cannot fathom. And also, perhaps, because there's power in the lengths to which you will go in a misguided attempt to secure your father's release from Guevara's hellhole of a prison, La Cabaña. It makes for a good story even if I inwardly cringe at the young girl whose hubris made her think a kiss could save a life.

"Did you enjoy it?" Golden Boy's expression is inscrutable, a clever and effective mask sliding into place. I can't tell if he's scandalized, or if he feels sorry for me; I far prefer society's scorn to his pity.

"The kiss?"

He nods.

"I would have preferred to cut his throat."

To his credit, he doesn't flinch at my bloodthirsty response.

"Then why did you do it?"

I surprise myself—and perhaps him—by opting for truth rather than prevarication.

"Because I was tired of things happening to me, and I wanted to make things happen for myself. Because I was trying to save someone's life."

"And did you?"

The taste of defeat fills my mouth with ash.

"That time, I did."

The wave of power brings another emotion with it, the memory of the life I couldn't save, of a car screeching to a stop in front of the enormous gates of our home, the door opening, my twin brother's still-warm dead body tumbling to the ground, his blood staining the steps we once played on when we were children, his head cradled in my lap while I sobbed.

"Is it as bad as everyone says?" His tone is gentled to something I can hardly bear.

"Worse."

"I can't imagine."

"No, you can't. You have no idea how fortunate you are to be born in this time, in this place. Without freedom, you have nothing."

"And what would you tell a man with only a few minutes of freedom left?"

"To run," I reply, my tone wry.

A ghost of a smile crosses his face, but it's obvious he isn't buying what I'm selling, and I like him better for it, for seeing past the facade.

"To savor the last few minutes he has," I answer instead.

I want to ask his name, but pride holds me back—pride and fear. Such luxuries have no place in my life at the moment.

I blink, only to be greeted by an outstretched palm, waiting for mine to join it.

"Dance with me."

I swallow, my mouth suddenly dry. I cock my head to the side, studying him, pretending my heart isn't thundering in my chest, that my hand isn't itching to take his.

"Now why does that feel more like a challenge than an invitation?"

The music is a faint hum in the background of the evening, the notes drifting out onto the empty balcony.

"Will you dance with me, Beatriz Perez, kisser-of-revolutionaries and thief-of-hearts?"

He's too smooth by half, and I like him far too much for it.

I shake my head, a smile playing at my lips. "I didn't say anything about stealing hearts."

He counters my smile with a spectacular one of his own, the full wattage hitting me. "No, I did."

Do I really even stand a chance?

He steps forward, obliterating the space between us once more, his cologne filling my nostrils, my eyes level with the snowy white front of his shirt. His hand comes to rest on my waist, the heat from his palm warming me through the thin fabric of my dress. He takes my hand with his free one, our fingers entwined.

My heart turns over in my chest as I follow his lead. Unsurprisingly, he's a natural, confident dancer.

We don't speak, but then again, considering the conversation between our bodies—the rustle of fabric, brushing of limbs, fleeting touches that imprint themselves upon my skin—words seem superfluous and far less intimate.

The thing about collecting marriage proposals is that people assume you're a flirt, and perhaps I was, once, long ago, but now it feels unnatural to play the coquette. I am somewhere between the girl I was and the woman I want to be.

The song ends, another beginning with far too much speed, the dance both stretching for eternity and ending with a blink. He releases me with a subtle heave of his shoulders, the cool air between us, my fingers missing the twine of his, the shock of his absence surprisingly sharp.

I gaze into his eyes, steeling myself against the onslaught of flirtation likely to follow, the invitation to lunch or dinner, the compliments about my dancing, the heat in his gaze. I have no use for romantic entanglements at the moment, even as I imagine I would very much like to be temporarily entangled with this man.

He smiles. "Thank you for the dance."

I watch him walk away, secure in the knowledge that he will turn around and look back at me.

He doesn't.

Surprise fills me as he disappears back into the ballroom, into the world where he clearly belongs. Minutes pass before I'm ready to return to the ballroom, to the glittering chandeliers, the harsh glint of the other guests.

I walk through the balcony doorway. Isabel stands to the side; Elisa is nowhere to be seen.

"She went home. She wasn't feeling well," Isabel answers when I ask about our sister's whereabouts.

A waiter approaches us, a tray of champagne flutes in hand, more waiters around the ballroom offering the same to other guests, a murmur resounding through the party, whispers tucked behind cupped hands, names on everyone's lips, the calm before a scandal breaks.

Curious as to the piece of gossip they've all seized upon, I scan the crowd, looking for Golden Boy, searching for—

He stands next to the orchestra near the front of the room with an older couple and a woman.

Oh.

Oh.

There's no point in dissecting her flaws, for I fear it would be a useless endeavor and do me no favors. It's clear as could be her family did hail on a great big ship at this nation's founding; she's stunning with her blond hair and delicate features, the perfect complement to his golden looks. Her gown is the height of fashion, her jewels certainly not paste, her lips curved in a pretty smile.

Who could blame her for smiling?

I join the rest of the ballroom in lifting my champagne flute and toasting the happy couple, as the bride-to-be's father announces his daughter's engagement to one Nicholas Randolph Preston III. He is not just a Preston; he is *the* Preston. The sitting U.S. senator rumored to have aspirations of reaching the White House one day.

Our gazes meet across the ballroom.

How could I not see this a mile away? In the end, life always comes down to timing.

It's New Year's Eve, 1958, and your world is parties and shopping trips; it's New Year's Day, 1959, and it's soldiers, and guns, and death.

You meet a man on a balcony, and for a moment, you forget yourself, only to be reminded once again how mercurial fate can be.

I drain the glass of champagne in one unladylike gulp.

And then I see *him*—the one I came for—and nothing else matters anymore.

Unlike Nicholas Preston, this man is short and stout, his hair balding at the top, his nose more suited to a larger face. He wears his tuxedo like it's strangling him. Through the research I've done, I've learned he's invited to these parties for one reason: his wife is the darling of the charity circuit, her maiden name whispered with reverence throughout the ballroom. He clearly prefers the comfort of the shadows, every inch of him reinforcing the intelligence I've received: he's a man unafraid to roll up his sleeves and dirty his hands, who enjoys moving world leaders around like they are pieces on a chessboard.

His last name is Dwyer and he's the CIA's man on Latin America.

I lied before when Nicholas Randolph Preston III—soon-to-be-married U.S. senator—asked me about freedom. I would savor it—for a moment.

And then I'd fight like hell to ensure it was never, ever taken away from me again.

As nice as moonlit dances with princes are, I came here with more important business at hand. I came to meet the man who is going to help me avenge my brother Alejandro's death and kill Fidel Castro.

chapter two

Same balcony. Different man. Same assessing gaze, except this time there isn't a glimmer of admiration or a spark of attraction. And there's certainly no dancing, even if the music lingers in the background.

"It appears we have a common enemy," says Mr. Dwyer. His rough-hewn features are arranged in a careful mask; his gaze lingers on my face, my body. He is every inch the spymaster in his perusal: unflinching, thorough, opportunistic.

The CIA's role in Latin America has been bloody and brutal, whispers of their involvement in places like Guatemala reaching the circles in which I now travel thanks to the mantle my brother has passed on to me after his death.

"We do," I acknowledge.

"And you think you can do something about him?"

Dwyer removes a slim cigarette from a gold case; the flame from a matching engraved lighter sends the paper crackling. The first puff of smoke makes its way into the air, the heady scent of tobacco filling the balcony, mixing with the perfume I dabbed at my pulse points.

"I do."

Maybe it's strange that at twenty-two and female, I am standing on this balcony rather than someone like my father, someone who has spent his life accumulating power and influence, but the very nature of my age and gender makes me an attractive weapon. For this to work, they need someone who can get close to Fidel, someone he will not view as a threat, who can draw his interest. After all, who is more easily discounted than a woman, and a debutante at that? Fidel has many vices, and it is well known his Achilles' heel is feminine beauty.

"You were involved with the rebels in Havana." Dwyer's stare is flinty and faintly disapproving. The CIA's relationship with former Cuban president Batista was a complicated one to say the least; I and others like me caused them their fair share of problems over the years.

War makes for strange bedfellows.

"I was."

"Because of your brother?"

Perhaps he means to catch me off guard with these details of my life he's gleaned, but I'm hardly surprised they know about Alejandro's involvement in the revolution or about his death. The Americans have meddled in Cuba's affairs for a very long time, their machinations pulling the strings for Batista and others like him.

"In the beginning," I answer, my tone considerably cooler.

Dwyer smiles, the effort unnatural on a face that looks as though it has little use for charming lines creeping in the creases and folds of his skin.

"I can do inscrutable with the best of them, Miss Perez, but you requested this meeting, so if you're going to convince me this is worth my time, you'd better start now."

In Cuba, people are suffering, dying, while here stands a man in a tuxedo idly plotting a coup between drags of his cigarette. That he's likely enjoying it adds insult to injury.

"You wouldn't be meeting with me if you weren't a little desperate." My confidence grows a bit with each word falling from my lips. "You wouldn't be here if you weren't looking for creative ways to get close to Fidel," I add. "If he hadn't rebuffed any and all diplomatic overtures you've already made. I'm the one risking everything—my reputation, my family's, my *life*—so please explain to me how I need you more than you need me. I could easily find a rich man to slide a ring on my finger and buy me a big mansion while the world around me burns, but you're the one with communism breathing down your neck, whose head will roll if Latin America falls. You have a potential powder keg sitting ninety miles away from America's shores. You need Cuba. And you need me. Let's not insult each other's intelligence by pretending otherwise."

He inclines his head in a mock salute amid a cloud of smoke. "Eduardo said you were more than just another pretty face."

Eduardo Diaz, the son of one of my father's friends, is the man who orchestrated this little meeting, one of the many who have helped my family acclimate to life in the United States.

Dwyer takes another drag on his cigarette. "Would you like to start over, then? Why do you think you can get close to Castro?"

"Because he is a man."

Is there really need to say more? You don't garner five marriage proposals without learning a thing or two about the management of men.

"Have you met him before? Has he proposed to you, too?"

It seems my reputation once again precedes itself.

"No, he's never had the pleasure. I've met Guevara a handful of times, though."

"And Guevara trusts you?"

I allow myself one very unladylike snort. "Hardly. I doubt he very much cares one way or the other, but isn't that the point? I'm the girl they know from the society pages. One of the infamous sugar queens they so despise yet cannot resist. No one considers me a threat, and given the size of their egos, their dislike of my family, and the cachet of my last name, the idea of sticking it to my father will be eminently persuasive. Besides . . ."

My voice trails off, but I don't need to finish the thought. Revolutionaries, tyrants, it doesn't matter. They are, at their hearts, men, driven by things other than their intellect.

Dwyer's gaze rakes over my appearance once more, examining the curves on display, taking in the signs that my circumstances have been reduced: the dress a blush removed from fashion, the ill-fitting shoes, the garish glint of the necklace around my neck.

For all my posturing, I need this, too, and he knows it.

"So how do you propose to get to him? In Cuba?"

He dangles it in front of me like a treat before a child. What wouldn't I give to return home to the only place I have ever felt as though I belonged? To return to my friends, my extended family, my people, to stop this endless waiting?

"Perhaps," I answer. "Or when he comes to the United States for a diplomatic visit."

Castro was invited to the United States last April, three months after he took power. To his credit, President Eisenhower didn't receive him, but Fidel did meet with Vice President Nixon. Judging by the man standing before me, their meeting did not go well.

"Castro isn't a reckless man. Not with his life, at least. It won't be easy to get close to him, even with your considerable charms," Dwyer cautions.

"I don't need it to be easy. I only need a chance."

"And if you don't succeed? If his guards stop you, they could kill you. They likely will. There are some places where your last name isn't going to protect you. Are you prepared for that?"

"If I don't succeed, then they kill me. I assure you, I'm aware of the stakes. I wouldn't volunteer for this if I wasn't."

"Didn't take you for an idealist."

He says "idealist" like it's a vulgar word.

"I'm not one."

"Your brother—"

"I don't talk about my brother. You don't get that."

Alejandro was the first to speak out when he began to see the cracks in the life we lived in Cuba before the revolution. His outrage over our family's wealth and position in contrast to the suffering of those around us spilled out at the dinner table. Eventually, he joined the Federación Estudiantil Universitaria, one of the student groups organizing at the University of Havana, and became involved with the resistance to then Cuban president Fulgencio Batista, participating in an attack on the Presidential Palace that ultimately led to our father disowning him. While most viewed Batista through a negative lens, our father chose friendship as a necessarily evil.

As with everything in our lives, where Alejandro went, I followed, until his anger became my anger, his dreams my dreams, his hope my hope, his death my death.

We left my brother behind in Cuba, buried in a mausoleum with countless other family members, his body interred beneath the same soil his killers now control.

I take a deep breath. "Are you interested in my help or not?"

Dwyer snubs the cigarette out on the ground with the toe of his evening shoe. "Possibly. We'll be in contact."

He's gone with a clipped nod, leaving me alone on the balcony, torn between hope and despair.

It's just me, Isabel, and Maria at the house with our parents now that Elisa has married. Maria spends her days in school while Isabel and I struggle to occupy our time. We volunteer with charities, the church, and then, of course, I have my political extracurricular activities. Still, it feels so aimless. I've resurrected the argument to allow us to attend university, asked to help out with the sugar company our father is resuscitating from its near demise thanks to Fidel's revolution.

Eight months ago, the regime passed the agrarian reform law, limiting the amount of privately owned land, redistributing the remainder or seizing it for government use. With a stroke of a pen, everything my family and others like us had built for centuries simply vanished. The rumors coming out of our country are harbingers of far worse. Thousands of my countrymen have been tortured, imprisoned, murdered.

"You should be careful."

The voice jolts me, and I pivot slowly, prolonging the moment a bit for female vanity, but mostly to clear my head.

He's no less golden now that I know who he is, or now that he's officially engaged. In fact, the only thing marring his handsome face is the scowl directed at me.

"Dwyer is not someone you want to get on the wrong side of," Nicholas Preston warns.

Given his influential position in the government, I'm not surprised he's familiar with a CIA official; from the interest I saw in his gaze, I'm not surprised he tracked my departure from the ballroom in the midst of his engagement announcement, either.

I bristle at the words, though, at the warning contained in his tone, at the implication that I need a keeper.

"I can take care of myself."

"Maybe you can, but that doesn't mean you shouldn't be more careful about the company you keep. Dwyer won't feel guilty about using you in order to achieve his ends, and he won't concern himself overmuch with what happens to you in the process. He doesn't play around."

"Good, because I don't play around, either."

His words feel a lot like all the ones my parents put before me, the barriers and obstacles—my gender, our family's status, the need to marry a man who reflects well on my family, the importance of always advancing our position in the world.

He steps forward, and I tilt my head to the side, studying him.

"Should you be out here, Senator Preston? I can't imagine your fiancée would be pleased to see you so concerned with another woman's affairs. Especially someone like me."

In this sedate little town, this insular island, I am a scandal.

A tic in his jaw erupts as the word "fiancée" falls from my lips. A full-body flinch at "affairs."

I smile, all teeth this time. "Like I said, I can take care of myself."

He doesn't speak, the silence yawning between us, and then he nods, the motion stiff, the familiarity that existed between us earlier on the balcony erased.

"Of course you can. I apologize for intruding." There's a hint of mockery in his tone and in the curve of his lips that suggests he bites, too. "As you said, my fiancée is waiting for me."

It turns out his is a remarkably effective closing line as I am met once again with the sight of his back and the rarity of watching a man walk away from me.

I never accepted any of those five proposals, never really considered them, because while most were nice enough men, some odious but in possession of perfectly nice *fortunes*, they never made me feel anything.

They never slid under my skin and rattled me.

In one evening, Nicholas Preston has.

chapter three

"How did it go last night?" Eduardo Diaz asks me in Spanish, his voice low, his gaze darting around the crowded restaurant as we debrief the introduction he arranged between Mr. Dwyer and me.

"I'm not sure," I admit. There hardly seems to be a point to lying to a man I used to blackmail into playing tea party when we were children. Eduardo is the sort of friend who is practically family.

"Well, how did you leave things?"

"Mr. Dwyer said he'd be in contact." I lower my voice. "I got the impression the CIA doesn't have a plan for getting close to Fidel, but he was intrigued by the idea of using me to accomplish such a feat."

Eduardo takes a sip of his coffee, a frown on his handsome face. "It's not enough."

"Maybe not, but what was I supposed to do? The man is suspicious. If I'd pushed too hard, he likely would have thought I was a Cuban agent or something."

The spying going on between Washington and Havana has been

particularly fervent these days, and Fidel is rumored to have inserted spies into the growing exile circles.

"Perhaps." Eduardo leans back in his seat, taking another sip of coffee. The instant he sets it back on the table, a server is there to refill it. He flashes her a smile, one I've watched him employ countless times. Women are forever falling in love with Eduardo Diaz, which I fear is a terrible mistake. He's a selfish bastard, albeit a lovable one, and at the moment, his focus is devoted to our cause, and a pair of fine eyes or other virtues won't sway him. Despite how much Eduardo likes women, he loves Cuba more.

A pink hue tinges the waitress's cheeks.

Once Eduardo's coffee mug is filled to the brim once more, the waitress leaves us.

"I heard you gained an admirer last night," he muses.

"I imagine I gained more than one; I was trying for my best damsel in distress—the princess without a throne, in need of a valiant knight to slay the dragon for her. Men love nonsense like that."

He grins. "Some do."

"No dragon slaying for you?"

"Hardly. You know I hate to dirty my hands."

"Well, presumably some of these American men don't share your sentiment."

They say Nicholas Preston was a war hero.

His gaze turns shrewd. "Speaking of American men, I heard you were the recipient of a ballroom proposal."

Eduardo wasn't at the party, but clearly, I'm not the only set of eyes and ears he has placed in Palm Beach society.

"You could just come to these events yourself, you know. Rather than relying on your little network of spies to tattle on us for you."

"I was playing cards last night. It turned out to be a very profitable endeavor."

"Cards? Is that what they're calling it these days? I'm sure there were other, shall we say, *distractions* to your evening."

Eduardo enjoys a position in society the rest of us haven't achieved. Despite the temporary lack of fortune, they view him as a catch, the sort of escort bored housewives and ambitious mothers love: his appearance handsome, his manners impeccable, a perfectly tailored dinner jacket at the ready.

"I can't help it if everyone finds me irresistible," he teases.

"Please. It's far too early for that sort of talk, and I went to bed far too late last night."

"So I wasn't the only one who had an *interesting* evening."

He manages to make "interesting" sound like a very naughty thing, indeed.

"I very much doubt my evening was as *interesting* as yours, considering I went home with my parents and sisters, and you went home with—who was she?—a lonely widow or aspiring cabaret singer? Perhaps a misunderstood, much younger wife?"

"Oh, I think your companion for the evening was a touch more interesting than mine."

My cheeks heat. Despite the lack of familial relation between us, Eduardo has always had a way of ruffling my feathers in a manner only older siblings can achieve.

"I'm quite certain I don't know what you mean."

"I think you do." His expression sobers. "They're a powerful American family, Beatriz. Influential in politics."

"They may be, but he's a distant cousin. I hardly think he's influential in their political decisions."

"I wasn't talking about the marriage proposal. I heard you also caught a certain senator's eye."

My voice cools. "Do you have spies among the staff at these parties, or guests you've converted to the cause?"

"You know I can't give away all my secrets."

"It was just a dance."

"Right."

"It was," I insist.

"The way I heard it, he spent the whole night watching you."

It shouldn't make me feel a sense of satisfaction, but it does.

"He spent most of the night getting engaged."

"Engaged men still have eyes."

"Oh, charming, exactly want I want, a philanderer."

"Yes, better if he is a philanderer—for our purposes, at least. I'm sure his pretty fiancée can fare just fine. There may be a day when we need his vote in the Senate, Beatriz."

It's a struggle to keep my voice light. "From a dance to votes in the Senate, my, you are ambitious. I thought the plan was to kill Fidel, not legislate him to death."

"We need to keep all of our options on the table. There's a party tonight. Senator Preston will be there. All I'm suggesting is that you entice him a bit, see if he's interested."

My gaze narrows, my voice hardened to steel.

"You might not have a hard time finding underlings to do your bidding, but I'm not for sale. I'm here for Fidel, not to sleep with politicians to help you regain your fortune."

"I thought you were here for Alejandro," Eduardo counters, not a hint of shame in his expression. What is it with people throwing my brother's name around as though I will simply bend to their will if they tug at my heartstrings? You can love someone and still not lose your reason. "And it's not just my fortune we're talking about here," Eduardo adds. "Don't you want a better life for yourself, your parents, your sisters?"

"I'm not going to sleep with Senator Preston for you, or for Alejandro's memory. Or because my sisters and I are forced to re-wear our gowns. There are other ways to defeat Fidel. Besides, I knew my brother better than anyone, and I'm fairly certain he would have objected to me prostituting myself for the cause."

Despite the manner in which Fidel has beggared us all, Eduardo's upbringing is enough to ensure he finally looks momentarily abashed. "Fine. Don't sleep with him. But see what comes from you holding his interest. Maybe he'll be more amenable to helping us if he likes you."

"He's getting married," I say for Eduardo's benefit, and perhaps a bit for my own, the reminder a necessary one in the face of the memory of how much I enjoyed myself on the balcony last night.

Was he really watching me the whole evening?

"And you're Beatriz Perez," Eduardo retorts.

"I'm not going to ruin a man's life or his marital ambitions. I'm not going to hurt innocent people."

"He's an American politician," Eduardo counters. "How innocent can he possibly be? The Americans have unclean hands in all of this. There's a party tonight. Your Senator Preston will be there. Come with me."

I hesitate.

He smiles. "What's the harm in trying? Like you said, it was only a dance."

Eduardo throws the gauntlet down with a knowing gleam in his dark brown eyes—both a challenge and a plea—and damn him for it, because we both know I never was one for resisting lost causes or walking away from a dare.

The crowd differs from last night; there are no matrons or gray-haired parents. This is the fast set, some of the faces familiar, most a far cry from the parties I attend with my parents.

"You look beautiful," Eduardo whispers, my arm tucked in his as we enter the room.

"That may be, but it's a little disconcerting when you say it like that."

"Like what?"

"As though you're dangling me in front of them like a cut of meat."

Eduardo chuckles, a lazy smile on his face that draws the notice of the vast majority of the women in the room. If they didn't hate me before, showing up on the arm of one of the season's most handsome bachelors certainly won't do me any favors.

"I really did miss you when you were still in Cuba," Eduardo murmurs, his manner affectionate and indulgent, giving the impression that we are either old friends or lovers.

Eduardo left Cuba before we did, before President Batista fled the country on New Year's Eve, abandoning us to Fidel's hands on New Year's Day. I always wondered if all the money Eduardo had slipped people throughout the years gave him advance warning that Cuba's fortunes were about to shift.

"Most women I meet these days spend their time flattering me," he adds, grinning. "It's exhausting, really."

I stifle a snort as I tear my gaze away from his and scan the crowd.

My breath hitches.

A pair of blue eyes bore into mine, and Eduardo is momentarily forgotten.

There's no fiancée tonight, or if there is, they aren't the sort of couple to dangle on each other's arms. More likely than not, she's at another more respectable venue like most unmarried girls of good families. It's that kind of party.

Nicholas Preston is just as handsome as he was last night, wearing a suit instead of a tuxedo, his skin hale and tan against the blinding white collar.

Polite society comes to Palm Beach during these winter months to escape the harsh temperatures farther north, and it's easy to envision Senator Preston hitting the links with the Kennedys in the early-morning Florida sun, or walking along the sandy beach in the waning hours of the day. He gives the impression he is happiest doing something: either behind the helm of a sailboat, gripping the stick of a plane, on the back of a polo pony brought down from some tony estate somewhere, or with a racket or club in hand, ready to thoroughly trounce his opponent.

I stand next to Eduardo while he greets our host, the heir to a newspaper fortune whose family is immortalized in the *Social Register*, which serves as my mother's unofficial bible as she pores over the names, searching for an eligible man to which she can affiance one of her remaining unmarried daughters.

Nicholas Preston's gaze follows me, lingering over the bare skin exposed by my gown, Eduardo's hand on my body, the point where our flesh meets.

When Eduardo leads me onto the makeshift dance floor, a shiver slides down my spine, the weight of Nicholas's stare unsettling, the curious looks from the rest of the guests pointed. Have they noticed the attention I'm drawing from Nicholas Preston's corner of the room? Or are their stares merely a reaction to the sight of Eduardo and me together, the manner in which our dark features complement each other, the familiarity with which we move a confirmation of their suspicions that I am Eduardo's mistress or something equally tawdry?

"He's going to ask you to dance," Eduardo predicts before releasing me into a twirl.

I peek over his shoulder.

Nicholas Preston is still watching me. Goose bumps rise over my arm, the twirling making me just a bit dizzy. Or perhaps it's everything else tonight: the man, the subterfuge, the want curling inside me.

The thing is—I want Nicholas Preston to cut in. I want him to cross the ballroom and ask me to dance, and I want to pretend I'm just a twenty-two-year-old girl, the girl I used to be.

I only want to dance with him. Fine, maybe flirt a bit, too.

The song ends without me glancing his way again; it's a Herculean effort, considering I feel his attention on me as surely as a physical caress. Eduardo was right; he does watch me.

Constantly.

Eduardo leaves me by myself in a corner with a wink and the promise to return with champagne. Thirty seconds later—

"Dance with me."

My brow rises at the smooth voice, the confidence contained in those words, as I fight to keep a smile from my red lips. I like him better for the fact that he, too, treats this as though it is little more than a foregone conclusion, as if we are two magnets drawn to each other, his arrogance tempered by the weight of his gaze on me all evening.

"Your asking has lost some of its polish. What was I before, 'thief-of-hearts,' wasn't it?"

He smiles. "I didn't think my charms worked on you."

I can't quite formulate a response to that one.

"People will talk," I say instead.

"Yes, they will."

"It's an election year."

He laughs. "It's always an election year."

"And you are an engaged man."

"I am. But have no fear, I won't lose my heart over a dance."

I grin, returning his verbal volley. "But I might."

A dimple winks back at me as he offers me his hand. His fingers are momentarily unencumbered by the weight of a thick, gold wedding band. "Then we will just have to risk it, won't we?"

I hesitate.

I wasn't merely being coy earlier. I walk a tightrope when it comes to my reputation.

And still, I can't summon the energy to deny myself this pleasure.

I place my hand in his, my fingers threading with his fingers, our palms connecting.

There are whispers; there are muffled gasps. Ironic, really, considering we're surrounded by men and women dancing with partners to whom they aren't lawfully wed.

But if I've learned anything in this past year, it's that there are different rules for those who were born into this enclave, and interlopers like me. If Andrew's proposal last night bothered them, tonight is likely to drive them to apoplexy. In the social hierarchy of the Palm Beach set, there is no higher an unmarried—or married—woman can reach than Nicholas Randolph Preston III. His is the lead they all follow.

He knows it, too.

He appears impervious to the looks, the wagging tongues, nary a hitch in his stride. At the same time, it's impossible to miss the way his breath catches as his hand settles on my waist.

"Are you enjoying yourself tonight?" he asks.

I cock my head to the side, studying him while we dance. "Are we to have polite conversation now?"

"Would you rather we had impolite conversation?"

"Perhaps. What exactly would that entail?"

"I imagine it would start and end with your dress."

I flush beneath said fabric. "It is a very fine dress."

A dress Marilyn Monroe herself would be proud to wear, form-fitting and decadent, perfect for highlighting the abundance of curves God gave me. My mother barely approved of the dress, her concern for gossip warring with her need to marry her daughters off with military-like precision. Pragmatism won out over propriety, as it so often does.

"Are you trying to steal my heart?" His expression is one of mock alarm.

"Only a little bit," I tease.

My gaze drifts to the other guests before returning to my partner. "Considering the way we left things last night, I thought you were angry with me."

"I don't think we've known each other long enough to be angry with each other."

"True," I acknowledge. "It occurs to me we've actually never been properly introduced."

"Then let me rectify that immediately. My friends call me Nick."

I turn the name over in my mind, savoring the sound of it, the private side to a very public man. How many women have used the moniker with him? Have known the casual side of him?

"Are we to be friends?"

"Something like that." His gaze turns speculative. "You seem to have other *friends* here tonight."

It's impossible to miss the question wrapped in those words.

"Eduardo is more like an old, dear family friend. Almost like a brother."

Almost, but not quite.

"With similar interests, I presume?"

It's easy to forget the man before me is more than the golden facade, that he sits on powerful committees in the Senate. Eduardo wasn't wrong; Nick Preston would make a powerful ally.

"Are you trying to get me to spill all my secrets?" I ask.

"Hardly. In my thirty-seven years, I've learned the art of patience. I have a feeling your secrets are best unwrapped one by one."

"I didn't realize you were so old." Etiquette is momentarily forgotten as I seize on that important fact and ignore the unmistakable hum of interest lingering in the background of our conversation. No wonder he's eager to marry.

"Is thirty-seven old these days?"

"It is when you're twenty-two."

He smiles. "See. My first Beatriz secret."

"My age is hardly a secret."

"Perhaps. But it is something about you, one more piece to the puzzle. Besides, I have a feeling you're an old soul at twenty-two."

"I don't think you can live through a revolution and lay much claim to innocence afterward," I agree.

"No, I suppose you can't. War has a way of sanding down your virtue."

"You fought in Europe, didn't you?"

He nods, his expression more guarded than before.

"So you know then."

"Yes," he replies.

It's different going to a place and fighting, seeing the destruction men can wreak all around you, and then returning home, to the sanctuary of a country that will likely never descend into such madness. Harder to live it in your favorite haunts, to watch death touch your friends and family. And still, war is war and misery comes to all men, natives and foreigners alike.

"It's hard talking to people who haven't lived it, who haven't seen the things you've seen, who don't understand."

He nods.

"What was it like? Going to war? You were a pilot, right?"

"It was like nothing life had ever prepared me for. It was terrifying the first few times I went up in the air. The first time I shot a plane down, knew I'd killed a man . . ." His voice drifts off for a moment. "I didn't think you could get used to a thing like that.

"After a while, though, you do get used to it. You know each time you go up that you may die, but you make peace with it, I suppose, learn to adjust to sitting next to a man in the bar one day, knowing he probably won't come home the next. And then it's all over, and miraculously, you didn't die, and you go home.

"Everyone wants to thank you for your service, and they call you a hero, and you struggle to find where you fit in this world again."

Our gazes lock.

"You go to balls, and parties, and drink champagne, and dance with pretty girls, but there's always a piece of you back there, amid the bombs, thinking of the lives you could have saved, but didn't, the sons, husbands, and fathers that should have come home, but didn't. And you begin to wonder why you were saved when all those good men weren't, if there's some reason for your life, something you're meant to do to pay back the debt you owe. It eats at you, over and over again, and it's hard to get those thoughts out of your head. It's hard to find people who understand."

Do I really even stand a chance?

It was so much easier to discount him as just another Palm Beach playboy, more style than substance, more privilege than responsibility, but the truth of it is in front of me, swimming in those blue eyes that are clearly in another time, in another place, haunted by images he can't erase, sounds that wake him in a cold sweat throughout the night.

I still hear the firing squads in La Cabaña executing Cubans with terrifying precision, still smell the stench of death, damp, and filth in the hellhole of a prison; the noise of the crowd cheering and jeering as men were condemned to death in the stadium wakes me in the middle of the night. It's the sound of fear that lives with me now, the refrain of uncertainty: a whirring engine as a plane takes flight, a body hitting the ground, a car screeching away.

"I'm sorry," I reply, knowing how little comfort the words offer.

"I know."

Silence descends, a prick of discomfort filling me, the sensation that he has indeed uncovered another one of my secrets—a real one—the pain beneath the diamond smile.

"They're not staring anymore," I comment, struggling to fill the silence with something innocuous and impersonal. Something safe.

"Who?"

"The rest of the party."

There's that smile again. "I didn't notice."

The song ends and he stills.

It feels unnatural to stop, to pull away from this man.

"Thanks for the dance," he says, his tone formal compared to the intimacies we shared moments ago, the veneer returned once more.

Which version of him does his fiancée know and love? The man with ghosts in his eyes or the composed one standing before me now?

There's faint pressure at my elbow, and I don't have to look to know Eduardo is standing at my side. The evidence is etched all over Nick's expression.

Nick inclines his head, not offering any words for Eduardo, a glance passing between them over my head. Seeing them together like this, I am struck by the sensation that Eduardo is a boy, whereas Nick Preston is a man.

And then Nick is gone, walking away from me once more, all broad-shouldered, long-limbed grace.

Eduardo hands me the champagne flute. My fingers tremble as I grasp the stem.

"I almost feel sorry for the man," he comments.

My gaze follows Nick's retreating back until the party swallows him up and he disappears completely.

"Why?"

"You'll break his heart eventually," Eduardo predicts.

"I highly doubt that."

If I had a heart left to lose, I'd fear he'd eventually break mine.

chapter four

Through the grapevine, word spreads that Nick Preston has left Palm Beach for Washington D.C., garnering political capital in preparation for the upcoming election in November. Weeks pass, the season insufferably dull in his absence. His pretty little fiancée remains behind, our paths crossing at a distance throughout the social whirl even if we do not speak. She is shepherded around Palm Beach by a host of Prestons and Daviesies; her own prestigious surname is enough to elevate her to a distinct social stratum from the sphere I inhabit.

Eduardo shows up on my doorstep one February afternoon, orchids in hand.

I shake my head at the sight of my favorite flowers, a smile playing at my lips; his reduced circumstances notwithstanding, Eduardo always did have style down to an art form.

"Come for a drive with me," he says when he greets me.

The flowers are likely more of a bribe than an attempt at romance, and if he thinks I can be bought with a pretty pair of orchids, he's sorely mistaken. Then again, the possibility of getting into mischief—and Eduardo always guarantees mischief—is far more entertaining than my alternative plans for the day: reading fashion magazines on the couch next to Isabel and listening to my mother bemoan our lack of prospects. That she's said little of the gossip surrounding my dance with Nick Preston speaks to how much our fortunes have fallen; even my mother realizes how far out of reach he is.

"Where will this drive take us?" I ask Eduardo.

"To visit a mutual friend. He wants to meet with you again. He's interested in your proposition and wishes to discuss the logistics."

I'd almost given up on the CIA man in the intervening month between our first meeting and now.

"He wants to move forward?"

"He's definitely interested. I told him we'd meet him for lunch."

"And you assumed I'd be available?"

"I assumed you'd be bored out of your mind and looking for an adventure." Eduardo holds open the car door for me. "Are you coming?"

I get into the car, the flowers dangling from my fingers.

The wind from the open road blows my hair as we speed down the highway. The weather is a bit cooler than I'd like; while many flock to Palm Beach to escape the colder weather up north, it's nothing compared to Cuba's tropical climes. I almost ask Eduardo to put the top up, but the question sticks in my throat as we whip around a curve.

Eduardo drives with the same carefree approach he adopts with everything else in life, and it is both his best and his worst quality. When you are along for the ride, that lassitude opens up a whole new world of possibilities. When you are caught up in whatever wreck his carelessness has caused, it is his tragic flaw. When I was younger, I fancied him a bit; indeed, among our set and contemporaries, I'm fairly certain having a crush on Eduardo Diaz was a rite of passage of sorts. The three years between us gave him an air of sophistication, the closeness between our families a constant comfort. He was always there in the background of my life in Cuba, as much a part of my memories as the sound of the waves off the Malecón, my sisters' laughter, my brother's voice.

I stole a kiss once when we were kids playing in the backyard of my house in Miramar and swore him to secrecy later. I never would have heard the end of it had Alejandro found out I'd kissed his best friend. Does Eduardo even remember? The edges of the memory blur. It feels like such a long time ago, as though the moment belongs to a different girl.

"Where are we meeting him?" I raise my voice to be heard over the sound of the wind and the waves near the road.

"A little restaurant up in Jupiter. Nothing fancy. He thought it would be better this way," Eduardo shouts back.

"How well do you know Mr. Dwyer?"

"Not well at all," Eduardo admits, his fingers strumming the steering wheel as the little car takes another sharp turn. My stomach lurches with the movement even as I welcome the speed, even as I weigh the odds of waking with a wicked head cold in the morning. Why are the things that are the most fun invariably the worst for you?

"And yet, you trust him."

"I wouldn't say I trust him, but we don't have many options available to us. He'll probably cast us aside when we're no longer useful, but at the moment, our interests align. Hopefully, they will continue to do so for long enough for us to get what we want out of the deal."

"And if we don't get what we want?"

"I don't know. We're working on some other things."

"Like what?"

"You'll see."

"So there are secrets between us now?"

He shoots me a sidelong glance. "You tell me. What did you and Senator Preston discuss during your dance?"

I turn away from him, casting my gaze out to sea.

"Nothing of interest."

He chuckles softly. "Now why don't I believe that? I saw the way he looked at you. That certainly wasn't nothing."

"We spoke of the weather. Of the party, the social season."

"Sure you did."

We spend the rest of the drive in silence as I stare out the open window, watching the scenery pass us by. It's a whole different world when you cross the bridge that separates Palm Beach from the mainland. It's nice to get off the island, to gain a reprieve from the prying eyes and snickers, not to mention to take a break from my mother. With each day in exile, she grows more despondent, more restless, the walls of our home closing in. I'm not sure she would have agreed to leave Cuba if she'd known we'd be gone this long. At the same time, after Alejandro was murdered, staying became even more impossible. Fidel and his men threw my father in prison and threatened to kill him. Who knows what would have happened to him or the rest of us if we'd stayed?

When we reach the restaurant, Eduardo pulls into the dusty parking lot, sliding the sporty car between an Oldsmobile and a Buick. The rest of the lot is barren, the building's exterior a far cry from the elegant restaurants on the island. The chance of recognition here is exceedingly low, what's left of my reputation at the moment safeguarded.

Eduardo walks me to the front door, steadying me when I stumble, my heels slipping on the loose gravel, kicking up dust in my wake.

"This is where I leave you."

"You're joking."

He shakes his head. "I'm merely the messenger. He only wants to meet with you. I'll wait for you in the car, and when you're finished, I'll take you home."

I've met with Mr. Dwyer alone, of course, but somehow, it felt different when we were ensconced in a balcony off a ballroom. This setting is another thing entirely, the sort of place my mother never would allow any of her daughters to patronize, and I hesitate at the entrance, the door battered, the restaurant's dingy interior visible through the glass hardly encouraging.

Eduardo leans forward, kissing my temple.

"You'll be fine."

He holds the door open for me, and I cross the threshold, my gaze sweeping over my surroundings, my dampened palms brushing against my skirts.

I've been on edge since the revolution took hold in Havana, since Alejandro's death, since I began wondering if one day they would come for me, too. We lived under Batista's rule for so many years in a constant state of conflict that it was easy to pretend as long as we displayed a modicum of sense, as long as we didn't dare too much, with our father's influence enough to keep us out of real danger, we would be safe. Alejandro kept me a step or two removed from the rebel movement, shielding me from Batista's ire. But then Fidel came and everything changed, our last name enough to cause real trouble, to threaten us all, my brother's death reshaping the way in which I view the world. Now when I walk into a room, I look for the danger first.

The restaurant is practically vacant. At one table sit two elderly gentlemen, newspapers in hand, cups of coffee beside them. On the other end of the restaurant, tucked away in a booth, sits Mr. Dwyer—CIA kingmaker.

Dwyer doesn't look up from his newspaper and coffee mug as I walk toward him, and I sweep into the booth with the Perez charm that has served me well thus far. When all else fails, pretend your palms aren't sweating, your knees not knocking beneath your skirts.

"Mr. Dwyer."

He looks up from his drink. I've no doubt he knew the moment I stepped into the restaurant.

"Miss Perez."

The waitress comes over and takes my order, bringing me coffee.

"Why did you call me here?" I ask once she leaves.

"Because I've spoken with others about your proposal." He takes a sip of his coffee. "They find it intriguing."

I lean forward in my seat, lowering my voice. It's time for some intelligence gathering of my own.

"Where do things stand with Fidel?"

It's hard to not be in Havana, to rely upon the word of others as to the mood of the country, the rumbles on the street.

"Not good," Mr. Dwyer admits after a pause. "We tried to open a secure communications line between Washington and Havana. Didn't take."

The fear that the United States will legitimize the regime and leave us Cubans to our own devices has been a looming specter over our plans for quite some time now. At the moment, any attempts to remove Fidel from power hinge on American support, or at least the possibility that the Americans won't come to Fidel's aid. We learned the hard way under Batista that the United States is a formidable ally with a seemingly endless supply of resources behind them.

"No, it likely wouldn't," I comment. "Fidel is not the sort to welcome someone else interfering in his affairs."

"In this case, he doesn't get a vote."

"Bringing him to heel will not be easy," I warn.

There were those of us who thought it useful to allow Fidel to defeat Batista and then simply eject Fidel from power. Many of my brothers and sisters in arms believed he could bring about the change we yearned for. When Fidel failed to do so, his removal became a necessity. Unfortunately, he's proven far more resilient than anyone ever imagined. Better the Americans learn the lesson now rather than later.

"He is an arrogant man," I add. "They are all arrogant men. Serving on bended knee will not be in Fidel's nature, and he's not a man born to compromise, either. He cannot afford to lose face in Cuba, to be a puppet to the American regime as Batista was. I'm not sure the people would stand for it."

"His arrogance is precisely why we need you."

"So now you *need* me."

"It would appear so."

"Why now? You didn't intervene last January when Cubans were being slaughtered in Havana. What's your interest in all of this? What has he done to push you to the breaking point?"

"Sugar," Dwyer answers.

The agrarian reform law. I should have guessed. The ground gives and Castro takes it away. The law is the final blow for my father, one he rants about over dinner and drinks, the unfairness of it a crushing defeat for all of us. Under the agrarian reform law enacted in the summer of 1959, the Cuban government nationalized estates and companies, restricting large-scale landholding, and prohibiting foreign ownership. While some of the land was distributed to the Cuban people, rumor has it the government kept the majority for itself.

"We'd hoped he would compensate the American companies he nationalized," Mr. Dwyer continues. "That he would be open to discussion, but he is not to be reasoned with. And now with these murmurs of communism spreading, with him cozying up to the

Soviet Union, well, we simply can't bide our time anymore. He has become a thorn in our side, and we must remove him from power. And when fair means have failed us, well, we are not averse to foul ones." He smiles. "I speak to the methods, not the instrument."

"Of course." I pause. "This isn't just about sugar, though, is it?"

Wars have been waged over far less, but somehow I can't quite envision the might of the American government this concerned with agrarian reform in Cuba, even if it does affect the fortunes of American companies. Nor can I envision them overmuch concerned with the well-being of Cubans.

"It's complicated," he answers. "Fidel has been speaking with foreign leaders, expressing his interest in helping them create similar discord in their countries."

I'm hardly surprised.

"We must be careful," Mr. Dwyer continues. "He is popular in Cuba. You're correct. We cannot create the impression that the ills of Batista's regime are being repeated through our intervention in matters of Cuban sovereignty."

His point is not lost on me, nor is the irony that I have become a willing participant in an arrangement that I spent much of my adult life decrying. When the Americans propped up Batista, I viewed them as villains. Now we will join forces to remove Fidel.

Eduardo's earlier allusion to his more secretive activities with the CIA comes to mind again.

"You have something else planned, don't you? Beyond my role in all of this."

"Effective diplomacy relies upon several contingencies. So yes, we have considered many options should this mission fail."

There are rumors—little more than idle whispers, really—that they're planning an attack of some sort, an attempt to wrest control away from Fidel.

"The Soviets are becoming a problem. This trade deal—it looks like there is to be friendship between Moscow and Havana. If Fidel gets his hands on enough of Khrushchev's arms, everything will change." Dwyer signals for the bill for our two coffees. "We're working out the details now. I must return to Washington, so it's likely we won't meet again for some time. In the meantime, we'll be in contact when we have something for you. Eduardo will work as an intermediary between us."

"And if I do this, what do I get in return?"

"I thought you were doing this for love of country, Miss Perez."

"Then you mistook me. I don't do anything out of the goodness of my heart. If I'm going to risk my life, I deserve to be sufficiently compensated, and I don't come cheaply."

I learned a thing or two about doing business at my father's knee.

Mr. Dwyer makes a grunt that almost sounds like approval.

"What do you want?" He pulls a shiny black ballpoint pen from his jacket pocket, sliding it across the Formica tabletop. He tosses a paper napkin to me, the restaurant's name scrolled at the bottom.

My fingers tremble as I write my demand down. I've thought about this since the night we met in Palm Beach, tried to imagine what would restore my family's position. You can't put a price on avenging my brother's death, but the rest of it—

One hundred thousand dollars and my family's property in Cuba returned to us.

I cap the pen, set it down on the table, and slide the paper back to him.

"Do we have a deal?"

He gives the napkin a cursory glance before he looks up at me and smiles.

"We have a deal."

. . .

"How did it go?" Eduardo asks when I slip back into the car.

"Well, I think. He wants to proceed."

Should I have made more demands? Did I ask for too much? Too little?

I've always prided myself on being fairly good at reading people—it's hard to get through the social whirl without that particular skill—but the CIA's man is inscrutable. After his parting words, he took the napkin, crumpled it up in his jacket pocket, paid the check, and walked out the door.

Rude, really.

"I don't like him."

"I don't think anyone likes him, Beatriz."

"Perhaps I should clarify then. I don't trust him."

"Do you trust me?"

"Sometimes."

Eduardo grins. "Smart." His expression sobers. "I made a promise to Alejandro when you got involved in this stuff back in Havana. I told him if something ever happened to him, I'd watch over you like I would my own sister. He was my best friend. I won't let anything happen to you."

Tears well in my eyes at the mention of my brother, at how much I miss him.

"I know."

Eduardo cups my chin. "It'll be fine. I promise. In a year, we'll be sitting at a table at the yacht club toasting your success. We'll dance at the Tropicana. You'll be a hero in Havana."

"I don't want to be a hero. I just want to go home."

"And we will," Eduardo vows.

"Do you ever feel like you're forgetting it?"

"Cuba?" he asks.

I nod.

"Sometimes," he answers after a pause.

"It's like that for me, too. Each day I wake up here it feels a little farther away." It's easier confessing these things to him than to my own family. Cuba is in its own way a difficult subject for all of us, any mention of Alejandro's death avoided by all. For my parents, there's the added complication that prior to his death, they'd cut off all ties with my brother due to his anti-Batista activities.

"I worry I'm forgetting Alejandro," I admit. "I woke from a dream the other night and couldn't remember the sound of his voice or his laugh. All of our photographs are back in Havana. Will I eventually forget what he looked like?"

Eduardo squeezes my hand. "It's normal to feel that way. Even harder still when we're away from home, from the places where he lived, the things he loved."

"That, too."

And at the same time, even as I'm loath to admit it, perhaps it makes things a bit easier, too. At least the ghost of my brother isn't haunting every room in our house, every street corner.

"Do you remember him?" I ask.

A sad smile crosses Eduardo's handsome face. "I do. I remember when we were kids running wild around Miramar. I remember the time we both fell for the same dancer at the Tropicana. I did everything I could to win her, but of course, I didn't stand a chance. Maybe because he was a Perez, but probably because he was so damned charming."

I smile. "He really was. He lost some of that, though. After the attack on the Presidential Palace, he was someone else entirely. He never laughed like he used to."

My brother killed in his fight for Cuba's future, and while he was passionate about the cause, he was at his core a kindhearted man. He didn't have it in him to take a life and not be shaken by the ramifications of it.

"You never felt the same way he did, did you?" I ask.

"What do you mean?" Eduardo brushes a strand of hair behind my ear.

"You were involved in those efforts to remove Batista from power. You're doing the same now with Fidel. But you never went through the"—I search for the right words—"self-loathing Alejandro experienced. How do you believe in the movement, in democracy for Cuba, and not hate the privileged society that caused it, the society we are part of?"

"How do you?" he counters.

I've never been the idealist my brother was. For all I objected to Batista, I never denounced my family like Alejandro did. I could never absolve us as entirely innocent, but at the same time, I couldn't consign us to the role of villains, either.

"It's my pragmatism, I suppose," I answer.

"You're a survivor. For yourself, your family, your country. That's how I do it. I figure it's going to take all of the energy I have to remove Fidel from power. I'll deal with the rest of it later."

"The note will come due for all of this eventually, won't it?"

Eduardo smiles sadly. "It always does. The trick is finding someone else who will pay it."

chapter five

My social calendar is full in the week following my meeting with Mr. Dwyer, the two parts of my life so distinct. In public, I am the carefree debutante. In the few private moments I am allowed, I wait and worry over my arrangement with Mr. Dwyer. My mother keeps me busy in her never-ending quest to find Isabel and me husbands. To that end, she's fixated on Valentine's Day.

Everyone who is anyone in Palm Beach commemorates Valentine's Day in a singular fashion: the Palm Beach Heart Ball, a charity event to raise money for the American Heart Association, chaired in previous years by Mamie Eisenhower herself. Considering the past guest list has included members of the illustrious Kennedy family, entertainers like Ed Sullivan, and sports stars of the same ilk as Joe DiMaggio, she couldn't have asked for a better occasion for her daughters to "see and be seen"—and to raise money for charity, of course. This year's chairwoman, the wife of a wealthy industrialist and a permanent fixture on the Palm Beach social scene, has outdone herself, and the stakes my mother has riding on this evening are great indeed, her eyes wide and calculating as though she has the personal net worth of each man in the party tucked somewhere in the recesses of her mind, their marital status jotted down beside the extraordinary sum. In Cuba, she was tenacious, but in Palm Beach, matchmaking has become her vocation.

We walk into the ball, a line of sugar queens, arranged by age, which auspiciously happens to coincide with the speed with which our mother hopes to see us married off. Isabel is first in line; she wears a Dior gown we've only repurposed once—an impressive feat given our current finances. Technically, she's still engaged—her fiancé, Roberto, is back in Cuba—but he was hardly our mother's first choice before, given his modest means, and I now imagine she's ready to jettison him from Isabel entirely whether Isabel wishes it or not.

I'm next, wearing a red gown in a nod to the holiday and my own inability to blend in with the background. Husband-hunting or not, there's nothing wrong with making an impression. And if a handsome senator happens to commemorate the holiday in the same fashion, well, there's no harm in looking nice.

Elisa trails behind me, her arm tucked in her husband's.

Maria is at home, likely cursing her youth and our mother's rules.

Our parents bring up the rear, watching over us with proud expressions. Elisa's wedding helped us gain a useful entrée to society, and no doubt they have even higher hopes for Isabel and me.

I scan the party like I always do, as though I'm heading into hostile territory and need to identify any and all threats, disappointed not to see Nick Preston's blond head towering over those around him. Surely, he wouldn't miss tonight, would he? There's no sign of the fiancée on a second sweep, either.

I turn toward Isabel, and suddenly, a tingle slides down my spine, joined by a prick of awareness, a hum in my veins.

He's here.

I swivel slowly until I see him.

Wherever Nick has been campaigning, he hasn't lost his tan or the easy smile on his face that augments his charm.

He really is too handsome by half.

Nick stills, mid-conversation, inclining his head for a moment until his gaze rests on me. The curve of his lips deepens, a gleam entering his eyes for an instant before it is gone, his profile to me, his attention returned to the group surrounding him, hanging on his every word.

A flash of heat rises over my skin.

I can't look away.

Because even though he isn't looking directly at me, even though there's nothing in his demeanor to suggest he's anything other than polite and solicitous toward his companion, I know the smile on his face—brighter than it was seconds before—is meant for me. I am immeasurably grateful I chose the red dress tonight.

Elisa sidles up next to me, her voice in my ear.

"Be careful with that one."

In the year since we left Havana, my little sister has become a wife, a mother, and where her admonitions to proceed with caution rang with a faint hint of disapproval in Cuba, now there is a sagacity behind her words conveying the impression she's the elder one.

"I will," I lie as Nick Preston breaks away from the group and walks toward me.

I take a step away from Elisa. Then another one.

In the five weeks he has been gone, I've thought about this moment, played it over and over again in my mind, wondered if he was thinking of me in his home state of Connecticut, or at work in Washington D.C., or wherever his travels took him.

Every time I crossed a threshold into one of these events, every polo match, every charity lunch, every performance, I looked for him.

And now he's here.

I'm vaguely aware of the other people in the room, my family somewhere behind me, but at the moment, they're little more than a hum lingering in the background. Nick Preston has a way of filling up a room I imagine is so very useful in his political and personal life.

"You look beautiful tonight," he says in greeting.

I grin, any hope of sophistication likely obliterated in the face of the giddiness his compliment brings. "Thank you."

I fear my crush has deepened since I last saw him.

"Happy Valentine's Day."

"Happy Valentine's Day," I echo. Neither one of us speaks, and I'm certain we flaunt matching embarrassed smiles.

My name is uttered in an urgent tone behind me, and I turn, in time to see Isabel flash me one of those looks we've developed for conveying whatever needs to be said without speaking at all. Sisterly intuition and all that. I shoot her a bland smile as if to suggest everything is fine, as though anyone who knows me well can't read the temptation lingering in my eyes.

I pivot back to face Nick.

He steps closer to me, his tall form shielding me from the rest of the room.

"I've spent the whole night watching the door," he murmurs. "Wondering when you would arrive." His voice is a silken caress. "And now you know one of my secrets."

I duck my head, my cheeks heating. "Everyone is watching us."

Perhaps tonight will be forgiven when the next scandal emerges, if he is seen on his fiancée's arm enough. Perhaps it will be forgiven with time, but his reputation will fare far better in this than mine will even though he's the one with the fiancée.

Does he love his fiancée? Does she love him?

"Does it bother you?" he asks as though he's just noticed the attention we're drawing.

"That people so vehemently dislike me? Not particularly. If I only went places where I was wanted, I'd hardly go anywhere these days."

"Then you're braver than I thought," he answers, his voice gentle—too gentle.

"Don't feel sorry for me."

"I don't. Not even a little bit."

"Liar."

He smiles. "For what it's worth, I don't think it's so much that they hate you as that they fear you."

"I'm the least fearsome thing I can imagine," I scoff.

"I suppose it's a matter of perspective then, because I'd disagree."

I am equally struck by the desire to laugh and the need to weep.

"You've been to war."

"I have."

"Don't tell me I am more terrifying than a blitz."

The corners of his mouth quirk up. "Perhaps not more terrifying. But you have a way of making a man doubt himself I never felt when I was in the sky."

"And that's scary?"

"Utterly terrifying."

We both know, how can we not? This is a hello and a good-bye all wrapped into one.

My sisters and my parents have moved on, but I'll probably get an earful about this encounter later.

"What are we doing?" I ask him.

"Right now?"

"Yes."

"Hell if I know."

"We should probably stop."

"Probably," he agrees.

"I have sisters, and they have reputations that need protecting. And at the moment, everyone is craning their necks to hear what we're saying."

Regret flashes in his eyes. "I'm sorry."

"I know."

"What was it you said earlier about savoring your last moments of freedom?" he asks. "Want to dance?"

I laugh despite the melancholy filling me. "It seems like all we ever do is dance."

"It's probably the safest activity of all the ones we could do. But perhaps not the most fun," he amends, a dimple winking back at me.

I hesitate. "One dance. And then no more."

"One dance," he agrees.

And suddenly, his hand is there, outstretched between us, and it seems the most natural thing in the world to place my palm against his, for his fingers to curl over mine.

Nick leads me out onto the dance floor as a new song begins.

Eduardo is on the dance floor with a pretty redhead, a smile on his face, his gaze trained on Nick and me. Eduardo inclines his head toward me in a mock salute.

I will tell Eduardo this part of his plan is off the table; I won't use the attraction I feel for Nick to advance our interests in Cuba.

Nick follows my gaze until his settles on Eduardo as well. "We both lead complicated lives, don't we?"

"What isn't complicated in this climate?"

"True. Not everyone understands, though." He looks out over the ballroom, his attention shifting away from Eduardo. "Some people are content to attend parties like these and pretend everyone is fortunate enough to live like this."

"We made that mistake in Cuba. For a time, at least. We learned our lesson in the worst possible way."

"What would you do if things were different? If Castro was gone?"

"I would go home," I answer without hesitation. "I don't belong here. I belong in Havana, with my old friends, the family still there. Our nanny, Magda. This—Palm Beach—is a temporary life, a purgatory of sorts."

"I've never been to Cuba. I've always wanted to go. I've heard it's beautiful."

"It *is* beautiful. The beaches, the countryside, the mountains, the city, all those old Spanish buildings—" In my memory, I see the island exactly as it was, the sun rising over the Malecón. "It's the closest thing to paradise. On the surface, at least," I amend. "We have much work to do."

"And you want to be part of that work?"

"Yes. Wouldn't you? It's my home."

"You feel a responsibility, then?"

"And a desire. I've received the benefit of an education, even if it wasn't quite the one I envisioned, even if my academic ambitions were thwarted due to my mother's beliefs in feminine endeavors. I should do something with that education, shouldn't I?"

"You absolutely should."

The sincerity in his voice surprises me. It hasn't escaped my notice that many women in the United States are, in many ways, nearly as restricted as far too many women in Cuba.

"Perhaps I'll visit you in Cuba someday. You can show me around the island."

I try to match his smile, imagining a date we will never keep between us. "Perhaps."

The final strands of the song stretch through the ballroom, and then it's over, and he releases me.

He hesitates, as though he, too, is reluctant to walk away. "Thanks for the dance."

His smile's erased now. Mine, too.

"It was my pleasure," I reply.

"Good luck with everything. I hope you're able to go home like you want."

Nick takes my hand once more, his lips ghosting across my knuckles, and then he's gone.

I walk back to my sisters; the stares cast my way are inescapable, the whispers far louder than is polite. They will eventually disappear; this indiscretion will be forgotten.

I will forget him.

chapter six

A thud wakes me from my slumber. The sound jolts me, and for a moment, I forget where I am, the darkness of my room adding to my confusion.

Three more thuds follow the first one. Then a whisper carried on the wind that sounds a lot like my name.

"Beatriz."

There it is again.

The sound is a familiar one, and my disorientation returns again, catapulting me to my old bedroom in the house in Miramar, to the days after Alejandro was disowned by our parents, when I used to sneak out to see him, slipping him food and money, exploring the city and engaging in revolutionary activities with him and Eduardo by my side.

I throw back the covers, grabbing my robe from the foot of the bed and slipping it on, fumbling with the tie at my waist.

Another thud. Louder now—

"Beatriz."

I walk over to the window and pull back the curtains.

Eduardo stands outside my second-floor window. He's removed the bow tie and jacket from the tuxedo he wore earlier tonight at the Heart Ball, has rolled the sleeves of his snowy white dress shirt, baring his forearms. He raises his arm to throw another rock—

I open the window.

"What's wrong?" I hiss.

My room is toward the front of the house, my parents' to the back, but I am surrounded by Isabel and Maria, and the last thing I need is for them to say something about Eduardo's nocturnal visit.

"Were you sleeping?" he whispers back, stepping closer to the window, his gaze raking over me, no doubt taking in the nightgown and robe, my disheveled hair, the vestiges of makeup I missed removing earlier this evening.

"It's almost two A.M."

"Is it that late?" He grins. "You're getting old. Once upon a time, you would have been out dancing somewhere at two A.M."

"You didn't come here to go dancing."

"No, I didn't. I need to pick up a shipment. Care to join me?"

"A shipment? At two A.M.?"

"It's a very discreet shipment. Germane to our interests—the Cuban ones."

The prudent thing would be to say "no" and go back to bed. But I've already done the prudent thing tonight by putting distance between myself and Nick Preston, and I'm still feeling the sting of that decision.

Small rebellions are the hardest ones to resist.

"Give me a minute."

Fifteen minutes later, we're barreling down the highway, headed farther south.

"What's in the shipment?" I ask Eduardo.

"I don't know. They don't tell me that part beforehand. It's brought in by boat and picked up by some guys—different ones each time. I meet them by the docks, and we confirm we are who we say we are. Then they move the shipment from their trunk to my car and we all go on our way."

"You've done this before?"

"Once or twice."

"Have you ever checked the shipment?"

"Of course."

"What was in the shipment those other times?"

Silence is his only answer.

"What do you do with it?" I ask, trying a different tack.

"I can't tell you that."

"What is it used for?"

"I can't tell you that, either."

"What can you tell me then?"

"Where's your sense of adventure? You said you wanted to be involved in my other activities. This is one of the other things we're working on."

"With the CIA?"

"Not exactly."

"Is it smart to make enemies of them?"

"I'm not doing anything to jeopardize our plans with the CIA. But what's in our interest is not always in theirs, and vice versa. You should always have a contingency plan, Beatriz. And be careful of who you trust."

"Are you warning me off you?"

Eduardo smiles. "Never."

"So what am I doing here? You didn't just drag me out in the middle of the night for fun."

"No, I didn't. Last time I did one of these runs, I got pulled over by a local cop. Nothing happened, but they asked more questions than I cared for. Now, if it happens again, I have the perfect excuse: they'll see us together and think I snuck out to be with a woman. No one would look at you and think anything nefarious."

I look down at my outfit: a simple pair of trousers, the pale sweater I threw on over my top, the serviceable pair of flats.

I see his point.

"We'll meet, pick up the package, drop it off where we're supposed to go, and I'll have you home and in bed by dawn. You can plead the aftereffects of this evening's festivities and too much champagne when your parents ask why you slept in so late."

"I doubt they'll notice."

"So what are you worried about then?"

"Everything."

Eduardo reaches between us and takes my hand.

"Trust me."

Our surroundings turn seedier, the impact heightened by the quiet streets, the dark night. We drive for nearly an hour before Eduardo makes a series of turns, until we're parked in front of what looks to be an abandoned marina.

"Wait here," he whispers. "And keep the doors locked."

"I thought you said this wasn't dangerous."

"It isn't. I can't say the same for the neighborhood."

He reaches across me, pulling something out of the glove box and thrusting it in my hand.

My fingers curl around cold metal.

"A gun?"

"Like I said, you can't be too careful with the neighborhood. If you see anything suspicious—anything not related to me," he amends with a grin, "shoot."

I'm beginning to wonder if he didn't just bring me here for cover, but also for backup, which is a worrying thought indeed.

As soon as he gets out of the car, I lock the doors, my gaze searching the darkness for Eduardo's form. I find him for a moment, visible in the soft glow of a light down by the docks, and then he is gone, and I am alone.

The distant sound of a car fills the night, somewhere far off on the highway, the sound of the water hitting the docks little more than a hum in the background.

It's too quiet. Too dark. There's too much potential for something to go wrong.

What has Eduardo gotten himself involved in? And if he's not working with the CIA, then who is he working with? Is he alone in this or is there a broader network of exiles on his side?

Time creeps on, the weight of the gun in my hand making my palm damp. The notion of me using it is preposterous, although clearly, Eduardo thought it necessary.

I straighten in my seat at the sound of tires on gravel, my palm gripping the gun more tightly. I look out the car window, trying to spot the new arrivals.

The light near the docks is too far away to be much help, and I sense more than see a vehicle pulling up beside Eduardo's little convertible.

I duck, gripping the gun more tightly, cursing Eduardo for dragging me into whatever this is. It is one thing to risk your life for something as important as Fidel, but I don't even know what tonight is about. Is it related to Cuba? Or is this little meeting a by-product of Eduardo's lifestyle: A gambling debt that must be paid? An enraged husband? He said it was about Cuba, but Eduardo isn't above bending the truth to get his way, either.

I should have asked more questions.

The sound of two car doors opening followed by the crunch of footsteps against the gravel fills the night.

Are they friend or foe?

My heart pounds, the gun growing slippery in my palm as I wait for the new arrivals to investigate Eduardo's car, to see me. But the sounds of their footsteps diminish until there is silence, the forms of two men visible as they cross in front of the light near the docks.

Heading toward Eduardo.

I reach into the glove box where Eduardo stored the gun, my fingers wrapping around a flashlight.

My hand is on the door handle before I can think through my actions, the gun clutched in my other hand.

I step out into the night.

The car door shuts gently behind me, and I crouch between the two cars, straining to hear any sounds.

The gun is surprisingly heavy in my hand for such a small thing, and my hand shakes as my finger grazes the trigger.

What if I accidentally shoot someone? Or myself?

The car parked beside Eduardo's is a four-door sedan—an American model by the look of it. I move closer to the car, crouching near the trunk.

I turn on the flashlight, shining it toward the car.

Florida license plates.

The night is silent.

How can I not look?

I walk to the driver's side of the car.

"What did you get me into?" I murmur under my breath.

The window is down, and I reach my hand into the car and pop the lock, opening the door.

Despite the lowered window, the car smells of cigarettes and sweat, the faint hint of cheap perfume on the air.

My heart pounds. Am I really doing this?

Using the flashlight to guide my path, I engage the trunk release inside the car.

Flashlight in hand, I get out of the car, shutting the door behind me gently, and walk around the car to the trunk, lifting the lid over my head.

Crates stare back at me.

I pause for a moment, listening for the sound of footsteps, voices.

Silence greets me. Curiosity gets the best of me.

I lift the lid of one of the crates. Shine the flashlight down.

It takes me a moment to reconcile the sight of the red sticks piled together, for my brain to put a name to them. When I do, a part of me wishes I hadn't.

The crate is filled with sticks of dynamite.

I'm halfway to the dock, gun and flashlight in hand, when I hear Eduardo's voice in the distance.

Followed by his laughter.

I do a one-eighty, killing the flashlight and using the moonlight to guide me back.

He didn't tell me to stay in the car, but now that I know explosives are involved, I'm not eager to be any more embroiled in his scheme than I already am.

I shouldn't have come.

I lengthen my strides as I head toward Eduardo's car, slightly out of breath by the time I slide into the bucket seat and shut the door behind me, my heart pounding madly.

A minute later, their voices become louder, their footsteps heavy.

Eduardo walks beside the two men who arrived, heading toward their parked car.

I flatten my body against the car seat, turning my head to the side, careful to keep my face shielded.

The trunk opens, followed by a thud, the car lowering slightly as the crates are loaded. The trunk closes, and a few moments later, Eduardo climbs into the driver's seat.

"Did you miss me?" he teases.

Miss him? At the moment, I could cheerfully kill him.

The other car leaves.

"What's the dynamite for?" I ask.

"Jesus, Beatriz." He shakes his head. "I should have known better than to bring you."

"Yes, you probably should have. What's the dynamite for?"

"One of those other plans I was telling you about."

"One of the ones the CIA knows nothing about."

He nods, turning the key in the ignition and putting the car in drive.

"Why do you need that much dynamite?"

He gives a short little laugh. "Why do you think?"

In Cuba, we weren't afraid to use violence to achieve our ends. We wanted to bring about a revolution and were willing to use a variety of means to do so. But this isn't Cuba. And if Eduardo is intending to use the explosives in the United States or to hatch a plot here that the CIA isn't privy to—well, that doesn't seem very smart.

"You can't be thinking of using it here."

"*I'm* not doing anything. I'm merely a facilitator. For the right price."

"It's for Cuba, though, isn't it?"

"There are other ways to get the Americans' attention, to bring the fight to their home."

"We can't afford to alienate the Americans," I caution.

"You let me worry about the Americans. You just do your part in catching—and holding—Fidel's interest."

I get out of the car when we arrive home, eager to head back to bed, annoyed with Eduardo, with myself for following him. He was reckless in Cuba, and it's clear he hasn't learned his lesson.

I don't have the appetite for unnecessary risks anymore.

"Beatriz."

I stumble at the sound of my name, at the sight of my father, our gazes connecting across the driveway. He's dressed in one of his suits, standing at the front door, car keys in hand.

Is he heading to the office? It must be five A.M. The rest of the household is surely asleep at this hour.

"Where were you?"

The hardness in my father's voice surprises me most. He's always been a firm parent, and I've certainly heard that same tone directed at my brother in the past, but he treats his daughters with a softer touch, and me most of all.

"I—"

No excuse comes.

"Out with some boy?"

That's the easiest—and safest—explanation I could provide.

I shouldn't be surprised by the sight of my father at this late—or early—hour, even if I wasn't prepared to give any explanations. I've heard he leaves for the office before the sun comes up and works late into the night, but there is a difference between hearing that my father is working harder than he ever has before and seeing it with my own eyes.

He's in his sixties now. In Cuba, he'd talked about retiring, turning the business over to Alejandro. Now he's starting over again, decades of work and sacrifice erased because of Fidel.

"I was with Eduardo. There was a party," I lie. "You know how he is."

"I do. That's what worries me." My father is silent for a moment. "This isn't Cuba, Beatriz. I can't protect you. Not that I could . . ."

My brother isn't here with us physically, but his presence consumes the family. Is my father's drive—his obsession with accumulating more wealth and power—his attempt to make up for the fact that his efforts in Cuba weren't enough to save his only son?

"I know," I reply, stepping forward and wrapping an arm around him, as though our roles have shifted, and I'm the parent comforting the child. "I am careful," I add, even as we both know my words are a lie.

I doubt I've been careful a day in my life.

"It's dangerous, Beatriz."

"I know."

"After Alejandro—don't let your mother see you sneaking out of the house at all hours of the night. There's been enough trouble in this family. No more."

"I won't."

My father sighs.

"I've always liked Eduardo. He comes from a good family. But you'll learn that people are all too eager to take advantage of what you can do for them, what you can give them. Even more so when they are desperate."

"Do you think Eduardo is desperate?"

My father gives me a sad smile. "Aren't we all?"

chapter seven

The season drifts on, February turning into March, the social scene in full swing. We're never really invited to the intimate events, the ones hosted by families that have wintered together for decades, are never admitted to the lofty inner circles people like Nick Preston occupy. I don't know if he's still in Palm Beach, or if he's gone up north to prepare for the coming election, but either way, our paths do not cross again.

After Easter, many will move on to the next whirl, another set of parties and charity events, to northern climates where the temperature is more bearable leading up to the summer heat wave that will make Florida a less palatable destination. Glittering homes will be shuttered, their running handed over to caretakers, billowing white sheets covering the expensive furniture until it is to be dusted off in the winter for the start of the next social season. Some families will remain, Palm Beach their home year-round, but the traffic on Worth Avenue will slow considerably, society's gaze shifting away from the locale that has been under a microscope these past few months. The newspapers will be filled with the same girls, the same families, different settings, new scandals.

My mother's displeasure over the fact that we are to remain in Palm Beach long past what is fashionable permeates the walls of our house, her complaints filling the room, her ire toward Fidel occasionally turning toward our father, his insistence that we can't afford another house, that he can't send us up north to compete with the venerable families, that his business keeps us here, Cuba a fading memory in the face of the new fortune he seeks to build.

My mother's religion is our family's status, the social capital she accumulates not nearly as adroitly as our father rebuilds his empire, his world dominated by sugar and land, the money he hoards in Switzerland and other places, his mistrust of the government magnified by the audacity of Fidel's actions. I choke on their messianic fervor, on the fever pitch in our house as my mother's growing insecurity over our diminished position in society and our father's need for more reach inexorable levels.

And then with the late April showers, it's over as quickly as it started; the world to which my mother desperately hopes to gain an entrée has moved on without us, the majority of her daughters still unmarried, Palm Beach a veritable ghost town compared to the golden months.

We spend our afternoons in the sitting room once Maria is home from school, the three of us flipping through magazines, reading books, our mother sipping her afternoon cocktail and deciding our futures. We've had nine days of rain, too many hours spent cooped up inside the house. The waiting wears thin, manifesting itself in the sharpness in our tones, sisterly glares, a thickening frost covering the veneer of my parents' marriage.

"I have a cousin in Spain," my mother announces one afternoon from her perch on the settee. "You could visit her, perhaps. Her husband is a diplomat. Surely, you could attend some embassy parties. There's your father's sister, of course. Mirta has offered her help. Her husband's quite wealthy, you know."

She frowns, as though she's just realized the flaw in that particular plan.

Our aunt Mirta, our father's younger sister, came to visit us in Cuba a few times, but I always gathered my mother didn't approve of her husband. For all his money, the American lacks the pedigree to satisfy my mother. No, there will be no trips to visit our aunt to marry us off.

"I don't want to go anywhere," Maria interjects.

"Don't worry. No one is sending you away. You have ages to go before you're considered a spinster," I tease. "Enjoy it."

"I wouldn't be laughing if I were you," my mother retorts. "At your age, I was already a wife. Had a child."

Isabel is silent through all of this conversation, as though not speaking will render her invisible, and keep our mother's attention off her.

My mother swallows. "Two more on the way."

Surprise fills me. It is the closest she has come to acknowledging Alejandro since his death.

"You will be older next season," she adds, sweeping past the moment, casting a worried look my way, as though twenty-three will bring with it a wave of wrinkles and gray hairs that will render me officially on the shelf. "Men like a younger girl. Before the bloom is off the rose."

My mother was just eighteen when she married my father.

Maria snorts at the comment, and I'm glad this is all a joke to her, that she hasn't had to face the reality of our situation yet, that our parents consider marriage to be the final goal for us, our success tied to the men we catch rather than our own merits. The realization will come, of course, likely when she is ready to advance her schooling, when she dreams of college or law school as I once did.

Our part-time housekeeper, Alice, walks into the room before my mother can continue telling me my golden years are behind me.

"Pardon me. Miss Beatriz, Mr. Diaz is here to see you. He's waiting outside."

Saved by Eduardo.

We haven't spent much time together since the dynamite night—Eduardo's been "traveling," his whereabouts a mystery, but at the moment, I'll take political intrigue over my mother's marital machinations.

I paste a smile on my face and rise from the couch, setting my magazine down on the end table.

"I shouldn't keep Eduardo waiting. After all, time isn't exactly on my side, is it?" I say, shooting my mother a pointed look.

From Isabel's position on the couch, a strangled laugh escapes.

"You saved me," I tell Eduardo later when we are walking side by side on the beach.

"Did I? I think I like the sound of that. Would you say I'm your hero, then?"

I laugh. "I wouldn't go quite that far."

"Humph. What did I save you from?"

"My mother. Voicing her displeasure that society has moved on and we are still here in Palm Beach." I cast a sidelong look Eduardo's way as we walk along the beach, my sandals in hand, the skirt of my dress clutched in my fingers as the sand slithers between my toes. "I'm surprised you didn't leave."

"Where would I go?" Eduardo looks to the sea, brushing a lock of dark hair from his forehead. It's grown longer since the season ended, the ends curling.

"New York, perhaps."

His lip curve with distaste. He knows the game as well as I do. "Trying to marry me off?"

"Would you marry? You have to eventually, don't you?"

He's three years older than me, not so old that his single status is unusual, but not so young, either, especially in these uncertain times. It's different for men, of course, their bachelorhood tolerated far more than our impending spinster status, but still, at the end of the day, we are all meant to marry, have children, live the lives our parents lived before us.

"Marry for love?" he asks.

"Love, position, security."

Eduardo stiffens slightly, and guilt stabs me. We don't speak of our reduced circumstances; our pride doesn't allow it. For a man like Eduardo, it's a great blow indeed. In Cuba, Eduardo's family lived like kings, their wealth in the land they owned, the businesses, the horses, an empire built over centuries. There are rumors that his father took money out of the country in the yawning days of Batista's presidency and before Fidel marched into Havana, but the bulk of their fortune is now in Fidel's hands.

"I didn't mean—"

"Would you?" he counters.

"Sell myself to the highest bidder?"

"Yes."

"Sometimes it feels like things would be easier if I did," I admit. "For my family, at least. It would certainly please my parents."

"Yes."

"What will you do when we go back to Cuba?" I ask, changing the subject.

This is one of my favorite games to play.

Eduardo smiles. "Sit on the patio of our house in Varadero and look out at the water, a cigar in hand. Breathe. Admire the legs of the dancers at the Tropicana. Marry some girl willing to put up with me. Have children. Watch them play in the water and know they won't live under the same fear we've experienced, that they will grow up in a world where they can put down roots, where they can hold on to something without the fear it will be ripped away."

"You want a family?"

"I do."

"I wouldn't have predicted that." Whenever I take Eduardo at face value, somehow he always seems to surprise me.

"Why?"

"I wouldn't have thought you'd be one for entanglements, that you would view a family as more of a burden than anything else."

I'm fairly convinced our father sees me, my mother, and my sisters the same way; he loves us, but we're another thing to manage and care for, to fret over.

"I suppose it would depend on why I married," Eduardo answers. "If I chose a wife to get me out of this mess, married some American girl with the right last name and the kind of connections that would ensure a lifetime of smooth sailing, it would probably feel more like a burden than a joy. Don't mistake me; money makes everything easier, and don't think I haven't considered taking the easy way, but—"

"You're a romantic." The notion surprises me.

He gives an embarrassed little laugh. "Isn't that the whole point? Why are we doing any of this if not for the romanticism of it?"

"I suppose I thought it was about reclaiming the things you lost," I admit, momentarily abashed by the possibility that I've misjudged him, that this whole time I've chalked his motives up to his own self-interest, when perhaps there was more there, his intentions more altruistic.

"It is. But those things aren't just the ones that can be bought. There are other things we lost, too. Ones you can't put a price on or replicate."

"No matter how much my father tries," I mutter under my breath.

"I wouldn't judge him too harshly," Eduardo says, surprising me once more. "He has a great deal of responsibility on his hands. Without Alejandro . . ." His voice trails off. "Your father isn't a young man, and now he has to ensure that when he dies, you, your sisters, and your mother are provided for. Most of the provisions he made for you in Cuba are probably gone. That must worry him."

And there it is: perhaps more than any of us, Eduardo is the ultimate intersection of the pragmatist and the dreamer.

"You're angry," he adds, surprising me yet again. He sees far more than I realize.

There's no point in denying it. Anger is my faithful companion.

"I'd hoped working with the CIA would help you," he says. "That it would make the anger more bearable somewhat, at least as it has done for me."

I always assumed Eduardo involved me because he knew I would be amenable to it and because my beauty and notoriety gave him a weapon he could use against Fidel. I never considered he was helping me, too.

Was that why he took me with him the night he picked up the dynamite? Did he notice how lost I felt in that ballroom after my dance ended with Nick? Or did he really just use me as a diversion to suit his own ends?

"It has helped a bit, I suppose," I answer. "Have you heard anything from Mr. Dwyer? Anything about Cuba?"

"There are rumors," Eduardo answers after a beat. "But one struggles with what to believe these days. With the explosion of *La Coubre*, they say Fidel is growing more paranoid. He's convinced the CIA is acting against him."

In early March, *La Coubre*, a French freighter loaded with weapons headed for Fidel, exploded in the Havana harbor. Many were killed, more injured. Fidel has proclaimed it an act of sabotage by the Americans, another grievance in a growing list of them.

"*Were* they responsible for the explosion?" It seems entirely plausible they would be, and at the same time, I am predisposed to disbelieve any words that fall from Fidel's lips.

Eduardo shrugs. "My contacts say 'no,' but who really knows with the CIA? I'm not privy to all of their schemes. I'm useful to them in my own way, but unfortunately, not powerful enough to be treated as an equal."

"What wonderful friends we've acquired."

"At the moment, they're the only friends who will have us."

"Perhaps we're foolish to put all of our faith in the Americans. There have to be others."

"Who else? The situation grows more complicated with each day. Now the Soviet Union is involved, and they're growing closer to Fidel; we're caught between two giants. There's increased concern about the ramifications intervening in Cuba will have on the tension between the Americans and the Soviets. It's a mess."

And even more, for Cubans it is an ongoing source of frustration and pain. Empires in one fashion or another have decided our history: first the Spanish, then the Americans, now Cuba lies in the balance of a proxy war between two powers.

"Do you think this plan will actually come to fruition? That they'll really have some use for me?"

"The CIA?"

I nod.

"I do. It will likely come down to timing. If they can arrange for you to meet Fidel, how they can get you into the country and extract you. I know the Americans aren't the best allies, but they won't risk your safety needlessly, won't risk the injury to their own reputation. With the current tensions between the two countries, they must be cautious."

With my history with Fidel, my brother's death, it will be easier for them to pretend I acted of my own volition, that I was motivated by anger and revenge rather than political machinations.

"Are you nervous?" Eduardo asks me.

"A bit. That I'll get a chance, that I won't."

"Sometimes I don't know what's worse: feeling like you did nothing or failing in the attempt," he acknowledges.

My gaze sweeps over the beachgoers sprinkled across the horizon. I seize on a mother and her two children playing in the sand. She barely looks older than me.

How differently would my life have turned out if I'd been born in this country, if I hadn't come into a fractured and divided island caught in never-ending turmoil? Would I wear the same contented expression on my face as she does? Or is there more there under the beach tan and flash of white teeth, the matching pair of children? Do we all have secrets lingering beneath our skin, private battles we fight? Does she look at Eduardo and me walking together and see a young couple in love, envy me the handsome man, the freedom my childless status affords me?

"We have a few things we're working on," Eduardo says, tearing my attention away from the woman and her children.

"Things you won't talk about."

Like the dynamite we picked up.

"It's complicated, Beatriz. There are some things it's best if you aren't involved in."

"Because I'm a woman?"

"No. Because the less people who know about our plans, the better. Fidel's spies are everywhere."

"I would never—"

"I know you wouldn't. But we need to be careful. I'm trying to keep you away from this as much as I can, trying to keep you safe. Alejandro always sought to shield you from as much of it as he could."

"And yet you've encouraged it. Took me with you to pick up those crates. Engineered my meeting with the CIA."

"Because I know how much this means to you. How much you loved your brother, how hard you fought against Batista. You believe in Cuba and the dreams you have for her future. Besides, you're Beatriz Perez. When have you ever wanted something and not gotten your way?"

"I can't tell if you're the only one who really knows me, who really believes in me, or if it's just that *you've* never wanted something and not achieved it, and I'm the easiest route from one point to another."

Eduardo laughs. "Maybe you're the only one who really knows *me* then."

He wraps an arm around my shoulders, pulling me against his muscular frame, leaning into me, and this time it isn't my imagination. The young mother casts an envious glance my way.

"Perhaps it's a bit of both," he concedes as his lips brush the top of my head, the affection in his voice belying the unvarnished truth in his words.

That's the thing about Eduardo—we are the same in so many ways, sometimes it's like looking at a mirror, and I'm not always prepared to face the reflection staring back at me.

chapter eight

Now that the season has ended, our days are stagnant, our boredom magnified by the heat and humidity. We practically live at the beach, the summer passing by with picnics and building sandcastles with my nephew. There are no more balls, no more elegant parties, and despite Eduardo's propensity for dropping by with bits of news between mysterious trips to undisclosed locations, our days are insufferably dull.

"We're thinking about moving to Miami," my sister Elisa announces one day in July when we're sitting on a big checkered blanket watching Miguel play in the sand, his nanny herding him around. In the past few months, my nephew's personality has transformed, and he's gone from a sleepy baby to an active little boy with a mischievous expression and an obstinacy that clearly reflects his Perez heritage. He's charmed the entire family, providing a rare spot of solace and hope in these tough times.

"Why would you move?"

Miami isn't far, but I've grown used to living near one another.

I always envisioned us living close together, our homes within walking distance so we could stop by for afternoon chats with ease.

"It's less expensive, and Juan heard about a good property from a friend of his. It would mean a bigger house, more space for Miguel. And it would be closer to Juan's work."

My little sister is a wife now, a mother, with considerations other than the family she was born into. It's the natural order of things, of course, and still—

I try to smile. "We'll miss you."

She squeezes my hand. "I'll miss you, too. It's not far, though. Really."

"It feels far." It's not merely the distance; she's building a life here, putting down roots that will tie her to America forever. I'm happy for her, but at the same time, she's moving on, and despite the age difference between us, I feel like she's surpassed me in life somehow.

"How are you?" Elisa asks, a knowing look in her eyes.

"I'm fine."

"Mm-hmm. The truth now. Not what you tell everyone else. How are you? Really?"

I sigh. "Miserable, mostly."

The wind kicks up sand near Miguel, and he wails, his nanny scooping him up in her arms. Elisa frowns before turning her attention back to me, even as I can tell a part of her is focused on her son.

I'm always a little amazed at how much she dotes on the baby, how naturally she seems to have adjusted to this change in circumstances, especially considering how quickly she went from wife to mother. It's even more impressive when you consider our own maternal example. Our nanny, Magda, was the one who soothed our cut knees, who wiped our tears away. Our mother was somewhere in the background of our childhood, swooping into the room in a beautiful gown, the scent of her perfume lingering in the air after she'd moved on to her evening entertainment.

"You're not happy here, are you?" Elisa asks.

"No, I'm not."

"Do you think you ever will be?"

"In Palm Beach? Permanently? How could I be? I didn't choose this. I didn't want this. It isn't home. This was just supposed to be temporary, remember? Father said it would take time for everything to sort itself out. Months, maybe. But now it feels like everyone has forgotten. You have a family now. Our parents are so focused on accumulating more money, building the company, our family name, but what about the things we can't buy back? I miss Magda. I miss my friends who are still in Havana, miss the old house." I push past the tears clogging my throat. "I want to visit Alejandro's grave. I want my life back. I want to go home."

"It's not the home you remember anymore." Elisa's tone is gentle, similar to one I've heard her adopt with the baby. There's acceptance in her voice, as though she has reached a conclusion I am unable to face.

"I know. And that makes me angry, too. It feels like Fidel has won."

"Not everything has to be a battle, Beatriz. You could just be happy."

"You say it like happiness is the easiest thing in the world."

"I didn't say it was easy. Just that it shouldn't be so easily discounted. There's nothing wrong with being happy. Alejandro wouldn't want you to suffer like this. Wouldn't want you to punish yourself on his behalf."

Is that what she thinks I'm doing? Playing the martyr because my brother was murdered? It was Elisa who found me first the day I discovered Alejandro's dead body; she should understand my motives more than anyone.

"Do you remember that day? Do you remember what I said to you?" I ask.

"I do."

"Fidel has to pay for what he did. Where is the justice? I can't live in a world where Fidel reigns over Cuba after all the Cubans he murdered."

"Beatriz," Elisa hisses, her gaze darting around the beach before her eyes widen, and it seems to occur to her that we aren't in Havana anymore, that every word need not be censored for fear of retribution.

For all that I complain about our presence here, I've grown used to the freedom to speak my mind.

"How are you not angry anymore? How have you forgotten?"

"I have not forgotten," Elisa replies. "I will never forget. I *can't* forget. But I don't have the luxury of languishing in my grief or allowing my anger to consume me. I have a son now. He needs me. This revolution has already stolen enough from him."

"I'm sorry. I shouldn't have—"

"You wouldn't be you if you didn't. I know how you feel, how you've always felt about Cuba. But I worry about you. You can't stop living just because we aren't home. Who knows how long we will be gone? We can hope for the best, pray one day we will return, but for the moment, that's all we can do.

"I know it's hard when our parents don't want you to go to school. It must be difficult to fill your days, but this isn't the way to do it. Hating Fidel is not a way to live."

"Then what would you have me do? I'm not like you. I don't know that I want to marry and have children. I've spent my entire life being told I'm only good at one thing: my role is to be beautiful and charming, but not to have a thought in my head—or heaven forbid, express a controversial opinion—and I'm tired of it. I don't want to end up married to some man who will want more of the same. I know you're happy with your life, but the thought of domestic bliss *doesn't* bring me peace. It terrifies me."

"You make marriage sound like a prison."

Our parents were hard on all of us, had high expectations for us to make excellent matches, but it was different with me. Whether deserved or not, I've always been the one who was touted as the beauty in the family, and while the moniker should have been a benediction, it always felt like a curse. Until now. Now it gives me an opportunity to use my reported beauty for something that actually matters.

"Maybe not a prison. But not something to aspire to, either."

"Does Eduardo know you feel this way?"

"Eduardo?" I laugh. "I very much doubt Eduardo cares one way or another about my thoughts on marriage."

"You're always together."

"We're friends of a sort. As much as Eduardo is interested in having friends anyway."

"He looks at you like there's more there."

There it is again, that note in her voice suggesting I've missed something important, lack the maturity she's acquired somewhere along the way.

"He looks at you like he wants you," Elisa adds, her voice low, a pink flush rising on her cheeks.

"Lots of men look at me like that. It doesn't mean anything. If Eduardo occasionally glances my way with something akin to interest, it's because he's a man, *not* because he has some secret feelings for me. I doubt Eduardo is even capable of losing his heart to someone. Do you remember what he was like in Havana? The dancers at the Tropicana? The married women they whispered about?"

"If you say so." Elisa's eyes narrow. "So if it isn't romance that's brought you two together so often, what is it?"

"We're friends."

"That's all it is?"

"That's all."

"Now why don't I believe that? You aren't ever going to give up on this, are you? Everything I just said to you? None of it resonates with you, does it?"

"I don't want you to worry about me, too."

"No matter what, you're my sister. I'm always going to worry about you."

I give her a wry grin. "It feels like I'm the younger sister these days."

"I feel old sometimes," she admits. "That's what comes from spending your days chasing after a child, telling him not to put random objects in his mouth, picking strange bits of food out of his hair, always being responsible for someone else's well-being, for keeping them safe."

Yes, Elisa is definitely adopting a new mode of motherhood than the example we received.

I laugh. "You're not exactly tempting me to embrace a life of domesticity."

"It has its moments."

"And you love him? Juan?" It seems a silly thing to ask, but I realize this is one thing I don't know about my sister.

She smiles. "Don't all wives love their husbands?"

"That would be nice if it were true."

But we both know better.

"He seems like a good man," I say cautiously.

"He is." She scoops up a handful of sand, the granules passing between her fingers, her gaze cast out to sea. I think she's some-where else entirely, and then she blinks as if to break herself from her stupor, and she's returned to me.

"I love him." There's both surprise and confidence in her voice, as though it's a new concept she hasn't quite gotten used to. And at the same time, I believe her. She looks happy. Happier than she's been in a long time, as though her marriage and son have erased some of the darkness that has followed us for so long.

"Good. I'm pleased for you. You deserve to be happy. To be at peace."

"So do you."

"I fear I am not a peaceful person by nature."

Elisa laughs. "True." Her expression sobers. "But it is not good to always be at war, to always be fighting."

"I will try to keep that in mind."

"Please do. And Beatriz?" She grasps my hand. "Whatever you do, promise me you will be safe. I can't lose another person I love to this madness."

Her words so closely echo my father's the night he caught me sneaking back into the house, that a lump clogs my throat, Fidel's impact on each member in my family indelible.

"I promise."

We walk back from the beach, Miguel chattering excitedly between us, his nanny in tow. At the intersection of our two homes, we part ways, Elisa heading back to her house, a few minutes away from ours. I will miss her desperately when she moves to Miami.

I turn right instead of left, walking past homes more modest than the ones that flanked our estate in Havana. We knew all of our neighbors in Miramar; Elisa's best friend, Ana, lived next door to us. Here, we are all strangers. Some of the houses are inhabited by seasonal residents, others by people who barely acknowledge us when we walk past.

We've tried to varying degrees to fit in—admittedly, my efforts have likely been the most half-hearted—but the differences be-

tween us and the Americans around us aren't the sort you can remove with a fashionable dress or the right conversation note. I've
seen things these girls haven't, lived through a revolution, and no
matter how hard I try, I can't mimic the carefree attitude they adopt
with aplomb; I lack the innocence they lay claim to. Perhaps that's
why their mothers shield them, why we have become pariahs of
sorts. They fear we will sully the pristine society they've created
here, separated from the troubles of the outside world, unencumbered by poverty, fear, violence, and death.

When we were younger, our mother instructed us to always have
a smile on our faces when out in society, to be polite, to laugh at
men's jokes and flatter their vanity. She raised me to be soft and
malleable in a time when she thought that would win me a husband.
Now I am all sharp edges and steel, and I can't imagine one of these
American men wanting me for their wife, can't possibly fathom why
they would take on all that weighs me down if not for the superfici-
ality of such a relationship—the realization that we have nothing in
common, that we are little more than strangers, an eventuality. No,
I can't say I have much interest in the sacrament of holy matrimony.

I trip on a pebble beneath my shoe, my gaze trained on a point
in the distance.

There's a car parked near our driveway. A nondescript black car.

A man leans against it, dressed in an equally unremarkable
black suit, a neat little hat.

My heartbeat picks up.

He turns toward me as though he's been expecting me, and a
chill slides down my spine. How long has he been waiting? Did he
see me at the beach with my sister? Did he watch us play with
Miguel? It's one thing for me to meet him at restaurants, for Eduardo to act as a go-between, but this—him standing outside my
family's home—unnerves me. It's easy to forget Mr. Dwyer is a
man who has eyes and ears everywhere, easy to look at his benign

appearance, the way he blends into his surroundings, and underestimate him.

Mr. Dwyer greets me with a false smile—congenial and casual—as though we are neighbors encountering each other on a fine summer day.

There are no preliminaries, no disinterested inquiries into my well-being, merely—

"Castro is coming to New York to address the United Nations General Assembly."

My heart pounds.

"We want you to go to New York and meet with him. We'll arrange for you to be at the same location: a party or restaurant, perhaps. The State Department will ensure he has a large American security detail present, and we will be able to monitor his movements quite effectively. What do you think?"

Fidel might not have pulled the trigger that killed my brother, but it was likely on his orders. Alejandro—intelligent, educated, well-connected, charismatic, passionate about Cuba's future—was a threat to Fidel's regime, to his ability to consolidate power and unite the divergent factions in Cuba. My brother's death provided a warning to anyone who dared challenge Fidel's stranglehold on the island.

Can I face my brother's killer, and smile, and flirt in an attempt to steal his heart?

Only if I get to watch the life drain from his eyes as I was forced to do with Alejandro.

"Do you want me to kill him in New York?" I ask.

"No. We've discussed this, and relations with Cuba are simply too tenuous at the moment for people not to suspect our involvement if his death occurs on American soil. We do not need this turning into an international incident that will reflect poorly on American interests in Latin America."

"Then what do you hope for with this meeting?"

"We want you to draw his attention. Like Fidel, you and your brother were critics of Batista and his policy. We want you to engage Fidel, to convince him you are open to the future he envisions for Cuba. Between your past, and your not inconsiderable charms, we hope that will be enough for him to be interested. After all, Fidel enjoys his women.

"Once you've made the initial contact, the next phase will be to send you to Cuba at an expedient time and arrange for him to meet with you there. After you've gained his trust, well, then you can remove him from the equation."

It sounds so simple, and yet, so very ambitious. The CIA's plan depends on a myriad of factors, each one contingent upon my ability to play the consummate actress.

"And how am I to convince Fidel I harbor no rancor over my brother's death? That I trust him? I may be able to sell a great many things, but no one in Cuba would believe I would cozy up to my brother's murderer."

"There was never any proof tying Fidel to your brother's death. Who's to say it wasn't one of Batista's men left behind when the president fled the country? That your brother's murder wasn't an attempt to strike back at the revolutionaries? Your brother wasn't involved with the 26th of July Movement, but there were so many groups of young, disaffected men. In the chaos, perhaps your brother was mistakenly targeted?"

Dwyer smiles at me, the effect somewhat chilling.

"We can make the truth be whatever we need it to be, make Fidel believe whatever we need him to believe. It really is quite simple."

"When it comes time . . ." I swallow. The words stick in my throat.

"To kill him?" Mr. Dwyer finishes for me.

"Yes. Will you help me? I don't know . . ."

It seems such a silly thing to speak aloud, because *of course* I don't know how to kill a man.

"Yes. We will. It will need to be done carefully. We will guide you." He cocks his head, taking my measure once more. "This is it, Miss Perez, the chance you wanted to take back your country and to avenge your brother. Do we have a deal?"

I clasp his outstretched hand.

"We have a deal."

chapter nine

I put away my summer dresses and floral prints, the casual shifts I
have begun wearing as a concession to the Palm Beach heat, in
preparation for my trip to New York. I raid my closet—and my
mother's and sisters'—for the most elegant pieces I can find. I even
have a dress made by a seamstress I discovered on one of my shopping expeditions on the mainland. It is sleek, sexy, and if anything
will catch Fidel's attention, this will be it.

Mr. Dwyer has devised an invitation to the Hamptons with one
of the many prestigious families his wife is acquainted with as my
cover for the weekend. My mother is overjoyed at the prospect of
me traveling in such prominent circles, my father too busy to be
concerned, my sisters bewildered by the surprise invitation and the
friendship I've failed to mention all season, yet too caught up in
their own lives to worry overmuch about my plans.

Elisa is distracted by her upcoming move to Miami, Isabel dating a local businessman, Maria busy with school and her friends.
Their distraction is fortuitous indeed, and they are happy to help me
shop and pack for my trip without it raising an alarm.

The flight to New York is pleasant enough. I land at Idlewild Airport and take a cab to the Midtown hotel Mr. Dwyer has arranged for me: an elegant enough structure a blush removed from the fashionable corner of the neighborhood. I'm unlikely to see anyone I know, but my reputation should be preserved should anyone learn I'm staying in the city alone.

Once I've checked in to my room and set my suitcase down, I head downstairs, where Mr. Dwyer is waiting for me in our prearranged meeting spot.

The hotel bar is a somewhat depressing place, filled with weary business travelers and men looking for a good time. A man sits in a corner playing the piano with little enthusiasm. There's nothing unsafe about the hotel, just a tinge of wear to its edges, and while I value the anonymity it provides, part of me wants to head over to the Plaza, where I stayed when my parents brought us on a shopping trip to the city so many years ago, anonymity and budget be damned.

I slide into the empty seat across from Mr. Dwyer.

He doesn't look up from his newspaper, folded to the crossword section, a black ballpoint pen in hand. He carefully, meticulously, fills a series of squares with block letters, his handwriting neat and just a touch oversize. When he finishes, he sets the pen down on the table, and looks up at me.

"Did you have a pleasant flight?"

"I did."

"Good. He's in Harlem." Mr. Dwyer frowns. "At a place called the Hotel Theresa. We had him at the Shelburne a few blocks away from your hotel, but he stormed out of there with his entourage in tow."

"What happened?"

"Something about a damage deposit. The press is talking about chickens. Who knows? Likely, he just wanted to thumb his nose at all of us. He claims we're harassing him. Even complained to the United Nations about it."

He mutters an invective about Fidel I can't disagree with.

"He'll look like a hero to the people," I muse. "Leaving the comfort and elegance of the Shelburne for Harlem."

"We're aware. We tried to get him in at the Commodore, but he wasn't amenable. The man's been prancing all over New York City, people fawning all over him like he's a damn celebrity. He's receiving world leaders in his hotel room: Khrushchev, Nasser, Nehru."

I almost feel sorry for the Americans.

"Fidel likes to cause trouble. His brand thrives on chaos, disorder, operating outside of the system. Don't underestimate him," I caution.

Mr. Dwyer shoots me a pithy look, conveying the distinct impression that at the moment he has little sympathy or tolerance for my countrymen and me.

"You leave the politics of this visit to me. You just worry about catching his interest."

"When?"

"Tomorrow night. He's holding court at the Hotel Theresa in an effort to get back at us for not inviting him to the Latin America summit. There will be women there, and we'll have one of our people put your name on the list."

"Are you sure you want me to go in under my real name?"

"It will be part of the appeal for Castro," Mr. Dwyer answers. "Besides, if you pretend to be someone you're not, the risk is too great that a member of his entourage will recognize you, if not Fidel himself. It is hard enough to gain his trust; starting out with a lie could kill the operation before it even begins."

Our waitress comes by with a new drink for Mr. Dwyer and asks me what I would like. I order a sidecar while she sets an old-fashioned beside his folded newspaper. The condensation from his drink has edged against the newspaper, blurring the letters in "two across." He frowns at the smudged ink.

"Any questions?" he asks, once she's left us alone again.

Only about one thousand.

"What happens next?"

"You talk to him. Flirt. Make an impression. Then you go home. Tell your family you had a wonderful time in the Hamptons. The money we agreed to pay you for this little jaunt will be in the account we opened for you in Palm Beach."

We settled on five thousand dollars and all of the expenses paid for this trip, deposited in a secret bank account the CIA helped me open.

"Then we'll look at more occasions to put you in Fidel's path," he continues. "It is unlikely he will return to the United States, so it will have to be in Havana. But that attempt will be much more successful if you've already established a rapport between you. We'll be in contact when we have more information."

Mr. Dwyer reaches into his pocket, pulling out a slim money clip and peeling off a few bills. He tosses the money—enough to pay for both of our drinks—on the table, sliding his chair back and rising. He picks up the newspaper and tucks it beneath his arm.

"It's 'fear to.'"

He pauses. "Excuse me?"

"Forty-seven across. The answer you were looking for is 'fear to.'"

What might be a smile flashes across his face. "So it is. 'Where angels fear to tread.' Imagine that." He winks, and with a quick "Good luck, Miss Perez," he is gone.

I drain my drink, resisting the urge to order another. My mother drilled the risk of overindulgence into all of us, but then again, she never would have approved of any of this, so in for a penny, in for a pound, as they say.

The same waitress from earlier returns to the table, clearing away Mr. Dwyer's drink.

"He'll never leave his wife," she says to me.

"Pardon me?"

She leans in closer, busying herself with wiping off the table. "Don't mind me saying so, but a young, pretty girl like you deserves better than a man like that. I see them come in and out of here; all of them have a story, you know. Their wife doesn't understand them, they're just together for the kids, it gets lonely traveling so much, but someone has to provide for the family." She makes a noise of disgust. "Creeps, if you ask me."

"I'm not—he's not my lover or anything. He's an old family friend."

"They'll say that, too, in the beginning. They'll say just about anything to get close to you." Her eyes narrow. "You're not from around here, are you?"

"No, I'm not."

"Just be careful. This city can swallow you up before you even realize it. Lots of pretty girls like you come here looking for adventure and find heartbreak instead."

Something about the waitress's manner, her maternal concern, reminds me of my nanny, Magda. My father told my sisters and me that Magda left Havana and went to the country to stay with her family. While I understand her reluctance to leave Cuba and her family, it doesn't feel right not having her in the United States with us.

"Thank you. I appreciate it."

"Would you like another drink?" she asks.

I order one more. The occasion calls for it.

The next evening, I peer out at Harlem from the comfort of a cab, the exterior of the Hotel Theresa looming before me. I spent the day exploring the neighborhood around my hotel, and now, the farther away we travel, the more my surroundings change. The hotel is a far cry from mine, the surrounding businesses anything but swanky. But the hotel is only one part of the picture, and at the moment, it's far from the most dramatic.

I never realized how much I viewed America as a haven, how much I enjoyed the freedom from having to hear Fidel's speeches, the absence of the yoke of fear we lived under those weeks before we left Cuba. Fidel's presence is a constant reminder of all we've lost, all he's stolen, and now, he's here, and this is another thing he's taken from us, as he invades our sanctuary, too.

Mobs of people carrying signs surround the hotel entrance, police barricades erected to maintain a semblance of crowd control. Except it doesn't look controlled at all. It's chaos, and the sight of those people takes me back to the streets of Havana in the days after the revolution, after President Batista boarded a plane for the Dominican Republic in the dead of night and left us in the hands of Fidel and his followers.

The energy here is palpable, the excitement and hope similar to the messianic welcome Fidel received when he marched into Havana. To these people he's a hero, a Robin Hood figure who has taken from the wealthy and given to the poor. It likely doesn't hurt that he is handsome in a rugged sort of way, his green fatigues heralding him a soldier, the beard exotic to some, the image he has so carefully cultivated designed to appeal to those rebelling against the old guard.

The sight of their fervor disgusts me.

These people don't have to live under his regime. They are free here, are able to protest against their government. They celebrate the man who has taken such liberties away from us.

"They say Khrushchev came to see him," the cab driver comments, a measure of awe in his voice. "Can you imagine that?"

I make a noncommittal sound, my attention on the scene before me.

Someone has hoisted up a Cuban flag, hanging it from the hotel, a symbol of defiance in a foreign land.

A few protestors are interspersed in the throng, their signs decrying the injustices in Cuba under Fidel's regime. And still, so many—far too many—of the Americans cheer for Fidel, their ignorance and glee a slap in the face. What will it take to make them understand, for them to listen to us?

Artists flock to him, world leaders praise him, the intellectual set fawns over him, writers and poets dine at his table, but for all of their "enlightenment," they do not bother to look beneath the green-fatigued facade. Is his uniform still so romantic when they learn how many men have seen those fatigues in the last moments of their lives, condemned to death without any semblance of justice? Would they still admire him if they heard the shots from the firing squads, the cries of the murdered, smelled the blood of their countrymen? Write a poem about that, our slow, never-ending death.

"Where would you like me to let you off?" the driver asks me.

"Up ahead is fine."

"Are you sure? The crowd is growing rowdier."

"I'll be fine."

He pulls over about a block away from the Theresa, and I pay him for the trip and step out of the car, wrapping my coat more tightly around my body, in part to ward off the late-September chill that the rest of the city appears immune to, and in part to cover my dress.

For the longest time, I've felt as though I hovered in the precipice between girl and woman. My mother has expected marriage from me—my little sister *is* a wife and mother—and society has pushed me into a grown-up state I am largely unprepared for, as though once I turned eighteen, I miraculously crossed some imaginary threshold that made me ready to go from my parents' house to my husband's house.

I've hovered in this in-between, staring at my reflection in the mirror and feeling slightly betrayed by the body that decided to grow curves and breasts somewhere along the way, that propelled me into this stage of life whether I was prepared for it or not.

Oh, I flaunted my newfound womanhood as soon as it came, because there was power in it. But still, I was always uneasy, as though my body belonged to someone else, never to *me*, as though it was a commodity to be bought and sold on my behalf.

Not tonight.

Tonight, I looked at myself in the mirror, and it occurred to me that perhaps adulthood had come not with a white gown and veil thrust upon me against my wishes, but rather in this moment, with this decision to claim my womanhood, to use it to get what I want rather than what everyone else wants for me.

Tonight, I feel powerful.

My heels click against the pavement, heads turning my way with each step. The crowd looks larger up close; a group of protestors shout at a pair of camera-wielding tourists. In my younger years, I would have stood beside them, holding a sign proclaiming Fidel a villain, shining a light on his human rights abuses for the world to see. I flash the protestors a quick, private smile, wishing I could commend them for the sense they have injected into this farce, the courage they're expressing standing up for their convictions.

A policeman wades over to the protestors and yells at them. I duck my head to the side as a reporter raises his camera and snaps a picture of the interaction. In Havana, my sisters and I were forever captured in the society pages, our faces well-known enough that circumspection became a necessity.

Security personnel stand outside the Theresa, men in serviceable black suits that practically scream "U.S. Government." A few more disreputable sorts are mixed in with the fray, bearded men in fatigues who must be part of Fidel's personal security detail. I scan their faces quickly, but no one is familiar to me.

I remove my coat once I'm inside, and one of the security men guides me through the hotel. With each step, people stare, whispers in English and Spanish reaching my ears. A man laughs somewhere in the background, a comment about my figure causing my cheeks to heat.

We follow the growing crowd, over the threshold to another room, my heartbeat kicking up with each passing moment, a tingle running down my spine.

There are more men dressed in fatigues here, another horrible reminder of what the streets of Havana looked like in the aftermath of Fidel's coup. The atmosphere is jovial, smoke in the air, fat Cuban cigars in hand. It's the scent of my childhood, my father smoking on the veranda of our home in Miramar, Maria playing in the backyard, the chef making paella in the kitchen while Isabel hit discordant notes on the piano. Tears well, and not just from the smoke.

And then the crowd shifts, and my eyes adjust to the dim light, the haze, and I step forward.

I've imagined this meeting for so long, steeled myself for the moment when I would face my brother's killer, Cuba's scourge, and now he's here, the villain of my days and nights slouched in a chair, his omnipresent green fatigues wrinkled and grimy, his beard scraggly, a cloud of cigar smoke surrounding him, and the shocking thing isn't the flash of hate I expected to feel or the wave of grief I imagined would carry me away, but rather the sheer banality of it all.

I don't feel anything. He could be a stranger on the street. And the truth of it hits me, the realization that somewhere along the way I have built him up in my mind until he has become a caricature of himself, likely more cunning, more intelligent, more formidable than he is in real life. He was the villain lurking under my bed, the ghoul in the closet, the proverbial monster used to scare children into good behavior, and the reality doesn't live up to the machinations of my imagination.

He is, after all, just a man. A flawed one, a dangerous one at that, but a man all the same. Confident, arrogant, easily led astray by a pair of fine eyes and a set of curves.

Fidel holds court seated at a long table against the wall, flanked by two of his cronies, plates of food in front of them. The audience is overwhelmingly male save for a few women wearing similar dresses to mine. The one closest to Fidel—a pretty brunette with chin-length brown hair—sizes me up as thoroughly as any debutante.

Fidel is in the middle of telling a story—his exodus from the Shelburne, I presume, based on the words drifting my way. He gestures excitedly, a cocky smile on his face, a cigar dangling from his fingers before he stubs it out on a cheap ceramic ashtray.

I square my shoulders, my body relaxing, my hips going languid, my eyes sharp.

Tonight, I am confident.

Tonight, he is mine.

chapter ten

Fidel's gaze flicks to me as I approach the table.

He pauses mid-sentence.

I don't allow myself to blink; I hold his stare and return his lazy perusal with one of my own. There's a glimmer of interest in Fidel's eyes that's not altogether unsurprising—a gleam, if you will.

He looks every inch of his thirty-four years, surprisingly young for a man who has wrought such havoc. Measured against men like the American president Eisenhower and the Soviet premier, Fidel is a marked change, as is his casual attire. The irony, of course, is that for all his pretense of being one of the people, a soldier in fatigues, he comes from a family similar to mine.

A smile curls on Fidel's lips.

Any greeting I might offer him sticks in my throat. I break eye contact, scanning the crowd for a familiar face. Thanks to my brother's protectiveness, my ties to the rebel groups in Havana have been more tenuous. I've met Che once or twice, but thankfully, he hasn't joined Fidel on this trip.

Fidel murmurs something under his breath to the man next to

him, and they both chuckle, their gazes running over my dress, my curves, the hints of skin exposed by the daring cut of the fabric.

"Miss—"

Fidel leaves it hanging between us like a lord dangling a treat before a peasant.

I allow the moment to draw out a bit, steadying my nerves and showing Fidel I have no problem keeping him waiting.

"Beatriz Perez."

I say the name proudly. My family is far from perfect, but I come from a long line of people who fought for what they believed in, and at the moment, I'm holding on to that.

It isn't instant recognition, but I see the attempt to place me in his expression, the last name familiar to him. It's strange to realize someone is your nemesis, and yet to them, you are little more than a faint murmur in the background of their life.

While I am likely insignificant to him, my last name conjures images of my father, his influence, his wealth. Does Fidel remember my brother, or was Alejandro insignificant, too?

"And what are you doing in New York?" Fidel asks.

If I am to be comforted by anything, it is the fact that I am wearing a new gown, that the seamstress I discovered in Miami has a gift with her sewing machine, that I look every inch the queen I was in Havana. Let him see us thriving despite his attempts to destroy us.

"Visiting friends. Shopping." I affect mannerisms that would have felt natural to me a few years ago when I was little more than a carefree socialite. "Why else would one come to New York?"

He quirks a brow at me, that taunting note in his voice slightly louder this time.

"And your quest for new gowns"—his gaze lingers on the low neckline of my dress—"brought you to Harlem? I had heard things were not going so well for Emilio Perez." He chuckles softly, pleased with his joke. The men beside him parrot the move.

"I came to Harlem because I was curious," I answer, forcing myself to keep my voice light, to push the tremor from my throat.

"And why were you curious?"

"Because you are Cuban," I answer. "And because once our interests likely aligned."

My involvement with the university groups organizing against the former Cuban president were not as flagrant as my brother's, but such views were certainly not uncommon among the children of the wealthy in Cuba.

"Did they? And now? Do our interests still align?"

"I don't know," I lie.

"I very much doubt your father feels this way."

"My father and I have different goals for Cuba's future. He wishes to live in the past, and I understand we cannot, that we must move forward, past our relationship with the Americans, past the hold sugar and its ilk have had over the country for so long."

Fidel's eyes widen with interest; no one listening could doubt the sincerity of my words. The truth is, on this we share a common bond, as much as it pains me to admit it. It's simply his methods I find truly abhorrent, even while I privately agree with him that Cuba needs to change.

Just not like this.

"My brother fought for Cuba's freedom," I add. "He died for it."

The passion blazing through my words has silenced the room. Let him think I am a foolish girl motivated by my quest for revenge, my ire at Batista and his loyal men; let Fidel think I am caught up in a world I don't understand.

"I am sorry to hear that. We lost many good men in the revolution."

He lifts his glass in a toast to the men who died, and something burns inside me, bright and sharp. One day in the not-too-distant future, I will toast his death with the finest champagne money can buy, and I will revel in it.

Someone hands me a glass at Fidel's command, and I swallow the cheap drink with an inelegant gulp, hoping the alcohol's bite will remove the bitter taste of death from my mouth.

"Join us." Fidel gestures toward a seat immediately vacated by one of his lackeys.

The brunette at the table is several seats away from Fidel, but her eyes narrow as I sit in the empty chair. Is she one of his lovers? Dwyer didn't mention anything about competition for Fidel's affections.

Fidel returns to the story he originally was telling before I interrupted him, his belly jutting out as he guffaws at his own joke, his hand stroking his beard, his gaze intermittently flicking to me.

My back is ramrod straight, my mother's voice in my head now. When I laugh, it is not too loud; when I smile, I keep a hint of reserve in my expression, as though I am attempting to gain his measure even as he does the same to me. Fawning over Fidel will do me no favors; if I want to be memorable, to pique his interest, I must treat him as though he is any other man, need to prick his vanity until his ego deflates, make him wonder what it is about me that keeps me from being in his thrall.

Men always want that which they cannot, or should not, have.

I speak to my neighbors at the table, engaging in small talk about world events, listening while Fidel decries the ongoing war in the Congo. He rails against the imperialist Belgians, the conversation becoming increasingly more difficult to follow. I confess my interest in world affairs is typically limited to Cuba and her concerns; my knowledge of the conflicts of which they speak is far more limited. Does Fidel consider the conflict in Cuba resolved, and is he now turning his gaze to other countries, hoping to replicate his revolution throughout the world?

102 · CHANEL CLEETON

I contribute little to the conversation, but then again, it's evident I'm not meant to. I'm here to look pretty and hang on Fidel's every word.

The seat I've taken comes complete with a full place setting of silverware, and the cutlery tempts me, the steak knife inches away from my fingers. If I grabbed it now, if I lunged across the table and stabbed Fidel with it, would I be fast enough before his security personnel could stop me? Would I have a chance?

I reach for the knife.

The brunette stares at me again, her gaze narrowed once more as though she is attempting to work something out in her mind.

I force my hand back to my lap.

As the evening progresses, the crowd thins, the conversation changing as the men and women group together. Fidel's gaze grows bolder with each glass of Chivas Regal.

Does he want the conquest of sleeping with one of Emilio Perez's daughters?

I—

I consider it.

How could I not?

Mr. Dwyer never specified how close I should get to Fidel at this meeting. Was this his intent all along? Sleeping with Fidel would be one manner of gaining his attention, but considering my lack of expertise in that particular area, I fear it might be one evening and nothing more, and if I am not to kill him on American soil . . .

Could I sleep with him?

"You should go home, girl." The brunette slides into the seat next to me, a glass of whiskey in hand.

"Excuse me?"

She smiles, her red lips curving as she leans closer to me, the scent of her perfume filling my nostrils. "You may be the toast of the society scene, but do you really think you could hold a man like Fidel's interest for very long? You're in way over your head."

And suddenly, sitting next to this woman, watching her move, the mannerisms she affects, the sheer confidence and sensuality that seemingly oozes from her pores, she's right. I feel out of my league.

She leans in even closer, her breath hot against my neck.

"Go back to where you came from, Beatriz Perez. Before you do something you regret."

She rises from the chair, offering me a polite, impersonal smile before she slides back into her seat, turning her attention to the man next to her. He hooks an arm around her waist, pulling her onto his lap, his mouth on her neck.

I look away, my cheeks heating.

The tenor of the evening is changing, the men becoming more amorous, the women welcoming their attentions—or at least pretending to. I can't make myself smile at Fidel, can't accept the invitation in his gaze. Now that the moment is here—the choice mine—I can't bear the thought of spending the rest of the evening on his arm and in his bed.

Fidel is accustomed to getting his way; I hope tonight I did enough to intrigue him. I hope our plan will be best served by keeping him dangling on the line.

I have nothing left to give.

I leave the party without a backward glance for Fidel, the weight of the brunette's gaze on me as I reenact my own Cinderella routine sans the discarded pump. If Cinderella had paid what I did for these shoes, she'd have made sure she left the ball with both, too.

The cab ferries me from Harlem back to my hotel in Midtown, the New York skyline passing me by. I have one more day in the city, my flight leaving tomorrow evening, and then I am back to Palm Beach, expected to regale my family with stories of my indulgent weekend in the Hamptons, my lies swirling out of control.

What will I do if word of my appearance at the Hotel Theresa gets back to my parents? My father disowned Alejandro for participating in the attack on the Presidential Palace when Batista was in power. What will he do to me for consorting with Fidel? It is commonly accepted that I am his favorite, but even my father's love has its boundaries.

We arrive at my hotel, and I pay the cab driver. I consider going up to my room, but the cramped space, austere walls, and ugly bedspread are far from appealing, and instead, I head toward the hotel bar. I was careful not to drink too much in Fidel's presence out of fear for the alcohol loosening my tongue and the tight rein I kept on my emotions, but now I need a drink to bolster my flagging nerves, the adrenaline crash coming on strong.

I glance around the room for the kind waitress from earlier. Maybe I came here for that all along, the simple companionship of someone doting on me.

I don't see her.

It's rowdier here at night than it was during the day, although after the crowded room in Harlem filled with revolutionaries and a tyrant, a loquacious business traveler hardly seems fearsome. And still, the looks sliding my way—curious, interested, hungry—are unsettling.

I take a spot at the bar, waiting until the bartender, a young, handsome man a few years older than me, comes over and takes my order.

He talks to me while he makes my drink, setting the glass on the bar top in front of me with a wink and a smile.

The first sip of alcohol hits me with a kick, the night returning to me in waves as I attempt to recall what I said, what I overheard.

I have a feeling Mr. Dwyer will want a thorough debrief. Fidel's interest in the Congo will surely be of note to the Americans, as will his apparent desire to replicate his "success" in Cuba around the rest of the world, even if his methods in doing so are less clear.

The alcohol slides down my throat, the ice clattering around in the thick glass as I take another sip, and then another. My mother would be utterly horrified if she saw me now, the perfect posture she drilled into me spoiled by the hunched slope of my shoulders, my body tucked away in a corner of this unremarkable bar. I dab at my eyes with the cheap cocktail napkin the waiter set beneath my drink, the hotel's name printed on the white square.

Perhaps I should have gone upstairs with Fidel. I likely should have killed him when I had the chance.

And suddenly, I feel almost unbearably alone here in this big city, far away from the familiar comforts from which I draw strength: the smell of arroz con pollo cooking in the kitchen, the sound of my sisters' laughter, the feel of the sand beneath my toes, the sight of my nephew's angelic smile. I should never have come here, never have attempted this. I want to go home, and at the moment, home doesn't look like Havana, but rather, Palm Beach.

A man sporting a garish orange suit and a gaudy watch jostles my elbow. He bumps into me again, no apology, gesturing wildly, the liquid from his glass spilling all over the wood. I press my body closer to the wall, wishing I could make myself invisible in this corner of the room I've carved out for myself.

Finally, the man moves away, leaving me to my solitude.

The barstool next to me slides back with a screech, and I turn away from the interloper.

A tear runs down my cheek.

A white linen square of fabric slides across the bar top in front of me, entering my line of sight. The fabric is followed by the flash of a tanned wrist, a light sprinkling of fine hairs, a crisp white shirt, the wink of a cuff link, the scent of sandalwood and orange. I reach out, my fingers trembling as I trace the monogram on the square of linen, the elegant whorls of the initials, goose bumps rising over my skin as a palm settles against the small of my back.

N. H. R. P.

I turn, his tall form blocking out the rest of the crowd, creating our own private alcove in a room full of strangers, the anonymity making me bold, the months between us overshadowing any embarrassment I might feel over the likelihood that I look far from my best.

I smile.

"Hello, Nick."

chapter eleven

Did I imagine running into Nick Preston in the city, albeit in much more glamorous surroundings than these?

Possibly.

Of course I did.

He looks tired, more so than the man I knew in Palm Beach, as though the campaigning and glad-handing has taken a toll on him. And still, he is every bit as handsome as I remembered.

"What does the 'H' stand for?" I run my fingers over the monogram on his handkerchief.

"Henry."

"It's a good name."

"It was my grandfather's."

"How did you find me?"

Does he know why I came to New York?

"I have the odd connection or two that can prove useful," Nick replies. "I asked at the desk, and they said you weren't in your room. I thought about leaving you a note, but then I overheard someone mention a beauty in the bar, and, well—" He smiles. "Have you eaten?"

I shake my head, sweeping the handkerchief across my lower eyelid, more than a little horrified when it comes away with the smudged black kohl of my eyeliner.

He holds his hand out to me. "Then we'll eat."

I take his hand, still slightly dazed by his appearance, and we leave the hotel, turning onto the busy New York street. I haven't adjusted to the pace here, the frenetic manner in which everyone walks, the sheer energy of it all. Nick's palm lingers solicitously at my back, guiding me out of the way of oncoming foot traffic, his tall form hovering over me.

I glance at him from the corner of my eye, admiring the manner in which his suit drapes his body, his coat in hand. Besides that first night on the balcony when we met, this is the longest we've been in each other's company, the most privacy we've had, and I can't resist the opportunity to indulge in the freedom of the evening.

After a few minutes of walking in silence, Nick stops in front of a nondescript restaurant shoved in between a flower shop and a bakery.

"It doesn't look like much, but they have some of the best steaks in the city. Is this all right?"

It also doesn't escape my notice that, like the hotel bar, it's not the sort of place where he's likely to be recognized.

"It's perfect," I reply.

I walk ahead of Nick, waiting while he speaks to the maître d'. With a handshake and a green president passing between them, we're whisked to a table in the back with dim lighting and a red leather booth in the shape of a clamshell. A squat candle in a glass votive flickers and sputters atop the cream tablecloth.

I remove my coat for the first time since Nick has seen me, handing it to the waiter hovering nearby.

Nick's gaze rakes me from head to toe.

I slide into the booth first, nerves filling me once more.

Once Nick sits next to me, the space feels much smaller.

The waiter hands us two leather-backed menus.

"So how are you?" Nick asks after we've perused the menu, after the waiter has taken our orders and retreated to one of the restaurant's dark alcoves, reappearing for a brief moment to set our drinks in front of us before disappearing once more. "Has your trip to New York been enjoyable?"

"I'm not sure 'enjoyable' is the word I would use. Hopefully, it has been productive, although it's probably too soon to tell." I hesitate. "How much do you know?"

"Enough."

Between his role in the Senate and his family's connections, I'm not entirely surprised, but it is a bit unexpected. There are players in the game unknown to me. Do I have a codename somewhere at CIA headquarters? Do men in suits discuss me: my family, my potential relationship with Fidel, my motives?

"I have a knack for getting into trouble," I admit.

Nick doesn't respond as he sips his scotch, his gaze steady on mine.

His fingers are bare. Is he married now or still engaged?

"Beatriz—" Nick's voice breaks off and he swallows, his Adam's apple bobbing.

"I don't think I'm the only one who has a penchant for getting into trouble," I say, acknowledging the utter impropriety of us being alone together.

"Touché." Nick raises his glass, clinking it against my champagne flute. "To trouble."

"To trouble," I echo, taking a sip of my drink. I study him over the rim of my glass. "I thought senators were supposed to avoid the appearance of trouble."

"That's what they tell me."

The waiter interrupts us, setting our appetizers in front of us. He's gone without a word.

"You were upset in the hotel bar earlier," Nick says.

"I—it's complicated."

"You're in trouble."

"It isn't anything I didn't go looking for, and it isn't anything I can't handle."

"I know you've lived through a lot in Cuba. I can't imagine what it must have been like for you to experience the revolution up close. The briefings we've received on the situation paint a dire picture. But be careful. These men you're involved with aren't always who you think they are, and their motives aren't always what they seem."

"Don't worry, this arrangement is convenient at the moment, but I have my eyes wide open."

For a moment, he looks like he's going to argue the point, but before he does, I can't resist asking the question that has been running through my mind for months.

"Are you married now?"

There's no ring on his finger, but not all men wear them, and while a wedding such as theirs would have likely caused a stir in the world of polite society, when you live on the fringes of such things, you do miss quite a bit.

He blinks, as though my question has caught him off guard. "No. I'm not married."

Relief fills me.

"Soon, though?"

"We haven't set a date yet." He gives me a wry look. "You can just ask, you know. Friends ask each other about the details of their lives."

"So we're friends now?"

"Something like that."

"Why the delay then, friend?"

"She wants a long engagement, a break before assuming the responsibilities that will go with our marriage. Can't blame her for that. There's some pressure, though, too, from both our families. At some point, it becomes as complicated as a merger between two entities."

My parents' marriage was conducted in a similar fashion. When you have a great deal of money, there is much more at stake than one's affections.

"My family wanted me to propose earlier, so we could be married before the election," he adds. "Voters tend to look favorably on married politicians, and ones with families even more so."

Don't do this. Don't go down this path. It's beneath you.

"Why didn't you propose earlier?"

"It turns out I have an inherent dislike to being maneuvered into anything I don't want to do."

I laugh. "I understand."

He makes a face. "I have a hard time imagining anyone maneuvering you into anything you don't want to do."

"And yet, they still try."

"Is that why you haven't married? The reason all those proposals never became engagements?"

"Just how much have you learned about me?"

"Not nearly enough. I used to think patience was one of my virtues, but I found myself unable to wait for answers about you."

"Why?"

He takes another sip of his drink, meeting my gaze once more.

"Because I wanted to know if you were with anyone. Even though I had no right to be, I found myself quite jealous of the man who might hold your affections."

I open my mouth to speak, and immediately close it; I don't have the words for such conversations, lack the experience to conjure a witty response. There's flirting, and then there's this, and there's not a hint of humor in his expression, nothing to suggest the earnestness in his voice and in his gaze isn't the truth.

He shakes his head. "I shouldn't say such things. I'm sorry. I—"

"No, you probably shouldn't." I take a deep breath. "I wondered about you, too. Constantly."

His hand pauses in midair, the glass halfway to his lips.

"Beatriz."

There it is again, a host of emotions contained in my name. It really sounds quite beautiful when he says it like that.

Before I can respond, the waiter returns with another staff member. They clear our appetizers away, bringing out the main course, the steaks juicy and thick.

"This is a mess," Nick says once we are alone again. He doesn't sound the least bit sorry.

"It is," I agree.

In this moment, with him, I'm not that sorry, either.

"I'm normally quite boring."

I grin. "I have a hard time believing that, and if it were true, it would be a sad thing, indeed. No rebellions?"

He laughs. "Sadly, no. My siblings are the wild ones. I'm the eldest, the head of the family now that my father is gone. They're forever getting into scrapes."

"And you run behind and clean up their messes?"

"Invariably." He takes another bite of his steak, and when he's finished chewing, his gaze reverts to me. "And you? Are you the troublemaker among your sisters or the one taking care of everyone else?"

"Do you really have to ask?"

He laughs again.

"You should try a little rebellion sometimes," I add. "It's really not so bad."

"I suppose I'll have to take your word for it."

And because I want him to know me, because I hate the idea of him seeing me as little more than the frivolous girl so many think me to be—careless, and reckless, and dangerous—I say—

"I took care of my brother. We were twins," I add, unsure of how much he knows about my life. Clearly, he's privy to most of it, but at the same time, my brother is the one topic my family never discusses.

Nick doesn't attempt to fill the silence with probing questions or meaningless platitudes, and perhaps it's his silence—steady, reassuring—that gives me the courage I need to continue.

"Alejandro was killed in Havana after the revolution. He was killed because he was a threat to Fidel's attempts to consolidate power. My family was influential in Cuba. Alejandro was well-known and popular, active in one of the other groups opposing former president Batista. He was a risk, and Fidel is a paranoid man."

"That's why you're working with the CIA?"

"Yes." I take a deep breath. "I found my brother. We had lost track of him during the early weeks of the revolution. Everything was so chaotic then, and my parents had disowned my brother a couple years earlier for his role in a plot to attack the Presidential Palace when Batista was in power. I saw the car pull up to the curb, watched them . . . They dumped his body in front of the gates of our home in Miramar as though he was garbage." I can still hear the sickening thud of my brother's dead body hitting the ground, can still remember the feel of the gravel cutting into my skin as I cradled him, as his blood covered my hands. "I vowed Fidel would pay. For what he did to Cuba, for what he did to my family: for throwing my father in prison until we feared he was lost to us, for his role in my brother's death. There were days, so many days, when that vow was all that kept me going."

Nick reaches between us, lacing our fingers together.

My mouth goes dry.

He gives my hand a reassuring squeeze before releasing me.

"And the CIA's going to help you destroy Fidel?" he asks, his voice low.

"Yes. I hope so, at least."

"Whatever they tell you, at the end of the day, their interests will always come first. You're expendable to them, and they won't hesitate to use you in order to further their own interests."

"Maybe I'm using them."

"It's not a game."

I laugh, the sound devoid of humor. "You think I don't know that? I come from a country where men are executed without proof, in travesties of trials without any respect for their legal rights, for nothing more than the fact that Fidel has willed it so. And before that? Batista was no better. And before that? I come from a long line of dictators. Trust me, your CIA can do their worst, and I seriously doubt it will come close to the things I've seen."

"And yet you want to return to Cuba?"

"Cuba is my home. It will always be home. I will always wish for it to be better, to be what I think it could be, but yes. It will always have my heart."

"I admire your loyalty."

"But?"

"Look, I understand. My family wanted me to be involved in politics, but at the same time, I wanted to do it for my own reasons. I was young when I went off to fight in the war. It was exciting in a distant sort of way, and it seemed like the sort of thing I *should* do. And when I saw what war was, outside of the books I'd read or the stories I'd heard, I understood just how important politics and diplomacy were. War should always be a last resort. That desire for more you speak of; I understand it. I hope my work in the Senate can help in some small way. But at the same time—"

"What? I shouldn't risk my life? You risked your life because you believed in what you were fighting for, didn't you?"

"I did."

"It's not really different then, is it? Or is it because I'm a woman?"

Perhaps it is better to be a woman now than it was when my mother was my age, but whatever progress has been made still doesn't feel like nearly enough, and I've learned that even in America, where democracy and freedom are preached with religious fervor, there are different definitions of "free." Women in Cuba and the United States alike are still viewed as extensions of other people—fathers, husbands—rather than as our own selves, to be judged on our own merits.

"No, I suppose it shouldn't be different," Nick answers.

The waiter collects our finished meals, interrupting the moment between us.

We peruse the after-dinner menu as though we both wish for this evening to continue, languishing over drink choices and ultimately deciding to order dessert.

Nick tells me about his work in the Senate, his desire for sound fiscal policy, for balancing the budget. He speaks of his concerns that the government doesn't do enough to support people when they need it most, his hopes to come up with a solution for Social Security to provide medical care for the elderly.

It is strange to hear him speak of these policies with such fervor and passion. I am more used to fiery rhetoric than sound policy, and balancing the budget is hardly a stirring topic. And yet, it is clear the policy inspires him, that he believes the best things that can be done to improve people's lives are often the small changes. I am so used to being surrounded by men intent on destruction and revolution that it is refreshing to hear a man growing excited about building something, however incrementally.

I admire him tremendously.

I talk about my sisters, about life in Cuba with the taste of pineapple on my tongue and a Brandy Alexander clouding my head. Or maybe the man is responsible for the feeling inside me, this giddy, achy feeling.

Once we've spent as much time as absolutely possible in the restaurant, tables clearing out, the night growing later, Nick walks me back to the hotel.

It seems as though it takes us far less time to get back to the hotel than it took to walk to the restaurant, and despite the late hour, I yearn to turn down side streets, to prolong my time in his company.

Our conversation tapers off the closer we get to the hotel, the building looming before us.

Will he be married the next time we see each other?

Nick follows me into the lobby, his hand on my waist. I wait for him to release me, for the evening to reach its natural conclusion: me tucked under the covers of my hotel room bed, him somewhere out in the city.

Does he keep an apartment here? Is he checked into an elegant hotel, or does he stay with his family when he's in the city?

A group of businessmen spills out of the hotel bar, their raucous laughter filling the nearly deserted lobby.

"I'll walk you up to your room," Nick offers, his gaze darting to the men, his hand tightening around my waist.

The men watch us walk through the lobby, comments about how lucky the man with me is reaching my ears.

Nick tenses beside me.

"Leave it," I whisper. The last thing either one of us needs is a scene.

He gives me a clipped nod, his strides lengthening until we reach the bank of elevators.

The elevator operator greets us as I tell him the number of my floor, and Nick releases me, his arm falling to his side. We take the elevator up to my room in silence, the car blissfully empty of other guests. I watch the buttons light up as we ascend to distract myself from the nerves rising in my stomach.

The elevator stops, and the door slides open. I keep my gaze trained on the carpet as I step into the hall, Nick behind me.

The elevator whirs to life as it continues its journey. In the distance, a baby's cry emanates from one of the rooms, mixing with the noise from a television farther down the hall.

I reach into my purse and fumble for my room key, pulling it out with shaky fingers.

I wish I'd met him a year ago, before he got engaged, when I'd just arrived in Palm Beach, before I became involved in this mess with the CIA. I wish I'd never met him at all so I wouldn't know what I'm missing.

"Thanks for dinner."

"It was my pleasure," Nick replies.

I wish I could read his mood, but his emotions are hidden, until the silence stretches on, and I summon the courage to ask the question that has run through my mind all evening.

"Why did you come find me?"

He's quiet for so long I almost think he isn't going to answer me.

"Because I wanted to see you."

He says it like a man unburdening himself of a great and terrible secret.

God help me, I do what everyone says I do. I push.

"Why?"

"Because I think of you. Constantly. Because I wonder what it would be like to kiss you. For you to be mine, even for a moment." His voice cracks. "Do you?"

My heart thunders in my chest so loudly I imagine he can hear it, too, the sound of it sputtering and racing, filling the empty hotel hallway, joining the baby's cries, the television's chatter, the hum of the elevator.

I nod, and then because I want to give him the words, because it seems right to match his courage and candor with my own, I say—

"Yes." I swallow, the key biting into my palm as I fist my hand, careful to keep from reaching out and touching him. "Constantly."

The elevator starts up again, coming back down. Anyone could see us like this. At any moment, the elevator door could open and someone could step out.

"I should go to my room."

"You should go to your room," he agrees, lowering his head as he moves closer to me, as he tucks me into the curve of his body.

I take a deep breath, and then another, steadying myself.

With my free hand, I trail my finger along the cuff of his elegant Burberry trench coat, curling under, brushing the suit fabric beneath, grazing the soft skin at the inside of his wrist.

He shudders against me.

My fingers tremble as I press my hotel room key into his palm.

I walk toward my hotel room door alone, leaving Nick standing in the hallway behind me.

My gaze rests on the wood door, my legs quaking beneath my dress, the sound of his footsteps filling my ears, the elevator whooshing between floors.

I close my eyes as his hand settles on my waist, at the scent of orange and sandalwood, his breath against my neck. I open my eyes to the sight of his tanned, naked fingers placing the key into the keyhole on my hotel room door.

chapter twelve

The hotel room door closes behind us.

I face him.

"We should talk about this." Nick sets the key down on the nightstand.

"I don't want to talk."

"What do you want then?" he asks.

"You."

"I'm a politician. There's scrutiny—"

"I'm used to the scrutiny. I don't care."

"It's different," he warns. "I don't want to hurt you."

I don't want to hear all the reasons this is a terrible idea. I *know* it is probably a terrible idea, that my actions this evening have been brazen to the extreme, that I am about to cross an invisible line for which there shall be no return. I don't want reality to intrude on this moment.

I sigh. "You think I'm too young for you."

Nick steps forward, and his lips brush the top of my head, his fingers clasping my waist, clutching the fabric of my coat, somewhere between pulling me closer and pushing me away.

"You're too everything for me. Young is probably the least of my worries."

My hand finds his, and he releases the fabric, threading his fingers with mine once more.

"This is a bad idea," I whisper, as I step into the curve of his body.

"The worst," Nick agrees, his hands moving to my nape, his fingers on the clasp of my necklace. His fingertips ghost across my skin as he removes the jewelry from my neck. He sets it on the nightstand before mimicking the motion with my earrings, his knuckles skimming my earlobes.

He leans down. His lips graze my ear.

I shudder, goose bumps rising over my skin.

I tip my head up, no longer content to wait for him to kiss me first. In truth, I've built up this kiss in my mind since the first moment I met him.

It doesn't disappoint.

There are kisses, and then there are *kisses*, and this one rests firmly in the latter category.

"I thought you didn't believe in rebellions," I whisper, tearing my mouth away from his, my fingers making quick work of his tie as he shrugs off his coat.

Now that I have the taste of him in my mouth, the feel of his body against me, I am greedy for more.

Nick groans, pulling me closer. "Maybe I just hadn't found the right one."

He strokes my nape, his fingers shifting to the buttons at the back of my dress, his knuckles soaring across the exposed bare skin.

I fumble with the buttons down the front of his white dress shirt, removing his tie from his collar, my heart pounding madly, madly, madly with each shudder, each caress.

When you're a young girl, from the right family, who sits in the wooden pew at Mass each Sunday alongside your parents, inhabiting a society that looks for reasons to cast a proverbial scarlet letter upon you, you're told to guard your virtue against such wantonness. No one tells you with the right man it can feel like heaven; in the right moment, it can make you feel more powerful than you ever imagined.

No one tells you how truly lovely it can be.

I thought I knew what it was to want, but now, his body above mine, well, now I know what all those men before him only hinted at, the stolen kisses by eager boys paling in comparison to the passion I find in his arms.

Is this love?

Who has time to worry about such things?

At the moment, it is everything, and that's all that matters.

"You're quiet," Nick says.

He dabs his cigarette in the ashtray on the bedside table, his other arm wrapped around my shoulders. My head rests against his bare chest.

When I remember this moment later, it will be the scent of his cigarettes, his skin warm against mine, the sheets scratchy against my skin, the bright light from the lamp we never got around to turning off that I conjure up. Those will be the colors, sounds, and smells that shape the memory, but what fills it, what fills me now, is how happy I feel, even as I know there will be heartbreak down the road, that I am the villain in this piece for going to bed with an engaged man, that as I once warned Eduardo, the bill always comes due at the end.

And still—I don't regret a moment we've shared.

"I'm happy," I reply.

"You say it like you're surprised by the emotion," he muses.

"I suppose I have a hard time trusting 'happy.'"

"I can understand that."

Despite his time spent fighting in the war, I have a hard time imagining he *can* understand, and at the same time, there are some things I don't know how to explain, don't want intruding on this moment.

My body was easy to share; the rest of it more difficult. Ironic, really, when you think of all the times my mother and Magda worried over my virtue, guarding my virginity as though it was the most prized part of me. They worried far less over my heart.

"You're still afraid," he says, his tone filled with surprise.

"I am."

"I would have thought—"

"That if I were afraid of Fidel and his men, I'd stay far away from them?"

"Yes."

"The only way to stop being afraid of something is to confront it. To take away its power over you."

"He doesn't have power over you anymore, though, Beatriz. You're safe now."

The earnestness in his voice almost makes me laugh, and for the first time all evening, I feel like the older, wiser one.

"I don't even know what 'safe' means anymore. I was so busy living in a bubble, I didn't realize how tumultuous the rest of the world was, how badly people wanted to tear down everything we'd built. None of it was real. It was all just a pretty illusion we fooled ourselves into believing. I won't make that mistake again."

"So you don't believe in anything anymore?"

"I believe in myself."

"Is that why you don't let anyone close? All those abandoned marriage proposals?"

I shrug.

"Don't do that. Don't push me away, too. You can let me in."

"Can I? What is this if not a fantasy? What good does it do to pretend it is anything else?"

"It doesn't have to be a fantasy," he replies. "It could be something more, something real."

He is a good man. That is a singular quality these days. He is a good man, and one day he will do great things.

So will I.

I roll over, resting my chin on his chest, trailing a finger down his jaw.

"We are both what ambition has made us. Let's not pretend otherwise. We have our goals, and the paths we are on are set. This is a moment. Nothing more."

"You don't want it to be more."

"It's not about what I want or what you want. Neither one of us would be content to have our plans derailed, and we don't fit neatly in each other's pockets. You have a fiancée out there somewhere." He flinches. "You can't afford a scandal. Not now. The election is, what, not even two months away? And I am nothing if not a scandal."

"You don't have to be, you know. It's not too late to back down from this insane arrangement you have with the CIA."

"It's not in my nature to back down."

"Sometimes I forget how young you are."

I sit up, the sheets dropping to my waist.

"Don't do that. Don't discount me because of my age. I am so tired of people telling me I don't understand the world around me because I am a woman or because I am young."

"It's not about your age or gender. I just can't reconcile the version of you that is smart and logical with this person who seems willing to throw herself into an utterly reckless and risky situation."

"That's because you have no idea what it's like to watch your country fall apart in front of you, and to feel so utterly powerless, so helpless to do anything about it."

I want him to understand this side of me, the most important part, perhaps. I want him to value the choices I've made as I do. I want his respect.

"No, you're right, I don't," he replies. "I can't imagine what you experienced in Cuba. But I don't understand why you feel the need to fix everything yourself. There are other people who can do that, Beatriz. You don't have to risk your life. If my brother told me he was involved with the CIA, I would warn him against it. Dwyer has a reputation."

"So do I. This isn't the first time I've participated in such activities and I doubt it will be the last."

"And your family? What do they say of your involvement with the CIA?"

"They don't know anything about it."

"They wouldn't be pleased, though, would they?"

"Probably not. They certainly weren't happy when I was involved with the revolutionary movement in Cuba. If I only did what my family wished me to do, I wouldn't have very much fun at all. I certainly wouldn't be here with you."

He has the grace to nearly blush.

"I'm not that strange, you know," I add. "There are plenty of women who have joined the revolutionaries in Cuba, who are fighting for what they believe in. I can admire their conviction even if our beliefs are not the same."

"And I can worry about you even if it annoys you. I can't help it, Beatriz."

I turn, capturing his mouth in another kiss.

"Let's not talk of such things. I don't want politics between us. Not now."

"What do you want then?" he asks. "From me?"

There's hesitancy in the question, and I imagine he's the sort of man from whom a great many people want a great many things.

"This."

"And what is 'this,' exactly?"

"I want you. Just you. No cash by the bedside table. No lies between us. No promises we don't intend to keep."

"Debutantes aren't what they used to be, are they?"

I roll my eyes. "Would you rather I let you take the lead?"

He laughs. "I'll manage just fine, but thank you. So I take it, even though I never extended the offer, that you have no interest in being my mistress."

"It's hardly personal. I don't want to be *anyone's* mistress."

"Then that's not the plan with Fidel?"

"You don't want to know the plan with Fidel."

"He'll be back in Havana soon. Will you still be here?"

"I'll be in Palm Beach."

"I want to see you again." He hesitates. "Can I see you again?"

"My flight doesn't leave until tomorrow evening. Do you want to stay with me until then?"

"Yes."

And just like that, we stop talking about politics.

It's different the second time. There's a familiarity between us that has sprung up in a remarkably short time, the kind of knowledge that comes only with intimacy.

Before we fall asleep, he turns to face me, his head against the pillow.

"Why tonight? Why me?"

"Because I wanted it to be you." I take a deep breath, staring up at the ceiling, lights from the street flickering through the crack between the curtains. "Why this? Why me?"

"Because I wanted it to be you."

"On the balcony?"

"Before that."

"When?" I demand, greedy and a little bit tipsy from the bottle of champagne we ordered from the bar and shared earlier.

"When I saw you in the ballroom. Andrew was on his knees making a fool of himself, and you just stood there, and I could see you were there, but you weren't, and I wanted to be wherever you were."

"It's an election year."

Now is not the time for recklessness.

"It is."

"And you're to be married."

Nick sighs. "I am."

He shifts, bringing me against his side, wrapping his arm around my waist. My eyes close to the sound of his breathing, to the beat of his heart against my back.

chapter thirteen

The dream starts as it always does—me sneaking out of our house in Havana, the money I stole from my father's safe to give to my brother stuffed in the little handbag I carry around my wrist. I'm in a hurry, worried about Alejandro, if he's safe, if he's well.

I spy one of the gardeners off to the side of the house, and our gazes connect. Fear pricks me. Will he tell my parents? Are his loyalties to my family or to the new regime?

The gardener breaks eye contact first, going back to his duties, as though he's aware of the trouble that usually follows in my wake and wants no part of it.

I'm almost at the front gates of our estate.

A car rounds the corner, going far too fast for our street considering the number of children that reside in the surrounding houses.

The tires screech. A door opens. A body hits the ground.

I am running, the purse abandoned somewhere on the gravel of our front driveway, my legs pumping, heart pounding.

I scream.

When I was younger, I followed Alejandro out into the ocean one day, and a wave overtook me, water filling my lungs, panic flooding my body as I attempted to save myself.

That's what the dream feels like—like I'm drowning, and I can't save myself, and I can't look away.

My brother's dead face stares back at me.

I jolt awake, my limbs weighted down like lead, chest heaving, my breath coming in harsh pants.

"You're safe. It was just a dream."

I shift in bed, my eyes adjusting to the semidarkness, momentarily disoriented and surprised to see Nick looking at me with concern in his gaze.

He strokes my back as I take deep breaths, trying to get my heart rate back under control.

"Can I get you something?" he asks, the kindness in his voice bringing a lump to my throat.

I shake my head.

"Do you want to talk about it?"

"No," I croak.

He sits up in the bed, making a space for me to curl into his body, and something turns over in my heart.

It feels like the most natural thing to lay my head on his bare chest, for his arm to wrap around my waist, holding me tight.

"When I came back from Europe, I had these dreams . . ." He flinches. "Still do sometimes."

"Does it ever get easier?" I ask.

He bends down, his lips brushing the top of my head.

"It does. It takes time." His grip around me tightens. "It never really goes away, though."

"No, I imagine it doesn't."

We don't let go of each other for the rest of the night.

. . .

We spend my last day in New York drinking champagne naked in bed, dining on chilled lobster and a thick cut of filet mignon. We don't speak of politics, or his fiancée, or Fidel, or the future, but I learn some of the answers to the questions that have filled my mind about him, and he learns some Beatriz secrets, too.

"Tell me about your family," he says.

"My family?"

"I'm curious."

"It's really not that exciting."

"Now why do I have a hard time believing that? I've seen your sisters in action."

I laugh.

"What was your brother like?" he asks, his tone gentler.

"He was fun. When we were younger, he always had a trick up his sleeve, always wanted to go in search of an adventure. He was charming. And he was kind. We all spoiled him, of course; he was the only boy with four sisters. He loved it."

"It's nice to be able to be friends with your siblings. You're lucky in that. It isn't always so."

"My sisters have always been my friends. And Alejandro was my best friend. I don't know how to describe it, but we understood each other in a way no one else in the family did. Maybe it was a twin thing."

"You must miss him terribly."

"Always. It feels wrong to move on with my life knowing he won't ever have the opportunity to do so."

Nick brushes a stray tear from my cheek. "I'm sorry."

"Tell me about your family," I say.

Nick leans back against the headboard.

"My family is big and loud, and full of expectations and plans."

"Was the Senate one of their plans?"

"It would be easier if I could say that, wouldn't it? No, that one was all my own. Sometimes I curse myself for it, but mostly I'm grateful for it. My work in the Senate saved me."

"How so?"

"When I came back from Europe, I was lost. During the war, I was surrounded by men who fought for the same things I did. There was a brotherhood there. It disappeared when I came home."

"And the Senate gave that back to you?"

"I suppose it did."

"I never got the impression senators were so chummy."

"We are and we aren't. And still, we're working toward a common cause. I missed that sense of purpose when I came back."

"Why politics?"

"I'm in a unique position. I was born into a family that hasn't had to struggle for the basic things other people in this country are fighting for. I have a platform and a voice thanks to my last name, and I want to use it to do some good in this world. I saw firsthand what comes of not speaking up for what you believe in when I was fighting in Europe, what silence can do to a man, and I want to make the world better than I found it."

"Is it true what they say? That you dream of being president one day?"

He shoots me a wry grin. "If you're going to have a goal, why not make it a big one? At the moment, though, I'm just hoping for reelection. It's not my time to run for the presidency, yet, and besides, the party is in good hands."

"You're friends with Kennedy, aren't you?"

"So you did ask about me."

I laugh. "Let's just say it's hard to make it through a season without hearing the name 'Nicholas Preston' on everyone's lips. They say you and Kennedy are great friends."

"He's a great man. He'll be a good president, will lead this country in the direction we need to go."

"And after that?"

Nick smiles. "Perhaps one day it will be my time."

"You'll need to be careful, then. Future presidents can't afford scandals."

"No, they can't."

"You'll need the right wife. The right family. The right image."

"Yes, I will. I do."

I swallow.

"Are there others? Other women like me?"

Even as I fear his answer, I make myself ask the question, because I will not go into this with anything less than my eyes wide open. He would hardly be the first man to have a woman in public and others in private.

"Have there been other women? Yes."

I'm hardly surprised, yet I appreciate the honesty between us.

"There aren't any other women now. There haven't been for some time." He sighs. "I wish I'd met you a year ago. I wish I'd met you before I made promises."

"We shouldn't do this again."

"No, we probably shouldn't," he agrees.

chapter fourteen

We say good-bye in my hotel room, one last kiss between us, Nick's arms wrapped around my waist, the body I've gotten to know so well pressed against mine, the business card with his private number scrawled on it clutched in my hand. Once Nick is gone, I head downstairs to the hotel bar, where Mr. Dwyer and I agreed to discuss my meeting with Fidel.

"I heard it went well with Castro last night," Dwyer says by way of greeting when I sit across from him at the table.

"I think it did."

"He liked the look of you."

My eyes narrow. "If you had spies there, why did you need me?"

"I have spies everywhere, and I haven't yet determined I need you."

"What comes next then? What else do I have to do?"

"You made an impression. My sources told me Fidel was upset you left early. Upset he couldn't enjoy some private time with you."

Heat creeps up the back of my neck.

"I thought—"

"You played it well. If you'd been too eager, he would have been suspicious. If it had been too easy for him, he would have dismissed you. You weren't impulsive, didn't blow your cover. You did better than I expected."

"So what happens now?"

"We wait on the right timing before you move on Fidel. In the meantime, I have another offer for you. A paying one."

"What is it?"

"The Cuban spying apparatus has proved more formidable than we anticipated. Simply put, Fidel has spies everywhere. I want you to infiltrate them."

"I'm not a spy."

"Which makes you even more useful to me. You move in the right circles, speak several languages, can blend in if you need to. No one will suspect you are a spy, and you will be able to insert yourself into places my professional assets might not be able to. We want you to become involved with one of the pro-Castro groups in South Florida. Someone has been feeding Fidel information on our plans to overthrow his regime, double-crossing some of the exiles you call friends. I want to know who it is."

"And why do you think I'm capable of getting this information? Don't you already have people in these groups?"

"I do. The problem with a double agent is that it's difficult to know whom you can trust. I don't have those concerns with you."

"Why?"

"Because you're a new player on the board, if you will. And because you learn to be suspicious in my line of work, but I would bet everything I have on the fact that you will burn the world down in order to avenge your brother. I like people I can predict."

"And I'm predictable?"

"Revenge is the oldest motive in the book."

This will certainly pass the time spent waiting, and if I really can gather intelligence for Dwyer that's helpful in removing Fidel from power—

"How much?"

"It will depend on the intelligence you feed us, but it will be worth your while. Was this trip not a sign of our good faith?"

They have paid me well. Like my father, I have begun to appreciate the virtues of becoming financially independent.

"We'll work this out as we go along," Dwyer adds. "I understand your need for discretion given your family's reputation, their feelings about Fidel. The appearance of you colluding with his regime will be a closely guarded secret. We will do everything we can to protect you."

"And our original plan?"

"Like I said, it will take time, but it is certainly still of the foremost importance to us. Besides, the more you infiltrate Fidel's supporters, the more he will begin to trust you.

"It will be dangerous," he adds after a beat. "Spying is a different beast altogether. It will force you to put your neck on the line for a long period of time, to lie to those you love, those who are close to you. Do you think you can do that?"

"That won't be a problem."

Fidel leaves New York days after I return to Palm Beach, his trip to the United States capped by his delivery of the longest speech in the United Nations' history: a four-and-a-half-hour-long denouncement of the imperialist Americans he accused of plotting his government's downfall. He praised the Soviets, his words reportedly met with enthusiastic applause from Khrushchev, who later offered Fidel a ride home on a Soviet airliner when American authorities seized Castro's plane at Idlewild Airport because of unpaid debts to American creditors.

It's becoming clearer and clearer which way the wind blows in Cuba, and I expect I will soon receive more instructions from Mr. Dwyer.

When the instructions arrive, they come in the form of an address scribbled on a piece of paper passed to me by a nondescript man who slipped the note into my pocket one day when my sisters and I were shopping at the Royal Poinciana Plaza.

My first order of espionage from Dwyer is to attend a meeting of suspected communists. I'm armed with an address, a name he assures me will help me gain admittance, and only my wits to guide me.

The communist meeting is held at a bright green house on a quiet residential street in Hialeah, the grass growing over the edges of the sidewalk leading up to the front steps. There are three cars parked in the driveway.

I take a deep breath, raising my fist to knock on the door.

In the distance, a dog barks.

The door opens, and a young man not much older than me stares at me across the threshold.

I had expected one of my countrymen, and am greeted instead by an American with a scraggly red beard, pale skin, and freckles, dressed in denim and a worn, paper-thin cotton T-shirt.

"Can I help you?" he asks.

I purposefully chose the plainest clothes in my closet: a pair of dark trousers and a white cotton blouse, a serviceable pair of flats. His appearance makes it clear I still missed the mark.

"Claudia sent me," I answer, following the instructions jotted on the note below the address even though I have no clue who Claudia is, and have a sinking suspicion she has no idea who I am, either.

Does Dwyer have other spies infiltrating this meeting? If I get into trouble, will someone come to my aid, or am I truly on my own here?

The man nods, stepping back to make way for me to enter the house.

I follow him past a galley-style kitchen, into a living room filled with four other people.

He jerks his thumb at me. "Claudia sent her."

I sit on one of the couches in the corner and listen while the man who answered the door—whose name is Jimmy—starts the meeting. From the bits of conversation going on around me, I glean that he studies at one of the universities in town; the two women in the room—Sandra and Nancy—are classmates of his.

Like Che, they are communists, not Cubans, and whatever their allegiance to Fidel, it stems from ideology, not nationality. When Mr. Dwyer gave me this assignment, I envisioned dangerous revolutionaries plotting violent attacks, not intellectuals—or pseudo-intellectuals—spouting dull rhetoric. Is this really what the CIA fears? Or is this all a test of my utility to them?

The other two men are brothers—Javier and Sergio—and from their introductions, I gather they left Cuba a few years ago when Batista was cracking down on the student groups at the University of Havana organizing against him. Of all of the group's members, the brothers seem the most likely to have useful intelligence on Fidel, and I smile at Javier, peek at Sergio a few times during my own introduction.

I give them my real name, talk about my activities in Havana prior to Fidel taking power, expound on my dislike of Batista, my wish for Cuba to be independent from American influence. The Americans' eyes are wide when I mention my brother was involved in planning the attack on the Presidential Palace. I very much doubt they've been anywhere near the kind of violence we lived through during the revolution.

There's a look of understanding between the two brothers, though, as if they were intimately familiar with Batista's personal brand of hell. That Batista is living out his days in lavish exile in Portugal without answering for his crimes, the men he killed, his role in delivering us to Fidel, is yet another injustice we're forced to tolerate.

Once the introductions are complete, and I am somewhat assured Claudia isn't going to appear and denounce me as an impostor and a spy, the conversation shifts to other topics: namely, the new trade embargo on Cuba.

President Eisenhower has restricted all American exports to Cuba except for a few humanitarian essentials like medicine and some foods. For a country that relies on so much of its foreign goods coming from the United States, it will be a blow to Fidel. But is it enough to destabilize him?

The Hialeah group rails about the embargo for nearly an hour, offering little in the way of meaningful plans or suggestions, and I still struggle to see the danger Dwyer alluded to. The Cuban brothers are largely silent through this discussion, and I follow their lead, contributing little, taking the time to get the lay of the land in an attempt to understand the inner workings of the group.

We agree to meet again in a month, and I head back to Palm Beach.

When I arrive at my parents' house, Eduardo is parked outside, leaning against his snappy red convertible.

"Have you been waiting long?" I ask as I step out of my car.

"Not too long," he answers.

Eduardo kisses me on the cheek, his gaze running over my appearance, a faint smile playing on his lips.

"What's so funny?"

"I'm just taken aback, that's all. I don't think I've ever seen you dressed so . . . austerely?"

"Very funny."

He's not wrong, but even in my plainest outfit, I still felt ridiculously overdressed at the communist meeting.

Eduardo trails a finger along the sleeve of my top. "Dare I ask, or are there some things I'm better off not knowing?"

Despite the fact that he's been my initial contact with the CIA, Dwyer stressed secrecy on the spying front, and the fact that he hasn't mentioned any of this to Eduardo gives me the impression I shouldn't, either.

"Better off not knowing," I reply. "Let me guess, you're here to whisk me away to acquire more explosives."

I've heard nothing of the dynamite we picked up that evening months ago, of his plans for it, or whether they've come to fruition.

"You're hilarious. I actually wanted to talk to you."

"Do you want to go for a walk on the beach?" I ask.

It's become a routine of sorts between us when he's in Palm Beach, and I've missed the time together.

"Of course."

I follow him down the path, exchanging small talk.

When we arrive at the beach, we both remove our shoes and walk barefoot in the sand.

"How was New York?" he asks.

"Confusing."

"Was it hard? Seeing Fidel?"

"Harder than I imagined it would be. In the beginning, he looked so ordinary sitting there with everyone else. I suppose I let my guard down a bit. And then it all came rushing back to me: Alejandro's death, the violence in Cuba, the fear we all felt. La Cabaña, everything. It was like a scream kept building inside me while I sat there staring at his smug, smiling face, and then I couldn't take it anymore and I had to leave."

"I heard it went well. That he was interested."

"I hope he was interested. It was difficult to tell."

"I have a hard time believing he wouldn't be interested. You're beautiful, Beatriz."

"He was interested as any man is interested, but will that be enough for me to get close to him at a later date? I don't know."

I am tired of waiting, of making incremental progress like going to the meeting in Hialeah, while the world around us shifts, Cuba drifting farther and farther away.

"Hopefully, you won't have to pretend much longer," Eduardo says.

"Did Dwyer tell you anything about their plans to send me to Havana?"

"No. At the moment, the CIA is preoccupied with other things, not to mention the American presidential election."

"And you? You've been absent quite a bit lately. What's kept you preoccupied? A woman?"

He laughs. "Not even close." He reaches out, tugging my hair affectionately. "Don't you know you're the only woman in my life?"

I snort. "Hardly."

"Would you believe I've missed you, then?"

I smile. "Perhaps that."

"I came back to see you. To see how you were doing. I was worried after New York." He stops walking, and turns to face me, his gaze turning serious. "I heard other rumors about your time in New York." His eyes narrow slightly. "Did you go to dinner with him?"

I struggle to keep my expression blank. "With who?"

How does he know about this? Was the CIA watching me while I was in New York? I confess I didn't even think of it, figured I was too far beneath their notice for them to exhaust their resources on someone like me. Did someone else see me and Nick together?

"I heard you looked beautiful. That he couldn't take his eyes off you."

Is this it? Have I finally ruined my reputation beyond repair? Do people know Nick Preston and I stayed in my hotel room together?

"I don't know what you're talking about," I lie.

"So after everything, all the secrets we've shared, this is how it is to be between us?"

The disappointment in his eyes strikes a chord within me, but then again, it's not just my reputation I'm protecting; it's also Nick's.

"It was nothing," I lie again.

"Be careful. He's a powerful man."

"Are you really one to lecture me about being careful?" I ask. "Where do you go when you leave Palm Beach? What did you do with the dynamite we picked up that night? Who are you working with? What's your plan in all of this?"

He sighs.

"Do you love him?" Eduardo asks, ignoring my questions.

I look down at the sand. "Fidel?"

"Beatriz."

"Don't be ridiculous. Of course I don't love him."

Everyone knows an affair is impermanent; I would be foolish indeed to risk my heart under such circumstances. I've already committed myself to one lost cause. Two seems exceedingly reckless.

chapter fifteen

October turns into November, and there is no word from the CIA, but I keep my scribbled notes from the meetings with the group in Hialeah in a box crammed in the back of my bedroom closet. The intelligence I've gleaned so far is hardly significant on its own, but perhaps Mr. Dwyer will view it through a different lens with his experience to guide him.

Eduardo is absent as well, and I am left to my own devices: wondering about Nick's whereabouts, helping my sister Elisa set up her spacious new house in Coral Gables, worrying whether Isabel will be the next one to marry, her romance with her American businessman boyfriend gaining speed. Our mother couldn't be more pleased, crowing over Isabel's future matrimonial success, while simultaneously readying herself for the upcoming season and her marital designs for me.

"Did you hear Thomas mention his cousin, Beatriz?" my mother asks me from her usual spot in the living room.

Thomas is Isabel's boyfriend, single-handedly bolstering the floral industry in Palm Beach with his wooing of my sister, and if I've ever encountered a duller man, I can't recall. Suffice to say, I don't have high hopes for the cousin.

"His cousin has his own firm. Accounting, I think," she adds.

I make a noncommittal sound, my attention on the television. Our father is off somewhere on business, but Isabel, Maria, our mother, and I are gathered around the television in the sitting room in the late hours of November 8, awaiting the results of the American presidential election.

It is strange to live in a place where election results are not a foregone conclusion, to hear the excitement in the Americans' voices as they wait to learn who their next president will be. Before the revolution, my childhood was dominated by Batista's presidency, and just prior to him fleeing the country, we had an election of our own, one that, despite our hope for change, was dominated by whispers of rigged votes and the knowledge that Batista had ensured one of his cronies would take his place.

Of all of us, Maria is the most excited for this election. She sits on the couch with a pad of paper and a pencil in hand, eager to record the early results. They've been studying civics in her school, and she comes home each day with a new piece of information she has gleaned about the American political process. Truthfully, her enthusiasm and fervor for the subject have caught us all a bit off guard. Perhaps by virtue of her youth, she has acclimated the easiest to our life here, even as we have all worried about the toll it would take on her. I try to remember myself at fifteen; did I have her resilience, or is the manner in which she bounds through life merely another facet of her personality?

The rest of us watch the election on-screen with varying levels of interest, Chet Huntley and David Brinkley reading off the early returns. My mother is unconcerned with politics; our father has been closemouthed about the entire affair. I wouldn't be surprised if he's hedged his bets, doing everything he can to forge relationships with both parties. I've learned from our experience in Cuba that in my father's eyes, business supersedes ideology.

If the media reports are to be believed, this contest between Kennedy and Nixon will be a close one indeed, the election dragging on into the early hours of Wednesday morning. My interest in the results is much narrower. Is the lack of communication from Mr. Dwyer a result of the upcoming election, the waiting game the CIA is playing to see how the administration changes hands? And if so, will the election's outcome affect our plans for Castro and Cuba?

Nixon's position mimics President Eisenhower's: that the administration has helped the Cuban people realize their goals of progress through freedom. Kennedy challenges the position, labeling Castro's regime as communist and decrying Eisenhower's—and Nixon's—inaction in preventing Cuba's slide toward the Soviets. I admit to a degree of hope when I hear Kennedy's thoughts on Cuba; there is comfort to be had in the fact that someone recognizes the political situation in my country for the farce that it is. Will Kennedy sign off on the CIA's plans if he's elected? Will he take military action against Fidel? The hope of it is enough for me to support Kennedy and his Democrats. That he and Nick share a political party in common doesn't hurt, either.

It's been a month and a half since I last saw Nick, his business card tucked away in a drawer, the number never called. What would I even say? There's no future in this flirtation, and I wasn't lying when I told him I had no desire to be a mistress, and even less to be a wife.

"Kennedy won Connecticut," Maria announces triumphantly, jotting down the result on her pad. "He leads in the popular vote, too."

I can't help but smile at her enthusiasm, even as a pang of sadness hits me.

How will she feel when we return to Havana? Even in the best

144 · CHANEL CLEETON

of circumstances, it's hard to imagine our country won't undergo a massive transformation period. Will she be able to experience the same level of freedom the Americans enjoy in their country? Will her vote truly matter in Cuba one day?

Change is all around us, both at home and here, and where I once fought so hard for change, now I must admit I fear it, a bit. Change is good in principle, but there is no guarantee in terms of what you will end up with, and I wouldn't wish our experience with Fidel on my worst enemy.

Tonight, the trend seems to be a growing movement toward a new guard replacing the old, a slate of handsome, young, privileged men with heroic military backgrounds ushered in on the wave of Kennedy's enthusiasm and success. Nick would fare well in such a climate, and I wonder where he is tonight, if he's sitting beside his friend Jack Kennedy in Hyannis Port waiting for the results, or if he's home in Connecticut surrounded by his family and fiancée.

"The race is tightening," Maria declares, the pencil between her teeth now.

"I'm going to sleep," our mother announces, sweeping from the room in a cloud of Chanel with a pat on the head for Maria and a nod for Isabel and me. Given our one-sided conversation about my prospects, I receive a frown my sisters don't.

"Senator Kennedy is still leading," Isabel says once our mother has left the room. "And the Senate results?"

I flush, staring down at the silk couch to avert my gaze from my sister's prying eyes, running my fingers along the floral pattern.

"I imagine they will come later," I reply.

"Things would probably be easier if he didn't win," Isabel whispers.

"I'm sure I don't know what you're referring to."

"Quiet," Maria admonishes. "I can't hear. Vice President Nixon is about to speak."

Isabel ignores her. "Beatriz."

"Isabel." I mimic her tone as I did when we were younger just to annoy her.

"Do you know what you're doing?" she asks.

"Right now? I'm watching the election coverage with my sisters."

"You're not going to be watching with your sisters for much longer if you both don't be *quiet*," Maria hisses through gritted teeth.

"Don't be obtuse," Isabel snaps, ignoring Maria once more.

Of all of my siblings, Isabel and I have always been the most likely to butt heads, our personalities the most distinct. There is an ease to Elisa, a youth to Maria, and my brother was the other half of me. But Isabel is surprisingly obstinate despite her reticence, and we've always been oil and water.

"Don't presume to know my affairs."

"Quiet," Maria interjects again.

"I saw you with him during the season," Isabel retorts, disapproval dripping from her voice.

"That was months ago. Do you think I've been carrying a torch for a man I saw a few times in a crowded ballroom?"

"And next month? When they all return to Palm Beach?"

Have I thought about how it will feel to see Nick again? Of course. Have I wondered if he thinks of me? If he regrets those days between us? If he's moved on to another girl, another affair?

Of course.

"I really don't know what you're talking about. You're making far too much of a casual flirtation."

"Your flirtations have a way of causing trouble for the rest of us."

"So is that what this is about, then? You aren't worried about me; you're worried about your reputation."

"So what if I am?"

"Let me guess. Your precious boyfriend doesn't want to be associated with a scandal."

"He's a senator, Beatriz. What did you think would happen? His fiancée is a debutante. Do what you want, but you are sorely mistaken if you think you can carry on an affair with an American politician and not feel the ramifications of it. That we won't all feel the ramifications of your behavior."

"And your own behavior is entirely above reproach? Does your boyfriend know about the fiancé *you* left back in Cuba? How many men are you going to get engaged to?"

Isabel reddens.

"Will you both please be quiet?" Maria shouts. "I'm trying to watch the election."

"Oh, who cares about the election?" Isabel snaps as she rises from the couch in a huff. I've crossed an invisible line by mentioning the fiancé she left back home. Our family is filled with secrets and lies, truths we're neither willing to face nor speak of.

Isabel leaves the room without a backward glance, and there's a moment where I consider going after her, only to be stopped by the expression on Maria's face.

"I hate the fighting," she says.

Something tightens in my chest. "I know. But sometimes you fight the most with the people you love. It doesn't mean you don't love them. It just means you don't always agree."

"It would be easier if we all could agree."

I laugh. "But much more boring. There's nothing wrong with having different opinions as long as at the end of the day we always remember we're on the same side. We're Perezes first and foremost."

"Do you think Isabel will get married and leave like Elisa?" Maria asks, the same fear and uncertainty in her voice that I've been ashamed to confront.

"Maybe."

"Are you going to get married and leave like Elisa?"

"Never."

. . .

I wake on the ugly floral couch in the living room to the sensation of Maria shaking me. I peer up into her excited eyes, my head foggy from sleep. I blink, my vision adjusting to the low light in the room, as I attempt to process what time of day it is.

"It's over."

The election.

My heart pounds.

"Who won?"

"Kennedy," she announces triumphantly.

So Nick's friend is to be this nation's thirty-fifth president, and the American people are to transition from a Republican leadership to a Democratic one.

"That's good," I murmur, my eyelids growing heavy once more.

"He won, too," Maria whispers.

Two thoughts go through my head right before sleep claims me—

One, even my youngest sister has heard the rumors about Nick Preston and me, and two, even though Isabel was right, and any hope I have of resuming things with Nick would likely be much easier if he wasn't reelected, I am immeasurably glad for him that he has won reelection.

chapter sixteen

Now that the election is over, everyone has turned their eyes to Palm Beach and what the press has dubbed the "Winter White House." Everyone wants a chance to rub elbows with a Kennedy, to catch the president-elect's ear.

There's a new cachet surrounding the venerable Kennedy compound, a certain pride in the way the yearly residents speak of the family. The Kennedys have been a fixture in Palm Beach for decades, and now it's official: the Kennedys are American royalty, and Palm Beach is eager to celebrate their coronation. A massive crowd was at the airport in West Palm to greet Kennedy when he arrived in town last month after the election, the images showing people clamoring for a chance to shake his hand, to see the man who has brought so much hope to the country.

Maria begged our parents to let us attend, but after the revolution, my mother has become quite wary of crowds. Perhaps we'll see the new president-elect up close at one of the many events this winter, even if the circles he and his family travel in are a bit more rarified than the ones we inhabit. Everywhere he goes, there are people eager to meet him, and if he seeks solace here in the sand and the sun, I fear he won't receive much of a respite. They're predicting it will be the best season in a decade.

In the mornings, I wake early and walk along the beach. Now that Elisa has moved to Miami, I'm left to my own devices far more often. Maria is in school, Isabel off being Isabel, and Eduardo is once again on a "business" trip. Our friendship is such that we don't keep tabs on each other's whereabouts, but I miss him more and more as the days go on. I've not really made any friends here in Palm Beach, have social acquaintances more than anything else. I miss the companionship of being around people with whom I can be myself.

I continue attending the meetings with the group in Hialeah, but I've come to realize they are little more than a social club, idealizing men like Castro and Khrushchev, delighting in reading the works of Lenin and Marx, rallying against the American president and capitalism. On the one hand, I have found the dialogue I craved when I argued for my parents to send me to university, but it comes at the expense of being unable to express my true opinions, unable to indulge the overwhelming desire to disagree when they cite communist rhetoric as gospel.

I am still most curious about the Cuban brothers and their role in all of this. Like me, they engage in the conversations, however, with much less fervor than the Americans. Their family appears to own some sort of business in Hialeah, but they are surprisingly reticent when asked about anything even remotely personal, and I've largely given up my attempts to do so for fear of arousing their suspicions.

Claudia has yet to make an appearance; her name has not been uttered again since my initial introduction to the group.

The group members speak of the Cubans who have left in recent months as traitors, "worms," and rage fills me. More of our friends have fled Cuba in the wake of Fidel's increasing limitations on their freedom; some have traveled to South Florida, others farther afield and overseas. What does Fidel think of the exodus? Does he gloat each time another prominent Cuban family departs Havana?

I find an empty stretch of beach and sink down on the sand, looking out at the sea, listening to the waves crash against the shore. It's early enough that it's breezy and cool, the sun nowhere near its full strength. A couple passes by me, deep in conversation, the obvious familiarity of years together marking their body language, their heads bent.

I pull my knees to my chest, their retreating backs now a speck in the distance.

A man walks a few hundred feet behind the couple, dressed in a pair of light linen pants and a white collared shirt, his shoes dangling from his hand. My gaze skims over him, returning back to the sea, the urge to dip my toes in the water overwhelming. I begin to rise, intending to do just that when—

The man has stopped walking, and is staring at me, and at once, it all comes together, like puzzle pieces falling into place: the cut of his shirt, the broad shoulders, the tanned skin, the solemn blue eyes, the body I know intimately.

I blink.

Still there.

He closes the distance between us in several long strides, and I rise on shaky legs, dusting the sand from my clothes.

"Hello," he says.

I wondered when he would come to Palm Beach, worried whether he would return this season at all, and now he's here.

"Hello," I echo.

The wind whips between us, and then Nick steps forward.

His lips brush my cheek for a moment before he pulls back.

My heart thunders in my chest.

"How did you know where to find me?"

"I called at the house. It was foolish, I know. Your sister Isabel told me you like to walk on the beach."

"Did you see my mother?"

Please, tell me he didn't meet my mother.

Nick shakes his head.

That's a blessing, at least. I can only imagine the fuss she would make over a wealthy senator calling on me.

"I didn't want to wait to see you for the first time at some party where everyone would stare at us, and whisper, and wonder. And I wasn't sure of your plans, if you were even in town for the season, if you'd gone back to Cuba, or moved on somewhere else, or if you'd—"

"It's good to see you again," I blurt out.

"It's good to see you again, too. Would you like to walk?" he asks.

It's still early out, the season not officially started. Surely, little harm will come from an innocent walk?

I nod.

We head east down the stretch of beach, Nick measuring his strides against mine.

I sneak a sidelong look his way.

"Congratulations on the election."

"Thank you."

"It must have been a relief."

Is there anything more awkward than making polite conversation when there are other things you wish to say?

Nick smiles as though he can read my thoughts.

"It was."

"And you must be pleased with the results of the presidential election."

His smile deepens. "I am." He's silent for a beat. "Are we to speak of polite topics like politics and the weather now?"

"Is politics a polite topic? I thought it ranked up there with discussing religion."

"True. The weather, then. It is a particular fine day we're having, isn't it?"

"Oh, fine. No, I don't want to talk about the stupid weather."

"Then what do you wish to talk about?"

The way we left things, what he's been up to since we last saw each other, whether he's in love with his fiancée, if they set a wedding date, if another woman has been in his bed since we parted.

"It's not fair, you know," I say instead. "You came looking for me today, and I wasn't expecting to see you, certainly not now, not like this. Give me a moment to catch up."

He bursts into laughter.

"You just described the way I've felt since I saw you in that ballroom. Sorry, but you won't find any sympathy here. I've been trying to catch up for nearly a year now."

Relief floods me.

"You missed me, then?"

"You have no idea how much."

"You didn't try to reach me."

"I didn't know if you wanted me to. You didn't call."

"It seemed imprudent. And I didn't know what to say."

"I thought you didn't worry about things like that."

"Maybe I'm trying to be more considerate."

"You're worried about my reputation?" His tone is fairly incredulous.

I shrug. "You're the one with something to lose."

"And what about your reputation?"

"I told you. I have no plans to marry. As long as my reputation doesn't trouble my family overmuch, I don't really care what people say about me here."

"Because this is just temporary. Because you're still planning on returning to Cuba."

"Yes."

"I'm trying to do the right thing here. I wasn't a monk before, but I've never been involved with someone so—"

"Young?" I finish for him.

"That's part of it, but not everything."

"Innocent?" It's a struggle to say the word with a straight face. Despite my lack of sexual experience, I find it hard to believe any-one would describe me thusly.

"No, I guess I just don't want to complicate your life."

"Don't worry on that front. Fidel already complicated it for you."

"I don't want to be the thing you use to make yourself forget, either. To numb the pain."

"You're not."

"Where does that leave us then?" he asks.

"Why do we have to worry about that? Can't we just keep this private, between us?"

"So there's an 'us' now?"

"You tell me. I'm not the one with the fiancée. I don't want to hurt her, either, although I suppose we're already far past that."

"I know. It's not like that. I know how that sounds. How seedy the whole thing sounds. But it's not—we're not—she doesn't love me. I don't love her. It's not about that. I don't want to hurt her, either, don't want to cause any gossip that will embarrass her. Or my family. Or you."

"Then we probably shouldn't be standing on the beach together. Take me somewhere," I say recklessly.

. . .

Nick leads me down the beach, past the mansions shuttered until their inhabitants return. We stop in front an empty house on a stretch of beach near the Breakers.

My family and I live in a less fashionable section of the island, although, really, there are no bad neighborhoods to be had. Once you cross the bridge, you're automatically in an enclave of wealth and privilege.

"Whose place is this?" I ask.

A spacious veranda and pool deck lined in hedges overlooks the water, the house set back a bit, the entire rear portion of the mansion a wall of enormous glass doors. It must be incredible to watch the sun rise and set from such a vantage point.

"It's mine," he answers, a touch of pride in his voice. "I bought it a couple months ago. I had my attorney offer on it when it came on the market in October."

"It's beautiful."

"It was the view that sold me. I imagined myself standing out here, listening to the waves crash. I was in the throes of the campaign, and the idea of finding some peace and quiet here was extremely persuasive. My family has a home on the island, but there's little solace to be had there. Relatives pop in and out all the time, the rooms filled with guests and interlopers. I figured it was time I found a place of my own."

"I can imagine. Sometimes I just want to escape my house a bit. My morning walks give me the chance to clear my head. It can be both a blessing and a curse being surrounded by family."

"Yes, it can. Do you want to take a look around?"

"I'd love that," I answer, even as I wonder if seeing this will make it worse. Will I now be able to envision him here with his fiancée?

"Katherine's father wishes to gift us a house as a wedding present when we do eventually marry," he adds as though he can hear the thoughts running through my mind.

"And this house?"

It hardly looks like a love nest with its vaulted ceilings and elegant fixtures, but is that what this is? An expensive house in which to situate a mistress?

"An investment. An indulgence. When I marry, perhaps I'll sell it or rent it out to those who come down for the season." His expression turns serious. "It's not what you think. I knew the family that owned it before, and I always loved this house. When it came on the market, my friend mentioned it in passing, and the idea of having my own place, of being able to relax, was eminently persuasive.

"And yes, perhaps I imagined you standing on the balcony next to me. I hoped when we saw each other again, we would have the opportunity to do so. I've thought of you every day since we parted in New York."

I've been on the receiving end of some truly magnificent flattery, but it is the truth in his words that speaks to me most. After being surrounded by subterfuge, his honesty is a welcome change, even when the very nature of our relationship demands secrecy and discretion.

I take his hand. "Show me the rest of the house."

I follow him from room to room, our fingers linked. The marble floor is cool against my bare feet, the furniture covered in crisp white sheets.

"The staff hasn't opened the house for me yet. I've been staying at the Breakers. It was easier than trying to get a household set up from Washington. Plus I was eager to get down here." He hooks his arm around my waist, his lips brushing my temple. "Desperate to see you."

"Be careful," I tease, even as a thrill fills me. "You're beginning to sound like a man prone to little rebellions."

He laughs. "Perhaps I am."

We end up in the master bedroom as though it was our destination all along. The big room boasts an impressive view of the ocean, the sound of the waves filtering in from the enormous windows dominating one of the walls. The bed is set on a raised dais, the sort of furniture that looks as though it belongs in a stately home in Europe. A single white sheet covers the mattress.

If I'm going to have regrets in this life, I'd rather them be for the chances I took and not the opportunities I let slip away.

I let go of his hand and sit on the edge of the bed, looking up at him, leaning back on my elbows.

I reach out, my fingers closing around his arm, pulling him toward me, his mouth capturing mine in a kiss I've waited months for.

It is everything I remembered, and once again, we are a train hurtling off the tracks, and I don't want to get off.

When I take my morning walks now, in the days that follow, I have a destination in mind, the solitude no longer bothersome when I am headed to him. Nick keeps these hours of his schedule open, the staff conveniently absent—limited to scheduled times a few days a week—the sheets off the furniture. I never intended to be a mistress, and as much as we have danced around the title, we act as though I am mistress of this house, as though it is our home. I have a key now, and sometimes when he's not there, I take a book and curl up in one of the couches, listening to the ocean, reveling in the view, the space from my family. Other days I sit and wait for him to return from the various meetings he attends.

Nick left early this morning to hit the links with Kennedy and some of their friends at the Palm Beach Country Club. The sound of the front door shutting, footsteps on the marble, startles me from my reading, and I set the book down, rising from the couch, just in time to see him walking into the living room.

"Hello, honey, I'm home," Nick jokes, as he walks over and kisses me.

"I made you a drink." I hand him his old-fashioned.

"How domestic."

I laugh. "Don't get too excited. I might know my way about the bar, but the kitchen is a mystery best left to more capable hands than mine."

"I happen to like your hands, and think they're very capable, thank you very much."

I grin and sit back down on the sofa, tucking my legs beneath me. "How was golf?"

"I've never seen anything like it." Nick takes a sip of his drink. "Crowds of people came out just to see him. They tried to shake his hand. It was a mob. I don't know how he goes around like that, can't imagine what it's like when he tries to go out with Jackie and the kids."

"They love him."

"Many do." Nick's mouth tightens into a thin line. "It makes the Secret Service's job harder, though. With all these bodies pushing at him, the crowds, well, it puts him at risk."

Kennedy and anyone with him.

They arrested a man a few days ago, a retired postal worker turned would-be assassin. Responding to a tip, the police pulled him over and found the dynamite he planned to use against the president-elect in his car. It's a sobering reminder that the security around Kennedy isn't foolproof, that men like Nick are at risk because of their career.

"Are you worried?" I ask.

"He's taking it seriously, thankfully. So is the Secret Service. Still, there is no perfect solution. Jack wants to be a president for the people, wants them to feel connected to him and his family. The more you open yourself up, the more danger you let in, too."

"Do you ever worry about your own safety?"

"Me?" He shakes his head. "I'm just a lowly senator from Connecticut. My office occasionally receives threats, but I highly doubt someone would ever act on them. The president is another matter, though."

I wrap my arms around him. "I still worry about you."

"Nothing's going to happen to me." He sets his glass down on the table next to me and takes me into his arms. "You're not going to be rid of me so easily."

We celebrate Christmas in private on December 26, after the family celebrations have ended. Palm Beach is brimming with the holiday spirit; the pews of St. Edward's Catholic Church are packed on Christmas Day, everyone clamoring for a peek at the president-elect.

Nick gifts me with an extravagant diamond tennis bracelet I will somehow have to pawn off as paste in front of my family. I bought him a watch I saw in a shop on Worth Avenue using some of my money from the CIA, enjoying the freedom of no longer relying on an allowance from my parents. I spin a tale to my mother and father about staying at an imaginary friend's house, and Nick and I enjoy the unique pleasure of spending the night together, sneaking out late in the evening when the beach is empty to swim in the ocean, waking beside each other the next morning with lazy caresses and breakfast in bed.

I don't ask for details on how he spent his Christmas, and he doesn't offer any, but I have heard the rumors that his fiancée is now back in town, and Nick and I perform an intricate dance to keep ourselves from bumping into each other during the social whirl.

My New Year's Eve is spent at home; after the last New Year's Eve party I attended, the one where we learned President Batista had fled the country leaving us in Fidel's hands, I have little use for ringing in the New Year with fanfare and champagne, the occasion one I mark with solemnity more than glee.

The next morning I read in the paper that Nick spent his evening at the Coconuts' bash, Palm Beach's oldest and most prestigious private affair. Reportedly, a secret committee rules the party, and members each invite a handful of guests. My mother lamented our lack of invitation for days; I can only imagine the blow it would be if she learned I was essentially sharing a mansion on the beach with one of the Coconuts and had failed to use it for my social gain at all.

Shortly after the New Year, Nick returns to Washington during the week, journeying down to Palm Beach on the weekends. I continue with my morning walks, spending hours by myself. We set up times for Nick to call the house daily now, and the distance that existed between us before is obliterated by the freedom the house provides us. I once decried the existence of a "love nest" between us, but I now appreciate the convenience it provides, practicality eclipsing pride. And still, the walls of the mansion are unable to keep the rest of the world and its problems at bay.

Nick calls on a Tuesday evening, distracted, his voice full of worry.

"What's wrong?" I ask.

"We've abandoned our embassy in Havana. The staff boarded a ferry and left. President Eisenhower made the decision to sever diplomatic and consular relations with Cuba." He's quiet as though he's weighing the benefits of trusting me, the line between lover and politician whisper thin. "There are rumors that there are pilots training in Miami, landing at night with their lights off, the operation being conducted in secrecy."

My heartbeat picks up. "They're planning for an invasion?"

Is this what has kept Eduardo occupied and away from Palm Beach?

I've been to two more meetings with the communists in Miami, and this is the first I've heard of any American plan to invade Cuba. Is it a matter of them not trusting me, or are they simply not well-connected enough to have spies placed among the exiles?

"I don't know," Nick answers.

"You could find out."

He is silent.

"Do you think there will be war?" I ask.

"I don't know. Everything is more complicated now that Fidel has cozied up to the Soviets. He is both more of a danger to us and someone we cannot afford to treat too harshly."

"Would war be such a bad thing?"

"Don't wish for war, Beatriz. War is a terrible, horrible thing, and you might not like what you're left with when it's over."

"I'm afraid I don't have that luxury. It will take an act of violence to separate Fidel from power now."

Nick's voice is grim. "That's what I'm afraid of."

chapter seventeen

On a clear and cold Friday in January, snow on the ground, John Fitzgerald Kennedy is inaugurated as the thirty-fifth president of the United States while the nation rejoices. Nick spends more time in Washington after Kennedy's inauguration, trading sand for snow. What little time Nick and I can cobble together between his work and social obligations, we do. I can't help but wonder:

How long can I keep up this secret life?

Nick's absence leaves me to my own devices, and I wander the Palm Beach house alone in my private time, escaping the wedding festivities overtaking my parents' home. Isabel's businessman proposed a week ago, and already she and our mother are planning the wedding with the efficiency and determination of generals commanding men into battle. I watch as my mother pores over the guest list, biting my tongue as she adds illustrious name after illustrious name that will likely sniff when they see the names on the ivory card stock and ignore the invitation altogether.

We don't speak of it, but for all of his wealth, Isabel's husband-to-be made his fortune owning a string of ice cream parlors, a profession that once would have been beneath my mother's notice even as the marriage is now viewed as a coup, the gaudy diamond on Isabel's hand something my mother can gloat about to her small circle of friends.

It is to be just Maria and me in the house soon, and my mother's not-so-subtle hints of fixing me up with Isabel's fiancé's cousin grow with each day that passes. She has started asking about my whereabouts more than usual, taking an interest in my daily activities she never expressed before.

My mother walks into my room without knocking as I am finishing dressing for a meeting with Mr. Dwyer.

I glance at my watch. I have to leave in fifteen minutes if I'm going to make it in time. I have a feeling Mr. Dwyer is not one for being kept waiting.

"Where are you headed?" my mother asks, her gaze running over me, taking in the knee-length skirt, the ivory blouse, the sensible heels.

Not my usual fare.

"Lunch with friends," I reply.

"Anyone I know?"

"I don't think so."

I dab perfume behind my ears and at my wrists.

"Thomas is coming over," she says, referring to Isabel's fiancé. "They're going to go over the wedding plans. I would like you to be here."

"I doubt they want my input considering Isabel and I don't exactly have the same taste."

My sister's wardrobe is unremarkably beige.

"I don't want you to give your input. I want you to make a good impression on Thomas."

"Why? Why does it matter what he thinks of me? He isn't marrying me; he's marrying Isabel."

"It's nearly February, Beatriz."

"It is."

"The season will be over before you realize it, and then where will you be? Another year lost, another year older, another year unmarried. Thomas's cousin would be a good match for you."

"Why? Because he has money? Because I need a husband? We've never even met. You know nothing about him."

"I know you might have a chance with him. If you continue the way you are, no man will have you."

"What's that supposed to mean?"

"Do you think I haven't noticed how many walks you go on now? How often you disappear for hours at a time?"

Is she suspicious of my political activities or my relationship with Nick?

"I could speak to your father about it. He gives you too much freedom," she snaps.

We've never been particularly close, my parents leaving the raising of their children to others, but the anger in her voice, etched all over her face, catches me off guard.

"Whatever you are up to, you will put an end to it. I will not let you ruin this family. Our reputation and good standing are all we have."

I laugh, the sound devoid of any humor. "This isn't Cuba anymore. And we aren't the same family we once were. Can't you see we're already ruined?"

Her cheeks flush with anger. "You go too far."

"I have to leave. I'm going to be late."

I don't give her a chance to respond before I walk out the door and head to my meeting with Mr. Dwyer.

. . .

"Tell me your impressions of the Hialeah group," Mr. Dwyer commands when we are seated across from each other at what is becoming our usual table at the restaurant where we met in Jupiter last year. I drove myself, Eduardo once again suspiciously absent.

I sip my coffee, still rattled from my earlier fight with my mother.

"They're children playing at politics."

"We said that of Fidel and his friends once," Mr. Dwyer cautions.

"That may be, but it doesn't change the reality that they sit around speaking of things they do not understand, their rhetoric bombastic and hyperbolic, but devoid of any practical considerations. They are children, with little understanding of the world outside of the books they read."

"They're not much younger than you, Miss Perez."

"Why do you want me to watch them? Is this another test?"

"Not at all. The group is a very real threat, their support for Fidel unshakable. Did you not feel the zeal rolling off of them?"

"What can they do at the end of the day? Two American university girls, a boy . . ."

"What about the brothers?"

"The brothers are more interesting," I admit.

"They are. What have you learned about them?"

"Not much."

"Come now, Miss Perez. You are a beautiful woman. Surely, they've expressed interest."

"They haven't."

"Perhaps you haven't given them enough of an incentive."

"I have plenty of experience knowing when a man is interested in me. They're not. In fact, I can't quite figure out why they're in the group besides their hatred of Batista. They speak little; they don't appear to have a relationship with the other members. They're—"

"The ones you should be watching."

"Why?"

"What do you know about Fidel Castro's father?"

"Are you always going to answer a question with a question, or will you ever give me an explanation straightaway?"

He smiles. "This is your training, Miss Perez. Preparing you for bigger and better things. Now, what do you know about Fidel Castro's father?"

"Not much beyond the salient points. Like my father, he made his fortune in land and sugar."

"He did. Those boys—Javier and Sergio—their father worked for Fidel's father. Fidel is older than they are, of course, but they knew him when they were children. They looked up to him. I believe they are loyal to him."

"They've never mentioned knowing Fidel. Not once. The rest of the group speaks of him as though he is a messianic figure, but the brothers have never shared that they have a personal connection to him."

Dwyer smiles. "It's curious, isn't it? You would think they would want to share their infamous connection with their newfound friends. And yet, they're silent."

"What do you think their aim is?"

"I think they're recruiting for Fidel. Now they're in the Hialeah group, but they've popped up in other places before. Fidel wants to spread communism through the world; what better place than to have it spring up in the United States, to have it infect our country."

"If they're recruiting for him, they're doing so in a curious manner. They aren't prone to flowery speeches or charismatic overtures. They don't have the tools Fidel has used so successfully to sway people to his cause."

"True. But what do they add to the group? A good spy sees everything, can peel back the layers to read a person's motivations, and to understand how to achieve their aims."

I consider this. "They tell stories of Batista's cruelty, portray an image of what Cuba was before. They make it look as though things were terrible when Batista was president."

"And is that image authentic?"

"You know it is. And at the same time, Fidel certainly isn't the savior they make him out to be. His brand of politics isn't much better."

"So what do they bring to the group?"

"Authenticity," I answer, thinking back to the youthful eagerness of the others.

"Exactly. They're the rallying cry. The danger here isn't that they have some secret connection to Fidel. You saw what happened with the president, the attempted assassination plot by that madman who was arrested in Palm Beach. All it takes is one man. They're attempting to sew discord in this country, trying to radicalize American communists. And it's not just the brothers. There are others, you know."

"The mysterious Claudia?"

He smiles. "Ahh, Claudia. No, Claudia is something else entirely."

"Your spy?"

"Something like that."

"So what do you want me to do about the brothers?"

"At the moment, I haven't decided. On their own, they are just two Cuban instigators. I want to know if they are part of a broader network, if there are efforts to expand the Hialeah group, if there are plots in place that must be stopped. I want you to be my eyes and ears. I want to parlay your role in the Hialeah group into something greater. Do they trust you?"

"I don't think so. They accept me because I am Cuban; I think they believe me when I speak of my hatred of Batista—that much is real, at least."

"But they don't trust you."

"I am no communist."

"No, you aren't. Here's a piece of free advice, Miss Perez. The best spies are the ones who can find a kernel of truth they can cling to, around which they can craft their covers. When their covers are threatened, their identities called into question, it's that kernel they are able to cleave to in order to see themselves through.

"Yours is your brother. Make them trust you."

"And if they don't?"

"Then I misjudged you. A good spy must be willing to do whatever it takes for the mission. To be frank, we've tried to get close to Fidel before with no success. I've learned from those failures. I will not send someone in who will bungle the job. You want your shot at Fidel? You must prove yourself first."

chapter eighteen

Nick and I celebrate Valentine's Day together in private. I purposefully avoid the society pages, knowing if I look, I will see a picture of him with his fiancée at the Heart Ball. I pleaded a cold to be excused by my family from the entire event. I thought my mother would insist upon my presence, but the fear of me out in public looking anything but my best dispatched with that problem.

Instead, Nick and I spend the weekend together, commemorating the occasion with my favorite champagne and moonlight swims when the beach is abandoned.

I wish I could say it was an entirely happy occasion, but as the weekend wears on, as Sunday afternoon looms before us, I sense a change in Nick; he is quiet when he would normally be flirtatious and affectionate, his expression grim. His mood is infectious, and a sense of melancholy descends upon both of us. I spend the weekdays looking forward to the weekends when he is home, but once we are together again, I can't help but feel a sense of dread that our time together is far too short and will rapidly come to an end.

"What do you do when I'm gone?" he asks, trailing his fingers down my naked back as I lie on my stomach beside him in bed on Sunday afternoon.

"What do you mean?"

"When I'm in Washington. How do you fill your days?"

The nature of our affair doesn't exactly lend itself to inquiring too closely about the other's whereabouts. Is he jealous, or is it an innocent question, an attempt to envision my routine when we are apart?

"What are you asking me, exactly?"

"Nothing. I'm just curious."

"Would you like me to ask the same of you? What you do when we're not together? How was the Heart Ball, for example?"

"You knew I had to take her."

"I did. And I didn't ask you anything about it. Nor did I hold it against you."

"You could have."

I search his expression, attempting to figure out what is prompting this. Despite what he says, there's more than simple curiosity in his tone.

"Are you jealous?" I ask, harkening back to my original guess. "Is that what this is, you're worried I'm with another man?"

"No, I'm not worried about another man."

"Then what are you worried about?"

He stops stroking my back.

"Why do you go to a house in Hialeah known for communists who are aligned with Fidel Castro?"

My stomach sinks.

"I don't know what you're talking about," I sputter.

"Don't you? I thought we didn't lie to each other. I thought we had honesty between us, at least."

"We do."

"You're lying to me now."

I am, but doesn't he understand how dangerous all of this is, that I am trying to protect him from the political scandal, trying to protect myself?

"This is Dwyer's doing, isn't it? Another plot you have going with the CIA. What do they have on you?"

"Nothing."

"Then you're just doing this out of what, the kindness of your heart? Please tell me you're at least getting something out of it, that you aren't so stupid as to risk your safety on Dwyer's say-so."

I bristle at the word "stupid."

"They pay me."

"How much?"

"Enough."

The deposit is made into the account the CIA opened for me monthly, my nest egg growing to a comfortable amount. I'm not even sure what I'm saving the money for, only that the revolution has taught me the importance of having a safety net.

"Why are you so worried about having money?" he asks.

"Spoken like someone who has never had to worry about not having money."

His family made their fortune in steel and railroads a long time ago, and by all accounts, Nick Preston could never work a day in his life and remain a wealthy man.

"And if someone paid you more to stop?"

I reel back as though he's slapped me.

"Don't."

"Don't what? Worry about you?"

"There's a difference between worrying about me and treating me as though I am for sale."

"We're all for sale, Beatriz. It's just a matter of finding the right price."

"And what's your price?"

"Have you really not figured it out by now?"

"Political ambition."

He almost looks disappointed by my answer. By me. "Hardly."

"Well, you can't afford my price."

"And Dwyer can?"

"For the moment, Dwyer and I are on the same side."

"For the moment," he agrees. "But you seem to forget *we're* on the same side, too."

"Are we? It doesn't seem like it."

"I'm trying to be on your side. I'm trying to understand. But it isn't easy. You're exhausting. You act as though your indignation makes you superior to the rest of us, as though you can look down your nose at everyone for not being Cuban, for not taking the risks you take. Not all of us have the luxury of setting the world on fire, simply because we're angry. We must work within the confines of the system, must make changes where we can."

"These are people's lives at stake. I can't stand by and watch what's happening over there. It's killing me day by day. It's time to fight back."

"Isn't that the whole problem, though? You wanted a revolution, and you got one. Now you're unhappy with what the revolution wrought."

"I didn't want Fidel."

"But he's what you have now. So let's say you get rid of him. Then what?"

"We have a chance."

"Do you really think that's what the CIA is fighting for? To give Cubans a chance? Do you think they're overthrowing him out of the goodness of their hearts? You're smart, Beatriz. How can you not see the deal you've made?

"They want Fidel out of the way because he has nationalized their sugar companies and threatened their businesses. They want to remove him because he won't play ball with them like Batista did. Because they don't want the Soviets to have an ally in our backyard. Because they don't want communism to spread to the rest of Latin America and the world. This isn't altruistic, and it isn't about Cuba. No one cares about Cuba, not really. They care about America's position in the world. And they're willing to sacrifice you to achieve their goals. You're going to get yourself killed. All because you can't see past your anger. All because you take risks no sane person would take."

"If I'm so reckless, why are you here with me? Why don't you walk away? Why don't you go back to your fiancée and your comfortable life?"

"You don't think my life would be a million times easier if I weren't here with you right now? If I were in Washington D.C. doing the job I'm supposed to be doing, the job I was elected to do, rather than here, fighting with you? Do you think I'm proud of the man I've become? That I don't feel sick every single time I look in the mirror? I've broken my vows before I've even made them."

"Then go."

"I can't."

"Why?"

"Because I want to be here with you. I want to be here with you more than anything else. And at the same time, you're never going to stop pushing me away, are you? You're not going to give us a real chance. You're just biding your time until you can return to Cuba. I'm what—a convenient distraction?"

"Of course not. And I hardly think I've been pushing you away."

"I'm not talking about your body, Beatriz."

There's a sharpness to his tone I'm not used to hearing when he speaks to me.

"I'm talking about everything else. The secrets you keep. The double life you lead."

"You have everything else."

"No, I don't." His mouth tightens in a thin line. "How far does this thing go? Are you involved with the planning of the invasion everyone is whispering about?"

"No." I hesitate. "Eduardo has kept me separate from most of it."

"Eduardo is the one who got you involved in this mess with the CIA, though, isn't he?"

"It's complicated."

"Is it?"

"Are we back on you being jealous again?"

"We're back to me being worried about your involvement with the CIA. You need to stop going to the meetings in Hialeah. You need to stop trusting Dwyer."

"Don't you understand? This is all I know. In Cuba, it was me and my brother and Eduardo going to meetings and organizing against Batista. This was my life before Castro. This is my future. My brother isn't here to carry on the work we once did. Now it's my job to continue the fight."

"Beatriz."

"I should leave. I can't do this. I can't compartmentalize these different parts of my life. I don't want to lie to you, but just like some things are off-limits to me—your fiancée for one, *your* job— this is off-limits to you."

I move to leave, but he reaches for me, and that's all it takes for me to hesitate.

"I'm sorry. I know how important this is to you. I'm just worried about you. I don't trust the CIA."

"I understand why you're worried, but I know what I'm doing. My eyes are open on this. I promise."

I lie back on the bed next to him, staring up at the ceiling, the fight draining out of me.

I lay my head on his chest, breathing in his scent, hoping something will change.

My mouth finds his in a fierce kiss, our limbs entwined.

Sex is easy. It's everything else that's so very complicated.

chapter nineteen

We see less of each other after Valentine's Day, Nick's week-ends in Palm Beach fewer and farther between, his time spent in Washington, working in the Senate, caught up in President Kennedy's political agenda.

Isabel's wedding continues to dominate our mother's interests, the unrelenting not-so-subtle hints about throwing Thomas's cousin and me together. I spend as much time out of the house as I can, splitting my days between the communist meetings in Hialeah and volunteering in the camps set up by the Diocese of Miami to accommodate the growing number of children being sent out of Cuba to protect them from Fidel's policies.

As I walk through one of the camps, I am struck by the sight of their young faces, see myself, and Maria, and Isabel, and Elisa in their eyes. Everyone is doing the best they can to make this situation as bearable for the children as possible, but by its very nature, none of this is bearable.

And when I sit in those meetings in Hialeah and listen to the communists spout ideology, it's these children's faces that I think of. I want to shout at those pampered students whose notions of war came from something they read in a book. I want to tell them that this is war: not some words scribbled down by Marx, but the haunted eyes of thousands of children who have crossed the ocean on their own, who are now crammed together in camps, waiting to be reunited with their families, waiting to go home, waiting for the revolution to end.

This is what Nick doesn't understand when we fight about politics. For him, politics is an external entity. It is his job, but it is not who he is. And for me, none of this is just politics. It's personal.

At the end of March, I accompany my parents and Isabel to a party thrown by one of my father's business associates. I'm eager for the season to end this year, for everyone to go up north and leave us alone. I've attended far fewer events than normal, but still, rumors are growing about Nick and me, and I look forward to the break from all the scrutiny.

He's stayed behind in Washington D.C. this weekend, preparing for an upcoming vote in the Senate.

"That's a pretty bracelet," Isabel comments, eyeing my outfit as we ride in the car to the charity event.

Perhaps it was foolish to wear the bracelet Nick gave me for Christmas, to attempt to pass it off as a piece of costume jewelry and nothing more, but I couldn't resist. I've missed him since he's been in Washington more frequently, the phone calls doing little to alleviate the distance between us. Maybe Nick was right; maybe the secrets between us are creating a gulf we can't cross.

"Is it new?" Isabel asks, her voice loud enough to threaten our parents overhearing. It's a trick we perfected when we were younger and wanted to get a sibling in trouble or bend them to our will.

I flash her a smile that's all teeth and plenty of bite.

"Did you go out last night? I could have sworn I heard footsteps outside your room."

Isabel has been less and less discreet lately, sneaking out of the house at all hours, a skill she never quite excelled at as well as the rest of us.

She returns my glare, but offers no more comments about the bracelet, and the rest of the car ride passes mostly in silence, save for our mother's occasional one-sided chatter about tonight's festivities. Our father is largely silent in the car beside her, his presence in the family a distant one. When my brother was alive, our father was more engaged, but now he is surrounded by women, and despite the love I know he feels for all of us, he treats us as though we inhabit a mysterious world and are best left to our own devices.

We arrive fashionably late, which really isn't so fashionable considering everyone else imitates the same unwritten rule until we're all tardy, the impact lessened as we push into the room at the same time.

"You look beautiful tonight."

I turn at the familiar voice at my ear, my social smile converted to a real one at the sight of Eduardo in a tuxedo.

"I didn't know you were coming tonight," I say as we exchange customary air-kisses.

"I wasn't planning on it, but my plans changed."

"I haven't seen you in months."

He smiles. "Have you missed me?"

"Perhaps a bit," I tease. "Is everything fine?" I take a step closer to him, my voice lowering to avoid being overheard.

My family has been swept up in the crowd, leaving the two of us alone, but I swear I can feel my mother's gaze on me, following my every move.

Eduardo nods.

"Where have you been?"

He hesitates. "Miami."

Nick's earlier words come back to me.

There are rumors that there are pilots training in Miami.

"You're going to Cuba," I whisper.

Eduardo doesn't answer me. His gaze rests on the diamond bracelet on my arm.

It was foolish to have worn it tonight. Foolish to have given in to my emotions, to missing Nick and needing the connection between us. I should have left the bracelet in my jewelry box at home.

I pull back, dropping my arm to my side.

Eduardo steps toward me. He snags my wrist, the pads of his fingers rubbing the diamonds.

"Everyone is talking about you," he murmurs.

I tear my gaze away from him and glance around the room. There are, indeed, quite a few eyes cast our way. Is it the proximity of our bodies? Do they think we are lovers? And why do they care? For all of Eduardo's popularity, neither one of us is particularly prominent in these circles. Besides, there are far more interesting scandals to be had.

"What are you . . ."

My voice trails off.

People aren't just staring at Eduardo and me. They're staring at Eduardo and me, but their attention also darts to a couple on the opposite side of the room, and then back again, as though they're watching a particularly competitive bout of tennis.

I cannot help but look, either: at a beautiful blond debutante and her handsome fiancé.

Nick's gaze meets mine across the ballroom, and a myriad of emotions cross his face—guilt, confusion, anger—as his gaze rests on the point where my arm is linked with Eduardo's.

. . .

I t takes every ounce of self-restraint mixed with a healthy dollop of the training I've received from Mr. Dwyer to tear my gaze away from Nick's. I take Eduardo's arm with a false smile on my lips, my head held high as I accompany him onto the balcony for some air.

Eduardo wasn't wrong—everyone watches our progress, and whatever I thought of my reputation, it's clear it is in tatters.

Nick lied to me.

He said he would be in Washington; he told me he couldn't make it to Palm Beach this weekend.

He lied to me.

"Beatriz."

There's pity in Eduardo's voice as he says my name—pity and worry.

"Are you all right?" he asks.

"I'm fine."

I *will* be fine.

I knew this would happen eventually, that he wasn't mine to keep. I knew all of this, and still, it *hurts.*

"People are talking," Eduardo urges.

"I see that now." I'm not even angry with Nick; I'm angry with myself. I should have known better. I *do* know better. I was so busy playing house; I stuck my head in the sand at a time when I should have been more cautious.

"Are the rumors true?" Eduardo asks.

"What are you doing in Miami?" I counter.

"Beatriz."

"You want to do this? You get my cooperation with Castro. You don't get the rest of it."

"I thought we were friends first," Eduardo replies. "I'm concerned about *you.*"

"We are friends. And if you're my friend, you won't ask me about this."

"I don't want you to get hurt."

"I'm *fine*. What is happening in Miami?"

"You are impossibly stubborn."

"You used to think that was one of my most charming qualities."

"I used to think a lot of things."

"Miami?"

There's no place for a broken heart in all of this.

"You already have an inkling, don't you?" His tone is faintly mocking. "What is it? Pillow talk?"

"They're training pilots. To invade Cuba."

"Yes."

"Are you one of the pilots?"

He laughs. "God, no. Far too much responsibility."

"But you're involved."

"Yes. As is your Mr. Dwyer."

"And President Kennedy? I assume you've secured his support?"

The president's approval rating is high, his popularity soaring. People like the image he presents: the young, handsome idealist with the beautiful, accomplished wife and the two adorable children. I mostly like the president. Idealists make me wary as a matter of principle, but there is a thread of pragmatism in Kennedy's policies that gives me hope. Besides, at the end of the day, he is merely one man. The coffers of the American political machine are lined with men like Mr. Dwyer who scoff at ideals and have no compunction about rolling up their sleeves and getting to work. If the president lacks the stomach to do what needs to be done in order to defeat Fidel, no doubt one of his advisors will do the trick.

"Allegedly, Kennedy supports it," Eduardo answers. "I imagine your senator would know more about the president's intentions, though."

"He's not my senator."

"That's not the story I've heard."

"Well, he's not."

"Trouble in paradise?" Eduardo's gaze returns to my wrist. "That's an expensive bracelet."

"For what? A mistress?"

"Don't call yourself that."

"It's what everyone else is saying, isn't it?"

"Well, what did you expect, Beatriz? He's here with his fiancée."

"Don't tell me your latent morality is outraged by an affair. Half the party is sleeping with someone they aren't married to, and everyone knows it. You've certainly had no compunction over doing the same thing."

"It's not about my morality. It's about your pride."

I laugh, as though my aforementioned pride isn't currently lying on the floor in disgrace. "Do you think I'm settling?"

"Aren't you?"

"Why does everyone assume I want marriage? That if I'm not someone's wife, I'm not worth anything."

"It's not about marriage. You shouldn't be anyone's second choice. Don't you want to be someone's first choice?"

"I don't want to be anyone's choice. I want them to be mine."

"And you choose him?" Disbelief threads through his voice.

"I choose myself. And right now I choose Cuba." I take a step back. "I should return to the party before people talk even more."

This is what Isabel attempted to warn me about in the car earlier. Have the whispers reached my parents' ears?

"Before he gets too angry, you mean. I saw the way he looked at us standing together. He's jealous." The smug note in Eduardo's voice throws me off. "He won't claim you, but he doesn't want anyone else to have you, either."

I laugh angrily. "And if that is true, how does that make him any different from the rest of you?"

I am hurt, and the image of Eduardo standing before me in his elegant tuxedo, an arrogant expression on his face, makes me want to hurt *him*.

"Is that what this is?" I taunt, understanding dawning. "You want me because you think he has me?"

Eduardo takes a step toward me, his hand coming to rest on my bare arm. "You have no idea what I want."

Why does that sound like a challenge?

He releases me just as abruptly as he touched me.

"You won't see me for a while. I'm leaving Palm Beach."

"Where are you going?"

"I can't say."

"Where are you going?" I repeat.

Our gazes meet.

"I choose Cuba. Every time. Where are you going?"

"Guatemala," he murmurs after a beat.

"And then?"

"I can't talk about this, Beatriz."

So it's Cuba, then. The stories in the paper are true, the whispers I've heard of a coming coup. A fierce stab of worry catches me off guard, replacing what should be excitement.

"Are you sure this is a good idea?"

What does he know about fighting? The things they did in Cuba against Batista are not the same as going to war, and I can't look at Eduardo in his elegant tuxedo and see a soldier. And the rest of them, the men going to battle to reclaim our island: Has the CIA trained them? Or are they simply being given guns and told to hope for the best?

"You're worried."

"You're not a soldier."

A faint note of amusement threads through his voice. "Have a care with my ego, Beatriz."

"You know what I mean."

Trust Eduardo not to take this seriously.

He cups my face, tilting my chin so our eyes are nearly level.

"The days of letting others fight our battles are over. If I don't fight, if I don't join my fellow Cubans, I will regret it for the rest of my life."

"And if you die? What do regrets matter then?"

"If I die, then it will be for something I believed in." His fingers brush my cheek. "Would you be sad if I died? Would you cry for me?"

His tone is idle, taunting as mine was earlier, playing with me as I did him. We are so alike, too alike. I would say that this is all a game to him, except—

There's something in his eyes that suggests otherwise.

"Of course I would cry."

"Because we're friends." Eduardo traces the curve of my lower lip with his thumb, brushing away a tear at the corner of my mouth. I've played too close to the edge this time, lost whatever temporary relationship I had with Nick. Elisa has gone to Miami, Isabel is getting married, Nick was never mine, and now Eduardo is off to war, and I am really, truly alone.

I shudder.

"You're feeling sorry for yourself," he says with an affectionate smile.

"I am."

"You never did like being left out. You would always convince me and Alejandro to take you with us when we went on adventures, even if it was somewhere your mother never would have let her daughters go, even if it was the most unladylike activity."

"I've never had much interest in being a lady."

He smiles. "No, you haven't. But try to stay out of too much trouble while I'm gone. I will worry about you."

"Be careful," I reply.

"I will."

Neither one of us moves, his thumb lingering on my lower lip.

"We'll be in Havana soon," he vows.

"We'll dance at the Tropicana," I counter.

I close my eyes, and let my imagination take me there, indulging in the foolish hope that we will turn back the clock, and everything will be simpler once again. When I open my eyes, Eduardo is staring back at me, his gaze intent, and now that I am older, more experienced, I understand the look there for what it is.

"Have you ever wondered—"

He dangles the words between us, the possibility of them—

Have you ever wondered what it would be like between us?

Perhaps.

"We've never—"

"Once," I correct him, the memory surprisingly sharp in my mind despite the intervening years, the image of two children playing at being grown-ups and the kiss I stole all those years ago.

A different life.

Eduardo's lips curve into a smile as he remembers that rainy day when the world was a different place entirely.

"Once," he agrees.

His thumb sweeps across my bottom lip again, hovering there.

"Haven't you wondered about all the things I've learned since then?" A hint of amusement threads through his voice, as though this is all a game, like the ones we played when we were younger, but there's an earnestness that belies the casual tone of voice, the playful smile on his mouth.

I can't force myself to say the words, feel as though I've stepped outside my body and am watching this happen. In the end, I only manage a shaky nod before his eyes darken, his mouth covering mine, his arms hooking around my waist, hauling my body against his.

He kisses like a man living on borrowed time, as though the coming war will steal his remaining days from him, and he knows it. He kisses without guilt or reservation, the legendary skills I've heard whispered about in powder rooms clearly not exaggerated one bit. It's *fun* kissing him, energy building inside me like a laugh bubbling up, and then the bubble bursts, and the fun is swept away by the sensation of my body coming alive, the intensity of his kiss drowning out everything else.

As quickly as Eduardo embraced me, he releases me, and where I expect to see the same confusion in his eyes that lingers inside me, I see only inevitability, as the realization that he has wanted me for far longer than I ever knew hits me full force.

In another life, we might have been magnificent together.

A smile plays at Eduardo's mouth, satisfaction in his eyes. "You haven't been paying attention."

I take an uneven breath, then another, attempting to steady myself, to clear my head after his drugging kiss.

"You're as good as they say you are."

He gives me an indulgent smile. "You're as good as I knew you would be."

So, not an impulse, then.

"No, not all," he replies, and I realize I've spoken the thought aloud.

"I don't—I'm not—"

I don't see you that way. I'm not looking to further complicate my life.

Both of those things would have been true a few minutes ago, but then he kissed me, and I realize I've underestimated him, been so focused on Cuba and Nick, that I didn't see Eduardo as anything other than a friend, a connection to the CIA, when the reality is, he could be so much more.

He knows it, too, his gaze sharpening, satisfaction in his eyes, and a hint of my lipstick on his mouth.

"Something to think about. For when I return."

He's gone without a second glance, leaving me on the balcony alone, my arms wrapped around my body, my lips swollen from his kisses, my heart heavy from Nick's lie, and the knowledge that if Nick was watching the balcony entrance, he just saw Eduardo walk out with a smudge of my signature red lipstick on the corner of his mouth.

I escape to a powder room off the ballroom, locking myself in one of the stalls, taking a moment to catch my breath.

I stifle the urge to cry.

I can't stay here the rest of the evening, can't risk running into Nick again, having to face his fiancée. Surely, I can convince my parents that we should leave. I should have left with Eduardo.

To say this night has been a disaster is an understatement.

Outside the stall door, women mill around, but no one speaks of me or of the spectacle earlier.

Once the bathroom has gone blissfully silent, the sound of running water from the faucets ceased, the chatter stopped, I take a deep breath, steeling my shoulders, and open the door—

I freeze, the stall door clanging shut awkwardly behind me.

Nick's fiancée sits in a chair in the waiting area, her gaze trained on me.

I glance around the room, looking for—an ally, one of my sisters, a distraction, anything—but the rest of the powder room is empty, and we are really and truly alone.

"I've been wanting to meet you for some time now," she says by way of greeting. There's an elegant lilt to her voice, her expression inscrutable. "I confess to a curiosity of sorts, I suppose. Nick wasn't planning on coming tonight, but when I heard you would be here, well, I orchestrated this little meeting. Although, to be fair, it didn't go quite the way I'd planned. He shouldn't display his feelings so clearly."

She looks to be about my age, or perhaps a bit younger, her skin dewy and fresh, her hair like spun gold, swept up in an elegant style, perfect for complementing the emerald and diamond earrings that match her green eyes, offset by the green silk gown.

I catch sight of my reflection in one of the bathroom mirrors.

Hair mussed from Eduardo's hands, lips swollen from Eduardo's mouth, eyes red from Nick Preston's deception, panic etched all over my face.

She rises from her seat.

"I'm Katherine Davies. Nick's fiancée. He's quite taken with you, isn't he? I've heard the rumors, of course. Men are never quite as discreet as they like to think they are. He bought the house on the beach for you."

"I—"

I am perhaps for the first time in my life truly at a loss for words.

"There's really no need to be uncomfortable. He's not the first politician to take a mistress, and I'm sure he won't be the last."

There's an unspoken hint contained in her voice: *I'm sure* you *won't be the last.*

"I'm not his mistress."

"Well, you're not his fiancée, so at the moment 'mistress' is the most appropriate term we can come up with, isn't it?"

The sharpness in her tone pricks me, shame filling me. I am inescapably the villain in this tableau.

"I'm sorry, I never meant to hurt you."

"Oh, please, let's not go down that path. It's beneath both of us. You haven't hurt me, although I will confess this little scene tonight has proved to be an embarrassing one. You might enjoy your notoriety in Palm Beach, but some of us have worked very hard to secure our reputations. He is to be an important man someday. He can't afford the scandal."

"I know."

She smiles. "There, you see, we are on the same side of things. I understand men have their urges, that they do things with women like you they won't do with their wives. You appeal to his baser nature, and that is all well and good, but I won't become a laughingstock in this town. Keep your relationship confined to the bedroom, and we won't have a problem. Flaunt it in society again, and you will learn what a formidable enemy my family can be. Have a good evening."

She's gone without a backward glance.

chapter twenty

I don't go to the house in Palm Beach.
   Our house.
   I can't.

The anger over Nick's betrayal burns fresh and strong for over a week, my own confusion and regret over the kiss with Eduardo a knot in my chest, the shame of coming face-to-face with Nick's fiancée inescapable. Finally, just two weeks after the party, I use my key to open the Palm Beach house, knowing he is in Washington for a vote in the Senate. I set the diamond bracelet and the house key on the bed, which looks as though it hasn't been slept in for weeks.

I don't leave a note.

What is there to say? We were over from the first moment we met, minutes before his engagement was announced.

I wasn't made to be a mistress, and even my recklessness has its bounds. It seems remarkably stupid to give my heart to a man who can never be mine.

I slip out one of the side doors, walking down the beach, the salt water mixing with the tears on my face. It is for the best. The season is ending, and Nick would have run out of excuses for his continued presence in Palm Beach. Surely, he will have to set a wedding date soon. Men are allowed their indulgences when their lives are unencumbered by wives and children, but once he has a family, everything will change, and I cannot envision inserting myself into such a situation.

Our affair has run its course.

I return to the house to find my mother and father seated in the living room, Isabel next to them, Maria at home when she should be at school.

"Where were you?" my mother asks as I walk into the room.

"On the beach. I went for a walk." I brush at my face surreptitiously, hoping the tears have dried, that they will chalk my disheveled appearance up to the elements.

"Why aren't you at school?" I ask Maria.

"Quiet," Isabel interjects, gesturing toward the TV.

I follow their gazes, as Maria rises from her perch on the couch, turning up the volume on the television.

My breath catches.

The rumors are true; there's been an invasion of Cuba.

The thing about hope is that when it fills you, when you hold it in the palm of your hand, the promise of it is everything. You can go for days, weeks, months, years on that hope, telling yourself everything will be fine, eventually, you'll have what you've been waiting for, this is just a momentary setback in your life, one you will overcome. After all, if there isn't a happy ending at the end of the story, what is the purpose of all of it?

Hope is such a beautiful lie.

The initial reports are scant, the news dire. The invasion at Playa

Girón—the Bay of Pigs, as the Americans call it—failed miserably.
Over a hundred men killed, over a thousand men captured. There
is little room for my broken heart in these times, and I spend my
days gathering whatever news I can on the situation in Cuba, while
my father calls friends and business associates trying to discover
what has happened to our island, while my mother and sisters pray
in the pews of St. Edward's.

Does Eduardo's body litter the shores of Playa Girón, or is he in
one of Fidel's prison cells?

The thought of him dead or injured breaks my heart.

We wait for news to trickle out of Cuba.

Days after the failed invasion, President Kennedy addresses the
nation.

We gather in the same living room where we once watched the
election night results with eagerness. Now, Maria is quiet and sub-
dued. Our father is here, grim faced and disappointed in yet another politician. And I—

I regret the way I left things with Eduardo. But more than that,
I am filled with anger again, the hope I had placed in President
Kennedy evaporated now. Did I place too much trust in him because he is a friend of Nick's? Or are we simply naturally predisposed to hope?

Is Cuba lost to us forever?

Kennedy offers words, but it is not words we need now. We need
weapons: planes and tanks. We need men willing to fight. Men
who are trained in the art of such warfare, who are adequately prepared, not men who are sent to be killed and captured, outmanned
and outgunned, abandoned by the Americans.

We need military action from the United States.

"We're never going back, are we?" Maria asks me as she readies
for bed that night.

And in my weakness, in my grief, I admit the truth that has plagued me all along.

"I don't know."

Days pass, my nights spent tossing and turning in bed, worrying about Eduardo, about Cuba. I've seen firsthand what those prisons are like. Surely, Dwyer and his colleagues will move forward with the assassination plot now. They have to. What else is left? Leaving Cuba for Fidel?

The emerging reports surrounding the failed invasion suggest Fidel knew we were coming, and I am reminded of Dwyer's earlier concern that Fidel has eyes and ears within the United States reporting back to him.

Were we betrayed by one of our own?

There's a meeting with the Hialeah group this week; perhaps they'll have information to share.

In the beginning, I doubted the value of such espionage, but if anything, the recent events in Cuba have made me appreciate the CIA's role in this. And if it's possible for me to make a difference, then how can I resist helping? My countrymen lie dead on a Cuban beach; languish in Fidel's prison. I can't stand by and do nothing.

The beach is mostly empty at this early hour, the season ended, the social set moved on to Newport, or New York, or wherever. I walk toward my usual spot, stopping in my tracks at the sight of a man standing near the palm tree where I normally sit.

The impulse to turn back home is strong, anger and nerves filling me. The impulse is there, but for all of my flaws, I've never been a coward, and so instead of running away, I walk toward him, stopping when we're so close he could reach out and touch me.

He looks awful.

Thinner than I remembered, shadows under his eyes, a wrinkle—*two*—in his normally flawlessly pressed dress shirt.

Neither one of us speaks as we look at each other, and I get the sense he's searching my appearance as much as I am his, looking for signs of—what?—I don't even know. It's been over two weeks now since that horrible night I saw him with his fiancée, but it feels like so much longer.

He breaks the silence first.

"You left me."

"You lied to me," I counter.

"I know. I'm sorry. I didn't want to hurt you; I didn't want to lose you. It's not an excuse, and I know it doesn't make what I did right, but that's why I did it."

"You didn't want to lose me so you lied to me? Do you realize how ridiculous that sounds? I knew you were engaged. I understood where I was in your life. At least, I thought I did. And then you lied."

"I didn't want to lose you by disrupting whatever balance we have between us. We'd fought recently, and everything is so complicated right now with Cuba. I didn't want to make things worse."

"Lying to me isn't the answer."

"I know that now."

A woman and her dog walk past us, her gaze on us, Eduardo's earlier warning coming back to me.

"This isn't a good idea—us being seen together. People are already talking."

"I know," he replies.

"I should go home."

"Please don't go."

"What do you want? Why are you here?"

"I came to talk to you. To fix this. I thought I'd give you time, I knew you were angry, but I didn't think we were over until I came home and saw your key and bracelet on the bed. You don't owe it to me to do this in person?"

"This isn't working."

"Because you don't want it to work. You don't want to do this in public, fine. Come back to the house with me. Talk to me."

Tears fill my eyes, and I brush them away. "You hurt me."

"You don't think I know that? You don't think it hurt me to see that look on your face, to see you—" His words fall off with an oath. "I barely sleep. I sit in on briefings, and my mind is only half on what I'm supposed to be listening to, and half here with you. Thinking about you, wondering if you've moved on. I was wrong. I want to make it right. Please just give me a chance. Talk to me."

The prudent thing would be to end things here and return to the house. And still—

Nick holds out his hand, and I take it, walking toward his house despite my misgivings.

We enter through the veranda; the white sheets are draped over the furniture once more, the familiar sight of where we spent so much time together bringing a pang to my chest. The first morning he brought me here, when the sheets covered the furniture, it seemed full of possibilities. Now everything is shuttered and dead.

I sit on the edge of the couch where we once made love, Nick opting for the opposite chair, waiting for me to speak.

I lead with the excuse because it's always easier to address what's on the surface, and not the pain that lingers underneath.

"People are talking about us. I didn't think it would bother me, but you're right—everything is complicated now. I need to think about my family. My actions could hurt them."

"I know things are complicated. That was why I came to Palm Beach and didn't tell you. Katherine's father had heard the rumors about us and was angry. He wanted me to put in an appearance at the party, to dispel the gossip. I didn't think you'd be there."

I can't decide if that makes it better or worse.

"We were a late invite."

I consider telling him what his fiancée said to me, that she threw us together on purpose, but what would such a revelation serve. She is to be his *wife*, and I am just the woman who appeals to his baser nature, as she so kindly put it.

"I never wanted you to be in the middle of this, never wanted anyone to try to hurt you because of me. I'm the one who's engaged, who is in the public eye. I'm responsible for this."

"It's not your fault. We knew this was temporary. How could it not be?"

"And the rest of it?" Nick asks.

"What do you mean?"

"You don't want me lying to you. Give me the same courtesy. This isn't just about the gossip. You're not done with the CIA, are you?"

"How can I be done with the CIA? Why don't you ask your President Kennedy about that?" My anger over the failed invasion pushes to the surface, hot and sharp. "Did you know?"

"Beatriz."

"So you knew."

"There's more at stake here than my feelings for you."

"There's more at stake here than my feelings for you, too."

"This isn't about us. It isn't personal. It's politics."

"It's personal for me. It must be nice being able to put it out of your head and pretend it doesn't matter, that it happened to other people, that it doesn't affect you. Some of us don't have that luxury."

"That's not what I meant."

"Isn't it, though? You want your Cuban mistress in your bed, but I'm not supposed to have my own thoughts on the subject, am just supposed to pretend my country isn't falling down around me. That my people aren't dying. That children aren't being sent away from their families."

"I've never treated you like my mistress."

"Your fiancée certainly sees me as your mistress."

He blanches.

"Oh yes, we had a nice conversation in the powder room at the party. It was reassuring to know she wasn't bothered about our affair as long as your—how did she phrase it—'baser natures' were confined to me."

A blistering oath escapes him.

"I'm not angry. It's the truth. And I can't pretend politics aren't between us anymore. What happened?" I challenge. "Men are dead, in prison, because your government didn't support Cubans when they had the chance."

"That's the betrayal you want to hold against me? The Bay of Pigs?"

At the moment, I can't tell if that's the one that cuts the deepest or is merely the easiest to face.

"What happened?" I ask.

"We screwed up."

"That much is obvious. It's also not an explanation."

"I didn't realize I owed you one."

Of all the things he could have said to me, that one stings.

"You're a member of the president's inner circle, aren't you? How does Kennedy feel about the invasion?"

"It's embarrassing for the president. At this point, no one believes the CIA wasn't involved, and the more the administration denies it, the more disastrous this will prove to be. He needs to get in front of this, to admit we made a mistake and that we are doing everything we can to fix it. Otherwise he will look like a fool."

"And will he admit it? Is he doing everything he can to fix it?"

"I don't know."

"So that's what this was, then? A mistake?"

"You can't think it was intentional. Kennedy wants Castro defeated as much as anyone."

"Please."

"He does."

"Then why didn't he give the men who landed at Playa Girón more support? Why isn't the United States throwing its weight and might behind removing Fidel from power? You and I both know that if they did, we'd be having a very different discussion."

"Because we can't look as though we are in the business of nation building, that we're dethroning governments simply because we don't like them."

"But isn't that exactly what the United States does throughout the world? Don't tell me Cuba is any different. Fidel isn't what the Cuban people want. Do you know how many Cubans were involved in his 26th of July Movement? A few hundred. A few hundred guerrillas took control of my country."

"And no one fought back. Those who opposed him left. Others are trying to leave even as we speak. This was our attempt to help you get your country back. And it failed."

"Don't put this on us like it's our fault, like the United States hasn't been behind the scenes the entire time. You have no idea what it was like under Batista. None. He created an environment where there was a vacuum of power so no one would be able to take his power away from him. And you helped him with your guns and your sugar—"

"Do you really want to talk about sugar?"

I flinch.

"I can't get past this," I add. "I can't compartmentalize these parts of my reply. I can't maintain some semblance of self-respect anymore and sleep in your bed while you take your fiancée out in society. I can't pretend I'm not angry with you for what your Congress isn't doing to help my country, for the mess your government has caused. I can't turn a blind eye to the president's handling of the situation or to your friendship with him."

"It's just politics. It doesn't have to affect us if we don't let it."

"That's the problem. It isn't just politics to me. It's my life. It was my brother's life. He died fighting for a better future for Cuba. How do I turn my back on that?"

"But what if that dream never comes true? What then? Are you to be a widow to a country that has only ever existed in your dreams?"

I'm tired. So tired. And more than anything, in this moment I am tired of attempting to explain something to someone who will not, cannot ever understand. He went to war, but then he left it, and came home to peace. He has no idea what it is like to live your whole life in war.

"This is personal to me. It's everything to me."

"It's dangerous."

"It is. I imagine even more so for the men who participated in the invasion, whose fate is now in Fidel's hands. I've seen what it is like in those prisons, what Fidel does to men he views as traitors."

"They aren't your brother."

"They might as well be. Where is the president on this?"

"He's working on a deal."

"And Fidel?"

"You can't tell anyone what I'm telling you. This can't get into the press. It's serious. Lives are at risk."

I nod.

"They think Fidel is open to negotiation. Keeping all those men prisoner will cause him more trouble than anything else. Besides, this gives him a bargaining chip, which he desperately needs right now. They'll come home; we'll just have to give up something in order to bring them back."

I take a deep breath, the words rushing out of me.

"Eduardo was part of the invasion. I don't know what happened to him—if he is alive or if he's sitting in a jail cell somewhere."

By the expression on Nick's face, I have a feeling this isn't news to him.

"I'm sorry. I know he's important to you."

I don't deny it.

His gaze narrows. "I saw him after you went out on the balcony that night. He wants you, doesn't he?"

The question lingers between us, unspoken.

Do you want him?

"He's a friend."

"He's a friend now, but that's not his endgame."

"You can't be jealous."

"Why?"

"We have no future," I say, carefully, gently, the anger filtering out of me, the words for his benefit, and perhaps, a bit for my own.

"You don't think I know that?" He laughs bitterly. "Perhaps one day, once he's out of prison, that friendship will evolve and change, and you'll look at Eduardo differently, see whatever the hell it is that had everyone else after him all season. And he's perfect for you, isn't he? You both share the same political views, the same history. He doesn't love Cuba the same way you do, anyone can see that, the man's an opportunist to his core, but in these times, there are worse flaws to be had. And God, given what an idealist you are, perhaps that is the best match for you—if he loves you, then he'll keep you from getting yourself killed."

"So we're back to that, then? Me needing someone to take care of me."

"Only you would view that as a bad thing."

"You don't get it, do you? People don't immediately dismiss you because of the way you look, don't flash you a condescending smile and tell you some conversations aren't meant for you, you're too young, too female, too pretty, too sheltered to understand the world around you. You aren't treated like a painting, or a delicate vase, or a broodmare, as though your worth only lies in your beauty and what they can barter for it."

"And how is using your body to trap Fidel any different?"

"Because it is *my* choice."

"Is it your choice? Or is that just what they've sold you: the CIA, Eduardo?"

"They murdered my brother. They have to pay for that. My father is doing nothing. He throws what little money he can be bothered to spare toward the exile movement, but he does *nothing*. He doesn't care about Cuba; he has his sugar company here to focus on, wealth to rebuild. No one is doing anything."

"Maybe what you think is inaction is doing something, Beatriz. These things take time. You can't storm in and expect everything to change overnight because you will it."

"*I* am doing something. The men who fought at Playa Girón and died for it are doing something. Eduardo did something. You and your government are the ones who aren't doing something."

"Did you kiss him that night at the party?"

I hesitate. We move from politics to intimacy with an ease that disproves his argument that we can separate the two. They are both tangled up in this impossible gnarl we have created.

"Yes."

"Did you sleep with him?"

"No."

"But you've thought about it."

"No—it wasn't like that."

"Did you like it? His kiss?"

Silence fills the room.

"Don't ask me that."

"Jesus, Beatriz." Nick moves over to the edge of the couch, his elbows propped against his knees, his head in his hands. "I'm going to go. I have no right to any of this, and I know that. But I can't imagine his mouth on yours, his hands on your body."

"It wasn't like that. And don't put this all on me. You screwed us up as much as I did."

"What 'us'? Has there ever been an 'us,' or are there just stolen afternoons and secrets? Was what we had ever enough?"

"How could it be enough? We decided this was to be temporary from the beginning. An affair. Nothing more."

"What are you looking for then? Who will make you happy? Eduardo?"

"This isn't about Eduardo. This isn't even about you, or us, it's about me. I'm not looking for anyone."

"Then why did you kiss Eduardo?"

"I don't know. He was there, and I thought it might be easier to be with someone who understood me, who wasn't so complicated. He was going to war, and he wanted me, and that meant something, so I kissed him. And I was angry with you. Angry with you for lying to me, for how hard everything is right now. I just wanted a moment where something could be easy."

"Easy? You want to talk to me about easy? I've run my reputation into the ground for you, and I'd do the same again. And you were looking for easy?"

"You're to be married. This was never anything other than a fling," I say, repeating the sentiments as though the sound of them will finally lodge themselves into my thick brain.

"Why can't it be more? I love you."

For a moment, everything comes to a screeching halt.

Nick takes a deep breath. "I love you, and it's driving me mad, and if you want more, just say the word."

We've been so careful for so long to dance around the word, as though it is a red line we cannot afford to cross. It was easier to pretend it was just sex. And yet, here we are.

And still, "love" isn't the magic word I thought it was when I was a young girl.

Mistress, wife, at the moment they don't feel all that different. Neither one means he will see me as an equal. He wants me to abandon the only thing that has given me a sense of purpose in my life; he cannot have the political career he envisions with someone like me by his side.

"I was honest with you from the beginning," I reply, a tremor in my voice. "I'm not looking to raise a family and have a quiet life. I won't be a political asset and host dinner parties for you. That's not who I am, not someone I care to be. I didn't want to be that girl when I was a debutante living in Cuba, and now that everything has changed, I *can't* be that girl."

"Fine. I don't care about any of that. Be yourself. Just be you and be mine."

"Don't." I swallow, my heart breaking as I do the kind thing, the right thing, even as it tears me apart. "You should go back to Washington."

He hesitates, as though there's more he can say, as if he can convince me somehow, his gaze searching.

"So this is it, then?" he asks, finally.

I nod.

There are so many things I want to say, so many feelings pushing inside me, but at the end of the day, it's the urge to run that drives me. I've never been a coward before, but this time, I make an exception.

I've never been in love before, either.

We are truly, irrevocably over.

chapter twenty-one

I'm sitting in the living room curled up with a book when Isabel enters the room, her heels tapping the marble floor in a distinctive cadence that indicates one thing and one thing only—she's in a tizzy.

"How could you?" Isabel snaps by way of greeting.

I look up from the book, reading becoming my refuge in the days following Nick and I ending things between us.

"What have I done this time?" I ask.

With sisters, you never know—it could be a dress that was borrowed and never returned, a scuffed pair of sandals, a stolen boyfriend—the possibilities are endless, really. Isabel has been even more on edge lately with her impending wedding, and where I thought the notion of becoming Mrs. Thomas Tinsley would fill her with nuptial bliss, it seems to have done the opposite and made her more irritable than ever.

"I just got off the phone with Thomas," she answers.

"And?"

Isabel can be so dramatic sometimes.

"Diane Stanhope saw you going into that house Nick Preston bought on the beach the other day."

My fingers curl around the spine of my book.

"Everyone is talking about it. Thomas doesn't know if he wants to be associated with our family now."

Her words come out with a strangled sob, the utter panic in Isabel's voice eliciting a stab of pity. In Cuba, marriage was expected of us, but here with our fortunes and future much less certain, marriage has become a much more serious endeavor considering the alternatives before us.

"I didn't realize Thomas was so concerned with my love life," I say carefully.

Eduardo warned me about this. So did Isabel.

"Lianne Reynolds saw you embracing under a palm tree on the beach."

"We weren't embracing."

"But you are his mistress. All those things people have been saying about the two of you are true, aren't they? He gave you that diamond bracelet. Bought the house on the beach so you could, what, meet up and have sex?"

If the situation weren't so dire, I would almost laugh at the outrage in Isabel's voice at the word "sex." If the situation weren't so dire, and my mother weren't standing in the doorway of the living room.

My mother's gaze is pinned on me. "Isabel, leave us," she says, her voice filled with ice. When my father loses his temper, it's a heady explosion. When my mother loses hers, it's a brutal freeze.

Isabel's face pales as it likely hits her that she's broken the cardinal rule between siblings—never air our dirty laundry before our parents.

"Beatriz—" Isabel whispers, an unspoken plea of apology in her eyes.

I ignore it.

There will be no undoing what has been done.

Isabel leaves us, and it's just my mother and me squaring off in the living room. We're practically mirror images, down to the style of dresses we wear, the only obvious distinction between us the intervening years, and even then, my mother has aged quite well, time clearly bending to her will.

"You won't see him again."

I don't respond.

"How could you do this, Beatriz? To your sisters, to your father, to me? After everything we've been through? After everything you've put us through? I knew you could be reckless, but I didn't think you could be stupid. He's engaged. His fiancée's family is wealthy, powerful, established. So is his family. He's a U.S. senator. What did you think would happen? You've ruined everything."

"Don't you mean I've ruined myself?"

There's no pleasure to be had in arguing with my mother, and any points scored never feel like a victory. It would be so much easier if we got along, if our temperaments weren't so different—or are they too similar? I could never tell the difference.

"What do you want from me? Is it the husband? The big house? The child? Do you want me to be like Elisa? Or Isabel? Just tell me what you want from me so I can be that."

"I want you to succeed. To marry better than your sisters have. To do what is expected of you."

"And what if I don't want to marry for social status? What if I just want to be happy? What then? What if I don't need some man to pay my way? If I want to be able to support myself?"

"Happiness." She makes an unladylike noise. "And what will happiness buy you, Beatriz? Do you think it will keep you in the fine gowns and jewels you've worn your entire life? In the grand mansions? Do you think happiness will keep your family safe when they come with a knock at the door that can't be refused? Don't talk to me about your happiness."

Stubborn. Willful. Reckless.

I've heard it all, and it's all true. But I can't let this go. Can't accept the words she says as truth, the lot in life she wishes to consign me to as enough.

"Why is happiness not enough?"

Why has there never been understanding between us? Why can you not accept me as I am rather than as you would make me?

"You've always been selfish," she snaps, her gaze darkening, her words a lash across my skin, because God help me, I know what's coming, could see it building a mile away. "Your father never should have indulged you as he did."

Parents aren't supposed to have favorites, but they are human, after all, subject to the same flaws and foibles as the rest of us. I have always been my father's favorite, an unspoken understanding existing between us that I could push him further than the rest of my siblings, test the limits of his patience—much like my mother had her favorite.

The storm has been building for a long time, simmering in my family, the air crackling with it as we all dance around the one subject we cannot bear to speak of—

"Alejandro might be alive—"

I know what's coming, cannot guard myself from the blow and the immense wave of pain it brings.

"—if not for you," she finishes.

There's something special in the relationship between mothers and their sons, especially Cuban mothers.

"You filled him with ideas," she accuses.

"Alejandro had ideas of his own."

Ideas he was proud of, dreams and beliefs he was willing to die for. I have no problem accepting my responsibility in the matter, that I was a coconspirator in all of this, but it seems wrong to forget Alejandro's own desires, to take away his agency.

"You pushed him. You could never leave well enough alone. Even when you were a child, you insisted on misbehaving, on getting into trouble. And now look what you've done."

"I didn't kill him."

I can understand the grief, even understand the anger to a degree—after all, haven't I felt it when looking at Fidel? But what I can't understand is the anger in her gaze when she looks at *me*.

"Things would have been different if you hadn't pushed him to go against his family. If you hadn't encouraged that madness. He listened to you. He followed you. Those were your ideas you fed him. He was a good boy."

I almost feel sorry for her. My mother is not the sort of person who understands those who are not like her, does not adjust well to change, cannot reconcile what Cuba has become with her world of parties and shopping. The truth is, she cares not for the struggle of the average Cuban, only seeks to protect the private enclave she inhabits.

"We are sending you to Europe," she announces. "To live with my cousin in Spain."

"Pardon me?"

"I discussed it with your father. With Isabel's wedding coming up, your presence would only serve as a distraction. I won't have you ruin this for your sister. This marriage is too important for her. For all of us."

"I'm not trying to ruin this for Isabel."

"And yet, you have. If her fiancé breaks off this engagement, there will be no more opportunities for her. She will end up alone and unmarried."

"Like me? We aren't all you. We don't all aspire to marry a wealthy man because we're incapable of making our own way in the world."

Her hand reaches out, connecting with my cheek with a loud crack.

My skin burns from the feel of her palm.

"You think you can do anything, be anything, that you can defy your family with no repercussions. My parents wanted me to marry your father, and I did. I did it because I would never have threatened my family's reputation as you have, would never have considered defying my parents' wishes the way you constantly defy ours. You *will* go to stay with my cousin in Madrid."

"And if I refuse?"

"Then you will walk out of this house with the clothes on your back and nothing more."

"I don't need your money."

"So you've whored yourself out for that man."

I don't bother correcting her.

"Father would never let you throw me out."

"You've gone too far this time. The Preston family is powerful. Senator Preston's fiancée's family is equally so. They can ruin everything your father has worked so hard to build. Ruin your sisters' futures. You can go stay with my cousin, or you can leave."

"Elisa would never cut me off."

"Perhaps she wouldn't. But Maria doesn't have a choice. And Isabel is just as angry with you as I am. I won't have you bring this family down. Not after everything we've already been through."

I want to leave. I want to storm out of here, and find Nick, and take back everything I said, tell him I'll be his mistress, want to wait for him to return to Palm Beach when he can sneak away from Washington—when he can sneak away from his wife.

It would be easier.

It would be easier, and it would be wrong.

I can't be that woman.

I don't know what I'll do in Spain, but at the moment, I'm all out of plans for my future, and the urge to outrun my problems is irresistible.

"Fine. You win. When do I leave?"

I sit in the Palm Beach airport, waiting for my flight to Spain. My mother was correct; my father put up no protest when he learned I would be joining my mother's cousin, the relief in his eyes palpable. I mailed a letter to Mr. Dwyer, but I've heard nothing back, my departure a rapid one. Elisa and Maria were sad when I told them the news, but I spun it as an adventure abroad. Isabel was more reticent; the guilt in her eyes did nothing to lessen my anger with her.

Does Nick know I'm leaving?

I've heard nothing from him since we last parted, and when I took my final walk down the beach, the Palm Beach house looked shuttered now that the season has ended.

The airport is certainly quieter than it was when President Kennedy was in town.

Someone sits next to me in the waiting area near the gate, and I shift in my seat, an arm pressing against mine.

"Where are you headed?"

I jolt at the familiar voice and come face-to-face with Mr. Dwyer.

"How did you know I was here?" I ask.

He smiles. "By now you should realize there's little I don't know."

"Did you receive my letter?"

"No. I heard the whispers. Madrid, is it?"

"I'm sorry. I know you had plans for me, for the Hialeah group."

Dwyer shrugs. "We'll just send someone else in. You were right—they aren't as useful as I'd hoped they'd be, their connection to Fidel far too tenuous." He glances at his watch. "You still have a bit of time before your flight. Are you here by yourself? No family to see you off?"

Maria is in school, Elisa busy with Miguel. They are the only ones I would have wanted here.

"It's just me."

"Good, then have a drink with me."

I hesitate, Nick's earlier warnings about Dwyer and the CIA coming back to me again. And still, I'm in this deep already—I agree and follow him to a restaurant. We both order martinis and then the waitress leaves us alone.

"Eduardo is alive," Dwyer says.

Relief floods me. "Are you certain?"

"Yes. He's in prison—La Cabaña. Fidel will negotiate his release along with the rest of the prisoners."

"Was he injured in the invasion?"

"His leg, I believe. But he is very much alive, and all things considered, doing well."

"Thank you for telling me. I was worried about him. We didn't know what had happened."

"I know you're close, and I thought you would like to know."

"There are those who say the CIA is responsible for what happened at the Bay of Pigs. Who would lay the blame at your feet."

"I am sure there are some who would say that."

"What happened?"

He takes a sip of his martini. "I wish I had the answer to that. It is not nearly as nefarious as some would have you believe. We made a plan. It wasn't adequate. And more than that, Fidel knew about our plan. Knew we were coming and was prepared."

"You have a spy in your midst."

He laughs. "Likely more than one. But how do you root out the spy? It is difficult when you have so many men and women working for you. It could be anyone."

"Why are you here?"

"Because this doesn't have to be the end of our relationship."

"Excuse me?"

He chuckles. "I didn't mean it like that. Please, Miss Perez, believe it or not, not every man is enraptured by your beauty."

"I didn't presume."

"I'm sure. What I meant was there are other opportunities for a woman like you within the Agency: smart, well-connected, and yes, beautiful."

"Such as?"

"At the moment, our plan to send you to Cuba is on hold. The timing is not good, the optics are not good, and quite frankly, the president is not pleased with the Agency. Besides, I have some business to take care of in the Dominican Republic."

"Trujillo?"

The Dominican president gave former Cuban president Batista a temporary safe haven when he fled the country in '59.

"It is a difficult time to be a dictator in the Caribbean," Dwyer replies, his expression bland. "Turns out they have short life expectancies."

I'm more impressed than horrified.

"But have no fear; Castro is still very much a priority. He has decreed that Cuba is to have a socialist government now. He's abolished elections."

"I heard."

"They're imprisoning rebels," Dwyer adds. "Executing hundreds. He still hopes to inspire others, to export his brand of revolution to other countries in Latin America. To that end, I have a proposal for you."

"And what would this proposal entail?"

He takes something out of his pocket and slides it across the table to me.

An airplane ticket.

I scan the details.

"Why London?"

"You once asked me who Claudia was."

Claudia was the name that got me into the meetings in Hialeah.

"The Cubans are ramping up their intelligence operations—there are rumors that they are establishing a new intelligence section designed to spawn communist fervor around the world," Dwyer explains. "Idealistic presidents, Congress, and the like don't hamper them. And don't think they're doing it alone. We're not just fighting the Cubans. We're fighting the damned Soviets, too."

"And Claudia?" I ask.

"Claudia worked for Cuban intelligence. Claudia became one of mine. Worked as a double agent of ours. Someone killed her for it." Dwyer is silent for a beat. "She was young, like you. From a good family—not as prestigious as yours, but still. She was a good agent for us. Her father was murdered by Batista. She believed in the revolution, but Fidel betrayed those beliefs."

He slides a photograph across the table.

I recognize the woman instantly.

"She was there that night in Harlem." The sensual brunette. "She warned me off Fidel."

He smiles fondly. "You were younger then. New to the game. I had to have someone there to keep an eye on you, make sure you didn't deviate from the plan, make sure you weren't impulsive.

"She liked you. Thought you had promise."

"When was she killed?"

"A week ago."

"I'm sorry."

"It's always hard to lose assets. But I'm also worried about Claudia's work for us being compromised, her sources at risk. It's never just one agent—it's all the people they were in contact with that you stand to lose as well."

"What do you want me to do? Why London?"

"Claudia's former boyfriend is there. His name is Ramon Martinez. He's a graduate student. He was a double agent for us as well, but his intelligence has been far less impressive, far less reliable."

"You think he's a mole; you think he turned her in."

"I do. At the moment, though, I don't have proof, and we have to be careful with these agents. We can't risk burning bridges. We need them to turn against Castro and spy for us. At the same time, someone is feeding intelligence to Fidel. The sort of intelligence that caused the disaster at the Bay of Pigs. I need to know who I can trust."

"What do you want me to do?"

"We want you to set up a life as a student in London. To cross paths with Ramon. Catch his interest. See if you can discern where his loyalties lie."

"I would go to university for real."

"You would. I imagined you would like to study politics."

"And my living expenses?"

He smiles. "You would be compensated for the work you do for us, of course. In addition to what we've already paid you. You're becoming a wealthy woman, Miss Perez."

It appears I'm headed for London, not Madrid.

NOVEMBER 26, 2016
PALM BEACH

In truth, the champagne does not taste as good as she'd imagined it would. It is a fine bottle, of course, an exceedingly expensive one, an exquisite vintage of one of her favorite brands. And still—when this moment had played out in her mind, hundreds, thousands of times, she'd drained the champagne flute under different circumstances, in different company.

Time has tempered the taste of victory, lessening it somehow as each bubble tells the tale of how much she has sacrificed to reach this point.

After so many close calls, near misses, assassination plots and attempts, Fidel Castro is dead. Time has accomplished what she and so many others like her failed to do.

And perhaps, if she is really honest, the champagne does not taste as fine because every other time she has drunk it she has been in excellent company, and this time she is alone. Victories aren't nearly as fun without the right person to celebrate with, and the lure of her youth is bright and sharp, the memory of champagne-soaked afternoons a siren song.

She glances at the clock, marking the time, hoarding the last few private moments she has left with her memories. Her family will be calling soon, friends from all over the world.

She sweeps into the master bedroom, heading for the walk-in closet, thumbing through the dresses there, the bright, colorful prints, settling on the perfect one for an evening like this.

He always did like her in red.

She dresses carefully, meticulous in her selections, as exuberant in her fashion choices as she was when she was a girl of twenty-two. She is equally deliberate with her hair, her makeup. She's never taken much stock in those ridiculous articles advising women to "dress their age." Everyone knows a woman should dress as she damned well pleases.

The phone rings as she dabs perfume on her neck, behind her ears, as she slips the diamond bracelet onto her wrist to complement the canary diamond ring that has sat on her finger for so very long.

She knows, of course, when the phone rings who is on the other end of the line, has been expecting his call for decades.

She smiles at the sound of the familiar voice.

"Hello, Eduardo."

chapter twenty-two

Dwyer keeps me updated on the status of the Bay of Pigs prisoners as the months drag on, until a year has passed since I
left Palm Beach, then a year and a half. Reportedly, President Kennedy is working on securing the prisoners' release. There is nothing
we can do but wait as the two governments negotiate, as these men
are moved around like pawns on a chessboard.

I never realized how lonely spies must be, how difficult it is to
wear a mask each day you go out into the world. And even as it is
lonely, as it is difficult, I like it. Like what it has made me—

Brave, strong, independent.

There is likely no better place for recovering from a broken heart
than London. In the time since I arrived, I've settled into my new
life, taking up residence in a cozy flat in Knightsbridge, adjusting
to university, my courses as interesting as I once imagined they
would be, my classmates equally so.

The anonymity I have craved for so long is finally available to me here, and I can just be Beatriz, politics student—and occasional CIA spy.

My parents were surprised by the news that I had settled in London rather than Madrid, likely more so by my announcement that I had no need for their money. I imagine they both think I've been pensioned off by Nick and the like, but we do not speak of such things, and quite frankly, it's none of their business anyway.

The chasm between my parents and me has never felt greater, in part, perhaps, due to the physical distance between us, but also a result of the fight between my mother and me. Now that we've aired our true feelings, now that we've said too much, we cannot go back to the way things were, and so we exist in a state of détente, largely ignoring each other, the ocean between us welcome.

Elisa sends me photos of Isabel's wedding, writes letters imploring me to return home, inviting me to stay with her and her family. I have little to say to Isabel besides a cursory note congratulating her on the wedding.

I write back to Elisa, and I tell her of my classes, the fun I've had perusing the markets on the weekends for pieces to decorate my flat. I tell her about my classmates, the friends I've made, the nights out at bars and restaurants where no one cares what my last name is, where no one is trying to marry me off.

I don't tell her about Ramon Martinez, Claudia's ex-boyfriend, or the signals I receive from Dwyer. If the phone I've installed in my flat rings three times, I'm to go to a drop in Hyde Park where a stranger will pass me a note from Dwyer. If I prop a plant in my windowsill, we are to meet in Hyde Park the next day, the information ferried to Dwyer by random assets with whom I never exchange more than a cursory "hello."

There are other ways I earn my paycheck from the CIA. I go to parties, observe persons of interest, and report back. The skills one adopts as a socialite—the art of making polite conversation while attempting to discern another's secrets, the art of observing those around you and using those observations to your advantage—have provided a nearly seamless transition to spy.

If there are hiccups in my life here, they are of a personal nature.

I don't read the American papers. In my weaker moments, when I lie alone in bed, staring up at the ceiling, I imagine Nick is married now, that they have a child together. That he's forgotten me.

There are men, of course. Men who take me to dinner, take me dancing, men I meet at the parties I attend. There are men, and the occasional kiss, and my never-ending faux flirtation with Ramon, but it is as though there is a hole in my chest where my heart used to be. There is laughter, and parties, and freedom. And there is homesickness—not just for Cuba now, but for Palm Beach, for my sisters.

For Nick.

Thanks to Mr. Dwyer's intelligence, I've enrolled in two courses with Ramon. Fortuitously, we're both studying politics, so it isn't strange for our paths to cross, and given our shared nationality, I made it a point to seek him out when our program started a year ago, under the auspices of two Cubans alone in London.

Since I've been here, the summer of '61 turning into the fall of '62, I've become more convinced Ramon is guilty of deceiving the CIA and sharing the intelligence he gathers with Fidel, that he was the one who blew Claudia's cover. I just need proof.

From the beginning, I built our friendship gradually, lest Ramon become suspicious, keeping my cover story as close to the truth as possible: my family left Cuba after the revolution, sent me to London to study due to a family estrangement. I alluded to the scandal in my background without naming it outright, knowing how easily he could place a call and discover I was involved in an affair with a prominent American senator.

If he truly is a spy, it galls a bit that Ramon has never made an effort to recruit me to Fidel's cause, but his oversight is my gain. I'd rather him underestimate me and lower his guard.

Months of casual friendship have finally converted themselves into a flirtation that has proved most advantageous.

I almost think he's beginning to trust me.

Silly man.

"Do you have plans for the evening?" he asks as we ride the Tube together after class.

We're both on the Piccadilly line. I get off at Knightsbridge, Ramon a few stops later at Barons Court. The Cuban intelligence service, the newly formed DGI, Dirección General de Inteligencia, must not pay as well as the Americans.

"Just studying," I answer as he wraps his arm around me, bringing me against his side. I've learned not to flinch, to pretend as though I enjoy his embrace, to mold my body to his.

"Do you want to come over for dinner tomorrow night?" he asks.

For a moment, I'm convinced I've misheard him. I've been trying to get into his apartment for months now, hoping for an opportunity to snoop around. The more he keeps me at arm's length, the more convinced I have become that he is a man with secrets, and given the rumors that the DGI is now being heavily influenced by the Soviets, the more valuable his secrets have become.

"I'd love to," I reply.

"Excellent. It's a date then."

I say good-bye to Ramon at the Tube station after we have finalized our plans for tomorrow night, and head home.

I shift my books from one arm to the other as I search my purse for the key to my flat. I live several Tube stops from the university's campus on the east side of London, but I prefer the distance, the privacy my flat affords, the view of Hyde Park from my bedroom window.

I walk upstairs, stopping when I reach the second floor. I put the key into the lock and turn it, stepping over the threshold.

I freeze.

I can't quite put my finger on it, but something feels *off* about my flat.

And then I see him—Mr. Dwyer sitting in the corner, in the big chair where I like to do my reading for classes.

I close the door behind me with a quiet thud.

"I apologize for the break in protocol." His tone belies his words; he sounds very much like a man who isn't sorry at all, but rather, is accustomed to people adjusting to the changes in his mood, in his eccentricities.

It's been nearly a year and a half since we last saw each other.

"Something has come up, and there wasn't time to go through the normal signal channels. Since I was in town on other matters, I thought it best if I came to see you myself."

"And how did you get into my flat?"

He smiles. "Old habits. Have to make sure the skills are still sharp."

"What's happened?"

"Have you been following the news about the buildup of Soviet military arms in Cuba?"

"I have."

"The situation has become more dire. There is a Soviet asset who possesses intelligence on that matter that could prove useful. He's a colonel in the GRU, the Soviets' foreign military intelligence service. He's been funneling information to the United States and

Great Britain. Due to his position in the Soviet government, we have to be careful how we connect with him. He travels to Britain as part of his job with the scientific delegation for the Soviets, and he's in town at the moment. We want you to attend a party he will be at tonight. He will slip you the information we need. Tomorrow morning, you will go to Hyde Park and follow regular procedure to give us the microfilm."

Dwyer slides a picture of a man in military uniform across the coffee table to me.

"You are to wear a red dress and to pin a red flower in your hair. We took the liberty of doing some shopping for you. The items are in your bedroom. The colonel will be on the lookout for you, and he knows what you will be wearing. He's very, very careful, given his precarious position, but he's also a professional. I know this is new for you, but we wouldn't send you if we didn't think you could handle it. You've done good work here, and it hasn't gone unnoticed."

"Why me? Why not one of your more experienced assets? Someone who has actually received formalized training."

"Because you aren't experienced. He risks his life helping us; if the Soviets learned what he was doing, they would execute him. I don't have to worry anyone has intelligence on you. Only a very small group of people I would trust with my life know what you do for me."

"Speaking of the people you trust—"

"I haven't heard anything about Eduardo. As far as I know, he is still doing well. Kennedy continues working on negotiating his release along with that of the other remaining prisoners."

"It's taking forever."

Eduardo and the other men have spent nearly eighteen months in prison.

"Diplomacy too often does. I prefer my methods for that very reason."

At the moment, I do, too.

"Will you go to the party tonight?" he asks me.

"Of course."

I dress in the gown they selected for me, torn between amusement and embarrassment over the idea of Dwyer choosing my outfits. The dress is elegant, and *red*, certainly not the sort of thing one wears to blend into shadows.

I tuck the flower behind my ear. I glance at the photo one last time before I leave, attempting to commit the Soviet's face to memory.

I take a cab to the house where the party is being held: an elegant structure in Mayfair. I show my invitation at the door, and as soon as I walk in, I accept a glass of champagne for courage from one of the waiters passing it around on silver trays.

The gathering appears to be mainly the intellectual and diplomatic set; how many of these people are operating under covers, how many of them are foreign intelligence officers?

I don't see the Soviet anywhere.

I take a turn around the home's elegant ballroom, curious and admiring glances thrown my way, flaunting myself in the hopes I will catch the Soviet colonel's attention and he will seek me out.

And then I feel it—like a palpable thing—a gaze following me, like a fingertip trailing down my spine. I scan the room, looking for the colonel, only to come up short, the image in the picture nowhere to be seen. And still, I can feel his gaze on me.

Where is he?

And then the feeling changes, the faint prick of awareness

transforming into something else entirely, and in that moment, I know.

How could I not?

Fate, and timing, and all that.

There's a tightness in my chest, a tingle that travels down my spine as my gaze darts around the room. There's an inevitability to this, too, the knowledge that the world is really and truly not so large, that eventually our paths would cross again—

Another year. Another ballroom.

His name travels throughout the room, a murmur in the background. There are those who hope to speak with him to curry favor, women who aim to flirt with him, others who simply want to glean whatever they can about him so they'll have an interesting tidbit to share, those who wish to bask in the glory of being in the presence of an influential, handsome, and wealthy man. These people cling to power like barnacles on a boat, and he is the pinnacle of that power whether he is in Palm Beach or London.

My gaze scans the ballroom once more, my feet rooted to the floor.

Where is *he*?

Is his wife with him?

"Beatriz."

Goose bumps rise over my bare arms at the sound of his voice— low, husky, familiar. It turns out eighteen months weren't nearly enough to forget him.

I turn, steeling myself for the blow that will come when I look into his blue eyes, when my gaze will rest on his ring finger and the gold band I will surely see there.

And come, it does.

He looks unchanged by the year and a half apart; remarkably similar to the man he was when we were last together in Palm

Beach. It seems silly to think marriage would have altered him all that much, that I expected someone different to stare back at me, but all I see is Nick. The Nick who has held my hand, kissed my lips, laughed with me, slept beside me.

My Nick.

His ring finger is bare.

Is he the sort of man who chooses not to wear a wedding ring?

I take a deep breath, steadying myself.

"Hello, Nick."

chapter twenty-three

"You look beautiful."

The sound of Nick's voice momentarily transports me back to our time together in Palm Beach. It's a not entirely welcome sensation to realize a person can feel like home—especially when they're just out of reach.

Time has been good to me, as it has been to him, and really, the last thing I want to do is exchange pleasantries.

"I'm surprised to see you in London," I reply, stumbling over the words.

Is his wife here with him tonight?

He smiles. "Are you, really? Surprised to see me in London?"

I incline my head in a subtle nod, acknowledging his point, the feeling of inevitability that has always pulsed between us.

Fate, and timing, and all that.

"No, I suppose not."

Nick steps toward me, his voice lowering for my ears only. "You look as though you're a bit warm. Would you like to get some fresh air?"

I hesitate. I've yet to make contact with the Soviet colonel Dwyer sent me here to meet. And yet, surely, taking a moment to myself won't matter?

"That would be lovely."

I follow Nick to the balcony, ducking my head, the weight of a hundred gazes upon us. Despite their curiosity, the Europeans have a much more laissez-faire attitude about these things than the Americans.

Nick's steps are quick, his strides sure as he leads me outside. I drink in the sight of him: his broad shoulders, long limbs, muscular frame, the elegant cut of his tuxedo.

I curl my fingers into a ball to keep from reaching out and touching him. Once we exit the party, the cool air hitting my face, I move away from him, striding to the edge of the balcony, leaning forward and resting my elbows against the railing.

Nick mimics my position, our arms inches apart.

I wait for him to speak, to pick up where he left off when he invited me out here, but he seems content for the silence to linger between us. In that time I acclimate to his presence again, my body shifting, fitting itself closer to him so the inches of stone between us disappear, and his sleeve brushes my wrist, our chests rising and falling in rhythm, our breaths in quiet tandem.

"I missed this," he murmurs finally. "Just being near you. Everywhere else feels exhausting these days."

"The world is exhausting these days."

"That's the truth," he acknowledges.

"I'm pretty sure you once said *I* was exhausting."

A faint smile plays at the corners of his mouth. "I did. Long ago. And you are. But it turns out missing you is the most exhausting thing of all."

"Are you happy?" I ask.

I'm not sure I'm prepared for either answer he could give me. I can't stand the idea of him miserable, and I'm equally uncomfortable with the notion that he is madly in love with his wife.

He shrugs. "Does it matter, really?"

Not for people like us. "Happy" has gotten lost somewhere in between plots and politics, nation building and regime change, family and fortune.

"Why did you leave Palm Beach?" he asks.

"You know why. I couldn't stay."

"Will you ever come back?"

"I don't know. It still feels like home, and it doesn't. Like it belongs to someone else."

"Are you not Beatriz Perez anymore?"

"I don't know. Sometimes I don't think I know who Beatriz Perez really is."

"I don't believe that. You've always known yourself better than anyone."

"I've been blown off course," I admit.

"London?"

"That, too."

"I probably don't want to know how you ended up here, do I?"

"Probably not."

"I scoured every intelligence brief, read every newspaper; I saw your sisters at parties, and I wanted to ask—and then I did—"

Elisa never mentioned speaking with him.

He takes a deep breath. "I missed you."

"I missed you, too."

"Eventually, I heard rumors that you were capturing hearts and conquering Europe."

I smile. "Not *all* of Europe. Just a corner of it."

"You're too modest. It wasn't just London. I heard tales of your travels to Paris. And Barcelona."

"I'm not the sort to sit at home crying over my broken heart."

"Was your heart broken?"

It takes everything in me to refrain from looking down at his hands, the heart in question beating madly.

"A figure of speech."

"Of course," he counters smoothly. "Did you enjoy it?"

"Europe? Or the heart capturing?"

"Both, I suppose."

"Sometimes."

"And the other times?"

"I was homesick."

"For Cuba? Or Palm Beach? Or me?"

He delivers the last question with the same smooth confidence that has equal parts amused and infuriated me throughout the course of our relationship.

"All of them, I suppose."

My gaze darts back to his hand.

Nary a tan line.

I can't take the suspense anymore.

"And your wife? Did she accompany you on this trip?"

Surprise flickers in his gaze. "You haven't heard?"

"I make it a habit not to keep up with the American papers."

"I wondered when I didn't hear anything from you—I'm not married."

I can't ignore the faint prick of hope.

"You're still engaged?"

"No. I'm not engaged."

For a moment, my world stops.

"Since when?"

"Since I realized I couldn't imagine marrying someone I didn't love. I wouldn't be happy in such a marriage, and it wasn't a matter of growing up, or settling down, but rather the realization that I wanted my wife to be a partner, someone I could enjoy growing old with, who would be my match in every way. It wasn't fair to make promises to someone if I had even a shred of doubt I would be able to keep them."

"That sounds like a tall order."

"Does it?" He swallows, and he almost looks embarrassed. "Katherine was a nice girl, but she wanted the senator."

"Lots of women will want the senator. In her defense, it sounds like you wanted the debutante. Just like lots of men want me because I have a pretty face and a pleasing figure."

"I'm not sure either 'pretty' or 'pleasing' do you justice."

I smile despite the urge to weep. "You always did possess more charm than God should give any one person."

His lips curve.

"Will she be all right?"

"I think so," he answers. "She's engaged again. She seems happy. I don't regret what happened between you and me, I can't, but I do regret the fact that I acted less than honorably with her."

It's impossible not to feel as though Katherine Davies was caught up in the wreckage of our affair.

"And you?" Nick asks.

"What about me?"

"During your travels did you meet anyone . . ."

"You know the answer to that."

"Do I? Maybe I do. The trouble is there were far too many nights when I struggled to fall asleep, that question playing through my mind over and over again."

"Why are you here? For work? Or something else?"

"Did I know you would be here? Did I come here to see you? To attempt to win you back? What do you think, Beatriz? I missed you. And I was worried about you."

"It took you long enough. I left Palm Beach eighteen months ago."

"You can't tell me you were waiting around for me to come to you."

"No, I wasn't."

There's a question in his eyes, one that shouldn't need to be asked.

Stupid man.

"There were men." No matter what is or isn't between us, I won't lie to him about this.

"Should I be worried?"

"I don't know. Should you? Are you asking as my friend—or—"

The rest of it dangles between us.

"As the man who has loved you every day since the first moment I met you," he finishes for me.

"Nick."

"I know. Nothing has really changed, has it? We're still on opposite sides, and we still want different things."

"And yet, here you are."

"And yet, here I am."

I'd thought time would lessen my desire for him, that it would augment the differences between us. I'd thought the emotions inside me would peter out without anything between us to sustain us.

I was wrong.

"We still want different things," I echo.

"Perhaps." He shrugs. "Who knows? The world might change and surprise us."

"And until then?"

"Until then, I want you. No one else." He kisses my cheek, his hand resting on my waist for a moment before he releases me. "I'm in London until Monday. I'm at the Ritz. If you want to see me, I'll be waiting for you. If you don't, I understand. I'll go back home. I won't bother you again."

And just like that, he leaves me standing alone on the balcony, wondering if I should go after him.

I walk back into the ballroom a few minutes later, more than a little rattled by seeing Nick again, searching the room for the Soviet colonel. All I want is to finish the mission I was sent here to complete and to go back to my flat, where I can be alone with my thoughts.

Where is he?

I weave my way through the crowd, casually sipping champagne, attempting to look as though I am not searching for a spy, a chill running down my spine.

And then I see him.

The colonel is tucked away in the corner of the room, his back against the wall, engaged in conversation with a woman whose hand rests on the sleeve of his dress uniform and another gentleman who gesticulates wildly.

"Beatriz?"

My stomach sinks at the sound of my name, at the voice I recognize too well.

I pivot, pasting a false smile on my face, my heart pounding.

"Ramon? What are you doing here?" I ask, not giving him a chance to pose the same question to me first.

If I've learned anything in the social whirl or as a spy, it's to bluff my way through everything.

"I—uh—I came with some friends," he answers. "What are you doing here?" he asks after a beat, and the time I've spent watching him stumble over his answer has given me ample opportunity to formulate my own response.

"I'm on a date."

Ramon blinks.

"I didn't think you and I were exclusive or anything," I say, feigning the apology in my tone. "I assumed you were seeing other people as well."

"I was," he answers, the surprise in his voice contradicting his words.

Out of the corner of my eye, I see the colonel break away from his companions, walking across the room.

Go away.

"I should return to my date." I lean forward, attempting to keep my tone light. I flash Ramon a peek at my cleavage before pulling back.

Is he here for the Soviet colonel? To spy on the colonel's movements for Fidel to pass on to the Soviets? Or is he here for some other reason entirely?

The decision is reached, quickly, no time for second-guessing. I glance over my shoulder, making eye contact with Ramon, channeling all of the inner turmoil and angst I felt when I saw Nick earlier, attempting to look like a girl who is torn between two men, a silly, foolish girl—and one easily discounted at that.

Confusion stirs in Ramon's eyes, confusion and a prick of male vanity. He never once considered I was indulging in other dalliances while *we* flirted, and I hope that misstep combined with his surprise at seeing me tonight is enough to throw him off the scent.

I need the microfilm.

I turn away from Ramon, my legs wobbling as though I am unsteady on my heels, as though I am a girl who is *rattled* by this.

I pitch forward, colliding with the Soviet colonel, upending my champagne glass all over his elegant uniform. I rear back, just in time for him to slip the microfilm in my clutched hand, my body shielding the handoff from the rest of the room. I babble apologies to the colonel while he dabs at his jacket with an elegant handkerchief. I don't look back at Ramon, but I feel his gaze on me, and I hope I have done a good job of convincing him I am just an innocent girl, even as a sense of triumph fills me, the microfilm curled in the palm of my hand.

With one last apology, I brush past the colonel, ready to be done with the party, to return to the safety of my flat and wait until the next morning when I can complete the dead drop.

I stumble, my heel catching on some nearly imperceptible fault in the flooring, and this time, the reaction is entirely genuine.

Nick stands near the front hallway, his coat in hand, his gaze riveted by the scene I've just made. His expression is one I've recognized countless times before, the mask he wears in public when he is the consummate politician firmly in place. And still—I know him well enough, have seen the personal side to him often enough, to register that he hasn't been fooled by any of this, and I almost feel sorry for him.

He fell in love with a socialite and has gotten a spy in return.

I sweep past the colonel, careful to keep from meeting Nick's gaze once more. I fear he will read the expression on my face, that he will do something to give me away.

The cool air hits me as I walk out the front door, scanning the line of sleek cars manned by drivers waiting for their clients to emerge. I glance around, slipping the microfilm into my clutch.

It's just my luck there isn't a cab to be had this evening.

I pick up my skirt in my other hand, steeling myself for the walk ahead of me.

"Need a ride?"

I turn slowly at the familiar voice.

"Actually, I do."

He smiles.

"Where should I tell my driver to drop you?"

I take a deep breath.

Fate, and timing, and all that.

"The Ritz," I tell Nick.

The door to the hotel room slams closed. Nick's tuxedo jacket hits the floor. My dress follows.

There truly is something indescribably *right* about coming home.

Would I have gone to his hotel if I hadn't looked up and seen him standing there? If there had been a cab, would I have returned to my flat and fallen into bed by myself?

Who knows?

If I've learned anything at this point, it's that life comes down to timing. Things happen the way they are supposed to, the seemingly insignificant moments stringing together to lead you down a path you never imagined traversing, with a man you can't let go of and you can't keep.

My back hits the mattress, Nick's body covering mine quickly. We left the hotel room lights off, and I'm glad for it, as our hands and mouths relearn each other, the sheets rustling beneath our weight, the rest of the world and all of its problems firmly locked out on the opposite side of the door.

I don't want reality now, don't want to worry about the microfilm tucked in my purse, discarded somewhere on the floor, or what we will say to each other tomorrow, or what will happen when the time comes for Nick to return to the United States.

I want this evening. We'll worry about tomorrow later.

. . .

I wake to sunlight creeping in through a slit in the drapes of Nick's hotel room, a bright sliver of sun bisecting the coverlet. Beside me, Nick sleeps on his back; his body is sprawled as it always is when he is in a deep slumber, after I have done my part to exhaust him. I shift in the bed, turning over onto my side to watch him, indulging in the moment. Mornings like this have always been a luxury for us, nights spent together typically reserved for husbands and wives, and the impulse to savor this one is inescapable.

He's as handsome as he ever was, but now I have the opportunity to view him up close and in private, and I study the subtle changes in his face. The lines that have cropped up in my absence.

In the time apart, I didn't truly let myself appreciate how much I missed him.

I rise with a sense of regret, careful to keep my footfalls quiet, not to wake Nick. I'm certainly not eager to explain why I'm sneaking out of his hotel room at this early morning hour or where I'm headed.

I bend down, gathering my clothing, the bag discarded on the floor, opening it to reassure myself the microfilm is still there. I glance at the elegant clock on a desk in the corner.

I dress quickly now, wishing I had more time to go back to my flat and change into something more suitable for the meeting than a red evening dress. The coat covers most of it, but there are other things I can't salvage: my hair in a messy bun on my head, my makeup smudged and faded from the night before.

I slip from the room, walking out of the hotel and onto Piccadilly. Thankfully, the Ritz is close to the park, even if the heels I donned last night make the walk mildly less pleasant.

Hyde Park is busy this morning, Londoners eager for a break from the towering buildings, the concrete sidewalks, yearning for a patch of green to call their own. My strides lengthen as I head toward the far end where we usually do our drops.

As much as I love the energy of London, the freedom of it, the anonymity of it, I am not a girl for overly large cities. To visit, perhaps, but I crave the salt air, the roar of the ocean, the sight of swaying palms. Havana was many things all rolled into one and I enjoyed her secrets, the hidden surprises on every corner.

I pass the Serpentine, my gaze drawn to my usual spot. The bench doesn't offer the best view of the park, so more often than not it's vacant, and today is no exception. We have a backup plan in place, of course, but I prefer the routine of the same bench, the notch in the third rung I have grown used to.

I sit on the cold surface and wrap my coat more tightly around me, attempting to ward off the cool fall air. London in October is far from the coldest I've experienced, but for someone more suited to tropical climes, I've learned just how thin my blood really is during these fall and winter months.

Minutes pass.

No one comes.

Thirty minutes pass.

An hour.

My contact has never been late. Not once.

I clasp my clutch in hand, hugging it toward me.

Did I make a mistake with regard to Dwyer's instructions? Did something happen? Did he attempt to contact me at my flat while I was with Nick?

I wait another few minutes, the park no longer feeling so bucolic or safe, the tourists and joggers no longer appearing so innocuous. When my contact still doesn't show up, I rise from my place on the bench, and head home.

The morning grows later as I exit the park, turning onto Kensington High Street, then another turn, and another, twisting my way through the neighborhood to the brick building I call home. The streets are busier now; more glances cast my way as the red silk skirt of my evening gown peeks out from the bottom of my coat. London is a city where nearly anything goes, but this part of town is more predisposed to the wealthy and conservative, and my appearance and the obvious impression it conveys—that I am wearing a gown more suited to the evening before—draws more notice than I would prefer. I make a terrible invisible spy, but then again I suppose Dwyer knew that when he hired me, imagine he was looking for something else entirely.

The sight of the brick row of buildings in front of me brings relief, the familiarity of my street a comfort now. I enter the edifice, and when I reach my floor, I slip the key in the lock, pushing the door to my flat open and letting it close behind me, the deadbolt clicking into place.

I shrug out of my coat, hanging it on the coat rack near my front door, and at once, I am met with the same feeling as before—the sensation that I am not alone. I take two steps forward, ready to greet Dwyer and be done with the microfilm, only to stop in my tracks.

My instincts haven't failed me.

I'm not alone.

But it isn't Dwyer staring back at me.

chapter twenty-four

"Ramon."

It takes a moment for me to attempt to reconcile all of the reasons he could be here, only to quickly come to the conclusion that whatever his reason, it isn't good.

Ramon rises from his seat, still dressed in the same tuxedo from last night. Even in that simple motion, I see the change in him, the mask slipping, the quiet student replaced by someone far more formidable.

"Sit down." He gestures to one of the vacant chairs at the little table that functions as my dining space.

A gun lies in front of him; his finger rests on the cold black metal. I don't move.

"I wondered, you know. When I first saw you at the party, my initial thought was you were there for the same reason I was. But I dismissed it, because, well, I didn't take you for a spy. My mistake, of course."

What am I going to do?

"CIA? MI6?"

He's going to kill me. Just like he killed his girlfriend Claudia. My great battle with Fidel has now come to this—me dying at the hands of one of his spies, a traitor to our country.

"It doesn't matter, I guess. We both know why you were there last night."

I scan the little flat, looking for salvation, for something to get me out of this mess.

"I'm going to need the microfilm now." His expression hardens to flint; he holds his hand out to me.

"I don't know what you're talking about." I don't have to feign discomfort as I stumble over the words, my fear all too genuine. "I told you why I was at the party. That man—we were together when I lived in the United States. We've been involved for a long time. Our affair is why my family sent me to London in the first place."

I walk toward the table, setting the purse containing the microfilm on one of the chairs.

Ramon's gaze follows the motion as I'd hoped it would, my bright red clutch like a cape before a bull.

I glance at the gun.

Leave it on the table. Go for the microfilm. Give me a chance—
He doesn't.

Ramon strides toward my clutch, the gun dangling from his free hand with the insouciance of a man who can switch from idle to killer with a moment's notice, and who doesn't view me as very much of a threat at all.

My gaze darts to the knife block sitting in the kitchen I never use, the blades still sharp. There's a sliver of time, a heartbeat of opportunity, and the odds that I will be able to overpower him are slim, if I fail—

What does it matter? I'll die anyway.

Ramon opens my clutch.

I lunge for the knife block.

He turns as my hand wraps around the largest handle, pulling it from its wooden sheath, adrenaline crashing through me.

In a flash of speed, he's in front of me, his hand on my wrist as we wrestle for the knife.

If he were a bigger man, I'd be dead by now, but with his slight build, we are on a more even playing field, even if he maneuvers me with a level of skill in which I am outmatched.

As quickly as it began, it's over, my hand empty, the knife tumbling to the floor.

I'm going to die.

I'm not sure if it's my life that flashes before my eyes, but it's something. Moments flicker.

The Malecón. A Havana sunrise. The ocean lapping over my skin. Nick's mouth on mine. My sisters' laughter. Our nanny, Magda, telling me there are untrustworthy men in the world, and that if I ever find myself in a situation where one tries to take advantage of me, I should hit him where it hurts, her voice low to avoid my mother overhearing her.

I bring my knee up as hard as I can, connecting with Ramon's groin, our gazes meeting, surprise and anger in his eyes—pain—as he doubles over, as his hand comes up, my fingers finding his, wrapping around cold metal, grasping—

We both grab the gun a moment before it fires.

chapter twenty-five

I slip my hand inside the pocket of my coat, hiding the cuts from the front desk receptionist, the spot of blood near my fingernail I missed when I scrubbed my skin earlier.

My old clothes were disposed of, the beautiful red gown ruined by Ramon's blood and mysterious pieces of body matter best left unexamined. I chucked my outfit in the bin after I called my contact and told them I needed a cleanup in my flat, the blood pooling around Ramon's dead body. His gun had a silencer on it, but still. It will only be so long before the neighbors investigate the sounds of our struggle.

How long before a dead body starts to smell?

I didn't bother waiting around for questions, or give myself time to contemplate how *lucky* I was, the sheer fortune of my finger reaching the trigger before his did, the fortuitousness that it was pointed at him and not me at that exact, precipitous moment.

Instead, I changed clothes quickly, scrubbing the bits of flesh and blood off my skin with a detached efficiency.

And I ran.

To the Ritz. To Nick.

Are the police waiting for me in my flat? Or did Dwyer's people get there before me? And why didn't anyone meet me in the park?

The microfilm is on my person now, tucked in the cup of my bra, against my pounding heart.

I ask the receptionist for Nick's room, wishing I'd paid attention to the number earlier, attempting to calm my voice as much as possible, my expression a blank mask.

I cannot stop the shaking in my hand.

The woman behind the front desk calls up to his room, and I listen to her side of the conversation, as I try to guess Nick's reaction on the other end of the line.

Will he be surprised I have returned? Was he angry when I left him this morning without a word? Or did he wake to my absence with a sense of resignation? The understanding that we are still, as always, an impossible match?

"I'll send her up, sir," the receptionist says into the phone and relief floods me. I didn't just run here because I'm in trouble; I ran here because I need *him*.

The receptionist gives me Nick's room number with a polite smile, gesturing toward the elevators. I gather the small bag I hastily packed when I fled my flat and board the lift, declining the offer to help with my luggage, nerves filling me.

The operator presses the number for Nick's floor for me, the carriage empty save for the two of us.

The doors slide open, and I step off the lift.

When I'm standing outside Nick's door at the end of the long hallway, I knock on the door. The speck of blood I missed earlier stares back at me, a stain on my skin.

I've killed a man now, and I don't know how I feel about it.

The door swings open, and I jump. Nick stands on the other side of the threshold, his appearance uncharacteristically disheveled—

his white dress shirt only partially tucked into his trousers, his blond hair tousled, a harried expression on his face.

I open my mouth to speak, to apologize for leaving early in the morning without a word for him, but he doesn't give me the chance.

Nick steps forward, wrapping his arm around my waist, hugging me against his body.

His mouth seizes mine in a swift, fierce kiss, the hotel room door slamming shut behind us as a sob builds in my chest, my knees buckling.

I killed a man.

As quickly as Nick kisses me, he releases me.

"Beatriz—"

His eyes narrow as he looks over my appearance.

"What happened?"

"I killed a man," I whisper. "There was a Cuban man, he was with their intelligence service. I was at the party last night to meet someone, to make an exchange, and he noticed. He was waiting in my flat when I went home."

Shock flashes across Nick's face for a moment, and then it's gone.

"Are you in danger? What happened to the body?"

"I don't know. I left word with Dwyer's people to clean it up. I was supposed to meet someone from the CIA this morning—that's why I left so early—but my contact never showed up, and I went home, not sure what I should do. The man, Ramon, was waiting for me with a gun. We fought."

I tell Nick the rest of it, no secrets left between us. With each word, I wait for his censure, to watch the love dim in his eyes. Instead I see calm, as though he always expected it would come to this, the truth behind his words, his warnings about the CIA, his fear for my safety, finally resonating.

Nick wasn't wrong; I have gotten myself into an intractable mess, and in this moment, I know—

I killed a man, and I don't feel guilty at all.

I am immeasurably glad *he* didn't kill *me*.

When I've finished with my tale, I apologize for the trouble I've brought to his doorstep. "If you want me to leave, I understand. This would be a problem for you if it got out."

"Don't ever apologize for coming to me. I am here for you. Always."

Tears well in my eyes. "Thank you."

I slip a hand into the front of my blouse, pulling the microfilm out of my bra.

"I need to get this to my contact. There's a mail drop I can use." I take a deep breath, trusting him with all of it. "I got the microfilm from a Soviet colonel at the party last night."

Nick's entire expression changes. "From a Soviet colonel?"

"Yes."

"I was just packing before you knocked. Something has happened, and I have to go back to Washington." He hesitates. "A U-2 plane found evidence the Soviets have installed nuclear-capable ballistic missiles in Cuba."

chapter twenty-six

"How bad is it?" I ask.

"It's bad. The weapons can reach the United States. I need to return to Washington, in case—" Nick wraps his arms around me, and I allow myself to lean into him, the world around us spinning madly out of control.

Was the colonel trying to prevent such an attack? The idea of nuclear war—

Will Fidel use the weapons? Will the Soviets?

I need to get the microfilm to the CIA immediately.

My family, my sisters, they're all in Florida, ninety miles away from Cuba. And in Cuba—there are family and friends there, too, Eduardo languishing in a prison somewhere, so many innocent people in jeopardy.

What will the United States do in retaliation for Fidel allowing the nuclear weapons in Cuba? How many lives will be lost as a result of the escalating tensions between our two countries, politicians threatening war and posturing with little regard for the potential destruction on both sides?

I wanted a war, wanted the Americans to do *something*, but not this. Nothing good can come of this. We learned about the bombs the Americans dropped on Japan in school, about the devastation it wrought, and it terrifies me to think of the same kind of destruction battering our shores.

Will Cuba be caught in the middle of a war between the United States and the Soviet Union?

"They think the Soviets are going to use the weapons to attack the United States?"

"I don't know," Nick answers, his expression grim. "I hope the Soviets know better than to employ the weapons, but even the threat of them—that they moved them to our backyard—well, it's extremely worrying, to say the least."

What is on the microfilm? It can't be a coincidence that Dwyer asked me to get it at this time.

"What will the president do?"

"He's planning on addressing the nation. He's meeting with his advisors, the Executive Committee of the National Security Council. I need to go home."

"I'll go with you."

"No, absolutely not. If the Soviets do attack, you'll be safer here."

"And the body I've left behind?"

A blistering curse leaves his mouth as he remembers that particular complication.

"Besides, my family is in Florida. *You're* going to Washington. I don't want to stay here. If there is to be war, I want to be in the United States. Close to those I care about."

"It's not safe, Beatriz."

"When are we going to stop having this fight? Either I go with you, or I go on my own, but either way, I'm going. My sisters might need me. You might need me."

The CIA might need me.

He hesitates. "If things get really bad, promise me you will go somewhere safe."

"I will."

I'm not sure either one of us really believes me. I don't say the rest of it, because I can easily imagine his response, but it occurs to me there are many solutions to this problem—not just military.

Mr. Dwyer wanted to use me as a weapon against Fidel. Here's his chance.

Nick arranges our travel with an efficiency and expediency only copious amounts of money and influence can facilitate. I slip the microfilm into a padded envelope, the urgency of world events no longer allowing for me to wait to possibly hear from Dwyer again before I act. Nick insists on accompanying me, as I follow the backup procedure we've established if a drop ever collapses.

I return to the Ritz with Nick while he finalizes our travel arrangements. I take a proper shower, the remainder of the blood scrubbed away, little to be done for the cuts and nicks on my skin from where Ramon and I fought for the knife. Then I busy myself with repacking the clothes I threw into my bag earlier, and count the money I grabbed from my secret hiding place in my flat for a day such as this. My father taught me the lesson of preparing for emergencies, quick exits and exile, of always having cash on hand for whatever life throws my way.

My hand brushes a lace dress as I shut the bag, and a memory takes hold, of my last night in Havana, as I packed for a trip that has turned into a never-ending exile. The tenor of our days is defined by this madness, as we rush from one crisis to another, from revolution, to crushing defeat, to the brink of nuclear war.

Perhaps it is my recklessness that causes me to go with Nick to

Washington now. Perhaps it is a folly best forsaken, and yet, when the last four years of your life have been defined by war and conflict, it is impossible to feel as though you're not living on borrowed time, as though you shouldn't eke out every last moment of pleasure before the things you love most are once again seized from you.

Nick hires a car to drive us to the airport as we leave London. We sit in the back, our hands joined, resting on the seat between us. Everything happened so quickly; thankfully, I had the foresight to bring my passport with me when I left my flat.

Have the police found the body? Or did Dwyer's people get to the flat in time?

"You could be considered an accomplice, you know," I warn Nick in a whisper, grateful for the privacy window separating us from the driver. "Once we get on that plane together—"

"Haven't we been through this already? I don't care."

"You should care."

"And yet, I don't. What does it even matter in the face of what we're up against with the Soviets? Besides, we've heard nothing to give the impression that a body has even been found. It's just as likely the CIA was able to dispose of your Cuban spy. I imagine Dwyer has plenty of experience in these matters."

"How well do you know him?"

"Dwyer?"

I nod.

"Personally? Not at all. But in certain circles, his reputation precedes him. I had a feeling you were here for him when I learned you'd come to London."

"He helped me register for school. It was my cover, of course, to get close to the Cuban operative, but I liked it. A lot."

"Politics?"

"Of course."

"I'm glad you've had that opportunity."

"I suppose I've just screwed everything up."

"I wouldn't worry about that yet. You have time to figure it out. You might be able to take a leave of absence; you might not even be gone that long. You can always return whenever you want. If Dwyer's people disposed of the body, you might have nothing to worry about at all."

"Perhaps."

At the moment, it seems foolish to worry about such mundane problems under the threat of nuclear war.

We speak little on the flight to D.C., our relationship taking a back seat to politics, the threat of the moment, and the things Nick cannot speak of in public. Surprisingly, though, I sleep, Nick's arm draped around my shoulders as I make up for the hours of rest I lost in his hotel room.

I dream of Nick, of his arms around me, his hands on my body, his lips on mine. I dream of the struggle with Ramon, the gun in my hands, the pop of the gunshot, only this time, when I look down, my hands are covered in *my* blood.

When I wake with a jolt, Nick kisses my forehead, worry etched all over his face, in the furrow of his brow, in the tension that radiates from his hand to mine, our fingers linked together. We don't bother with pretense surrounding the nature of our relationship; there hardly seems to be a point with the threat looming before us.

We arrive in Washington, and Nick takes me to the apartment he keeps in Georgetown, pausing to change his suit for a fresh one, leaving me with a brief kiss before he is gone to work.

Once I am alone, I call Elisa and explain the situation to her with as little detail as possible.

At first, she peppers me with questions about my relationship with Nick, how we saw each other again, what happened, why I decided to accompany him to Washington. I say nothing of my extracurricular activities, of course, nor do I say much about the current diplomatic crisis, other than to warn her to be on alert.

The buildup of Soviet weapons has been monitored for the past week now, but the news that they are capable of launching a nuclear strike on American soil is grave indeed.

"You're scaring me, Beatriz. What are you suggesting?" Elisa asks.

"Just that you might want to get supplies. The president is addressing the nation tonight." I swallow as I think of my little nephew, whom I have not seen in a year and a half now. How much has he grown? How will we survive this? "Just get some supplies. And think about where you could go if you needed to leave Florida quickly."

It takes little convincing to get Elisa off the phone so she can call the rest of the family, so they can prepare for the coming days. We have lived through enough horrors to know better than to take such warnings for granted. We were caught off guard once; let it never happen again.

I occupy my time exploring Nick's apartment, running my fingers over the suits in his closet, the scent of his cologne on the fabric, learning this part of his life. We slip into domesticity each time together with an ease that simultaneously thrills and terrifies me.

There's a market a few blocks away where I buy some groceries with the money I exchanged when we landed in D.C., grateful once more for the independence my arrangement with the CIA has provided to me.

I return to Nick's apartment to cook dinner, sitting down in front of the television for the president's announcement.

Just one day after we left London, at seven P.M. President Kennedy addresses the country; he is seated behind his desk in the Oval Office, his manner grave. He possesses a calm temperament that, despite his relative youth, suggests he is not the sort to be rattled by these affairs, that he has a firm hand behind the helm of the nation. I envy the Americans their steady leadership contrasted against Fidel's fiery rhetoric and erratic outrage. When I was younger, I embraced the fury, fought for radical change, but now I find comfort in the calm manner of Kennedy, even as I cannot forgive him for the way he handled the Bay of Pigs.

My hand trembles as I swallow the drink I poured earlier, my gaze riveted to the television as the president tells the world Soviet missile sites in Cuba are capable of reaching Florida, and Washington D.C., among other places, a chill sliding down my spine. Military bases in Cuba are standing up with offensive capabilities, prepared to launch a nuclear weapons attack against the United States and the world.

Fidel is the wild card in this, the man who courts chaos and revels in strife. What is his aim in allowing the Soviets to establish such a position in America's backyard?

The Soviets engage in the fiction that they are supporting Cuba, providing a defense for a defenseless country faced with a great power's impressive military might. However, there is no doubt they are challenging the Americans, taunting them, and Cuba is the easiest method to do so, even if so many innocent lives hang in the balance.

And yet, as I listen to Kennedy's words, his condemnation of the Soviets' actions, decrying their attempts to insert themselves in the affairs of other countries, to amass power by proxy, I cannot help but think of the United States' own actions, their role in Cuba's current condition. Is the distinction between the two powers that the Soviet Union does so brazenly and with flagrant disregard for international condemnation whereas the United States does so covertly and secretly with the use of the CIA and other organizations like it, while maintaining the moral authority on the world stage?

I struggle to see much difference at this point, and at the same time, feel a sense of shame at my own involvement with the CIA. Am I guilty of the same things the Americans are? Do necessity and desperation change our moral fabric so much that we no longer recognize ourselves?

According to the president, the Americans are to quarantine any ships containing offensive weapons en route to Cuba and send them back to their countries of origin. Thankfully, Kennedy announces there will be no attempt to keep humanitarian items from reaching the Cuban people. And still, the United States has taken the position that the launch of nuclear weapons from Cuba against any nation will constitute an act of aggression against the United States, and is fortifying its military base at Guantanamo, preparing for war, families evacuated from the base, everyone on standby.

Kennedy calls for the Organization of American States to view this as a hemispheric threat, and for the United Nations Security Council to meet in an emergency meeting with the aim of passing a resolution to dismantle all nuclear weapons before the quarantine may be ended. His final words to Khrushchev and the rest of the world are spoken with resolve, and a stated desire for peace. Once again, I struggle to reconcile the image of the stalwart American presidency tasked with preserving peace throughout the world and exporting democracy, and the version of the United States I have known for much of my lifetime: the country giving weapons and aid to former president Batista and turning a blind eye to his abuses of power and the subjugation of the Cuban people.

It is Kennedy's closing words that speak to me most, though, the ones he addresses to Cubans, broadcast to the island through secret radio communications. How must my people feel, caught between two giants, subjected to the whims of great powers once more? Kennedy speaks of the deep sorrow the American people have felt at how the revolution has turned out, and all I can think of are firing squads and fraudulent trials, of families ripped apart by violence and bloodshed. I do not want his sorrow. It is of no use to my brother lying dead in the ground, to the men and women sentenced to death by politics. What we need now is action. The same kind of power the United States is willing to employ when their own interests are at stake, yet far less so when others are involved.

I thought my love for Cuba would be the hardest thing for me to reconcile, but in truth, it's the anger that's the hardest to dispense of. Love ebbs and flows, a low-level hum in the background, but anger sinks its claws in you and refuses to let go.

And suddenly, I can't take it anymore, and I rise from my position on Nick's elegant couch and turn off the television.

I wake to a kiss against my cheek, Nick stroking my hair. It takes a moment for me to acclimate to my surroundings, the leather couch beneath me, the wool blanket covering my body, the dark stillness of Nick's D.C. apartment, and the scent of his cologne— sandalwood and orange.

I sit up abruptly, grasping his arm, my fingers ghosting across his wrist, the faint sprinkling of hair there, his jacket discarded, his sleeves rolled up.

"What time is it?" I fumble for the light on the table beside me with my other arm.

"Late. Or early, depending on your perspective, I suppose."

"You sound tired."

"I'm exhausted."

"What can I do?"

"Just be with me."

Nick lifts me from the sofa, my body cradled in his arms, my hands threading through his hair, my mouth devouring his. He carries me through the apartment and sets me down on the soft mattress in his bedroom, the sheets covered in the scents I've come to associate with him, the familiarity of it causing a sob to rise in my chest.

I'm angry with the world, and so afraid, and I've missed him so much, these emotions inside of me threatening to splinter me, pulling me in so many different directions, my loyalties divided between logic, my family, my nationality, my heart.

"I love you," Nick whispers, his lips grazing my earlobe. "So much."

And in the dark stillness of the night, the threat of nuclear war pounding at the door of this enclave we've carved out for ourselves, I am brave enough to voice the emotion that has lingered in my heart for so very long.

"I love you, too."

We settle into a domestic routine of sorts in Nick's apartment in Georgetown despite the madness of the world surrounding us. Nick spends his days after President Kennedy's address to the American people working with his fellow senators, the president, and the president's advisors. Nick returns from work, worried and weary, our dinners taking place late in the evening, our conversations focused on politics.

"How is the president?" I sip my wine as we lounge in the living room after another midnight dinner.

"Cautious. These meetings with his advisors—" Nick shakes his head. "Right now we desperately need calmer heads to prevail. The president is providing that, at least. He knows what is at stake, how much a wrong and reckless move could cost us. He favors a blockade with the hope it'll buy us time."

These are the deals and negotiations weighing heavily on Nick's shoulders and those of the others trying to find a diplomatic solution to this mess. Whether Castro and Khrushchev are willing to be reasonable men remains to be seen.

"And how are you?" I kiss his cheek, wrapping my arms around those broad shoulders, bringing him closer to me, his heart thudding against my chest.

"Tired. So damn tired."

I take the glass of scotch from Nick's hands, setting it down on the end table, reaching between us and loosening the knot of his tie. He lays his head on my lap, his eyes trained to the ceiling, his jaw clenched. The heavy load of concerns he carries is evident in his tense body, in the knots I massage in his shoulders.

I no longer remember what it feels like to stand on solid ground.

I speak to Elisa daily now—she tells me stories of Maria doing duck-and-cover drills at her school, of my parents' worry and fear. This all feels so very familiar—the pervasive uncertainty a harbinger of worse to come.

The newspapers tell the tale of people stocking up on supplies, of shortages and fear, the *Washington Post* describing the political climate in D.C.—men and women working late into the night, like Nick, the lights in the executive office buildings on far later than normal.

There is talk of people leaving Washington, and at the same time, life seems to go on as usual. When I walk in the mornings, after Nick has left, before the sun comes up, I am struck by the people going about their daily lives—heading to school and work— despite the specter looming before all of us, the sense that the world could end at any moment. There's some comfort in this civility, in the enduring sense that people must carve out joys where they can, undertake the responsibilities to which they have pledged themselves.

I have heard nothing from London. Nothing from the CIA. Their silence, the unknown ramifications of me shooting Ramon, is just another trouble in a heap of them. We don't speak of Ramon; Nick is carrying the world on his shoulders enough as it is.

And still—the dreams haunt me. Sometimes when I look down, I see my brother's dead body. Other times when I look down, I see Ramon's. Have I killed someone's brother? A beloved friend? Am I the villain in their life as Fidel is in mine?

Nick's eyes flicker open, staring up into my face, a faint smile on his lips, renewed interest in his expression.

I smile. "I thought you were tired."

"I'm not that tired."

I remove Nick's tie, my fingers traveling to the buttons of his dress shirt, loosening the collar, undoing the line down his chest, exposing his undershirt.

He sighs again as my fingers trail down his abdomen.

In this moment, he is mine to care for, his worries mine to soothe, his aches mine to heal. It's so very dangerous to fall into the false promise of this, and yet, in the face of the world ending before us, I cannot find it in me to care.

I'll pay the bill for this dalliance when it comes due, but right now, I can't regret one single moment we've spent together.

Four days have passed since the president addressed the American people. Four days of wondering if the Soviets will accede to Kennedy's demands and dismantle the weapons, of waiting to see if I will hear from the CIA, if the microfilm I sent them was of any use, of fearing the police will show up on Nick's doorstep to arrest me.

While war has not yet come, the threat is still present in all of our minds. Nick refers to ExComm meetings, speaks vaguely of talks with the Soviets, but the world he inhabits now is one I am not allowed to enter, and the toll it has taken on him is all too obvious.

I attempt to stay busy while he is at work, settling into a routine even as I long for my days in London spent attending classes, rather than this sitting and waiting for a man to come home. The moments when we are together are perhaps the happiest I have ever known, but in the moments when he is gone, when I am alone with my thoughts, the doubts creep in.

On the one hand, it seems foolish to worry about such prosaic things given the current state of the world, and on the other hand, I can't not worry about them even as I lock the doubts inside me—our relationship is the last thing Nick needs to concern himself with in the middle of this mess.

And yet, I do worry.

I am not the sort of woman who is happy when relegated to the fringes of a man's life—what woman is, truly?—and the uncertainty of our future together weighs on me more than I imagined it would, the insecurity of my future equally so. This life in Washington is not permanent.

In December, society will move south to Palm Beach for the season. Will Nick return to the big house on the beach, and if so, should I go with him? And if I do, how will I handle seeing my family again? I miss Elisa and Maria desperately, perhaps even Isabel, but my parents are another matter altogether, my inability to forgive my mother an emotion that has not lessened with time.

I turn down Nick's street, offering a smile for a man passing by me, shuffling the bags of groceries I purchased from one hand to the other. I don't know when Nick will return home from his meetings tonight, but I have a dinner planned regardless, even if my culinary attempts so far have been less than stellar. Somehow, I've become the housewife I never wanted to be.

I pull the apartment key Nick gave me from my purse, and when I look up, a man is in front of me, sitting on the steps outside the brownstone, his hat in hand, his face unmistakably familiar.

As I suspected, I didn't need to go looking for the CIA.

They've found me.

chapter twenty-seven

There's no point in engaging in pleasantries with Mr. Dwyer, and I have no desire to do so. We greet each other perfunctorily, and he waits behind me as I slip the key into the lock, a slight tremor in my fingers as I turn the key and push the heavy wooden door open, Mr. Dwyer trailing behind me. I set the bags down on the round table in the entryway. He closes the door.

"You can imagine my surprise when I learned you were here in Washington D.C., residing with our esteemed and *virtuous* young senator," he drawls in a voice that is decidedly unsurprised.

I ignore that.

"What happened back in London? Did you find the—"

"Dead body in your flat? Yes, we did. Luckily for you, we disposed of it before anyone realized what happened there." His gaze sharpens. "How exactly did you kill a trained Cuban intelligence agent?"

"I have no idea," I answer honestly. "Luck, I suppose."

"That, and I imagine he didn't see you coming."

"That, too. Did you get the package?"

"We did."

"What happened to our scheduled drop?"

"World affairs."

"What happened in my flat—"

"You did well. Did what you were supposed to do."

"I killed a man."

"It's regrettable, but it happens. Based on your reports, I gather you were fairly convinced he had double-crossed us, that he was working for the Cubans, that he was the one who blew Claudia's cover."

"I *thought* he was, but I didn't have any proof, didn't—"

He huffs a little laugh. "Proof? What is it you think we do, Miss Perez? We don't operate in the world of signed confession letters and guarantees; we trust our instincts, draw our own conclusions, make the best of the information we are given. You did what you were supposed to do. You did what we needed—the intelligence you got from the Soviet colonel will prove very useful in the coming days. I'm not here to litigate your decision to kill Ramon Martinez. It was the right call."

"Then why are you here?"

"To appeal to your patriotic sense of duty."

"Because of the nuclear weapons."

"Partly. If it isn't the nuclear weapons, it will be something else. Fidel has become a dangerous threat. If you have a rabid dog in the neighborhood, you put it down before it bites someone. We need to put Fidel down. After London, you've proved yourself to be more capable than I anticipated. We're ready to send you into Cuba."

"I thought the president favored diplomacy in this course."

Nick speaks of international organizations and calls to world leaders, not assassination plots.

"There are factions within the Agency that do not share the president's views on this matter. This is an opportunity to rid ourselves of this problem once and for all. Castro wants to export his particular brand of revolution to Latin America and the rest of the world. For obvious reasons, we cannot allow that to happen. Nor can we allow the Soviets to use Cuba's proximity to the United States to antagonize us or the rest of the region. The Soviets wish to establish their dominance throughout the world, and they've brought the fight here in order to do so."

"What does that mean for me?"

"We want you to go to Cuba. By our estimation, the majority of the island does not support Castro. If we can destabilize him, if we can kill him, then, well, it's all over. You and your family can go home."

"If I go now, won't it look like it was an assassination attempt? I thought you wanted to avoid that."

"This nuclear situation has changed everything. Fidel has shown how far he is willing to take this, and we can't let such an action stand."

"How soon do you want me to move against him?"

"It depends on how the negotiations proceed. We are willing to give the president a few more days to reach a peaceful solution, but if he cannot do so, we will send you in regardless of the appearance it conveys. And if he does reach a peaceful solution, we still have need of you. We all know it is only a temporary solution; another crisis will arise shortly. If you want your chance against Fidel, this is it."

"What will I do? Will I receive training? How will I get close to him when I arrive in Cuba?"

"One of our sources will make sure you are granted access to Fidel. We have assets embedded in the Cuban government who are not loyal to Fidel, who support our cause. I have vetted them thoroughly. Mistakes like Ramon won't happen again.

"We'll use a fishing vessel to sneak you into Cuba. Once you arrive, there will be someone waiting for you who will assist you and help you gain admittance to Fidel's suite. From there on, it's a matter of slipping one of the pills in his drink, and that's it."

"How will I get out? Presumably, I will be captured if they find me in a room with Fidel Castro's dead body."

"We'll have an extraction plan in place, same as with any other asset."

"And if that plan doesn't work?"

"Then you will likely die. Either at the hands of one of Fidel's security forces or Fidel himself."

"And what happens after that? Is there another assassin waiting in the wings?"

"We have other plans in place, other assets we can send in."

"Have there been others before me?"

"Yes."

"Women?"

"A woman. Yes."

"And what did Fidel do to her once he learned of her intentions?"

"He let her go." Dwyer's expression darkens. "We made the mistake of trusting a woman who, despite her agreement, held too much softness for Fidel in her heart. We won't make the mistake again."

"Because you don't believe I possess such softness?"

"Because you strike me as the kind of woman who never forgets when she is crossed, and what Fidel did to you and your family was a truly abominable thing. Who could forget a murdered twin?"

"Have I ever told you how much I dislike being manipulated?"

He smiles. "Do you, now?"

"I do."

"Besides, given the London incident, we now know you aren't squeamish about taking a life."

I flinch.

"You know, despite what you may think, I like you. You did good work in London. There's no reason that we can't make this more permanent, that we can't continue the job we're doing together if—when—Fidel falls.

"You could be one of my assets. You speak several languages. Know the right people to be able to travel in influential circles and pick up interesting tidbits of conversation. It doesn't even have to be Cuba; we could send you to Europe. Your mother has a cousin who is married to an ambassador there, doesn't she?

"Besides, even if you succeed with Fidel, things will be tumultuous in Cuba for a very long time as the power struggle shakes itself out, as people adjust to their new leadership. Having eyes and ears within the country would be useful to us."

"You don't know me as well as you think you do, if you believe I would spy on my countrymen and help the Americans."

He laughs. "The Americans? Look around you, Miss Perez. You're practically living with an American senator. Who took you and your family in when your lives were in danger? Where do you call home now? Do you really think your father's going to leave his growing sugar empire behind? What about your sister Isabel, who is married to an American? Or Elisa and her child? Juan Ferrera has never set foot in Cuba. Do you really think he will move his family to Cuba if Fidel falls? How many of your friends have left and found new lives abroad? Do you really think things will go back to the way they were before? That people will simply accept the old way of doing things without a fight?"

"I didn't agree with the old way of doing things."

"Perhaps not. Maybe you liked to tell yourself that, even as you benefited from your father's wealth and power.

"There is no room for idealism in this world anymore. This fight with the Soviets is not about Cuba. It is broader, and the Soviets are a formidable enemy. Do you think they will simply let their dreams of supporting communism in Cuba fall? We will not defeat them in one blow, in one country, but over many, many years. You look to Cuba, and I look beyond that to the world. You have an opportunity here to do more. Cuba is one island. If you work for me, you will accomplish far more than that."

"You look too far ahead. I have not yet killed Fidel, and there is no promise that I will be able to do so."

"Whether you kill Fidel or not, the battle *will* continue on. Only a fool would not look ahead. Is your hesitation your focus on Cuba, or is it something else entirely?"

"I'm not sure what you're referring to."

"Is your relationship with Preston going to be a problem?"

"Why would it be a problem? And how did you know to find me here?"

Dwyer smiles. "We've known about the two of you for quite some time, of course. That we've chosen to remain quiet about it is a testament to our belief in your ability to complete this mission. If you were unable to, however . . ."

The threat lingers in the air between us, unspoken yet so very clear.

"At first you dangle a carrot in front of me—the opportunity for a more permanent job—and this is, what, the stick?"

"If you'd like to look at it that way, then fine. Senator Preston's political ambitions are quite impressive. That former fiancée of his would have been a great help. Her family was so well-connected, and she was quite lovely. Why did their engagement end so suddenly?"

I flinch again.

"The public wants a moral man. A family man. Your Senator Preston has the right look, the desired pedigree, and a voting record that truly is quite impressive. It would be a shame for anything to tarnish the reputation he's built, to threaten his dreams of reaching the White House."

"I wouldn't threaten me. I could also go to the press about your involvement in all of this."

"You could," he acknowledges. "But then I would be forced to share the details of our arrangement, and Senator Preston's involvement wouldn't look good from any angle. Nor would the events in London, your involvement with the Miami group. Scandals do have a way of removing that layer of shine he's worked so hard to develop."

I laugh, despite the sinking feeling in my stomach, the urge to cry.

"You do realize the vast majority of Washington is sleeping with someone they aren't married to," I bluff. "He's a single man now."

"Yes, but that's Washington. Perhaps your affair was contained to whispers at parties, and yes, he is now single. But you vastly underestimate the damage something like this can do when the secret of it is not protected within tight circles. Besides, it's not the same as a man having some fun with one of Hollywood's most prominent actresses or the like. People can understand that even if they denounce it in their church pews on Sunday morning.

"But a future president being involved with an assassin? A woman who leaves dead bodies in her flat? A senator entangled in espionage? Who's to say you aren't working for Fidel's government? After all, you were involved with that communist group in Miami. Who is to say a foreign asset hasn't already compromised Senator Preston? People believe what you tell them, Miss Perez. They don't want to concern themselves with matters of government and policy; they simply want someone to tell them that the men for whom they do their civic duty and cast a vote are good, God-fearing men. My voice can be a powerful one."

"And you won't hesitate to use your voice if I don't go to Cuba."

"Exactly."

"You must be very good at your job."

He smiles again. "I am."

And I was very foolish to let my heart get in the way of all this.

"Nicholas Preston is a good man."

"He is. Hopefully, he will continue to be one. However, it really doesn't matter at the end of the day. All that matters is whether he is a useful man, whether his interests align with ours—"

"And whether you can control him."

"You can control anyone, Miss Perez. It is merely an exercise in finding their weakness. Yours is him. His is you. And Fidel's is that he likes women and has an ego that clouds his judgment."

"And what's yours?"

"That I like the game far too much."

"How do you do this? Do you never feel the weight of the lives you wreck, of the countries whose destinies you change on a whim?"

"A whim? Hardly. This is just one country in a long line of them, Miss Perez. One threat in a never-ending series of dangers that keeps me up at night worrying about the nation I have sworn to serve and protect. You see us as the villains in this piece, and perhaps to you Cubans we are, but ask yourself this—

"Have you not seen the lengths to which you would go in order to protect your country, your family, those you love? How is what we do any different? I do not do this for some evil machination, nor do the men and women embedded with our enemies at this very moment, learning their secrets and gathering intelligence that will save American lives, do it for theirs. They risk their lives, their families, everything because they believe in the cause that they support.

"It's not a matter of politics or ideology, but a duty to one's country, a sense of patriotism that supersedes all else. A willingness to engage in great sacrifice and risk great personal peril. We are a nation at war—the Soviet Union seeks to destroy our way of life, to reduce our position in the world, to spread communism far and wide. It is my duty to defeat them, and I owe it to the men and women fighting in the field to make sure they are protected and supported.

"So here's your chance. What are you willing to do for your country? Your family? Your people, Miss Perez? For Senator Preston? What will you sacrifice for Cuba?"

All in all, it's a pretty enough speech, and he knows it. But at the end of the day, it's not his words that convince me, not even close. It's the fact that I've given so much of my life to this cause that the need to see it to the end is inevitable.

In the end, it's my decision, and I already made it a long time ago.

"We have a deal."

chapter twenty-eight

The thing that has always surprised me most about politics is the sheer unpredictability of it all. Events creep by slowly; so slowly you're convinced nothing is happening at all, change moving at an unbearable snail's pace. And then, suddenly, a transformation comes, moving so swiftly, so unexpectedly, that your world shifts, and you struggle to play catch-up, to understand how everything altered so quickly.

We move from President Kennedy warning the nation of the threat of nuclear war to waiting. So much waiting. And then, just five days after he addressed the nation, we receive the news that an American reconnaissance plane was shot down over Cuba, the pilot, Major Rudolf Anderson, killed, and war appears inevitable.

"They're preparing to invade Cuba," Nick announces over dinner late that evening.

"Do you think the invasion will really happen this time?"

"I don't know. The president's advisors whisper different things in his ears. Kennedy favors peace, diplomacy. And at the same time, there is much fear surrounding him. We cannot afford to be weak in front of the Soviets."

It's the entrée I need to tell him of Mr. Dwyer's visit. I've kept it from him since yesterday, nervous to shatter the fragile peace we've developed between us.

"They want me to go to Cuba."

Nick sets his glass on the table gently.

"They?"

"The CIA."

"So Dwyer is hard at work. I didn't realize you were in contact with him again. What did he say about London?"

"They took care of it. It won't come back on me. Everything is handled."

"Good."

We've spoken little about the day I killed Ramon since we returned to Washington, but the relief in Nick's voice tells me that it's been on his mind as it has been on mine.

"Dwyer came to the house yesterday," I add.

"He turned up here?"

"Yes. He was waiting on the steps for me when I arrived home from the market."

"That man has no shame, does he?" Nick pauses. "So they know about us."

"I think everyone knows about us at this point. We haven't necessarily been discreet. Does it bother you?"

"It doesn't bother me, but it complicates things."

"I think everything is already pretty complicated now."

"Yes, it is." With careful precision, he slices into the meat I overcooked, his knife forced to saw to and fro to cut through the dried bits.

"What did he want?" he asks.

"They want me to go to Cuba," I repeat.

"Of course they do. And what do you want?"

Silence falls between us.

"You didn't tell him 'no,' did you?"

"No, I didn't."

"Don't you see what a mistake this is?"

"The only mistake is the fact that Fidel has been able to remain in power for so long."

"Are those your words or the CIA's? After London, how can you put yourself at risk again? You saw what comes of the work you do for them. You saw what the stakes are. You got lucky. You could have been killed. Do you really think you can make it into Cuba and back out again? That you can kill Fidel Castro?"

"I have to try. The CIA thinks I have a chance. What do you expect? I've always been clear with you where my loyalties lie."

"And what about *my* loyalties? Or that this is bigger than Cuba? The Soviets have nuclear weapons trained on us. They shot down one of our reconnaissance planes. The situation is volatile enough as it is, and the only way a safe conclusion will be reached is if cooler heads prevail. This is no time for the Agency or for Dwyer to insert themselves into the diplomatic solutions being crafted. The CIA has been allowed to run rampant for far too long. They've become too powerful, too arrogant. They think they're the ones running the show these days."

"And perhaps the president has allowed it by doing so little and creating a vacuum where the CIA could step in. The administration is talking about potentially invading Cuba. That's hardly a diplomatic solution. Why can't I be one of those solutions? Why are some more acceptable and others not?"

"Because you're risking your life heedlessly. You aren't a spy, and you aren't an assassin."

"Are you sure about that? Because I did a pretty good impersonation of one in London. You killed men in war. Why is what I am doing any different?"

"This isn't war, Beatriz. Not yet."

"Why isn't it war? Because we're fighting with other weapons? Because we don't have planes and tanks?"

"Tell me you aren't seriously considering this. That you can't be this foolish."

"I'm not foolish. You knew this about me all along."

"I hoped you would realize your life was worth more than this. I thought after what happened in London, after you killed a man, you would come to your senses."

"And I thought you would understand, considering how much you're devoted to your work, the things you're passionate about."

"I do understand. But that doesn't mean I don't worry about you. You won't let anyone take care of you."

"I am neither a child nor an invalid. I don't want to be taken care of."

"Then what do you want?"

"You, you stupid man. Just you." I reach for him, my fingers connecting with the warm skin at his neck, threading through his silky hair, pulling him close to me.

"When will you go?" he asks, as though he knows my answer was given a long time ago, his mouth against mine, his arms holding me tight.

"When they send for me," I answer.

"Then I will pray for peace."

Perhaps it was Nick's prayers, or Kennedy's cool head, or the success of diplomatic channels, or assets run by men like Mr. Dwyer, but it appears we are to have peace.

"Can you believe it?" Elisa asks over the phone the next day, after the crisis has ended.

The Soviets are to move the missiles out of Cuba. The invasion plans are abandoned, and whatever my role is in all of this, I've yet to hear anything from Dwyer. If President Kennedy is to have the appearance of peace, then the CIA will likely have to put their plans on hold. I can't imagine Mr. Dwyer is pleased. In a way, neither am I.

While I certainly didn't want a nuclear war to break out, I had hoped that this was the final straw, that the United States would finally rid us of Fidel. And once again, we are disappointed. Nothing is changed. Fidel lives to fight another day.

"I thought we would die," Elisa says.

"I wondered it myself a time or two," I admit.

"And now that the crisis is passed, will you stay in Washington D.C.?" Elisa asks. "Or will you go back to London?"

"We haven't spoken of it. I haven't decided."

"What do you want to do?"

"I don't know. I liked London, but it didn't quite feel like home. I'm not sure what does anymore, to be honest."

Now that the mission with Ramon is over, there's really no need for me to return. As much as I enjoyed attending school, there are other universities I can attend, other places to live. The problem with a cover is that it's really not a life. You wear it like a second skin, make yourself believe the truth of it, but once the mission is over, the cover is gone, and you're left with a sudden need to reinvent yourself.

"It's funny how your sense of home can change, isn't it?" Elisa muses. "Havana was home, and it still is, but there's something about this house, the life Juan, Miguel, and I have built here, that feels right, too."

"I'm glad you're happy, Elisa. Glad you found what you were looking for."

"Sometimes it's a choice, Beatriz. You can't always predict how things will work out, but you can still forge a life for yourself, still find a way to be happy."

"I'm too tired to speak in riddles, Elisa. Too confused."

She laughs. "Patience was never your strength, was it?"

"So you think I should marry and have children?"

"No."

"Then you think I should go back to London?"

"No, I don't think that, either. I don't know what you should do. But I want you to be happy. You've been stuck since we left Havana, since Alejandro died, and you have to move forward."

"Maybe that's the problem then. Maybe I want to be stuck. Because I can't move forward. This thing with Nick and me—I don't fit in his life. And I don't want to hurt him. He's a good man, and the things he wants, his dreams for this country, are important ones, too. I don't want to damage his chances of becoming president one day."

"Then you have to let him go."

"I don't want to do that, either."

"I know. It was easier when we were girls, wasn't it? When we could do as we wished with little regard for the consequences. I miss those days. The freedom of them. But we're not girls anymore. At some point, you will have to choose. I know you've never liked being backed into a corner, but sometimes you have to make a choice. It's not fair to him otherwise."

"I know."

"And you can always come home. Despite what you may think, you aren't alone. What our parents did, the way they handled this—it doesn't mean I feel the same way. You will always have a home here. Maria misses you so much. So does Isabel."

"Somehow I doubt that."

"She's as stubborn as you are, albeit in a different way, but Isabel does miss you. You can't stay angry with each other forever."

"We'll see about that."

"Come home. You can visit your nephew. He misses you. I miss you. You should see Maria now. She's all grown up and ready to break hearts. Besides, the season is about to start. Your Senator Preston will likely return to Palm Beach. You can still see each other."

"And our parents?"

"They'll get over it. They'll have to. You're a Perez."

"Our mother blames me for Alejandro's death. For getting him involved with the rebels. I don't know how either one of us can move past that."

"What happened to Alejandro was *not* your fault. Getting involved with the rebels was his choice, and more than anyone, you did everything you could to help him. She is wrong to insinuate otherwise."

"Wrong or not, it doesn't really matter, does it? She'll always look at me and see his death, always consider me responsible."

"No one else feels that way, I promise you."

"Father is angry about the scandal of my affair with Nick."

"He's changed since Cuba," Elisa admits. "Business always mattered to him, but now it's become more like an obsession. I think he's afraid of what will happen next, attempting to shore up his resources and defenses before the next crisis strikes."

"Is this to be our life then, existing between tragedies?"

"I hope not. I want better for Miguel. I want better for myself."

Mr. Dwyer's words come back to me now.

"You're never going to leave Miami, are you?"

"I don't know. I would love to go back to Cuba. I want to walk along the Malecón, want to see our house again, see Ana, and

Magda. I want to go home, but things are different now. Juan has never been to Cuba. It's not his home. And Miguel—

"I'm afraid for my son. Afraid to return after everything that has happened. And it's hard. Too many ghosts. Too many memories."

We've never spoken about it, but in the weeks after Fidel took power, something changed in Elisa, the revolution affecting her in different ways than it did the rest of us. We all cried, all mourned our brother, but her tears came before Alejandro was killed. I used to hear her crying quietly in her room at night during those weeks.

"Come home. You don't have to make any decisions; it can just be to visit. I'll ready the guest room."

"I hardly think returning to South Florida will quell the gossip."

"What gossip? Isabel is married. A fool for marrying a man who was more concerned with his reputation than her heart, but married all the same. Maria is older now. She'll have to learn to survive in society on her own merits. And quite frankly, I couldn't care less. And if our parents are embarrassed, that's their problem. Come home."

chapter twenty-nine

Now that the missile crisis is resolved, our attention turns to other things, the real world intruding, the problems we once faced creeping back in. When I was a child, I believed if you wanted something badly enough, if you worked hard enough for it, if you pushed your way past the obstacles presented to you, well, it would be yours. But now I'm learning it's not simply a matter of will or desire; some things are perpetually out of our reach, and no matter how badly we wish it were otherwise, there are some battles whose outcomes are decided not in our hands, but in the stars.

As much as I wish it were otherwise, we are defined by these roles we play; the tensions between Nick and me creep into our relationship despite our best wishes.

"Have you heard anything from Dwyer?" Nick asks when we're lying in bed one night in November, two weeks after the missile crisis has ended.

"No, I haven't."

Each day that I've walked home from the market or the store,

I've wondered if Dwyer would be waiting for me on the front steps again, only to be greeted by bare stone.

"You sound disappointed."

"Not disappointed—just—it felt good to be doing something," I finally answer. "To not be so helpless."

"Is that how you feel? Helpless?"

"How could I not? There are still men suffering in Fidel's prisons." I don't say Eduardo's name, but it doesn't matter. He lingers between us anyway. "So many of my countrymen and women still suffer under Fidel's rule."

"I know they do, and I understand your frustrations, but you have to be patient. These things take time. We're doing everything we can."

"Are you? You worry about the United States looking weak in front of the Soviets, and yet, Kennedy hasn't felt the same way about appearing weak in front of Cuba, has he? Where do the Bay of Pigs prisoners fit in all of this? They're still there, languishing in Fidel's jails, and Kennedy hasn't exactly flexed his might.

"We've been patient. It's been almost four years since Fidel took power. Don't tell me to be patient."

"There are other problems going on in the world, Beatriz. Other battles to be fought. It isn't just Cuba."

"At least some people are willing to do something."

"Who? The CIA? The CIA isn't the answer to all of your problems. The Soviets knew about the Bay of Pigs a week in advance. The CIA knew they knew. They chose not to tell the president, to let it play out even when they had to realize what the outcome would be. You want to be angry at someone, be angry with your Mr. Dwyer and his friends."

"What is Kennedy doing to get them out?"

"These things take time, Beatriz."

"Fidel wanted tractors for the men. How hard is that to do?"

"Yes, he did, and now he wants sixty-two million dollars. For now. But no one knows what Castro really wants. He aims to make trouble more than anything else."

"Then do more."

"I'm trying. We're all trying. Bobby Kennedy is personally do-ing everything he can to help. As are many others."

"Are you?"

"What's that supposed to mean?"

"Just that Cuba and its people feel like an afterthought. You were all content to send Cubans to Playa Girón to risk their lives in order to solve your Castro problem for you, but now that you've all failed them, you aren't willing to do what you need to in order to save them."

"Is that really what you think of me? That I've turned my back on Cuba?"

I hear the unspoken words in his voice—

That I've turned my back on you.

"They've been rotting in cells for over a year and a half," I reply. "They're sick; they're suffering."

"And we've been working on it."

"Really? Your President Kennedy seems far more concerned with other matters. From what I hear, the family members of the prisoners are doing more to get them out than the U.S. Govern-ment that started all of this."

"It isn't just Cuba Jack has to worry about. You have no idea how many troubles he has on his plate.

"This plan was put into motion before he even took office. He had his reservations, but it was the CIA's baby, and your Mr. Dwyer certainly did what he could to push it along."

"He isn't my Mr. Dwyer."

"Isn't he? You're a part of my life, Beatriz. Do you really think I'm not going to worry about you?"

"Don't act like I'm some problem you have to fix, another person for you to take care of, some silly woman who needs a man to look after her."

"I never said that."

"But it's how you make me feel. Like we can't be equals because I'm a woman and you're a man."

"It isn't like that. You know it isn't like that. I worry about you. Constantly. You think you can take on Fidel, but you can't."

"Eduardo thought I could."

"Is that what this is about then? Eduardo?"

"He's in prison. Fighting for our country. He's like family. What kind of friend would I be if I didn't think of him?"

"I don't begrudge you for being his friend. But don't tell me it's just friendship between you."

"He's been sentenced to thirty years in prison. I hardly think he is preoccupied with romance at the moment."

"And when he's released? Is he going to pull you back into his world?"

"You cannot possibly be jealous of a man in prison."

"It's not jealousy. It's concern. There are groups of exiles who are being monitored closely for their activities inside the United States. And before he left for Cuba, Eduardo's name kept turning up on those lists. They're smuggling things into the country. Weapons. Explosives. There are rumors that they have planned attacks inside the United States to make it look like pro-Castro forces are at work in order to spur our action. Eduardo was in the thick of everything. I don't want him dragging you down with him."

Considering the night I went with Eduardo to pick up the shipment of dynamite, I'm not exactly surprised by this information. "The CIA trusts him," I retort.

Nick laughs. "The CIA doesn't trust anyone. They're using Eduardo because he's well-connected, but don't think for a second that they aren't also watching him, that they aren't also watching *you*."

"So, what, you'd rather he stay in Cuba because he's fighting for his country?"

"Of course not. I'd just rather him stay out of our lives for good."

"He was my brother's best friend. We grew up together. He's like family."

"I know. And I love how loyal you are. But he doesn't deserve your loyalty. Not when he risks your safety over and over again. So yes, I worry about what will happen when the prisoners come home. When he's back in your life again." Nick is silent for a beat. "We haven't talked about it, but let's be honest. You came back here because you had to leave London, because the world was on the brink of ending, and neither one of us was thinking clearly. But neither one of those things are at issue anymore. So what happens next?"

"I don't know. I spoke to Elisa the other day, and she mentioned me coming home. Said she missed me."

"Would you like to go to Palm Beach?"

"Only if you come with me."

In December, we return to Palm Beach for the start of the social season. Nick opens up the giant house on the beach I have always thought of as ours. The house was shuttered the day we said goodbye after the Bay of Pigs, everything as I remembered it, nothing out of place, a museum of sorts to our affair. The few clothes I had kept there still hang in the closet and reside in the dresser, and I am grateful for the signs that he did not attempt to erase me in my absence, the evidence of the role I play in his life and the space I occupy in his heart.

Now that the missile crisis is over, the town is abuzz with the glamorous Kennedys, decorated by women walking down Worth Avenue in brightly colored shifts designed by Lilly Pulitzer. The threat of Soviet aggression is, for the moment, contained, and the party is back on, dinners at Ta-boo followed by lunch at the Seminole Golf Club the next day.

Nick travels between D.C. and Palm Beach regularly, and I entertain myself with my sisters when he's gone. It's surprisingly easy to fall into a routine again, to greet now-married Isabel as though nothing has happened between us even when so much time has elapsed—the wedding I should have been a part of yet never received an invitation to pushed from both of our minds. As for my parents, we do the careful dance of politely ignoring and avoiding each other when we are on the island, an arrangement that works surprisingly well. I see Maria when I am visiting Elisa and Isabel, spend my days with my sisters or sunning myself on the veranda of the Palm Beach house as I once again settle into a version of the life I had before I left Nick. A few days before Christmas, Nick returns to me, and we spend most of the holidays curled up in each other's arms, looking at the tree we decorated, our gifts for each other piled atop the skirt. The domesticity is, once again, both comforting and terrifying.

"We should do one Christmas in Connecticut," Nick muses, twirling a strand of my hair around his finger.

"Isn't it cold in Connecticut at Christmas?"

Never mind the implication contained there.

He laughs. "You don't have to sound so horrified by it. It is cold, but everything turns white from the snow. You should experience at least one white Christmas in your lifetime."

Will we have another Christmas together? Somehow, I can't bear looking so far ahead. I still have not heard from Dwyer, but I feel as though I have a date with Fidel penciled in on my calendar, my future already set.

On Christmas Day, Nick goes to see his family, and I borrow one of his cars and drive down to Miami to Elisa's house in Coral Gables. She's hosting a big celebration for the holidays—and to celebrate the resolution of negotiations between Cuba and the United States.

Nick and I don't speak of it, but there's another reason for my visit to my sister.

Fidel has finally released the Bay of Pigs prisoners. Eduardo is coming home.

I'm standing in Elisa's living room, staring at the tinsel on their tree, when I hear my name in a familiar voice I haven't heard for a long time.

"Beatriz."

Eduardo takes a step toward me, and then another one, a limp in his stride that wasn't there before.

He's slighter than I remembered, not nearly as bad as I expected, though. My father had that same hollowed-out look about him when he was returned to us after his stint in prison, and that was only after a week or so. Eduardo spent over eighteen months in Fidel's prison.

Despite the weight he's lost, he looks much the same as I remembered him. Still handsome. Still Eduardo.

I swallow past the tears clogging my throat.

The weight of the stares on us is heavy, the curiosity there, and the whispers, causing my cheeks to burn. I am notorious—the lover of a prominent politician, the rumored lover of one of the Bay of Pigs prisoners. The gossip about us will be all over town by tomorrow.

Eduardo doesn't speak, but then again he doesn't have to. Time has not lessened the bond between us, the friendship that once felt so much more like family. I can read the tilt of his head, the question in his eyes.

I nod.

I follow Eduardo out of the room, down the hall, to Juan's study. Eduardo closes the door behind us.

I sink down on the couch, the tremor in my legs finally getting the best of me. Even though I knew Eduardo would be here, even though I came here for this, the shock of seeing him has caught me off guard in ways I never expected.

"You look well," he says.

My heart clenches.

"Beautiful as always," he adds.

The words hurt, and somehow, I have a feeling he means for them to hurt.

"I thought of you. Every day I was in that hellhole. I told the other men about you. Beatriz Perez. Sugar queen. Too beautiful to be believed."

"What was it like?" I ask as some part of me embraces the pain.

"You don't really want to know that. Don't you have enough dead bodies haunting your dreams as it is?"

"What was it like?" I repeat, my voice growing stronger with each word he hurls my way, as I embrace his pain, cultivating it inside me. Perhaps I have grown too complacent, too sedate, these days and nights I have spent in my lover's arms, Cuba and her future somewhere in the back of my mind. Perhaps I have lost my edge somewhere in all of this.

Eduardo turns from me, striding over to one of the bookshelves that flank Juan's impressive desk. My sister's husband will likely be chosen by our father to take over the management of Perez Sugar when our father dies, to pass it on to Miguel when he comes of age. It was Alejandro's legacy until he didn't want it anymore, until he was murdered, and now it is to be my brother-in-law's.

I've never felt the pull of sugar the way our father has; the industry has done enough damage to Cuba and its people. I'd wash my hands of the whole thing if I could, but I suppose there are larger practicalities at play here.

"It was hell," Eduardo finally answers, his back still to me. "The moment my feet hit that beach, I regretted the stupid impulse of heroism that pushed me to take such a ridiculous action. I should have stayed here, and drunk champagne, and danced with homely girls looking for husbands." He pivots, and his lips twist in a sneer, his gaze running over me, condemning me for dancing and drinking champagne while he bled.

"What a damned waste," he mutters, more to himself than to me.

"They knew," he continues. "The Americans. From the beginning, they had to have known we were outmanned, outgunned, that we had no chance without their involvement and support. That the little they gave us was not nearly enough. They abandoned us, left us to die on that beach, and for what? So they could rid themselves of the exiles causing trouble in South Florida. So they wouldn't get their hands dirty. So they could preserve their ridiculous image in front of the international community. As though the rest of the world doesn't know all too well what they are capable of, where their loyalties lie, how they prioritize their own national interest above everyone else's.

"'What was it like?'" he mimics. "You know what Fidel does to his prisoners. You know what it was like."

I do.

"Perhaps it was better because they were bargaining for us, because we had some value, at least—what was it they wanted first? Tractors for our lives. Then money. So much money. I should be grateful, of course, that I had some value. That they didn't just let me die there. Kennedy and his powerful political friends *saved me*."

It's coming. Like a storm building over the water, it's coming. I recognize the anger in him, the uncontainable, dangerous whiplash of rage pushing and shoving its way outside of him.

We are so very alike.

"What good allies we have in these Americans. They said we would hit the beach and we would march straight to Havana. They told us people would join us along the way, come out of their homes and greet us as liberators just as they did for Fidel and his men." He snorts. "We should have known it sounded too good to be true. That when they told us the sky would be filled with planes, that we would have more support than we needed, than we knew what to do with, it was just another empty promise from the Americans. We should never have been foolish enough to hope."

Does he see me as one of them—the Americans—because I love one of them? Does he view me as a traitor to my people?

"After we were captured, Fidel and his lackeys marched us with their guns trained on us, our hands tied behind our backs, surveying us as though we were animals being led to slaughter."

It's not enough to take our country from us; Fidel and his compatriots are also determined to take our pride, to break our spirit.

"They attached monetary value to each of us as though we were chattel. The lowliest among us were worth a mere $25,000. The rest of us, well, it turns out I was very expensive."

"Eduardo."

My heart breaks for him.

"Did he know?"

I flinch at the question, at the condemnation contained in his gaze.

"I don't know."

Liar.

"You don't want to know. Which is, in its own way, answer enough, isn't it?"

"I left him. When it happened, we fought. I left him. I understand the anger you feel right now. You don't think I was angry watching what happened to all of you, helpless, stuck here? I wanted to go with you. I wanted to fight. This is my fight as much as it is yours."

"Then do your part. This is no time to sit on the sidelines. To wait. This is the time for action. You can't claim to be loyal to Cuba and sleep with one of the men responsible for this mess we're in. You must choose. Are you loyal to him or are you loyal to your people? To Cuba? You say you left him, but that's his bracelet on your wrist, isn't it? You left, but you went back."

"What would you have me do?"

"I don't know, Beatriz. You always complained you weren't allowed to participate in our plans, that you were shut out because you were a woman. Here's your chance. You're sleeping with one of the most influential men in the Senate, a man who has the ear of the president; do something with it."

"We're back on that, then. You want me to whore myself out for some votes in the Senate, for a new policy on Cuba."

"There are worse ways to serve our cause," he snaps, his gaze darkening.

"It changed you. Playa Girón."

"How could it not?"

The flash of guilt is back again. I made love to Nick while Eduardo went to war, while he languished in one of Fidel's prisons. Perhaps I owe him this.

"What do you want from him?"

"The same thing I want from all of them. For them to fix this."

I once asked the same thing of Nick, for the Americans to use their power and intervene against Castro, but now, hearing such a request fall from Eduardo's lips, I am struck by how much we continue to rely upon the Americans, and the likelihood that doing so will never be in our best interests.

"Shouldn't we fix it ourselves?" I ask.

"I don't think we can fix it ourselves. The failed invasion only helped Fidel, gave him more power. If anything, he's stronger now, and he was a formidable opponent before. He has the Soviets backing him. How do we stand a chance if we don't have a great power backing us?"

"I've been in contact with Dwyer. I've been working with him."

"It's not enough. We're past the point of espionage. We're past the point of assassination attempts. If Fidel dies, someone else will merely take his place—his brother or Che."

"Fidel killed Alejandro. Have you forgotten that?"

"No, I haven't. But you're a fool if you think this is about your brother. This is bigger than your grudges, Beatriz."

"I'm aware of that. But don't pretend you don't have your own debts to repay, that you're driven by some altruistic need to save Cuba. I know you far too well for that. You want to see them suffer for what they did to you."

His tone is mocking. "You figured me out."

"We were friends once. I cared for you. We're not friends anymore, are we?"

He laughs. "Friends? I think it's a bit more complex, don't you? I loved you once."

"I didn't—"

"What? Love me back?"

I stumble over the words. "I didn't realize you felt that way about me. That you were serious about us. I thought . . ."

"I've loved you since we were children."

I gape at him. "You never said anything. There were always other women."

"I thought we were inevitable. That I could have my fun, and when we both grew up, we would get married. Start a life together. And then your senator came along; I admit I never saw that one coming. Never thought you would fall in love with a man like him.

"You'll hurt him, you know. You'll hurt him, because no matter how much you think you love him, you're not right for him. You want different things, and in the long run, you'll never make each other happy. He's an ambitious man; he'll need the right wife."

"I know." There's no point in arguing with him, in denying the truth.

Eduardo's expression changes, and suddenly, he looks like the man I remember.

"Did you ever—could you have ever—"

It's easy to read the question in his voice, contained in his eyes.

"I don't know," I answer honestly.

"And now?"

My silence is answer enough, I suppose.

He gives me a sad little smile. "If things were different, if we were in Havana, if Fidel had never taken power, so many 'ifs.'"

In the end, life always comes down to timing.

"It's only fair, I suppose. At one point or another, I was due to have a woman break my heart. Seems fitting it should be you."

"I'm so sorry."

He shakes his head. "Nothing to be sorry about. I should go." He hesitates, a flash of worry in his eyes. "Tread carefully, Beatriz. All of this is likely to get worse before it gets better."

His warning sounds a lot like a good-bye.

"And what will you do now?"

"Keep fighting, of course."

He closes the distance between us, his lips brushing my forehead for a heartbeat before he releases me.

"Will you go?" he asks.

"Where?"

"To Kennedy's 'welcome home' ceremony at the Orange Bowl?"
I shake my head.

He smiles, and in an instant, he looks like the Eduardo I re-member.

"Can't say I blame you. Wish I didn't have to participate in the farce, either. Good-bye, Beatriz."

"Good-bye," I echo, watching him walk away, leaving me alone in my brother-in-law's study, tears trickling down my face at some unknown emotion I'm unable to name.

chapter thirty

After his return home, Eduardo is conspicuously absent from the season this year, not that I blame him. His name is still on everyone's lips; clearly, he's missed by the female half of Palm Beach, his actions in the Bay of Pigs adding to the mystery of it all as he cuts a dashing figure for those who are too ill-informed to know better and see our plight as something to romanticize.

I enroll in university in Miami, relieved to discover my course work will indeed transfer, that I am able to pay my tuition on my own thanks to my arrangement with the CIA. It feels good to be back in the classroom again, strange, though, to discuss in an academic setting the subjects that dominate so much of my private time.

I avoid the social whirl altogether, spending my days and nights with Nick when he isn't in Washington, preferring quiet time with my sisters to the pressures of being on display. There's really little point in secrecy these days—I'm fairly certain the entire town knows I'm living here with Nick, has dissected the fact that Eduardo and I disappeared from Elisa's party at the same time. Nick and I have yet to speak of Eduardo's return, or of my conversation with him at my sister's house. We dance around the things of which we cannot speak—our future, the tension between our countries, the pressures from outside pushing at the seams of the private world we have created here.

When the season ends, I choose not to accompany Nick back to Washington, remaining in the Palm Beach house, spring turning to summer, summer turning to fall. I am a weekend mistress, visited on holidays and congressional recesses.

In the mornings, I walk on the beach, sometimes meeting Maria in the halfway spot between our two houses before she goes to school. If our parents disapprove or think I am a bad influence on her, they've said nothing on the matter. Sometimes I wonder if it is love for me that keeps them from speaking out, or fear for Nick's formidable position in society. While his influence hasn't been able to repair my reputation, he's made it impossible for the old guard to cut me directly.

This morning when I return from my walk, there's a man standing on the veranda. My steps falter as I get closer, as I recognize him, something clenching in my heart. When I was a young girl, our relationship was so much easier; I looked up to him as a larger-than-life figure, wanted to please him, for him to be proud of me.

"I'm surprised you're here," I say, a lump in my throat.

"I wanted to see you," my father replies, his voice rougher than I remembered.

"Why?"

It's the first effort either one of my parents has made to see me since I left Palm Beach over two years ago.

"Because I'm worried about you. Everyone says you're living here with Preston."

"I am."

"I can't say I'm surprised."

"Because you always knew I would come to a bad end?"

"Because you always did as you pleased and cared little for what others thought of it."

"Let me guess, you fault me for being reckless and impulsive."

"No, on the contrary. That quality of yours has always been one of the things I love most about you. Unfortunately, society does not always see things the same way. If you were a man, such indulgences would be praised as bold, ambitious, daring. If we were still in Cuba, you could get away with such behavior as the eccentricity of a wealthy and beautiful woman who has the luxury of doing as she pleases. But we are not in Cuba. And though you are, and always will be, a Perez, that does not mean what it once did. Not here. We must do more. Work harder. We must advance ourselves, because if we do not, these people will trample us. They don't want us here, and they won't let us forget it. Luxuries, and eccentricities, and indulgences are no longer feasible. They are foolish and dangerous."

"You're worried I'm shaming the family name."

"I'm worried about *you*," he counters. "I will not be around forever. When I die, I need to know my family will be taken care of. That my wife will be able to support herself in the manner in which she has grown accustomed, that my daughters will be taken care of, that those I love will be safe."

He turns from me, looking out to the sea.

"I couldn't protect your brother. I won't make that mistake again."

"I'm not Alejandro. Nothing will happen to me."

"You don't think I've heard about the risks you're taking? That your name isn't just being whispered in Palm Beach circles, but in other ones, too?"

"I thought you didn't concern yourself with politics anymore."

"Then you thought wrong. Business is political. Politics is business. I am just very careful now about the friends I make and the alliances I enter into. I wish I could say the same for you."

"You object to my relationship with Nick."

"I object to your relationship with Senator Preston, but that's not why I'm here. That's not the relationship that will get you killed."

"You want me to stay out of Cuba."

"Yes."

"Why?"

"Because if I have heard whispers of your involvement, don't you think Fidel likely has? Don't you think he has spies all over, reporting back to him with possible threats? He is a very dangerous man. I underestimated him once, and it was a costly mistake."

"You once called him a foolish man."

"And now he has proven himself to be dangerous, too, and the United States has foolishly made an adversary out of him, elevating him to more of a threat than he ever was."

"He killed Alejandro."

"Yes, he likely did."

"How do you live with that? How can you stand not avenging your own son?"

"Because you will one day learn the cost is not worth the payoff. Would it bring me pleasure to see Fidel burn? Of course. But what would it cost me in order to bring such an outcome about? What would I lose?"

"I'm in too deep now to turn back. I have to try. Don't you see that?"

He sighs. "I do. But I still worry. Be careful. Be careful of who you trust. At the end of the day, none of these people have your best interests at heart, and they won't hesitate to put you in jeopardy if it furthers their aims.

"And no matter what happens, you are always a Perez. Your

mother . . ." His voice trails off. "I made my mistakes with your brother. I regret them more than you can ever know. I don't agree with your mother's perspective on this, and while I had hoped her sending you to Spain would get you away from this mess with the CIA, would keep you safe, I never wanted you to feel like you didn't have a part in this family. You are my daughter. You are a Perez. My fortune, my name, all of it will always be yours. You will always be my daughter."

Tears fill my eyes. "Thank you."

"And because you are my daughter, and because I know you, I understand what you must do. Be safe, Beatriz."

"I will," I whisper.

"If you have a chance to see the house again—"

His eyes grow wet, and I am struck by how old he looks, how unfair it is that my father has been put in this position at the end of his days, that he is forced to rebuild, a lifetime of work eradicated by the winds of revolution. His legacy has been stolen from him, along with his son.

"I might not be able to keep you safe, may not be able to go with you on this journey, but if you get in trouble when you are in Havana—"

I listen closely as my father shares another Perez family secret with me.

NOVEMBER 26, 2016
PALM BEACH

She hangs up the phone, a smile on her face. There is something special to be found in conversations with old friends, former lovers, and family. That sense that you are known, that there are words that need not be said, emotions that need not be voiced, yet are felt from miles away. Despite the differences between them, the choices Eduardo has made, at the end of her life, there is still love and respect between them. At her age, there is a reckoning of sorts, and a need to heal old wounds.

They are, after all, countrymen.

Family.

She finishes getting ready, putting on the last piece of jewelry—

The diamond earrings she bought herself to celebrate when she graduated from law school all those years ago.

She studies her reflection in the mirror, pleased with the image staring back at her, her heart quickening as the phone rings once more, this time the voice on the other end of the line inviting her to an impromptu celebration—expected, yet long overdue.

It is, perhaps, poor taste to celebrate a death, even Fidel's. It might be tempting fate to rejoice in the misfortune of another who has succumbed to the travails of time when she stares it down herself. But this is both celebration and mourning—not for Fidel, never for Fidel, but a way of laying all she has lost to rest now that the villain has finally been brought to a justice of sorts for his crimes.

It's not the justice she wanted, of course, but she's learned life doesn't always give you what you want; time has a way of sorting things out in its own peculiar, indecipherable manner.

When Fidel dies . . .

She goes out into the night.

chapter thirty-one

The letter is delivered in the waning days of November, as the weather turns cooler, Palm Beach readying itself for another season—minor royals and Kennedys, steel magnates and celebrities, descending on the island.

The messenger is Eduardo himself, the intervening months since we last saw each other restoring him to his prior health, his skin tan, his body less slight, more muscular than when he returned from Cuba.

His expression is dark.

"Bad news?" I ask, letting him in.

"Is Preston here?"

"No, he's in Dallas with the president."

Eduardo stops in his tracks. "What do you mean he's in Dallas?"

I hesitate. Nick's purpose on the trip isn't exactly secret, but at the same time, I'm not sure he wants me sharing his affairs with Eduardo of all people.

"There are problems within the Democratic Party in Texas. One of the men was Nick's roommate at Harvard. Kennedy thought Nick could help smooth things over."

Eduardo is silent.

"What happened? Why are you here?"

"Dwyer couldn't come himself, but he asked me to deliver this to you personally."

Our fingers brush as I take the letter from him, and I open the envelope, unfolding the paper and reading the words written there.

You're getting your chance.

My heart pounds as I look up at Eduardo.

"What does this mean?"

"They're sending you to Havana. In four days. We'll bring you in by boat."

"We?"

"What do you think I've been doing the past few months? I wasn't going to stop just because Fidel had the temerity to throw me in prison."

"I would have thought—after Playa Girón—"

"That I'd give up? Go back to my dissipated ways?"

"That you wouldn't want to risk any more."

"Why would I care about the risk? It's not as though I have anything left to lose."

"That's not true. You have people who care about you. Your parents—"

"And what about you? Do you care about me?"

"You're a good friend," I answer carefully.

He sighs. "Ah, Beatriz. Sometimes I can't tell if you think you're lying to me or if you know you're lying to yourself."

He inclines his head toward the note. "I'll pick you up at six A.M. on the twenty-sixth."

I knew it was coming, suspected it might be close after my father's visit. But now this is really happening. I will have to tell Nick *something*; will have to say good-bye to my sisters, to my family. This might truly be it; I might go to Cuba and end up in a cell somewhere like Eduardo, or dead on the street like my brother.

Suddenly, four days doesn't feel very long at all.

Eduardo turns and walks toward the front door. He stops, his hand on the wood, turning back to face me.

It's the kindness in his voice that catches me off guard.

"There was a shooting in Dallas."

My heart drops.

"The president was shot in his motorcade with the First Lady by his side."

"Is he—?"

I can't finish the thought, even as I worry for Nick. He surely wouldn't have been in the motorcade. He was there for meetings.

I sway, and Eduardo reaches out, steadying me.

"The president is in surgery," Eduardo answers. "You should turn on the news. I'm sorry. I don't know anything else."

A knock at the front door pulls me away from the living room, where I sit watching the television, waiting for news of the president, the phone silent beside me.

I open the door, surprised to see Maria standing on the other side, still dressed in her uniform from school, her eyes red, her skin blotchy.

"Why aren't you in school?"

I usher her into the room.

"I left."

"You left? You can't just leave school. They'll be worried about you. You have to tell someone when you go, you can't just—"

"They shot him," she says. "The president. They shot him."

Her eyes well with tears, and I am reminded of the night we watched the election together, of the excitement in her eyes, of the pad of paper and pencil she held as she kept a tally of the electoral college votes. I am reminded of what it felt like to be young and hopeful, and unable to make sense of the world around me when that hope was dashed.

I wrap my arms around her, letting her hug my waist, tears pouring down her cheeks.

"I'm so sorry, Maria."

She looks up at me, and in that moment, so many things flash before me, and I am transported back to a different time, a different place, a different memory: of the uncertainty in her eyes as we left Havana that fateful morning, the fear in mine, the sense of powerlessness that overwhelmed me that day.

Perhaps it is foolish to think we are ever in charge of our destinies.

"Is the president going to be fine?"

"I don't know," I answer. "They broke into *As the World Turns* with the news that the president had been shot. He's in surgery. I don't know anything else. They just broke in again a few moments ago, but they haven't given an update on his condition. We can watch it together."

The phone rings from its place in the living room, and we pull apart as I race to answer it.

"Hello?"

"Beatriz."

My eyes close at the sound of Nick's voice on the other end of the line, at the reassurance that he is alive. I sag against the arm of the sofa.

"What happened?" I ask.

"I wasn't with the president, but he was shot in his motorcade while sitting next to the First Lady."

"Was she injured?"

"No. She's waiting at the hospital for word of the president's condition now."

"Where are you?"

"With some of the others who came on the trip with him. Governor Connally was shot as well. It's a mess here. No one knows what's going on. I have to go, but I didn't want you to worry. I'll call you as soon as I can. I love you."

"I love you, too," I echo.

Maria's voice interrupts me as I hang up the phone.

"Beatriz."

Before I even look at the television, Maria's cries tell me all I need to know.

At two thirty-eight in the afternoon, Walter Cronkite confirms the news we have all feared.

President Kennedy is dead.

I sit with Maria while she sobs, holding her head in my lap, stroking her hair as I did when she was younger.

As horrible as the events of today are, there is numbness inside me. Maria is too young to have truly experienced the terrors of the revolution, but they've inured me to the horrors of life. And still, I mourn the president. Even though I disagreed with him on some of his policies, as I imagine his wife, his children, those who loved him, his friends like Nick, a country now thrown into the grip of something so unexpected, I feel a deep sadness. He was not a perfect man, but I do believe he was a good one, and we are the worse for his loss.

Kennedy gave a nation—the world, really—so much hope. And despite the fact that his life was cut short before many of his promises could come to fruition, a pall of sadness has been cast across all of us. Perhaps he was the idealist men like Mr. Dwyer criticized him for being, but he was at his core a good man who cared about his people, who wanted more for his country and genuinely sought to bring that change about, and in this world, those are qualities to be honored and venerated indeed.

I walk Maria home, her eyes red. I don't have the energy to go inside with her and face our parents. Not today.

When I am back in the comfort of the house on the beach, I curl up on the couch with a glass of wine, the events of the day hitting me in waves. Is this why Dwyer wants me to go to Cuba now? Does the CIA suspect Fidel's involvement in the assassination attempt, in Kennedy's death?

I am to leave with Eduardo in less than four days, to see Cuba again. Once, it was my greatest wish. Now, I am afraid of what will be waiting for me when I do.

I doze off at some point in the night, only to be awakened by the sound of the front door opening, heavy footsteps against the marble floor.

I sit up, fumbling with the lamp on the end table.

Nick freezes, his overnight bag dropping to the ground.

"Beatriz."

He says my name as though he's reassuring himself I'm not an apparition; the keys drop from his hand and hit the table with a clunk.

He looks exhausted, his clothing rumpled from travel and wear.

I rise from the sofa and walk toward him, wrapping my arms around him, burying my face in his chest, tears trailing down my face, wetting his shirtfront, the haze surrounding me finally pierced.

"I'm so sorry," I whisper. "I'm so sorry."

He hugs me, his hands fisting my hair, his mouth finding mine, his hands fumbling with my clothes as he bends me over the couch and we sink into oblivion.

chapter thirty-two

Grief surrounds us in the days following President Kennedy's death. On the streets, people break into tears; in private, we are reduced to a state of somber shock.

On Sunday, just a few hours ago, the news announced that the president's assassin, Lee Harvey Oswald, was shot and killed by Jack Ruby, a Texas nightclub operator, in the basement of the Dallas police station en route to a more secure jail facility, the entire situation too bizarre to be believed. The chaos of the past few days reminds me so much of the hectic times between Batista's departure from Cuba and Fidel's arrival, when the news was simply too outlandish and erratic to be predicted. There's a sense of helplessness that can be found in such turmoil, the feeling that you have been swept up in the unrelenting curl of a massive wave, carried on against your will with no choice but to wait and see where the wave will take you.

Kennedy's state funeral is tomorrow.

Nick's anger is a palpable thing, and though we speak little of the president, his grief is a palpable thing, too.

"I don't want to leave you, but the funeral—" He swallows. "I need to be in Washington."

"I know. I understand."

"I wish you would come to Washington with me."

My heart aches. "I can't."

"Why?"

Since Kennedy died, the timing hasn't been right to explain about my mission to Havana, to compound his grief. And yet, I'm running out of time. I received a note from Eduardo yesterday morning.

The mission is still scheduled for us to leave for Havana the morning of the twenty-sixth.

"Because I can't."

I lean back against the pillows, watching Nick pack his suitcase. Is this the last time we will ever see each other?

Long ago, I thought I'd come to terms with the idea of martyring myself for Cuba, but now death is not as easy to reconcile as I once imagined. When I originally became involved with the CIA, I was so upset over Alejandro's death that I didn't think it mattered if I lived or died, as long as I took Fidel out with me. But now, I don't want to die. Somewhere in this waiting to go home, I've made a life for myself.

"Will you be here when I return from Washington?" Nick asks.

I can't lie to him.

Nick sets the final shirt down in his suitcase and looks at me across the bed.

"Are we going to talk about it now? Eduardo has been sending you messages, hasn't he? He came here to see you the day Kennedy was killed. What's going on?"

"I didn't know how to tell you; Kennedy was your friend. What happened was so horrible, and I know how much you're hurting. I didn't want to add to your grief."

"We have to talk about it, though, don't we?"

"The media has already made the connection between Oswald and his involvement in pro-Castro groups," Nick says. "He was involved with a group in New Orleans known as Fair Play for Cuba. The FBI is already looking into his ties, to see if his connections to Cuba were more nefarious. They aren't the only ones. Everyone is looking at Cuba. At Fidel. They're calling it a communist conspiracy.

"Oswald didn't agree with Kennedy's policies on Cuba," Nick continues. "He was a communist. Perhaps he did this on Fidel's orders. Perhaps he merely read Fidel's interview in September and thought he was carrying out Fidel's wishes by making good on Fidel's threat to strike against Kennedy after all the assassination attempts on *his* life.

"And perhaps, it was simply the act of an unwell man," Nick adds. "No one knows. But the suspicion is enough to exacerbate this entire situation. Negotiations were improving, but now . . . there will be no peace between us."

"But will there be war?"

"I don't know."

He's silent for a beat.

"There are other theories being bandied about."

"Such as?"

"Some in the administration believe Kennedy could have been targeted by a group of anti-Castro Cubans looking to provoke a conflict between the two countries. That they had the help of the CIA. Or that they did it because they believed Kennedy to be a traitor for not doing enough with respect to Cuba when he had a chance. Because they're angry about the Bay of Pigs."

"I've heard nothing—"

"From who? People like Eduardo Diaz? Your friend Dwyer? Do you know what they say about him, the rumors that the CIA has been acting against Kennedy's wishes this whole time? That Dwyer and his ilk are running South Florida with their own proxy war?"

"Eduardo did not kill President Kennedy. Nor did Dwyer, indirectly or otherwise."

"You don't know that. Right now, we don't know much of anything. All we know is the president is dead, and his killer had ties to Cuba. And the same day Kennedy died, Eduardo contacted you. Let me guess, they want you to go to Havana? That's why you won't come to D.C. with me.

"You nearly died in London. That was up against one man. Do you think Fidel's security detail will let you get close to him? That if you are successful, they won't kill you in retaliation? That if you aren't successful, they won't kill you all the same?"

His words so closely echo my father's from months ago that I pause.

"I don't know," I admit. "But this is the best chance I'll have."

"So you've already said yes."

"I have. I gave them my word."

Nick grips the edge of the suitcase. "And when do you leave?"

"Tuesday morning."

"Were you going to say good-bye?"

"I didn't know what to say. Good-bye seems so final."

"How about that you love me?"

"I do love you. But why does that mean I have to give this up, too? Why does my love for you have to eclipse all else?"

"I hoped things would get better."

"That I would change."

"No—I don't know."

He sinks down on the edge of the bed, his head between his hands. He looks up at me.

"Tell me. If you go to Cuba, and you successfully remove Fidel from power, if you kill him—what will you do?"

"What do you mean?"

"What happens after Fidel is dead? When Fidel dies, do you

come back here? To me? Do we end up together, do we grow old together, do we marry?"

A knot forms in my stomach.

"I go home," I answer, my voice weak.

How can I explain to him that a part of me wants to spend the rest of my days with him, but at the same time, another part of me knows there is more work to be done? That if Fidel dies, there will be an even greater fight for Cuba's future, a fight I want to be involved with.

Men go off to war and are lauded as heroes for sacrificing their lives for their country, for their dedication and patriotism. But women—why are our ambitions designed to end in marriage and motherhood? If we want something else, if our talents lie elsewhere, why isn't that dedication equally praised and respected?

If I had two lives, I would live one with him and one in Cuba. But I just have this one, and I've already committed it elsewhere.

"And if you fail?" he asks.

"I keep fighting."

He's silent as he reaches into his pocket and pulls out a little red box. I recognize the gold design instantly; my mother is quite fond of the French jeweler, the elegant necklaces, rings, bracelets, and earrings my father once bought her buried in the backyard of our home in Havana waiting for us to return.

"Open it." Nick waves to the box carelessly, as though my heart isn't bleeding out all over the elegant bedspread, as though this isn't the final blow to an affair that never should have started.

My fingers shake as I flip open the lid.

The ring stares back at me.

It's a canary diamond, the stone so large it teeters into vulgarity, flanked by fiery diamonds, absolutely perfect for me.

"I figured you wouldn't want something understated. That you would want something beautiful, unique."

"It is beautiful."

"But not right for you."

"It's perfect for me." I take a deep breath. "You asked me about the future I envision. What does your future look like?"

"You."

"It isn't just me, though, is it? Kennedy's death changes things in the party. Johnson isn't a man the people will be inspired by."

"No, he isn't."

"Who will carry on Kennedy's mantle? Who will fulfill the dreams you once had? There's his brother, of course, but there will be others, won't there?"

Nick nods.

"You can't have a wife who is involved with the CIA, who has been acting as a double agent against the Cubans, who attended communist meetings. You said it yourself, after what happened to Kennedy, all eyes are on Cuba. You can't have a wife who has killed a man. If you weren't in the Senate, if you didn't have ambitions for more, maybe it wouldn't matter. But it does."

"And you want nothing to do with this side of my life."

"I love you. I will never love anyone as much as I love you. But I don't want to wake up one day and no longer recognize the person looking at me in the mirror. I don't want to be relegated to being a silent, pretty ornament like my mother—never respected."

"I respect you."

"I wouldn't respect myself if I gave everything up. Do you want to know the truth? I like what I'm doing. I like what it has made me, the power it has given me, the freedom it affords me. Am I afraid? Of course. But I have been powerless for far too long. At least now, I have a chance to shape my own destiny."

"And where does that leave us?"

"We keep having the same fight."

"We do."

"I'm not going to change."

"I know. That was my mistake. I realize that now. I thought it was something you would move past, something you would forget, but now I see that this will always be your mission."

"And politics will always be yours."

"We're doing good work. Things I can be proud of. It's slow, and it's frustrating as hell, but I believe in my work in the Senate. I think I could do more. What happened to Kennedy—you're right, I want to continue his legacy of fighting for those who have suffered for far too long. He was my friend. I owe him that, I think."

Nick is a good man, and despite the time we've been together, the countless moments we've shared, I still feel that spark of excitement, the humming in my veins that I experienced when we first met. He still dazzles me, but Elisa was right. At some point, you must do the right thing, even when it hurts.

"I will always be a liability for you."

"I *would* marry you."

A tear spills down my cheek. "I know." I brush at my skin. "Part of me wants that more than anything, thinks I could be happy as your wife. If I could be happy as anyone's wife, it would be yours."

His eyes water.

I take a deep breath, my heart breaking at the pain in his gaze. "But I know it would only be a matter of time before I grew restless again, before world events became such that I could no longer turn a blind eye to the U.S.'s actions, before I became involved in something that would hurt you."

I lay my palm against his cheek, my fingertips growing wet.

"You know I'm right. And you wouldn't be happy. I don't want that. I don't want to wake up one day and feel like we've grown apart, become strangers. I don't want to ruin your career, your chance to fight for the things you believe in. I don't want to ruin the love we have for each other.

"Your wife—" The words hurt coming out. "Your wife should be someone who shares your hopes for the future, who makes you happy, who supports you, who wants the same things you want."

"Christ."

"I'll clean my stuff out before I go to Cuba."

He clears his throat, his voice rough. "No. The house is yours. It always was."

"I can't accept a house."

"Sure you can. You can do whatever you want. This house was my dream for us. Maybe that dream didn't come true the way I envisioned, maybe I only got to hold it for a moment before it slipped through my fingers, but I was happy here with you."

Another tear slides down my cheek. "I was happy here with you, too."

"Then hold on to it for us. Be happy here. I don't want to throw it away, and I can't imagine another woman walking through these rooms."

The truth is, I want the house. I want to hold the memory of us close if I make it out of all of this.

"I will."

"I should go. My flight leaves soon."

A tremor wracks my body as Nick wraps his arms around me, holding me against his chest once last time, as I wet his shirtfront with my tears.

"Be safe," he whispers, stroking my hair. He pulls back, and our lips meet, in one last kiss that feels so familiar, and is yet filled with such finality.

Nick releases me, bending down and zipping his suitcase. My gaze settles on the red box sitting on the bedspread, the diamond sparkling in the afternoon sun.

I hand the box to him.

He shakes his head. "Keep it. Please."

I curl my fingers around the ring box.

A sob escapes. "This feels too much like good-bye. Like we're over."

He swallows, his Adam's apple bobbing, as though he, too, is attempting to keep it all together.

"We will never be over. Not good-bye. How about until we meet again?"

"I think I like that even better," I say through the tears. "Until we meet again."

And then he's gone.

chapter thirty-three

In the nearly five years since I last saw Havana from atop my perch in the airplane carrying us to Miami, it seems as though the island has changed. At first sight, I cannot quite put my finger on the differences, only that it feels as though I am looking at a stranger, one's beloved who is now almost unrecognizable.

The sensation is expressed in overlapping waves—the past and present converging together on an image that is just out of focus, a moment one beat off where it should be.

The Malecón is still there, and El Morro, and La Cabaña in the distance. The buildings are still there, visible in the moonlight, and yet, the city feels different. Eduardo is silent beside me, as though he recognizes the changes, too, as though he is bracing himself for them.

"Is it always like this?"

He told me on the boat ride over that he's made this trip a dozen or so times since he was released from prison, smuggling others into the country.

"Yes."

He says the word as though it pains him as much as the image of Havana pains me now.

I imagined relief and a sense of closure at the sight of my homeland, but I confess to only feeling a tremendous sense of loss. I thought it would feel like coming home.

The tiny boat ferrying us bobs with the rising seas.

The journey has been fairly uneventful, no run-ins with the Coast Guard, the waves not too choppy, the stars and moonlight breaking through the inky dark night. Minutes ago, the sun receded over the horizon, bathing Havana in its glow for one beautiful moment before night came.

In an hour or so, I will be on my way to see Fidel.

Eduardo and a Cuban man who greets him with a quick smile whisk me through the city in a blue Buick, no names exchanged between them, the entire mood of the evening one of urgency. I yearn to linger, have to remind myself this is not the time to explore, that if I am successful in my mission, we will have plenty of days and nights in Havana.

Our destination is the Habana Hilton, now renamed by Fidel to the Habana Libre, a ridiculous moniker if there ever was one.

The capsule of poison Eduardo handed me when we left Palm Beach is tucked securely in my bra. My heart beats against it erratically.

I thought the time spent living in London as a spy had better prepared me for this, imagined that after my experience with Ramon, little could rattle me.

I was wrong.

"You have the plan down?" Eduardo murmurs to me.

I nod, my gaze on the city as it passes us by. If I'm to die in a few hours, let me enjoy these last few moments in Havana.

We arrive at the hotel quickly, and I am ferried in through a service entrance in the back, where another man in a hotel uniform meets us. He doesn't offer his name, either, merely tells me to follow him up to the leader's room.

I can't tell what either of these men think, if they believe I am another one of Fidel's women and they're merely arranging a romantic tryst, or if they are also affiliated with the CIA. In the absence of such knowledge, I opt for silence.

"This is where I leave you," Eduardo says, his words reminiscent of the first time he took me to meet Mr. Dwyer at the restaurant in Jupiter so many years ago.

How far we've come.

"You'll be fine," he whispers, although I get the sense he is saying it more for himself than for me, and at the moment, I don't need his reassurance.

I've had this date for a long time, and just as when I was a young girl, afraid of the dark and the monsters I imagined loomed beneath my bed, there is power in facing this horror head-on.

With a quick kiss on the cheek, I leave Eduardo behind me, and follow the man in the hotel uniform to an elevator bank, where Fidel's security men stop us.

I stand still as their hands run over my curves, checking me for weapons, their movements more perfunctory than anything else.

They ask my name, a few more questions, their mood jovial, and I do my best to answer them, to keep my voice steady, relying on the experience I gained from my time in London.

And then we're boarding the elevator, going up, up, up until we reach Fidel's floor and the doors slide open, revealing more security men.

They pat me down once more, and then the door at the end of the hall opens, and I cross over into Fidel's inner sanctum.

. . .

I've imagined this moment for so long, run over the possibilities of how it would transpire hundreds of times, and now that it's here, I want to savor the moment, but it runs by me too quickly, flashes registering before they're gone.

Fidel lounges on one of the couches, a customary cigar in hand, flanked by security men.

I stiffen at the sight of them.

Eduardo mentioned Fidel would be alone, that he often entertains his women in the privacy of his suite, this whole evening arranged by a spy embedded in Castro's government.

Why isn't he alone?

"Beatriz Perez, we meet again."

I walk toward Fidel on shaky legs, attempting to steady myself in my heels, a smile affixed on my face. A drink sits in front of him on the coffee table, and my gaze sweeps over it as I run through the possibilities in my mind of how I can slip the poison into the glass.

Why isn't he alone?

"Sit." Fidel gestures toward a chair opposite the couch. "You can leave us," he says to his security personnel. "We won't be long."

My legs tremble as I sink down into the chair. Was Eduardo's intelligence wrong? Is Fidel interested in me as a woman or not? And regardless, will there be an opportunity to slip the drug into his drink?

"It seems we have friends in common, Miss Perez," Fidel says smoothly when we are alone.

I can hear the sound of his security personnel talking just outside the door. According to Eduardo, the drug should take effect in minutes, giving me a narrow window to escape before they capture me.

I had envisioned an opportunity to take my clothes off, to slip my hand inside my bra and remove the pill. How do I get Fidel to turn his back to me?

"Do we?" I ask, my pulse jumping.

"We do. Two childhood friends of mine who found their way to Miami to escape Batista's cruelty."

And just like that, I know. Like a line of dominoes falling into place, it comes together.

Mr. Dwyer wasn't wrong to be suspicious of the communist group in Hialeah. The Cuban brothers were indeed the ones to watch.

"Javier and Sergio."

Fidel nods.

The lingerie I carefully chose, the seductive gown, the time spent perfecting my hair and makeup, none of it matters. The plan was over before it began. All along, Dwyer said Fidel's espionage was formidable. Apparently, more so than even we imagined.

It appears I am to die in Cuba at the hands of the same man who killed my brother.

Fidel takes another puff of his cigar. "The Americans sent you to kill me, didn't they?"

I don't answer.

Everyone warned me not to get involved. Told me this was dangerous, that I was in over my head.

They were right.

"You're hardly the first they've sent to kill me. I imagine you won't be the last."

Should I take the pill myself? What will Fidel do to me? Throw me in prison? Sell me back to the Americans? Will Nick pay my ransom?

Will Fidel hurt me to teach me a lesson?

"I wondered why they sent you," he continues. "Besides the obvious physical charms, of course. And then I remembered that there once was another Perez, remembered you mentioning a brother when we met in New York."

"His name was Alejandro," I say, my voice growing stronger. "He was with the Federación Estudiantil Universitaria."

He nods. "Some of my men were with the FEU. They remembered him. Said he was a good man."

He was a great man.

"I never had the opportunity to meet him. But I want you to know that I didn't kill your brother. Or order his death."

White noise rushes through my ears as I attempt to reconcile his words with every single thing I have held to be true, with the sight of my brother's dead body, the sound of a car screeching down the road.

"I don't believe you."

He shrugs. "Believe what you want. The truth is, it never happened. Maybe it would have eventually, but it had nothing to do with me."

Even as everything in my nature tells me not to believe him, that he is a man not to be trusted, there is something in his manner, in his voice, in his eyes, that gives me pause.

"I'm not going to believe the word of a murderer and a traitor."

"That's your choice. But ask yourself this, why would I lie? What do I have to lose? I'm not afraid of your family, of your father's reputation. His power isn't what it once was, is it?"

He takes another puff of his cigar. "In war, these things happen. Men die."

"At your hands."

"Do you forget what it was like under Batista? How many Cubans he killed? I did what had to be done. But I didn't kill your brother. And I didn't kill your President Kennedy. And because I did not, because your government must know that I did not, I will let you go back and tell them so. I will give you your life."

I gape at him.

"You will tell them that Cuba had nothing to do with this."

"I doubt my word will count for much. They suspect Cuban involvement. They're still going to be looking for answers, trying to understand who did kill Kennedy."

"Perhaps they should look closer to home then."

My eyes narrow. "What are you saying?"

"I'm merely suggesting your CIA might have a motive behind Kennedy's death. That there are groups within your country that viewed the president as a traitor and might have desired to strike at him because of it. I'm sure you don't know any people like that, do you, Miss Perez?"

"I don't know who killed President Kennedy, and I am sorry for his loss. But it wasn't on my order." Fidel gestures toward the door. "Go back and tell the men who sent you what I told you. And don't come back again. If you do, I won't be so generous."

I exit the Habana Hilton alone, my stomach in knots, bile in my throat, the poison pill in my bra. My gaze darts around the street looking for Eduardo, for the blue Buick.

It's nowhere to be found.

I can't stop trembling, the adrenaline crash ripping through my body.

I've spent years preparing for this, sacrificed so much, and for what? I spent five minutes in Fidel's presence and then it was all over.

So much for saving Cuba. So much for avenging my brother.

A lump forms in my throat as I glance down the street, looking for Eduardo, for the blue Buick.

Where is he?

Eduardo is responsible for the connection at the boatyard, for getting us out of here.

Has something happened to him?

A car whizzes past me, and I flatten my body against the wall, my gaze darting around the street once more.

The streets of Havana no longer look so friendly now that Fidel is in power.

And then I remember my father's words, the family secret he passed on to me.

It's about two miles from the Habana Hilton to Miramar, but I spent years sneaking out of the house at night, know the streets of Havana better than anyone.

I could sit here and wait for help, or I could—

I head home.

My childhood home is still much as I remembered it, the windows of the big house dark.

I cross the street in a hurry, glancing over my shoulder, once, twice.

I don't even know who lives here now. The staff is long gone, the house likely taken over by Fidel's cronies.

It feels as though I've time-traveled, back to the days when I used to sneak out and meet Eduardo and Alejandro at political meetings. It's both familiar and completely foreign to me.

I walk toward the house. When I reach the gate, I still. This is where I found Alejandro. This is where they dumped his body. This is where it all started.

My brother's blood is now stained in the gravel, soaked in the earth, and while there are no longer Perezes in the house where we lived for generations, a part of him is here, watching over it for us.

I push the gate open, wincing at the creak of metal.

My gaze darts around once more. I almost expect to see Fidel's men burst out of the darkness, come to take me away.

The street is silent. The house looms before me.

In the darkness, I travel by memory.

Does the painting of the corsair still hang on the walls? He was the first Perez ancestor of note and we used to make up stories about him when we were children; I think Elisa fancied herself a bit in love with him. Is the painting of his wife still there beside him— the woman who sailed from Spain to marry a man with a fearsome reputation, whose blood runs through my veins now?

Is the house just as we left it the morning we left Havana nearly five years ago, or have the new residents changed it?

There's a shed near the back of the property where the gardeners used to keep their supplies. I walk over to it, stumbling over the uneven ground, the changes in the landscape since I left.

I still once more.

The palms sway in the breeze, the bushes and grass rustling around me.

I have an hour or two at most before the sun rises and I lose the cover of darkness. The current climate in Cuba is one of fear and uncertainty, and I don't trust that anyone who finds me back here won't turn me in to the police. If my life rests on Fidel's word, I'd rather not take my chances.

I open the door and quickly riffle through the items in the shed, my hand gripping the handle of a shovel.

I close the door behind me.

I follow my father's instructions, stopping in front of the old palm tree where we used to play when we were young girls, where I first snuck a kiss from Eduardo when we were children.

I stake the shovel into the ground, digging out a plot of dirt. I freeze at another sound in the distance, struggling to remember the noises the estate used to make.

Is it the swaying palms?

What if can't convince someone to smuggle me out of Havana?

What has happened to Eduardo?

Silence fills the night.

I keep digging.

My gaze drifts to the Rodriguez house as I dig. Are our neighbors and old family friends still in residence? I yearn to see Ana once more, even though it would be too risky to embroil her in our affairs.

Cuba is perhaps now more dangerous than it ever was.

The shovel hits something solid beneath the ground.

I fall to my knees, the dress I bought to seduce Fidel covered in dirt. My fingers brush the wooden box my father used to keep in his study. I recognize it instantly. He hid money there sometimes, too, and after Alejandro was disowned, I used to steal cash from the box to give to my brother. My father always replaced the money, and even though we didn't speak of it, he had to have known.

I pull the box from the ground, lifting the lid and flipping through the contents.

My father is not one for sentimentality, and at the moment, I am grateful for it. The box is filled with jewelry, money, things that were once our family legacy, valuable items we couldn't take with us when we were forced to leave Havana.

It's enough to convince someone to risk their life to take me back to Florida.

There's a brief instant when I hesitate, the thought of using our family heirlooms to save me a painful one.

And yet, the truth is, at the moment, I can't think of a better use of them, and I'm fairly certain my father would agree. What we once held as so valuable no longer seems to matter anymore.

I gather the box in my hands.

The rustling sound is back, the palm trees, I imagine.

The moonlight shifts.

A man steps in front of me, a gun pointed at my chest.

chapter thirty-four

The box slides from my hands, hitting the metal shovel with a clunk as I stare down the barrel of the gun, and face the man holding it.

We haven't seen each other in over two years, but it only takes a moment for me to place him.

We've both come a long way since those meetings in Hialeah.

"Javier, isn't it?"

He grunts in acknowledgment.

"Did you come here for me?" I ask.

"I've been in Cuba for some time now. And then I heard you had shown up."

"Who told you that?"

"Does it matter, really? The CIA thinks they're so good at keeping secrets. Their arrogance prevents them from realizing that others are good at learning them."

"Fidel won't let you get away with this," I say with more confidence than I feel. "He wants me to carry a message back to the Americans."

Javier shrugs. "He won't know what happened to you. It's not like there will be a body to find."

"What will you do with me?"

"Shoot you. Throw your body in the ocean."

"Why?"

"Ramon was my cousin."

So that was the connection between Claudia and the Hialeah group. It would have been helpful for Dwyer to give me a little warning, though at this point the secrets have become expected.

"He was a murderer."

"Claudia had it coming. She was a traitor to her people."

"I suppose it's all a matter of perspective."

"She worked for the CIA. Like you. She was a traitor, like you."

I laugh. "And you're what, exactly? A hero to the Cuban people? That group you were involved with was a joke. A bunch of kids playing at revolution who knew nothing."

"Like your Lee Harvey Oswald?"

A chill slides down my spine.

"It's so easy to inspire these Americans when they're desperate to belong to something bigger than themselves. So easy to recruit them to the cause when you fill their heads with notions of glory in battle. I imagine it's not that different than the approach the CIA took when they recruited you. What was it, 'a chance to save Cuba'? The CIA has no problem involving themselves in Cuba's affairs, sending agents to meddle in our national sovereignty, attempting to destabilize our government. Why shouldn't we do the same to them?"

My eyes narrow. "Were you the one who blew my cover?"

"Ramon contacted his handler with questions about you the night before he disappeared. He saw you at some party, talking to a Soviet colonel. My aunt asked me to look into what happened to him. I recognized your name from our meetings in Hialeah.

"Ramon was my aunt's only son," he adds. "I made her a promise that I would see his killer dead. Given what I've heard about you, I would think you would understand that."

"So this isn't just about Cuba. It's personal for you, too."

He cocks the gun in response.

I reach for the shovel, swinging it in the air, high above his head.

It's unlikely I will escape death twice, but I have to try.

I bring the shovel down, but before it can connect with his head—

A shot fills the night air.

The shovel drops to the ground, and I brace, but where I expect to feel pain, there is nothing.

No blood.

Javier crumples to the ground in front of me.

Eduardo stands behind him, a pistol in hand.

"Did you kill him?" I ask, a tremor in my voice.

"I hope so."

Eduardo checks the body.

My legs tremble.

He nods. "He's dead."

"What happened? Where were you? I looked for you when I left the hotel."

"We got hassled by some officers. By the time they let us go, you were already gone. I guessed you might come here."

"He was going to kill me."

"You had it in hand."

"Not this time."

"What happened with Fidel?" Eduardo asks, his voice grim.

"He knew. Before we came, he knew. My cover was blown. He

met with me because he wanted me to pass a message on to the CIA. It's over. It's all over. I'm sorry."

"It's not your fault." Eduardo's gaze sweeps over the backyard. "Someone will have heard the shot. We need to get out of here. Now. We've missed the boat that was scheduled to get us out, but—"

"I have our boat passage here," I say, picking up the wooden box from the ground. My fingers slip against the edge.

They're covered in the splatter from Javier's blood.

I shudder. "Let's go home."

chapter thirty-five

Eduardo finds a man at the docks who is more than happy to run us back to South Florida for the remainder of my family's fortune. It's an absurd amount of money, but I don't have another option.

Who knows what happened with the rest of our valuables, if my father entrusted them to family friends, or other family members, of if those items simply disappeared, swept away by the revolution that took everything else? Does it really even matter anymore? You can't put a price on everything we've lost.

I wait while Eduardo and the sea captain negotiate the details of our passage, doing my best to clean myself off with the rag the boatman provided me, my gaze on the city, on the Malecón, the five miles of seawall between the city and the sea.

I grew up along this seawall, dangling my legs over the edge, feeling the ocean spray on my skin.

Will I ever see it again?

I turn as Eduardo comes to stand beside me, his gaze cast out to sea as well.

"He says there are only a few minutes left before it will be too dangerous to leave."

"I'm ready. Let's go."

Eduardo snags my wrist. "Beatriz—" He swallows. "I'm not coming."

"What do you mean, you're not coming?"

He doesn't say anything else.

He doesn't have to.

I can read it all over his face and in his eyes, and where I always thought looking at Eduardo was like looking in a mirror, now a stranger stares back at me.

"When?"

"After Playa Girón," he answers.

"Why?"

"Because I was sick of losing. Sick of being used by the CIA. Of the Americans making promises they don't keep. Because I wanted to go home."

"Fidel took everything from you and your family."

He has the grace to look embarrassed. "It turns out he's willing to make some amends on that front."

"In exchange for you selling secrets, double-crossing the CIA."

Everyone has their price. Eduardo's was always his pride.

"And me?" I ask. "Did you sell me out to Fidel?"

"He wanted to know about any assassination attempts on his life."

"It must have been valuable information to him. Did I win you back your estates?"

I want to slap him. I want to scream.

I'm too numb for any of it.

"He said he wouldn't hurt you. I would never let anyone hurt you. When Kennedy died, Fidel was desperate to make sure the Americans knew he wasn't responsible for it. He said he just wanted to talk to you. So you could carry the message back to the CIA. Dwyer trusts you."

"He trusted you, too."

"He used me," Eduardo retorts.

"We all used one another. And if I'd been successful? If I'd killed Fidel? What would you have done then?"

He gives me a sad smile. "I wasn't opposed to that happening, either. You always have to hedge your bets."

"So what? You're a communist now? You think Fidel is a great man? I don't understand how you could change your opinion so drastically, so quickly."

"Quickly?" He laughs, the sound devoid of humor. "I'm tired, Beatriz. We left almost five years ago. What's changed? Maybe we were wrong all along. Some of Fidel's ideas aren't that far off what we dreamed of years ago."

"You can't believe that."

"Maybe. Maybe not. You're in bed with the CIA now. Who would have imagined that five years ago? We all do what's necessary to survive."

"He killed my brother. Your best friend."

"He says he didn't."

"He told me the same thing. Do you believe him? How can you trust him?"

"Of course I don't trust him. I don't think I believe in anything anymore."

I give a bitter laugh. "That makes two of us then. After all, I always did see myself in you."

"I'm sorry."

"No, you're not."

"No, I suppose I'm not. Please don't hate me. I never meant to hurt you."

"What's happened to us? How did we get here?" I shake my

head. "When we left Cuba, it was supposed to be temporary. A few months at most."

"The world changed. Left us behind. I have to change with it. I want to be home. And maybe things will get better. Maybe he will bring freedom to the country."

"And if they don't get better?"

He doesn't answer me.

Once, I would have felt anger. But we've all come too far, seen and done too much, for there not to be a sliver of understanding inside me.

I can't agree with what he has done, can't condone it, but I know more than anyone how far one will go to return home.

And that is enough.

"She's a beautiful city," I say softly, taking Eduardo's hand, lacing our fingers together.

Saying good-bye.

"A heartbreaker," he replies.

"Do you think I'll ever see her again?"

Eduardo squeezes my hand, pressing a kiss to my cheek before he releases me.

"Of course you will. We'll dance at the Tropicana someday."

The boat begins to move, cutting through the sleek water, through the dark night. The waves hit the sides with thick slaps. Havana drifts farther and farther away, until the city is little more than a speck in the distance, the open water ahead.

Dreams never die all at once. They die in pieces, floating a little farther and farther away each day. So there's no longer an island before you, no longer Havana, the crash of waves along the Malecón vanishing, until the speck disappears completely. All you once clutched to your breast and held so deeply in your heart ceases to exist, slipping through your fingers like the sand that once lay beneath your feet.

And you are alone. And in that moment, you have a choice—

You can either succumb to the deep dark, cast yourself unto the sea, the weight of all you have lost simply too great and impossible to regain. Or you can turn around, putting the past behind you, and look forward.

To brighter days, to the future, to freedom.

To home.

chapter thirty-six

When I return from Havana, the Palm Beach house is as I left it, save for the fact that Nick's things are gone. And still, I am immeasurably grateful for the comfort and familiarity of it in the face of all that transpired while I was gone.

Even now, without Nick here, it feels like home.

I send my report off to the CIA, hearing nothing in return from Dwyer. A week passes, and I spend my days alone, but for the occasional walk with my sisters. I crave the solitude now, a mourning of my own, perhaps. I don't tell them about my trip or about Eduardo. We all have our secrets.

A man waits for me near the veranda when I return from my walk one morning.

"Beautiful house," he comments when he sees me.

I smile. "It is, isn't it?"

"Yours?"

"It is. Would you like a drink?"

Dwyer nods, following me through the enormous glass doors, into the sitting room, where he sits while I pour him a drink.

I hand him the glass and take a seat opposite his, sipping the mimosa I poured for myself, needing the liquid courage.

"I'm glad to see you are alive," Dwyer says after a beat. "I heard things were complicated in Cuba. You have my apologies. I didn't know about Eduardo. We do our best to prevent these things from happening, but sometimes they're outside of our control."

"I don't blame you. I've known him since we were children, and I never suspected he would work with Fidel."

"You were close."

"I thought we were," I admit.

"I read your report. You said he saved your life."

"He did. Javier would have killed me. I doubt I would have gotten lucky twice."

"Then perhaps there was still enough of the man you knew in him."

"How do you do it?" I ask. "The secrets? The lies? How do you trust anyone? How do you stomach it?"

"It's a cliché, of course, but it becomes easier. And you learn. Not to trust anyone but yourself."

"Are you saying I shouldn't trust you?"

"You most definitely should not trust me, Miss Perez. Eduardo was a lesson for you. A hard one. We all have one in our career. You won't forget it."

"But how could I have been so wrong about him? I thought we understood each other, that we were the same."

"The truth is always so very complicated. I'm supposed to say people rarely surprise me, that I've become so good at reading them that I can predict their actions and all that nonsense, but that's not true at all. People are constantly surprising me. The world is not so black-and-white, Miss Perez. There is a great deal of gray. And the truth is, there is a possibility that you and Eduardo Diaz are similar, that you do understand each other, and that you still stand on opposite sides."

"So where does that leave us then? Is this all for nothing?" I take a deep breath. "I failed. Fidel is still alive."

"I wouldn't judge yourself too harshly. You're in good company. Everyone we've sent in has failed. Some men are simply harder to kill than others."

"It seems unfair that he should live when so many good men have died for his revolution. I wanted revenge for my brother. Where is the justice?"

"There is very little fairness in my job. There is luck, and planning, and grueling hours, and hard work, but sometimes these things happen. It can be discouraging. Can make you question why you do the work."

"Why do you?"

"Because I like it. Because I'm good at it. Because I believe everyone has a purpose to their life and this is mine. Because sometimes we do win, even if we lose a fair share, too. There's always another fight. Another problem to solve. Another country to fix."

"You could always let them fix their own problems."

"We could. But often their problems are America's problems. Besides, no one complains when we intervene in situations where our presence is needed, where it's welcomed. The line between villain and hero is whisper thin and, very frequently, a matter of perspective. Gray, Miss Perez. We operate in the gray."

"And Cuba? What will you do about Fidel?"

"Keep trying. There's always another plot in motion."

"I'm surprised he didn't kill me."

"These are dangerous times for Castro. He has to know we're looking at him for Kennedy's assassination. He can't provoke us further. We've shown a remarkable amount of restraint so far, but if we throw the weight of the American government and military behind removing him from power, he stands no chance."

"Do you think he killed the president?"

"I don't."

"But you saw it as an opportunity to remove him regardless."

"That's my job, Miss Perez. Seeing opportunities." His gaze drifts around the room. "This really is a beautiful house." He turns his attention back to me. "What will you do? What are your plans for the future?"

"I don't know. Continue my education now that I have the means to do so regardless of my parents' wishes. I wanted to be a lawyer when we lived in Cuba. Perhaps I'll go to law school one day."

He smiles. "For what it's worth, I think you would make an excellent lawyer. I take it then our days of meeting in roadside diners and hotel bars are behind us?"

"My cover was blown. Fidel knows everything."

"That cover is useless to us, yes. But that's the beautiful thing about covers. You can always reinvent yourself."

"But Fidel—"

"Not Cuba, no. Indirectly, perhaps, you could still keep a hand in, but it would be too dangerous to have you actively involved in missions now that your cover is blown with Fidel. But like I said before, the world is full of many conflicts, and someone like you would be well-placed to help your country."

"I'm not American."

"Aren't you? Building a home here does not make you less Cuban. Even spies need a home to lay their head every once in a while. You could still go to school, visit your family, live the life you've chosen. We would be in regular contact, would look for ways our relationship would benefit each other. It wouldn't be Cuba, but this war with the Soviets will be a long one, carried out by proxy in many countries. Communism has destroyed Cuba. This is your chance to keep it from destroying the rest of the world. You said you wanted to avenge your brother. There are other ways of honoring his memory. Other ways to serve.

"Our work is often thankless. Soldiers come back from war and are praised for their heroism. We live in a constant state of war and operate under a cover of invisibility. But what we do saves lives. If you're looking for something to give you purpose in the future, for what it's worth, I think you would be very good at this line of work. And you would enjoy it."

"Where would you send me?"

"How do you feel about Europe? I believe your mother has a cousin in Spain, correct? Married to a diplomat?"

He smiles, as though he knows I am already his, the decision already made. Perhaps Cuba is lost for now. But there's still a fight to be had.

"When do I leave?"

NOVEMBER 26, 2016
PALM BEACH

She slips her key into the lock of her Palm Beach estate in the early hours of the morning, the evening spent celebrating with her family and thousands of her countrymen on Calle Ocho. As her palm pushes against the heavy wood, as the door swings open, she knows.

How could she not?

The front door shuts behind her, and she follows the light ahead of her, down the long hallway, the artwork she's amassed throughout the years flanking her, the antiques collected from her travels abroad, the framed photographs of her family—the next generation—the diplomas she's earned and proudly hung—

A life well lived.

When she reaches the floor-to-ceiling glass doors that lead out to the veranda, she hesitates, the canary diamond on her ring finger glinting in the light. She's worn it nearly every day for over fifty years, save for the days when she was in Havana, keeping him close to her, even as her path has taken her farther away.

She turns the doorknob, stepping out into the cool night air. She should be tired considering the late hour, and the fact that she's no longer a girl of twenty-two, accustomed to creeping into the house as the sun comes up.

They'll have an hour or so before daybreak, before the sun rises over the water in a brilliant explosion of colors.

She should be tired, but she's not, running on adrenaline and hope now.

The patio door shuts behind her, and the man standing on her veranda shifts, as though he's coming to attention. He suddenly seems taller, more broad-shouldered, and for a moment, the image of the man she loved and lost, and the man who stands before her now, his back to her, his gaze cast out to the sea, become one. She's transported to another time, another place, and another balcony. Another life.

And then he turns.

They've seen each other throughout the years, of course.

In a world such as theirs, complete and total obscurity is simply impossible. But there has always been a distance between them, an understanding that they were on separate paths.

Did he read the magazine spread on her? Did he keep up with her legal career? The human rights cases she was involved with? Did he wonder about her other career, the one she lived in shadows, blacked-out reports crossing his Senate desk?

His image has filled her television screen throughout the years, until he retired from the Senate a decade or so ago, the newspaper articles mentioning him tucked away in a scrapbook in her closet, the pages worn with time and frequent turning. And then there are the stories she read about his children in the society pages, a family that held her affection from afar because they were his.

"Have you been waiting long?" Her voice is thick with emotion, the words clumsy to the sound of her own ears.

"Not too long," he says, a smile playing on his lips and mischief in his eyes, as though he knows they aren't just talking about this evening, of course.

He is one of those men who have aged with grace, whose handsomeness is like a fine bottle of wine or an exquisite vintage of champagne. It is supremely unfair, of course, but if she has learned anything during her time on earth, it is that life is rarely fair. It simply is.

She crosses the distance between them, her heart pounding at the light in his eyes, at the love shining there.

"I've missed you," she says once barely a whisper separates them.

"I've missed you, too," he replies.

He reaches out and strokes her hair, his fingers grazing the curve of her cheek, and even though her skin is no longer that of a young woman, all the years between them fall away, and they are once again two people standing on a Palm Beach balcony under a moonlit sky.

They both look their fill, the luxury of just being in each other's company one that is impossible to ignore in the face of such a separation.

"Do you feel at peace now that Fidel is dead?" he asks her.

"I thought I would," she admits. "Thought victory would taste so sweet. Of course, I didn't think it would take this long, either."

"You've been happy, though?"

She smiles. "Yes. I have."

"Good. I'd hoped you were. That the years were kind to you."

"They were." She takes a deep breath. "I was sorry to hear about your loss—about your wife."

Her obituary was printed in the Palm Beach papers six months ago.

"Thank you. Your note meant a great deal. We were blessed with a good marriage. Wonderful children. We had a good life."

"I'm glad."

And she is. In her youth, perhaps, she would have been plagued with jealousy. But time has taught her many lessons, chiefly, the ability to put someone else's happiness above her own. After all, does not the very nature of love demand sacrifice?

He smiles and holds his hand out to her, and her heart skips and sputters in her chest, and it is perhaps the loveliest thing of all that after all this time, the spark between them still burns hot and strong, that eventually they have found their way back to each other.

Fate, and timing, and all that.

"Will you dance with me, Beatriz Perez, kisser-of-revolutionaries and thief-of-hearts?" he asks, and she laughs, the familiar words catapulting her back in time.

He's still too smooth by half, and she loves him for it. However much time they have left on this earth, however many days, weeks, months, years, she wants to spend them with him.

Beatriz shakes her head, a smile playing at her lips, tears welling in her eyes, joy in her breast.

"I didn't say anything about stealing hearts."

He smiles again, that full wattage hitting her, the love on his face and in his voice enveloping her in its warmth.

"No, I did."

Does she really even stand a chance?

"Of course," Beatriz answers, giving him her hand, letting him pull her into his arms, as they begin to dance, the sun rising over the water, time receding with each crashing wave.

epilogue

The secret to dating a man with whom you have been in love nearly your entire adult life is to still somehow maintain an aura of mystery, to ensure that even though he knows your affections are a constant thing, there are still dates, and flowers, and romantic letters you can read in the privacy of your sitting room. There are some who might say that at my age, romance is a ridiculous frivolity, that we must race through the remaining time we have left together, a concession to our declining health and advancing ages.

Fortunately, I've never been much for listening to what other people say.

The truth is, time is a luxury—yes. But like so many other luxuries in life, it is best savored rather than gorged, and so I spend ages doing my hair and makeup in preparation for our dates, take shopping trips with my great-nieces to buy new outfits, keeping the secret of Nick close to my heart.

He is punctual when he picks me up, flowers in hand, and the look in his eyes says time has not dimmed his impression of me, has not lessened the romance of our younger years. And I suppose, at a period when our lives are supposed to be winding down, there is something altogether delicious about rekindling a flame that never died.

After nearly two months of dating, he and his driver pick me up in his gleaming gray Rolls, and we drive out to Wellington for my great-niece Lucia's birthday.

It's time for him to properly meet the family.

It's a happy occasion for the Perez clan—my great-niece Marisol has returned from her trip to Cuba, scattering my sister Elisa's ashes where they belonged. We're all proud of Marisol and happy to have her back.

I introduce Nick to the family, more than a little amused by the faint look of discomfort on my nephew's face, as he clearly comes to terms with the fact that his aunt still has romantic affairs.

"Was this your very important date?" Marisol asks, her eyes wide as she leads me away from the rest of the family.

I've always considered my great-nieces to be like granddaughters to me, never having the opportunity to miss the children and grandchildren I never had with them around.

I smile, remembering our conversation when she came by the house last week. "Yes."

"He was nearly president, wasn't he?" A fair amount of awe fills her voice.

I smile. "Nearly. He would have been an excellent one, too."

"How long have you known each other?"

"A very long time. Since I was a young girl."

"Did you—"

"What? Love him before?"

Marisol nods.

"Always."

"I'm glad he's here. And that you're happy."

Lucia walks up to us, a glass of champagne in hand, and takes a seat next to me.

"Open your gift," I tell her, gesturing toward the wrapped square package sitting against the dessert table.

"I thought I'd wait until later."

"Forget etiquette. If you can't do what you want on your birthday, then what's the point? Besides, one of the benefits of being old is that the rules can hang. I give you full permission to open one gift—my gift—before the allotted time."

Marisol laughs. "I have a feeling you never had much use for the rules."

"Life's simply too short. Open it," I say, nudging Lucia.

She tears open the package, the paper revealing a pair of brown eyes, the curve of a cheek, glossy midnight-colored hair, a whispery gown floating around her, diamonds dripping from her neck.

"It's a gorgeous painting," Lucia proclaims.

"It is, isn't it? I won it at an auction a few weeks ago. Well, won it back, I should say. It used to hang on the walls of our house in Miramar, although it's had quite a journey. There was another painting, a companion piece—her husband."

"Who was she?" Marisol asks.

"Isabella Perez. The first female Perez ancestor that we know about."

"She married the corsair," Lucia says.

"She did. In the mid-eighteenth century. She boarded a ship from Spain headed for Cuba, was sent off to marry a man she had never met, a man she had never seen."

"Can you imagine?" Marisol muses. "She must have been so brave. And terrified."

"I agree. This painting was always my favorite," I add. "Your grandmother favored the corsair, but I always wondered about the woman who left her home, her family, everything she had ever known and set out across the ocean."

"I love it. Thank you," Lucia says, pressing a kiss to my cheek.

"Good. I'm glad."

"Who took it from our home in Cuba?" Marisol asks.

"I don't know. Somehow, it ended up in the estate of a man in Virginia. When he died, it went up for auction. The family might know more, and I've put in some discreet inquiries, but so far, I haven't heard anything. At least she's home now, where she belongs."

As am I.

Nick and I link arms as we join the rest of the family in singing "Happy Birthday" to Lucia, as we raise our glasses in toast to the beginning of her thirty-fourth year. My gaze meets my little sister Maria's across the party, and a smile passes between us, a gleam of pride in her eyes that matches my own.

I always thought Cuba would be my legacy. That I was destined to play a role in its future, that I was destined for great things. And perhaps, if things had played out differently, that would have been the case. But there's power here, too. An enduring legacy that has been passed on to the next generation of Perez women.

Men come and go, revolutions rise and fall, and here we stand.

Maybe it will come in the waning hours of the night, those wicked, magical hours. Or perhaps it will come with the break of day, stirring the sleepy from their beds with a shout. It may come as a ripple spreading quietly through the countryside, cloaked in fierce whispers and bridled hope. Or perhaps with a spark in the city, carried through a crackling radio station, a song on the breaths of those who need it most.

But come it will.

Our time will come.

Author's Note

From the first moment I introduced Beatriz's character in *Next Year in Havana*, I knew she had to have her own book. At the time, there were no plans for another entry in the lives of the Perez family, but Beatriz changed that with her wonderful, passionate, headstrong manner. Halfway through drafting *Next Year in Havana*, I had to stop and write the first chapter of Beatriz's novel, because her story was pushing its way out, demanding to be told. Whereas *Next Year in Havana* focused on the events of the revolution, I wanted *When We Left Cuba* to focus on what happened after, on the fight to reclaim Cuba and the role it played on the world stage.

While the Perez family and their friends are entirely fictional, the events in the novel were inspired by the tumultuous Cuban-American relations of the 1960s. Likewise, Mr. Dwyer is a fictional character, but he was inspired by many of the CIA's efforts in Latin America at the time. Declassified documents have uncovered numerous CIA-sponsored plots to assassinate Fidel Castro, including using one of his weaknesses—beautiful women—to get close to him. While these attempts failed, they were the inspiration for Beatriz's exploits.

The period of time surrounding the Bay of Pigs, the Cuban Missile Crisis, and the Kennedy Assassination was fraught with tension between Cuba and the United States and was a heyday of sorts for the spy game. Cuba's intelligence service was and continues to be a formidable force, and Castro was known for embedding double agents in the Cuban exile community and for being well-informed due to his intricate network of spies. The United States was equally fervent in their efforts, and of course, the specter of the Soviet Union added to the importance of intelligence gathering. Many of the incidents in the novel—including that of the Soviet colonel in London—were inspired by real efforts made by both governments, and often the details read like something out of a spy novel, proving that truth is often stranger than fiction. Castro's concerns that his regime would be targeted in retaliation for Kennedy's assassination were also genuine, as were the many theories that have sprung up surrounding the motivations behind the assassination including the involvement of groups on both sides of the Cuba issue.

Originally, I intended for the espionage to be in the background of *When We Left Cuba*, but of course, Beatriz wouldn't allow it, and when she saw the events unfolding around her, she demanded a seat at the table, and I couldn't shut her out of the game.

ACKNOWLEDGMENTS

One of the most amazing parts of this publishing journey has been the wonderful people I've met along the way who have made my books possible. I am so grateful to my agent, Kevan Lyon, and editor, Kate Seaver, for their support, wisdom, and enthusiasm for my work. It is such a pleasure to work with both of you, and I couldn't have asked for a better team to guide me and my career.

I am forever thankful my books found a home at Berkley. Thank you to Madeline McIntosh, Ivan Held, Christine Ball, Claire Zion, Jeanne-Marie Hudson, Craig Burke, Tawanna Sullivan, Fareeda Bullert, Roxanne Jones, Ryanne Probst, and Sarah Blumenstock, as well as the subrights department and the Berkley art department, for all of their extraordinary efforts on my behalf.

Thanks to the amazing authors who read *Next Year in Havana* and offered their kind words and support for the book: David Ebershoff, Kate Quinn, Stephanie Dray, Shelley Noble, Jennifer Robson, Renée Rosen, Heather Webb, Stephanie Thornton, Weina Dai Randel, Alix Rickloff, Alyssa Palombo, Meghan Masterson, and Jenni L. Walsh. Thank you to my lovely friends A. J. Pine, Lia Riley, and Jennifer Blackwood.

I am so grateful to the booksellers, bloggers, librarians, readers, and reviewers who have embarked on this new adventure with me. I've loved hearing from all of you and am so glad the Perez family has found a place in your hearts.

The Perez family came to life thanks to the stories passed down to me by my family and the inspiration of their love for their homeland. Thank you for sharing these pieces of Cuba with me and for your strength and courage.

To my family—thanks for your love and encouragement, for the inspiration you give me on a daily basis. You're the heart of every book I write.

❧ ❧

WHEN WE LEFT *Cuba*

CHANEL CLEETON

❧ ❧

QUESTIONS FOR DISCUSSION

1. In the first chapter, Beatriz says that she is somewhere between the girl she was and the woman she wants to be. How do you see her character grow and change throughout the novel?

2. When Beatriz arrives in Palm Beach, she feels out of place in society and cut off from the familiar people and things she loves. Can you relate to her experience of being a fish out of water? Have you ever experienced something similar, and how did it affect you?

3. Beatriz is motivated by her desire to avenge her brother's death as well as her love of her country. Which of these motivations is stronger for her, or do you believe they are intertwined? Do you agree with her actions or not?

4. When Beatriz becomes involved with the CIA, she acknowledges that war makes for strange bedfellows as she is now aligned with an organization she once decried. Do you agree with her decision? Do you believe in the axiom, "The enemy of my enemy is my friend," or do you disagree?

5. Beatriz and Eduardo have a close relationship, and the possibility of a romance between them simmers in the background of the novel. If things had worked out differently, do you think they could have had a future together? Do you think the bond between them is bolstered by their common interests, or is it mainly a product of nostalgia for the life they lived in Cuba? What similarities do you see between their personalities? What differences?

6. Throughout the book, Beatriz struggles to understand Eduardo's motives. Do you think he acts out of self-interest or patriotism? Do you think he has Beatriz's best interests at heart, or do you think he uses her for his own ends?

7. Which Perez sister do you identify with: Beatriz, Elisa, Isabel, or Maria? What traits do the sisters share, and in what ways are they different?

8. Each member of Beatriz's family takes a somewhat distinct approach to exile. Elisa builds a new life for herself in the United States; Isabel leaves her fiancé behind in Cuba; Maria adjusts to life in the United States with ease; their parents become obsessed with shoring up their financial and social influence to protect themselves from future ruin. How do you think Beatriz's feelings about exile differ from those of her family? How is the theme of exile explored in the book?

9. Beatriz chafes at the constraints placed on her by her family and their desire that she find a suitable husband. Can you relate with her desire to please her family while still following her heart? How much of the limitations placed on her are a product of the times and her background?

10. Beatriz and Nick are defined by their loyalties to their respective countries. How do you think this affects their relationship? Do you think timing plays the biggest role in their relationship, or are there other factors that keep them apart? What if they had met in Havana? Or before he was engaged?

11. Both Beatriz and Nick are shaped by war. He's influenced by his experiences serving in World War II, Beatriz by the Cuban Revolution. How has war shaped them? Has it influenced them in different or similar ways?

12. Mr. Dwyer plays a formative role in Beatriz's life and almost represents a paternal figure for her. How does their relationship change as the book progresses? Do you think he truly cares for Beatriz or only cares for her utility to the CIA? Is he motivated by self-interest or a sense of patriotic duty?

13. The CIA's role in Latin America and their efforts in Cuba heavily influenced the events of the early 1960s. What do you think about their motives and policies? Do you agree with their involvement in Cuba's affairs?

14. Beatriz's life is defined by the time period she grows up in and the events she experiences: the Cuban Revolution, Bay of Pigs, Cuban Missile Crisis, and Kennedy Assassination, to name a few. What world events have played defining roles in your life? What memories do you have of them? How have they influenced you?

Photo by Chris Malpass

Originally from Florida, **Chanel Cleeton** grew up on stories of her family's exodus from Cuba following the events of the Cuban Revolution. Her passion for politics and history continued during her years spent studying in England, where she earned a bachelor's degree in international relations from Richmond, the American International University in London, and a master's degree in global politics from the London School of Economics and Political Science. Chanel also received her Juris Doctor from the University of South Carolina School of Law. She loves to travel and has lived in the Caribbean, in Europe, and in Asia.

LOOK FOR THE NEXT CAPTIVATING
HISTORICAL NOVEL FROM
CHANEL CLEETON,
COMING WINTER 2020 FROM BERKLEY!

Ready to find
your next great read?

Let us help.

Visit prh.com/nextread

Penguin
Random
House